TH
EARNE ... AYS

"The truth is rarely pure and never simple."
(from *The Importance of Being Earnest*, p. 13)

"In married life three is company and two is none."
(from *The Importance of Being Earnest*, p. 15)

"To lose one parent may be regarded as a misfortune . . . to lose both seems like carelessness."
(from *The Importance of Being Earnest*, p. 23)

"Relations are simply a tedious pack of people, who haven't got the remotest knowledge of how to live, nor the smallest instinct about when to die."
(from *The Importance of Being Earnest*, p. 26)

"All women become like their mothers. That is their tragedy. No man does. That's his."
(from *The Importance of Being Earnest*, p. 27)

"I am sick to death of cleverness. Everybody is clever nowadays. You can't go anywhere without meeting clever people. The thing has become an absolute public nuisance. I wish to goodness we had a few fools left."
(from *The Importance of Being Earnest*, p. 27)

"I never travel without my diary. One should always have something sensational to read in the train."
(from *The Imp*

"I can resist everything except temptatio
(from

"How marriage ruins a man! It's as demoralising as cigarettes, and far more expensive." (from *Lady Windermere's Fan*, p. 142)

"We are all in the gutter, but some of us are looking at the stars."
(from *Lady Windermere's Fan*, p. 142)

"Experience is the name every one gives to their mistakes."
(from *Lady Windermere's Fan*, p. 144)

"One should never trust a woman who tells one her real age. A woman who would tell one that, would tell one anything."
(from *A Woman of No Importance*, p. 178)

"One can survive everything nowadays, except death, and live down anything except a good reputation."
(from *A Woman of No Importance*, p. 180)

"Duty is what one expects from others, it is not what one does oneself." (from *A Woman of No Importance*, p. 198)

"To love oneself is the beginning of a lifelong romance."
(from *An Ideal Husband*, p. 294)

"I do not believe in miracles. I have seen too many."
(from *Salomé*, p. 354)

The Importance of Being Earnest and Four Other Plays

OSCAR WILDE

With an Introduction and Notes by KENNETH KRAUSS

GEORGE STADE
Consulting Editorial Director

BARNES & NOBLE CLASSICS
NEW YORK

JB

BARNES & NOBLE CLASSICS

NEW YORK

Published by Barnes & Noble Books
122 Fifth Avenue
New York, NY 10011

www.barnesandnoble.com/classics

Lady Windermere's Fan was first published in 1892, *A Woman of No Importance* in 1893, and both *An Ideal Husband* and *The Importance of Being Earnest* in 1895. *Salomé*, written by Wilde in French, was published in English in 1894.

Published in 2004 by Barnes & Noble Classics with new Introduction, Notes, Biography, Chronology, Comments & Questions, and For Further Reading.

The Importance of Being Earnest and Four Other Plays
ISBN-13: 978-1-59308-059-4
ISBN-10: 1-59308-059-X
LC Control Number 2003109445

Produced and published in conjunction with:
Fine Creative Media, Inc.
322 Eighth Avenue
New York, NY 10001

Michael J. Fine, President and Publisher

Printed in the United States of America

QM

7 9 10 8 6

OSCAR WILDE

OSCAR FINGAL O'FLAHERTIE WILLS WILDE was born on October 16, 1854, to an intellectually prominent Dublin family. His father, Sir William Wilde, was a renowned physician who was knighted for his work as medical adviser to the 1841 and 1851 Irish censuses; his mother, Lady Jane Francesca Elgee, was a poet and journalist. Wilde showed himself to be an exceptional student. While at the Royal School in Enniskillen, he took First Prize in classics. He continued his studies at Trinity College, Dublin, on scholarship, where he won high honors, including the Demyship Scholarship to Magdalen College, Oxford.

At Oxford, Wilde engaged in self-discovery, through both intellectual and personal pursuits. He fell under the influence of the Aesthetic philosophy of Walter Pater, a tutor and author who inspired Wilde to create art for the sake of art alone. It was during these years that Wilde developed a reputation as an eccentric and a foppish dresser who always had a flower in his lapel. Wilde won his first recognition as a writer when the university awarded him the Newdigate Prize for his poem "Ravenna."

Wilde went from Oxford to London, where he published his first volume of verse, *Poems*, in 1881. From 1882 to 1884, he toured the United States, Ireland, and England, giving a series of lectures on Aestheticism. In America, between speaking engagements, he met some of the great literary minds of the day, including Henry Wadsworth Longfellow, Oliver Wendell Holmes, and Walt Whitman. His first play, *Vera*, was staged in New York but did poorly. After his marriage to Constance Lloyd in 1884 and the birth of his two sons, Wilde began to make his way into the London theater, literary, and homosexual scenes. He published *Intentions*, a collection of dialogues on Aesthetic philosophy, in 1891, the year he met Lord Alfred Douglas, who became his lover and his ultimate downfall. Wilde soon produced several successful plays, including *Lady Windermere's Fan* (1892) and *A Woman of No Importance* (1893).

Wilde's popularity was short-lived, however. In 1895, during the concurrent runs of his plays *An Ideal Husband* and *The Importance of Being Earnest*, he became the subject of a homosexual scandal that led him to withdraw all theater engagements and declare bankruptcy. Urged by many to flee the country rather than face a trial in which he would surely be found guilty, Wilde chose instead to remain in England. Arrested and found guilty of "homosexual offenses," Wilde was sentenced to two years' hard labor and began serving time in Wandsworth prison. He was later transferred to the detention center in Reading Gaol, where he composed *De Profundis*, a dramatic monologue written as a letter to Lord Alfred Douglas that was published in 1905. Upon his release in 1897, Wilde retreated to the Continent, where he lived out the rest of his life under a pseudonym. He published his last work, *The Ballad of Reading Gaol*, in 1898 while living in exile.

During his lifetime, Wilde was most often the center of controversy. *The Picture of Dorian Gray*, which was serialized in *Lippincott's Monthly Magazine* in 1890 and published in book form the next year, is considered to be Wilde's most personal work. Scrutinized by critics who questioned its morality, the novel portrays the author's internal battles and arrives at the disturbing possibility that "ugliness is the only reality." Oscar Wilde died penniless of cerebral meningitis in Paris on November 30, 1900. He is buried in Père Lachaise Cemetery, Paris.

TABLE OF CONTENTS

The World of Oscar Wilde ix
Introduction by Kenneth Krauss xiii

THE IMPORTANCE OF BEING EARNEST 3
LADY WINDERMERE'S FAN 95
A WOMAN OF NO IMPORTANCE 161
AN IDEAL HUSBAND 235
SALOMÉ 333
translated by Lord Alfred Douglas

Endnotes 369
Inspired by Oscar Wilde's Plays 373
Comments & Questions 377
For Further Reading 383

THE WORLD OF OSCAR WILDE

1854 Oscar Fingal O'Flahertie Wills Wilde is born on October 16 in Dublin to William Wilde, a prominent ophthalmologist, and Jane Francesca Elgee, a renowned poet and journalist.

1864 Wilde enters the Portora Royal School in Enniskillen, where he excels, and subsequently takes First Prize in classics and Second Prize in drawing.

1867 On February 23 Wilde's sister, Isola, dies of a sudden fever. Profoundly affected by the death, Wilde keeps a lock of her hair until the end of his life.

1871 Wilde enrolls as a Royal School Scholar at Trinity College, Dublin, where he earns the Foundation Scholarship (the highest honor bestowed on an undergraduate) as well as the Berkeley Gold Medal for Greek and the Demyship Scholarship to Magdalen College, Oxford.

1874 As a student at Magdalen College, Wilde finds a mentor in Walter Pater, a tutor and writer whose works, along with those of the Pre-Raphaelites, inspire Wilde to subscribe to the Aesthetic movement, which promotes "art for art's sake." Wilde develops a reputation for his flamboyant mannerisms, including his dandyism and long hair.

1876 Wilde's father dies.

1878 Wilde wins the Newdigate Prize for his poem "Ravenna," as well as "First In Greats" by his examiners. Wilde's eldest brother, Henry Wilson, dies.

1879 Upon graduation, Wilde moves to London with Frank Miles, a friend and portrait painter, and begins his writing career.

1881 Wilde publishes his first volume of verse, *Poems*, which is well received by critics. He becomes the subject of the Gilbert and Sullivan comic operetta *Patience*, which satirizes the Aesthetic movement. He embarks upon a series of lectures in the United

States; originally scheduled to last only four months, the tour is extended to fifty lectures and lasts nearly a year.

1882 Wilde meets Henry Wadsworth Longfellow, Oliver Wendell Holmes, Walt Whitman, and Henry James. He also arranges for his first play, *Vera*, to be staged in New York; it is a commercial flop.

1883 Wilde continues his lecture tour throughout the United Kingdom.

1884 On May 29 Wilde marries Constance Lloyd, the heiress of a Dublin barrister. The couple resides in Chelsea, a London neighborhood popular with artists, writers, and intellectuals. Wilde writes his second unsuccessful play, *The Duchess of Padua*.

1885 Wilde's first son, Cyril, is born. The Criminal Law Amendment Act, under which Wilde would later be prosecuted for engaging in "gross indecency," is passed.

1886 Another son, Vyvyan, is born.

1887 Wilde accepts an editor's position with *Woman's World*, a popular magazine, where he remains for two years.

1888 A collection of fairy tales, *The Happy Prince and Other Tales*, is published.

1889 Wilde's story "The Portrait of Mr. W. H." appears in *Blackwood's Magazine*; it asserts that the poems have a homoerotic subtext. "The Decay of Lying," a dialogue on Aesthetics and other subjects, is published in *The Nineteenth Century*, a literary review.

1890 *The Picture of Dorian Gray* is serialized in *Lippincott's Monthly Magazine*, published in Philadelphia.

1891 The publication of *The Picture of Dorian Gray*, an extended version of the magazine serial and Wilde's only novel, arouses controversy over the work's morality but makes little money. Wilde also produces several works that reflect his varied interests: *Intentions*, a collection of dialogues on Wilde's Aesthetic philosophy, *Lord Arthur Savile's Crime and Other Stories*, a volume of short fiction, and *The House of Pomegranates*, a collection of short stories. He meets Lord Alfred Douglas, an undergraduate at Oxford, and they soon become lovers. Wilde also befriends André Gide, the French writer and spokesman for homosexual rights.

1892 In February the first of Wilde's domestic comedies, *Lady Windermere's Fan*, opens at the St. James's Theatre to accolades. The financial success enables him to continue writing plays, and he completes *Salomé*, a reinterpretation in French of John the Baptist's martyrdom; he is unable to produce the play because of a law prohibiting theatrical depictions of biblical characters.

1893 Wilde again enjoys theatrical success with his second domestic comedy, *A Woman of No Importance*. He becomes friendly with Max Beerbohm, a fledgling writer at Oxford who soon becomes Britain's foremost caricaturist; his first subject is Wilde.

1894 In Paris, actress Sarah Bernhardt gives a performance of *Salomé*. In April "A Defence of Cosmetics," Beerbohm's parody of Wildean Aestheticism, appears in the *Yellow Book*, an alternative journal.

1895 Wilde is immensely popular on the London theater circuit: *An Ideal Husband* is performed at the Haymarket Theatre, and *The Importance of Being Earnest* is at the St. James's. Wilde becomes involved in three trials: In the first he sues the Marquess of Queensberry, the father of his lover Lord Alfred Douglas, for libel after the marquess refers to him in a note as a "somdomite" (*sic*). The defense counsel denounces *Dorian Gray* as an immoral book, and enough evidence is presented to try Wilde for engaging in homosexual activity. After two trials he is sentenced to Wandsworth prison for two years' hard labor. Wilde's wife and sons relocate to Italy and adopt an old family name, "Holland."

1897 Wilde is transferred from Wandsworth to Reading Gaol. While detained, he writes *De Profundis*, a dramatic monologue and biography addressed to Alfred Douglas that is published in part in 1905. Upon his release from prison, Wilde goes into exile to the Continent, where he lives under the alias "Sebastian Melmoth."

1898 *The Ballad of Reading Gaol*, Wilde's final work, is published. Wilde also publishes two letters on prison reform. Constance dies. Wilde briefly reunites with Douglas but spends most of his time traveling throughout Europe, occasionally writing for Parisian journals.

1900 Wilde is said to convert to Roman Catholicism on his deathbed, after a lifelong flirtation with the religion. He dies of cerebral meningitis at the Hotel D'Alsace in Paris on November 30. He is buried at Père Lachaise Cemetery, Paris.

1905 Wilde's play *Salomé* inspires German composer Richard Strauss to write a one-act opera of the same name.

INTRODUCTION

OSCAR WILDE: PLAYWRIGHT, INVERT, AND AESTHETE

IF OSCAR WILDE, whose best dramatic works are contained in this volume, had never existed, we would not have been able to invent him. The world-famous, and infamous, Wilde, the witty social commentator and outcast, the fabulous fop and invert, as well as the poet, novelist, and (certainly not least) playwright—the immortal Oscar Wilde whom we may come to know through his writings and reputation is, in fact, himself the invention of the very mortal Oscar Fingal O'Flahertie Wills Wilde, who came into this world October 16, 1854, and sadly departed it on November 30, 1900. The all-too-human man created the perfect persona of the quintessential Aesthete. Yet what Wilde the man made in his own image will never die.

The facts regarding the author's early life may seem, at first glance, pure and simple: Born to the celebrated (and ultimately knighted) Irish eye doctor William Wilde and his wife, Jane, who had penned verses for revolutionary newspapers, Oscar grew up in Dublin, eventually attending Trinity College and finally winning a scholarship to Magdalen College, Oxford. After his great triumph in classics at the great English university, he moved on to London, where he published a slim collection of poems that received great praise.

Still, as Algernon asserts in act one of *The Importance of Being Earnest*, "The truth is rarely pure and never simple." Although Wilde would achieve enormous success in the British capital, he never forgot his roots, which always made him feel different from others. "I am not English," he declared. "I am Irish—which is quite another thing." Furthermore, his time at Oxford was not completely occupied by his studies. Although he submitted a poem that was rewarded a major prize (the Newdigate) and did exceptionally well in his exams, his extensive social activities at university paved the way for a brilliant literary career in London. And by the time his little book of poetry had reached the hands of admiring critics, Wilde had already gained a reputation as a young man of celebrated drollness and fine feelings.

He was, in fact, publicly regarded as the quintessential Aestheticist, that is, as a typical member of the artistic movement that swept across Europe in the 1870s and 1880s. In contrast to Victorian idealists, who preached that Art should have a morally positive and uplifting influence, the Aestheticists believed great art was in itself, regardless of its moral implications, important and beautiful. Their motto, "Art for Art's sake," quickly became associated with all they stood for.

The basis of the literary and visual artwork of the Aestheticists, known also as the Decadents, was their preoccupation with the expulsion of human beings from Eden. Since the fall of man, they firmly held, Evil was ever present. Like the Romantics, they cherished the grotesque, but unlike them, they thought that the universe was imbalanced, that both health and innocence were very much overrated, and that Nature, like Man, had fallen and was not "pure." Thus, they championed the unnatural, the artificial, all things deliberately calculated and constructed.

The art of the Aestheticist movement emerged from an acceptance of an imperfect world. In both poetry and painting, dreamlike imagery predominated. The images were artificial and contrived, including, on a personal level, such trappings as elaborate jewelry, clothing, makeup, and hair (all the artifice that went into creating the exterior of the well-groomed fop). Aestheticist imagery culled from Nature never displayed natural simplicity. Instead, the images were grotesque or highly intricate specimens: exotic, delicate flowers; rare, bizarre birds; and fabulous cut gemstones. The butterfly, the clouding night sky, and falling leaves all reflected a fleeting beauty and the approach of death.

The Aestheticists thrived on being poseurs; they relished the artificial, and doing what oppressive Victorian society looked upon as "evil." After all, such socially reprehensible acts were supposedly unnatural—and thus, by the Aestheticists' own definition, superior to nature. Perhaps they were aware that much of what people said and did, how they appeared, and what they claimed to believe, were all poses anyway; perhaps their sense of superiority derived from their awareness that they harbored no pretenses about their "nonnatural" thoughts and behaviors. Wilde's poseurs, for example, in both fiction and drama, never apologize for their facades and affectations. This central contradiction, that one is conscious of one's pretensions but continues to hold on to them, echoes through the lines of Wilde's plays: The most hilarious passages of dialogue resound with polished paradoxes and heightened ironies. Indeed, it is this brilliant mix that makes so much of Wilde's comedy still so funny more than a century later.

Yet such irony could be serious as well. As Aestheticist poet Richard Le Gallienne (1866–1947) wrote in "The Décadent to His Soul,"

> Sin is no sin when virtue is forgot.
> It is so good in sin to keep in sight
> The white hills whence we fell, to measure by . . .
> Ah, that's the thrill! . . .
> First drink the stars, then grunt amid the mire.

Wilde, as it happened, put the same idea more positively: "We are all in the gutter," he agreed, as expressed by Lord Darlington in *Lady Windermere's Fan*, "but some of us are looking at the stars" (p. 142). Such an approach negated most nineteenth-century attitudes about Art, both the deep sentiments of the Romantics and the logic of the didactic, or morally improving, Victorians. It also stood in clear opposition to the techniques of more traditional artists. For instance, Romantic or Victorian poets might choose specific images drawn from nature to express, in a logical way, their feelings and ideas on Nature. An Aestheticist poet, however, would choose images that made more of an emotional, rather than an intellectual, impact. Readers of Wilde's poetry may observe how images in series may seem totally irrelevant but nonetheless provide an extraordinary parade of vivid, intense sensations. Take, for example, the beginning of his poem "The Grave of Shelley":

> Like burnt-out torches by a sick man's bed
> Gaunt cypress-trees stand round the sun-bleached stone;
> Here doth the little night-owl make her throne,
> And the slight lizard show his jewelled head.
> And, where the chaliced poppies flame to red,

> In the still chamber of yon pyramid
> Surely some Old-World Sphinx lurks darkly hid,
> Grim warder of this pleasaunce of the dead.

The cypresses are turned into ceremonial torches, and the owl reigns as queen of the night. The lizard is studded with gemstones. The red poppies burn. Such usually natural imagery resembles the result of deliberate human handicraft—complicated artifice. In sequence, each new image makes a distinct and separate impression on the reader.

Aestheticists became fixtures in London's social scene. Their deliberate affectations made them targets of much ridicule by the more conservative press. By the early 1880s, Wilde had become so well known that when William S. Gilbert and Sir Arthur Sullivan decided to create an operetta lampooning these "artistic" young men, many in the audience noticed a similarity between the main character and Oscar Wilde. *Patience, or Bunthorne's Bride* was a hit in London, but Gilbert and Sullivan faced the possibility of an enormous flop when the play was transported across the Atlantic. Americans, they reasoned, had little or no idea what an Aestheticist was; audiences in the United States would be unable to recognize the object of their lampoon. As a solution to their problem, the composer and librettist decided to send, as advance party, the man who embodied all the qualities of the most aesthetic Aestheticist, Wilde himself.

From the instant Wilde arrived in December 1881, Americans took note of this extraordinary figure. When asked by a customs inspector, "Have you anything to declare," Wilde immediately quipped, "Nothing but my genius." One reporter, in New York, observed (before Wilde's departure in 1883) in *The Tribune*,

> The most striking thing about the poet's appearance is his height, which is several inches over six feet, and the next thing to attract attention is his hair, which is of a dark brown color, and falls down upon his shoulders. . . . When he laughs his lips part widely and show a shining row of upper teeth, which are superlatively white. The complexion, instead of being the rosy hue so common in Englishmen, is so utterly devoid of color that it can only be described as resembling putty. His eyes are blue, or a light gray, and instead of being 'dreamy', as

some of his admirers have imagined them to be, they are bright and quick—not at all like those of one given to perpetual musing on the ineffably beautiful and true. Instead of having a small delicate hand, only fit to caress a lily, his fingers are long and when doubled up would form a fist that would hit a hard knock, should an occasion arise for the owner to descend to that kind of argument. . . . One of the peculiarities of his speech is that he accents almost at regular intervals without regard to the sense, perhaps as a result of an effort to be rhythmic in conversation as well as in verse.

If Americans were unfamiliar with Aestheticists, Wilde offered a very striking picture of who and what they were. He visited and lectured in seventy cities across the continent, in large metropolises and small towns in rural Kansas, Utah, and California. In Leadville, Colorado, he noted a saloon sign that read, "Please do not shoot the pianist. He is doing his best"; Wilde remarked, to the delight of the miners who had come to hear him, that this was the only rational method of art criticism he had ever seen.

Coast to coast, he became a celebrity. In San Francisco *The Wasp* published, on March 31, 1882, a vicious cartoon entitled "The Modern Messiah," in which the lanky, long-haired poet appears on horseback, a halo of sunflower petals above his head. (Wilde had let it be known wherever he traveled that he had a penchant for blue china and sunflowers.) In this caricature, awed notables from high society surround the divine Oscar. Tied to his horse's tail hangs a money bag, marked $5,000 (which would have been £1,000, an amazing sum at the time), the price Wilde was paid for his trek across North America. According to *The Daily Chronicle* in San Francisco, in an article dated March 30, 1882, he was followed everywhere:

MOBBING THE ESTHETE.

A scene of considerable excitement occurred yesterday afternoon when Oscar Wilde ventured out in search of Celestial handiwork. In company with a lady and an escort, he called at a Chinese store on Sacramento Street, below Kearny. No sooner had he been seen to leave his carriage than a general rush took place, and in a moment the street in front

> of the store was utterly impassable, and it required the bear-efforts of Officer Curtis to prevent the spectators from precipitating themselves into the store. The purchases completed, Oscar Wilde advanced through the passageway that had been cleared and entered his carriage followed by the lady and her escort. The blinds were pulled down, but the spectators, bent on seeing the esthete at closer quarters, crowded forward and pulled aside the curtains, revealing the apostle leaning back convulsed with laughter. Late in the evening Oscar Wilde fulfilled his duty as a visitor from afar by making a tour of the Chinese quarter.

In the United States Wilde gained a huge reputation and even a following, but had little to show for it. Before setting sail from New York, he was able to drum up interest for a production of his pseudo-Russian political thriller, *Vera, or the Nihilists*, but critics' and audiences' negative reactions gave it a short run. Wilde sailed back to Europe but fled England quickly. After spending time in Paris, working on a verse play that he had been commissioned to write, Wilde returned to London and began lecturing across Britain and Ireland. On his tour he met Constance Lloyd, the daughter of a deceased Irish barrister. She was educated and intelligent; like Wilde's mother, Jane, she spoke several languages and had independent views. The two married in 1884, and in 1885 their first son, Cyril, was born, followed by another son, Vyvyan, the following year. Now the head of a household, the Aestheticist turned to editing and writing—largely criticism, poems, and stories—to make a living.

In 1890 he brought *Dorian Gray* to the stage. Although it was a failure, Wilde turned the script into a novel published the following year. *The Picture of Dorian Gray*, in which a handsome young man's evil deeds disfigure his portrait's face (rather than his own), outraged and delighted a prudish public. A year later he tried the theater again, this time with *Lady Windermere's Fan*, which proved to be an unqualified success. The next year, his play *A Woman of No Importance* appeared. About the same time, Wilde wrote, in French, his most "decadent" dramatic work, *Salomé,* which was banned in England but appeared for a short run in Paris in 1894. In 1895 came the hit *An Ideal Husband* and the play that is generally regarded as Wilde's masterpiece, *The Importance of*

Being Earnest. Now, at last, Oscar Wilde was not just famous for being Oscar Wilde—he was also famous for being a brilliant playwright.

In 1892, on the opening night of *Lady Windermere's Fan*, Wilde again ran into an Oxford undergraduate, Lord Alfred Douglas, nicknamed Bosie, whom he had first encountered the year before, during one of the playwright's frequent visits back to the university. Bosie, the athletic and good-looking younger son of the Marquess of Queensberry, was not on good terms with his father, and Lord Alfred's time at Oxford made him despise the Marquess even more vehemently.

Wilde's marriage to Constance had dissolved around 1886; an upright and decent life seemed too much for any self-respecting Aestheticist to endure. Wilde found he was depressed and unhappy. Simultaneously he questioned his sexual orientation. A Canadian houseguest, Robbie Ross, who would remain a loyal friend to Wilde until the end, seduced him. Wilde's realization that he was more homosexual than heterosexual changed his life. He and Constance lived separately, he joking that he never came home because he couldn't recall the exact address. Wilde began to drink and would visit Oxford to meet and befriend young men. His association with Bosie, which in modern terms is difficult to define, became the center of his life. More than just lovers, the pair were friends, partners in crime, and fellow writers; Wilde's play *Salomé*, which Wilde composed in French, was (according to the credit given) translated by Douglas. Their shared interest in members of the same sex fueled their relationship in a variety of ways. Indeed, the most important phase of Wilde's theater career came during the three years when he and Bosie were together.

Yet the triumphs during this period precipitated Wilde's tragedy. In 1895 the Marquess of Queensberry, who finally tired of his son's involvement with the older man, tried to denounce Wilde in the theater where *The Importance of Being Earnest* had just opened. Because the box office would not sell him a ticket, the Marquess went directly to Wilde's club and, finding that the playwright was not there, left him a conspicuous message: "For Oscar Wilde, posing as a somdomite" (*sic*).

His lordship's bad spelling aside, Wilde, at the insistence of Bosie, sued the Marquess for libel. Yet Queensberry's attorneys shifted the crux of the case from libel to something very different. By calling as witnesses male prostitutes whom Wilde had known, the libel trial ended and a new trial, in which the Crown accused Wilde of the crime of homosexuality, began. This proceeding resulted in a hung jury, so there followed another, in which Wilde was ultimately found guilty and sentenced to two years in prison. Official Victorian society regarded homosexuality as an unspeakable abomination—during one of his trials, Wilde himself referred to it as "the love that dare not speak its name." Yet in court Wilde argued that homosexuality was neither shameful nor unnatural. Nonetheless, the scandal of his being branded a "somdomite," along with his sentence, ruined his career.

In prison Wilde waited nineteen months for paper and pen. Then, in his cell he composed *De Profundis*, a long essay, partly autobiographical and partly a letter to Douglas, that explained why they must never meet again; it was, in its subject matter and directness, considered so indecent that it was not published until five years after Wilde's death. The scandal of the trial and the shame of Wilde's imprisonment drove Constance to take the children and live abroad under an assumed name. Although she hoped Wilde would someday return to her (she died waiting), he was unable to fight his obsession with Bosie, who before the trials began had also taken up residence across the English Channel. (Douglas never testified on his friend's behalf, although he boasted that if he had, he could have saved Oscar.) On his release, Wilde assumed a new name and moved to France. He met with Bosie, and their relationship, which *De Profundis* had seemed to exorcise, resumed.

Yet Douglas's treatment of Wilde was now different, for Oscar was no longer the successful writer and dandy. The years in prison had changed him, both physically and mentally. Overweight and ill, he was shunned everywhere, and except for a long poem denouncing imprisonment, *The Ballad of Reading Gaol*, he no longer wanted to write. Bosie's cruelty to and ultimate abandonment of Wilde left him penniless. He died in a cheap hotel room in Paris in November 1900. Nonetheless, even at the end, Wilde could not resist his own wit: "My wallpaper and I are fighting a duel to the death," he told a visitor shortly before he expired. "One or the other of us has to go." Rumors circulated that on his deathbed Wilde converted to Roman Catholicism. He was forty-six years old.

Many critics looking back at Wilde's playwriting career have thought that the work that comes closest to his Aestheticist beliefs is *Salomé*, composed originally in French. This extraordinary one-act drama has been known primarily through its languid English version. The biblical story of King Herod's stepdaughter is refigured here to emphasize the princess Salomé's obsessive attraction to John the Baptist. John's rejection of the girl prompts her to demand the future saint's death from her stepfather, Herod, who harbors feelings of lust toward her. After Salomé has performed the sensuous dance of the seven veils, Herod agrees to have John beheaded, but when Herod sees her kissing the severed head, he is so revolted that he orders her death.

To this highly eroticized retelling, Wilde adds an array of minor characters whose own longings infuse the stage with a keen, unrequited passion. The dialogue, though clearly prose, is reminiscent of Wilde's dreamlike poetry. The language is marvelously purple in tone—vivid, deliberately antiquated, replete with intricate and sensational images. With its sexually charged descriptions of the changing phases of the moon, *Salomé* was banned in England but found a select audience at the Théâtre d'Art in Paris, a small playhouse devoted to Symbolist drama. The script served as libretto for the German composer Richard Strauss, whose haunting 1905 opera *Salomé* is frequently performed.

However, while *Salomé* may be the most obvious theater work by Wilde to reflect his Aestheticist preoccupations, all his plays in some way embody his artistic leanings; unfortunately, there has been a long history of critical half-understandings. For example, when *Lady Windermere's Fan* first opened in London, it was championed by one of the most important drama critics (and playwrights) of the time, George Bernard Shaw. Shaw, like Wilde, was an Irish Protestant writing in England. Although Wilde and Shaw were acquainted, Shaw's commitment to socialism took him into different circles. On the whole, Shaw tended to look askance at the affected fops who commanded the drawing rooms of London. (Wilde, for his part, noted, "As yet, Bernard Shaw hasn't become prominent enough to have any enemies, but none of his friends like him.")

But when Shaw attended *Lady Windermere's Fan*, he observed how amusingly it satirized the upper classes and criticized modern morality. Indeed Shaw, whose own interests lay in exposing the evils of capitalist culture, tended to see the realist dramas of Henrik Ibsen also as social commentary—and of course, to an extent, Shaw was right not only about Ibsen but also about Wilde. Thus Shaw thought highly of *A Woman of No Importance* and *An Ideal Husband*, both of which he saw as consonant with his own devotion to social change, but *The Importance of Being Earnest* seemed to him shallow. This comedy of manners did not appear to be about anything. Rather than analyze real life, the play, for Shaw, trivialized reality. Audiences, however, did not agree: They enthusiastically embraced *Earnest*, but the play closed suddenly as news from Wilde's trial was released.

If Shaw was only partly correct about Wilde, what about those who for the last century have loved *Earnest* precisely because it is so perfectly silly? Generations of theatergoers have welcomed this hilarious play, and the majority who have seen or read it have been content to accept, if not applaud, its apparent lack of significance. *The Importance of Being Earnest* is considered "safe" reading matter for high-school, even middle-school, students and deemed appropriate fare for spectators of all ages. It remains frequently performed on stage and television and has been filmed several times. Perhaps those who have come to adore *Earnest* look at the earlier plays, which Shaw liked so much, as flawed, hilarious merely in part, and consumed by vestiges of Wilde's social conscience, which now, at least to some, seems dated.

Again, this view of Wilde's drama is only partly accurate: Without the ballast of a traditional, meaningful plot, *Earnest* soars to comedic heights. Its surface is so polished that we easily may be blinded or taken in by the notion, so often articulated throughout the script, that surface alone matters. Yet beneath the superficial brilliance, Wilde manages to create a subtle interplay of ironies that add up to more than the wit so prominently on display. After all, Wilde was a serious Aestheticist, and while that may strike readers as a contradiction, it is exactly that hilarious paradox with which *Earnest* is so seriously concerned.

Lady Windermere's Fan was first performed in 1892 in a theater located near London's most fashionable neighborhoods, Mayfair and Belgravia (where the play is set). Before Wilde reveals how Lady Windermere and her husband are connected to Mrs. Erlynne, spectators observe the private world of the upper classes and the strict (and often hypocritical) social rules governing them. Modern readers may detect how one did not speak before the servants or how (as at the end of acts two and four) the need to inform the host that the carriage should be brought round might give one a brief respite. The domestic argument between husband and wife and the dilemma at Lady Windermere's birthday party may appear today as overly stagy, in part because of their use of soliloquies (in which a solitary character's thoughts are expressed aloud) and asides (in which the character speaks directly to the audience). Such conventions are reminiscent of the broader acting required by Victorian melodrama. Wilde's own dramatic style had yet to be influenced by the Realists, whose conventions we today accept as drama as usual.

By act two, however, we recognize Wilde: The dancing party is glib and amusing, with marvelously ironic exchanges. Still, the tension that ends act one, when Lord Windermere exclaims to himself, "I dare not tell her who the woman really is. The shame would kill her," hangs over the festivities. Although Lady Windermere has earlier promised her husband that she will strike Mrs. Erlynne in the face with his birthday gift—the fan—if she appears, we are not yet aware why this would be such an outrageous act.

Luckily, Lady Windermere remains civil, though cold, and the fan mentioned in the play's title, of which she tries to rid herself several times, changes hands onstage repeatedly. By the close of act two, we not only see how Lady Windermere's jealousy and moral indignation make her an easy prey for the unscrupulous Lord Darlington, but also, as the curtain falls, we hear from Mrs. Erlynne exactly why Lady Windermere's suspicions are so wrong.

Wilde's technique, as the plot tightens, of allowing one character to have one important piece of the puzzle and letting another possess a very different one, permits the audience to understand more than any of the characters onstage. Although there was debate during rehearsals as to when the crucial revelation regarding Mrs. Erlynne's identity should occur, readers and spectators alike already may have gleaned from hints in act one some notion of what is to come. Yet whether we are reading the play or watching it, we eventually become omniscient interpreters of the dramatic irony. In the end, we alone know the truth about Mrs. Erlynne, and we can detect, better than the characters themselves, the great change that has occurred inside Lady Windermere.

Yet there are traces of Wilde's Aestheticist sympathies and of his "secret" life. There are moments when the cleverness of the dialogue masks some of the deeper issues in the play. For instance, recall Lord Darlington's explanation of good and evil from act one:

> Good people do a great deal of harm in this world. Certainly the greatest harm they do is that they make badness of such extraordinary importance. It is absurd to divide people into good and bad. People are either charming or tedious (p. 103).

The idea is that one ought to judge others as an Aestheticist might judge a painting, not by how morally edifying it may be but by how interesting and beautiful it is. Form is as important, if not more so, than content. The result is, then, not *im*morality but *a*morality: Morality does not, according to Darlington, exist at all. A little later, after the Duchess of Berwick has entered the room and Darlington has exited, she (almost gleefully) expresses her sadness about Lord Windermere's supposed infidelity. Along the way, she manages to forget which sex the Windermeres' baby is; finally she remembers:

> Ah, the dear pretty baby! How is the little darling? Is it a boy or a girl? I hope a girl—ah, no, I remember it's a boy! I'm so sorry. Boys are so wicked. My boy is excessively immoral. You wouldn't believe at what hours he comes home. And he's only left Oxford a few months—I really don't know what they teach them there (p. 108).

Again, the comedy is delightful, but beneath the laughter lie references to what boys may pick up at Oxford and how some, on coming down to London, might spend their nights prowling its more sinister districts. The fashionable world of Belgravia and Mayfair is, in Wilde's plays, never very far from the exciting, yet immoral, demimonde in which reside illicit love and crime and all that was never to be spoken of, such as homosexuality, prostitution, drinking, gambling, and drugs. The violet haze that fogs this "degenerate" subculture, which late Victorians feared and yet dreamed of entering, is never as palpable in Wilde's social comedic dramas as it is in *Salomé*. Still, whenever this intriguing and ambiguous haze wafts through a line or a speech, it is always subversive.

There are two important character "types" who appear in *Lady Win-*

dermere's Fan and reappear in Wilde's next two "social" plays: Mrs. Erlynne is an outcast, someone—specifically, a woman—who has made a bad choice and has been punished far beyond what she has done by the brittle code governing relationships between people. The script makes clear that, although Mrs. Erlynne played a role in her own downfall, the people who condemn her are incapable of following the same rules. They do, however, manage to keep their transgressions secret; thus, Mrs. Erlynne's great sin is not that she has committed adultery but that she is known to have done so. Although the "fallen woman" was familiar to late-nineteenth-century theatergoers, who would recognize in her Marguerite Gautier, the tragic courtesan of *The Lady of the Camellias* (1852), by Alexandre Dumas (the younger), and a host of successors, Wilde's version of this "type" demands from the audience not just pity but respect.

The second "type" is the dandy or fop. Such characters were familiar to English audiences from Shakespeare's time and from Restoration comedies. Wilde's fop is a late-nineteenth-century version: In *Lady Windermere's Fan*, Lord Darlington, with his languorous paradoxical humor and confessions of evildoing, best embodies what Wilde's first audiences would have recognized quickly as the Aesthete. In a way, both types are the opposite sides of the same coin, for in Victorian times a man might claim all sorts of sexual adventures with temerity, but a woman would be reviled if there were any suspicion of her acting improperly. The double standard—one rule for males and quite another for females, as discussed by Lady Windermere and Darlington in act one—was yet another layer of hypocrisy.

Thus Wilde was successful in using irony both in the droll contradictions that sparkle in his characters' dialogue and in his systematic condemnation of late-Victorian social rules. Shaw liked Wilde's work because of his social consciousness and his exposé of how capitalist culture controlled the lives of the people who were supposed to set a good example for those beneath them. At the same time, Wilde's aristocratic and middle-class audiences were drawn to his plays' wit and dynamic plots. In addition, however, Wilde, the man who always felt Irish among English people, who at this time was struggling with issues of his own sexual identity, the much-mocked Aesthete and now aging young man, incorporated the theme of the outsider into his plays.

In *A Woman of No Importance*, the good but fallen woman, Mrs. Arbuthnot, is juxtaposed by the nasty fop Lord Illingworth. Gerald Arbuthnot's choice, whether to take Illingworth's offer for success or remain loyal to his mother, is influenced by his love for Hester Worsley, who at first seems a caricature of a rude American heiress. Yet as the play develops, Hester and Mrs. Arbuthnot convince Gerald that the world as it is currently constituted is immoral. By the final curtain, the three are on the verge of their own utopian future.

As if to make it clear that not all fallen women must be good and all fops bad, Viscount Goring, in *An Ideal Husband*, even with his witticisms and checkered background, emerges as heroic, while Mrs. Cheveley, in spite of her bad reputation and exclusion from society, appears to be nothing more than an unscrupulous blackmailer. Indeed, it is Goring's excursions into the disreputable underworld (which his future wife finds horrid and enticing) that have made him the one character capable of fighting the villainous Mrs. Cheveley. His varied experience makes Goring, rather than the tortured and narcissistic Sir Robert Chiltern, the ideal husband.

As with *Lady Windermere's Fan*, these subsequent dramas explore social issues through dialogue that sparkles with humor. They too look at the so-called Victorian "double standard" and the social inequality of the sexes. The issue of class always forms part of the social landscape, and there are hints of Aestheticist values and of a world beyond the drawing room, where exciting, evil things occur. Yet the crowning masterpiece of Wilde's career, what should have been in his own lifetime his most honored work, *The Importance of Being Earnest*, was neglected for years not because it was not a great play but because it happened to have been written by the notorious Oscar Wilde.

Many have accepted *Earnest* for what it seems to be, a comedy of manners that exquisitely and almost lovingly satirizes the upper classes. The apparent froth of the piece—its trivial and illogical plot, its grandly superficial characters, and its stunning contradictions—has proved little detriment to its success. Yet even in this play, which delightfully makes so much out of so little, Shaw might have recognized some of the features of Wilde's earlier work. Indeed, much of the humor critically characterizes the very issues that Shaw held so dear. Years later, with the world on the brink of World War I, Shaw perhaps understood better the absurdity of the play. He recycled many of the unpredictable plot twists and comedic ironies that had made *Earnest* initially seem so trivial; Shaw's masterpiece, *Heartbreak House*, owes an immense debt to Wilde at his silliest.

On a very immediate level, *Earnest* explores the nature of the connection between a symbol and what it represents. Both Gwendolen and Cecily assert that they cannot marry men whose names are not Ernest. Their superficiality, however, may obscure the wordplay inherent in the name itself: The word "earnest" and the name "Ernest" sound exactly alike. Is it men who have not been arbitrarily assigned the name "Ernest" by their parents whom the girls reject, or is it perhaps men who are not in "earnest"? In the play itself, it would appear both girls are looking for Ernest, and yet what the name has come to represent for them is the honest and open—that is, the "earnest"—acknowledgment that their suitors are just what they say they are: attractive, stylish, and wicked men of the world.

Missing is the outcast female from the earlier dramas: In *Earnest* none of the female characters, neither Gwendolen nor Cecily, nor Lady Bracknell, and certainly not Miss Prism, have gone far beyond the boundaries that Victorian society had set up for ladies and young women. Curiously, however, their well-bred innocence includes an awareness of that underworld into which fallen women fall. Cecily's diary, written to describe her imaginary courtship with the nonexistent but immoral Ernest, suggests an attraction to what her elders characterize as sinful. Miss Prism fears lascivious content in Cecily's economics text.

Still, if their lack of worldly experience appears slight, the women in *Earnest* have mastered the art of surfaces. Gwendolen's passion for Jack is based largely, perhaps completely, on his assumed name (and so, as we later learn, is Cecily's attraction to Algernon). Lady Bracknell, who may be regarded as a more terrifying version of the Duchess of Berwick or Lady Caroline Pontefract, becomes the epitome of upper-class snobbism: Her commands and judgments are based purely on how she anticipates she (or those around her) will be perceived by others. Her egocentricity is so enormous that her presence in a room makes young lovers quake. And yet her amazing and hilarious contradictions suggest there is little beyond the formidable facade. Lady Bracknell is merely a collection of other people's social prejudices.

The men in *Earnest* have devised tactics to protect themselves from the Lady Bracknells of the world. Masquerading as someone else, they manage to enter the demimonde of ill repute (or at least of pleasure). They manage to invent excuses (say, an uncontrollable brother or an invalid friend) that allow them to exit propriety and enter the gray area between good and bad, where they may enjoy themselves. The fopperies of Darlington and Illingworth, along with their mutual fascination with evil, are present in both Ernests. Yet Jack and Algernon are positive examples of young men-about-town who look upon upright Victorian morality with justified cynicism; like Goring, both seem capable of becoming husbands who, if not ideal, have been made better by their encounters in the shadier world.

If the complicated yet improbable plot appears to carry minimal meaning, spectators must look elsewhere for substance. That little if anything seems to go deeper than the surface is in itself significant. In *Earnest* people act as if they have no concern with what lies beyond the way things look to others. The ironies that give the play much of its humor, then, resonate with the notion that these characters are inhabitants of a universe in which bizarre contradictions make perfect sense. Their obsession with how things appear, and their need to disguise their real and private lives, have shaped them.

Here as in all else, the comedy assists the audience in gliding through the more searing social commentary. In the end, however, as the plot resolves through the revelation of Jack's true identity and Algernon's, the happy ending appears as unbelievable as the rest of the play: Is Gwendolen going to marry her first cousin? Will Cecily really settle for a man not named Ernest? Perhaps Wilde is implying here that none of the elements of the previous conflict mattered anyway, and that all has been, is, and will be nonsense. Or perhaps Wilde is asking us to accept that the action adds up to a comedic plot—or not even a comedic plot but a parody of a comedic plot. The play itself, then, may seem an accurate picture not of what life is really like but of what life is supposed to be like—and of how very silly that is. If what happens on the stage is supposed to mirror what happens in the world, the image thrown back by *Earnest* is distorted. Nevertheless, in an environment where appearances are everything, Wilde uses the stage to reflect just how ridiculous this preoccupation with externals is.

Today we may be less likely to judge Oscar Wilde's conduct and more likely to see him as an extraordinarily brave man, given his circumstances. Perhaps we can better understand how his wonderful dramatic works do very much relate to his life's experiences. Not only can we enjoy his plays, but we can embrace them as entertaining and meaningful.

Wilde's genius as a dramatist is not merely historical. Like all great playwrights, he is still widely known today because his work (like Shakespeare's) continues to be performed. Audiences continue to laugh at his work, and readers, with much delight, persist in quoting him. Students study him, and his name is generally well known. More than a century after his passing, Oscar Wilde remains in the present tense. Although rooted in the Victorian era and its institutions and customs, Wilde is nonetheless a very modern man. Some of him remains with us even now.

Kenneth Krauss was graduated from Sussex University, Brighton, England, and received his Ph.D. from Columbia University in New York City. He teaches drama at the College of Saint Rose in Albany, New York, where he also directs and produces. His books include *Maxwell Anderson and the New York Stage* (which he coedited), *Private Readings/Public Texts*, and *There's a War Going On*, a play produced in New York. In addition to numerous scholarly and unscholarly articles, he has written such plays as *Boudoir Philosophy, Bodybuilders in Jockstraps, Out of Nowhere*, and *A Season of Fear*. His most recent book is *The Drama of Fallen France: Reading La Comedie sans tickets*, on French theater under the German Occupation.

The Importance of Being Earnest

and

Four Other Plays

THE IMPORTANCE OF BEING EARNEST[1]

THE PERSONS OF THE PLAY

JOHN WORTHING, J.P.
ALGERNON MONCRIEFF
REV. CANON CHASUBLE, D.D.
MR. GRIBSBY, Solicitor
MERRIMAN, Butler
LANE, Manservant
MOULTON, Gardener
LADY BRACKNELL
HON. GWENDOLEN FAIRFAX
CECILY CARDEW
MISS PRISM, Governess

ACT ONE

SCENE: *Morning-room in Algernon's flat in Half-Moon Street, London, W.** TIME: *The present. The room is luxuriously and artistically furnished. The sound of a piano is heard in the adjoining room.*

LANE *is arranging afternoon tea on the table, and after the music has ceased,* ALGERNON *enters.*

ALGERNON: Did you hear what I was playing, Lane?

LANE: I didn't think it polite to listen, sir.†

ALGERNON: I'm sorry for that, for your sake. I don't play accurately—any one can play accurately—but I play with wonderful expression. As far as the piano is concerned, sentiment is my forte. I keep science for Life.

LANE: Yes, sir.

ALGERNON: And, speaking of the science of Life, have you got the cucumber sandwiches cut for Lady Bracknell?

LANE: Yes, sir.

ALGERNON: Ahem! Where are they?

LANE: Here, sir. (*Shows plate.*)

ALGERNON (*inspects them, takes two, and sits down on the sofa*): Oh! . . . by the way, Lane, I see from your book that on Thursday night, when Lord Shoreman and Mr. Worthing were dining with me, eight bottles of champagne are entered as having been consumed.

LANE: Yes, sir; eight bottles and a pint.

ALGERNON: Why is it that at a bachelor's establishment the servants invariably drink the champagne? I ask merely for information.

LANE: I attribute it to the superior quality of the wine, sir. I have

---

*Very fashionable address with a view of Green Park.

†Lane's dry humor (which emerges from time to time in this act) suggests that his relationship with Algernon is somewhat complex.

often observed that in married households the champagne is rarely of a first-rate brand.

ALGERNON: Good heavens! Is marriage so demoralising as that?

LANE: I believe it *is* a very pleasant state, sir. I have had very little experience of it myself up to the present. I have only been married once. That was in consequence of a misunderstanding between myself and a young person.

ALGERNON (*languidly*): I don't know that I am much interested in your family life, Lane.

LANE: No, sir; it is not a very interesting subject. I never think of it myself.

ALGERNON: Very natural, I am sure. That will do, Lane, thank you.

LANE: Thank you, sir. (LANE *moves to go out.*)

ALGERNON: Ah! . . . just give me another cucumber sandwich.

LANE: Yes, sir. (*Returns and hands plate.*)

LANE *goes out.*

ALGERNON: Lane's views on marriage seem somewhat lax. Really, if the lower orders don't set us a good example, what on earth is the use of them? They seem, as a class, to have absolutely no sense of moral responsibility.

Enter LANE.

LANE: Mr. Ernest Worthing.

Enter JACK. LANE *goes out.*

ALGERNON: How are you, my dear Ernest? What brings you up to town?

JACK: Oh, pleasure, pleasure! What else should bring one anywhere? Eating as usual, I see, Algy!

ALGERNON (*stiffly*): I believe it is customary in good society to take some slight refreshment at five o'clock. Where have you been since last Thursday?

JACK (*sitting down on the sofa*): Oh! in the country.

ALGERNON: What on earth do you do there?

JACK (*pulling off his gloves*): When one is in town one amuses oneself. When one is in the country one amuses other people. It is excessively boring.

ALGERNON: And who are the people you amuse?

JACK (*airily*): Oh, neighbours, neighbours.

ALGERNON: Got nice neighbours in your part of Shropshire?

JACK: Perfectly horrid! Never speak to one of them.

ALGERNON: How immensely you must amuse them! (*Goes over and takes sandwich.*) By the way, Shropshire is your county, is it not?

JACK: Eh? Shropshire? Yes, of course. Hallo! Why all these cups? Why cucumber sandwiches? Why such reckless extravagance in one so young? Who is coming to tea?

ALGERNON: Oh! merely Aunt Augusta and Gwendolen.

JACK: How perfectly delightful!

ALGERNON: Yes, that is all very well; but I am afraid Aunt Augusta won't quite approve of your being here.

JACK: May I ask why?

ALGERNON: My dear fellow, the way you flirt with Gwendolen is perfectly disgraceful. It is almost as bad as the way Gwendolen flirts with you.

JACK: I am in love with Gwendolen. I have come up to town expressly to propose to her.

ALGERNON: I thought you had come up for pleasure? . . . I call that business.

JACK: How utterly unromantic you are!

ALGERNON: I really don't see anything romantic in proposing. It is very romantic to be in love. But there is nothing romantic about a definite proposal. Why, one may be accepted. One usually is, I believe. Then the excitement is all over. The very essence of romance is uncertainty. If ever I get married, I'll certainly try to forget the fact.

JACK: I have no doubt about that, dear Algy. The Divorce Court was specially invented for people whose memories are so curiously constituted.

ALGERNON: Oh! there is no use speculating on that subject. Divorces are made in heaven—— (JACK *puts out his hand to take a sandwich.* ALGERNON *at once interferes.*) Please don't touch the cucumber sandwiches. They are ordered specially for Aunt Augusta. (*Takes one and eats it.*)

JACK: Well, you have been eating them all the time.

ALGERNON: That is quite a different matter. She is my aunt. (*Takes plate from below.*) Have some bread and butter. The bread and butter is for Gwendolen. Gwendolen is devoted to bread and butter.

JACK (*advancing to table and helping himself*): And very good bread and butter it is too.

ALGERNON: Well, my dear fellow, you need not eat as if you were going to eat it all. You behave as if you were married to her already. You are not married to her already, and I don't think you ever will be.

JACK: Why on earth do you say that?

ALGERNON: Well, in the first place girls never marry the men they flirt with. Girls don't think it right.

JACK: Oh, that is nonsense!

ALGERNON: It isn't. It is a great truth. It accounts for the extraordinary number of bachelors that one sees all over the place. In the second place, I don't give my consent.

JACK: Your consent! What utter nonsense you talk!

ALGERNON: My dear fellow, Gwendolen is my first cousin. And before I allow you to marry her, you will have to clear up the whole question of Cecily.

JACK: Cecily! What on earth do you mean? (ALGERNON *goes to the bell and rings it. Then returns to tea table and eats another sandwich.*) What do you mean, Algy, by Cecily! I don't know any one of the name of Cecily . . . as far as I remember.

Enter LANE.

ALGERNON: Bring me that cigarette case Mr. Worthing left in the smoking-room the last time he dined here.

LANE: Yes, sir.

LANE *goes out.*

JACK: Do you mean to say you have had my cigarette case all this time? I wish to goodness you had let me know. I have been writing frantic letters to Scotland Yard* about it. I was very nearly offering a large reward.

ALGERNON: Well, I wish you would offer one. I happen to be more than usually hard up.

JACK: There is no good offering a large reward now that the thing is found.

Enter LANE *with the cigarette case on a salver.* ALGERNON *takes it at once.* LANE *goes out.*

ALGERNON: I think that is rather mean of you, Ernest, I must say. (*Opens case and examines it.*) However, it makes no matter, for, now that I look at the inscription inside, I find that the thing isn't yours after all.

JACK: Of course it's mine. (*Moving to him.*) You have seen me with it a hundred times, and you have no right whatsoever to read what is written inside. It is a very ungentlemanly thing to read a private cigarette case.

ALGERNON: Oh! it is absurd to have a hard and fast rule about what one should read and what one shouldn't. One should read everything. More than half of modern culture depends on what one shouldn't read.

JACK: I am quite aware of the fact, and I don't propose to discuss modern culture. It isn't the sort of thing one should talk of in private. I simply want my cigarette case back.

ALGERNON: Yes; but this isn't your cigarette case. This cigarette case is a present from some one of the name of Cecily, and you said you didn't know any one of that name.

JACK: Well, if you want to know, Cecily happens to be my aunt.

ALGERNON: Your aunt!

JACK: Yes. Charming old lady she is, too. Lives at Tunbridge Wells. Just give it back to me, Algy.

ALGERNON (*retreating to back of sofa*): But why does she call her-

---

*Even in the nineteenth century, London's police detectives were located at Scotland Yard, though in a different building than today.

self little Cecily if she is your aunt and lives at Tunbridge Wells?* (*Reading.*) "From little Cecily with her fondest love."

JACK (*moving to sofa and kneeling upon it*): My dear fellow, what on earth is there in that? Some aunts are tall, some aunts are not tall. That is a matter that surely an aunt may be allowed to decide for herself. You seem to think that every aunt should be exactly like your aunt! That is absurd! For Heaven's sake give me back my cigarette case. (*Follows* ALGERNON *round the room.*)

ALGERNON: Yes. But why does your aunt call you her uncle? "From little Cecily, with her fondest love to her dear Uncle Jack." There is no objection, I admit, to an aunt being a small aunt, but why an aunt, no matter what her size may be, should call her own nephew her uncle, I can't quite make out. Besides, your name isn't Jack at all; it is Ernest.

JACK: It isn't Ernest; it's Jack.

ALGERNON: You have always told me it was Ernest. I have introduced you to every one as Ernest. You answer to the name of Ernest. You look as if your name was Ernest. You are the most earnest-looking person I ever saw in my life. It is perfectly absurd your saying that your name isn't Ernest. It's on your cards. Here is one of them. (*Taking it from case.*) "Mr. Ernest Worthing, B.4, The Albany, W." I'll keep this as a proof that your name is Ernest if ever you attempt to deny it to me, or to Gwendolen, or to any one else. (*Puts the card in his pocket.*)

JACK: Well, my name is Ernest in town and Jack in the country, and the cigarette case was given to me in the country.

ALGERNON: Yes, but that does not account for the fact that your small Aunt Cecily, who lives at Tunbridge Wells, calls you her dear Uncle. Come, old boy, you had much better have the thing out at once.

JACK: My dear Algy, you talk exactly as if you were a dentist. It is very vulgar to talk like a dentist when one isn't a dentist. It produces a false impression.

ALGERNON: Well, that is exactly what dentists always do. Now, go on! Tell me the whole thing. I may mention that I have always

---

*Town in southwest Kent, near Maidstone.

suspected you of being a confirmed and secret Bunburyist; and I am quite sure of it now.

JACK: Bunburyist? What on earth do you mean by a Bunburyist?

ALGERNON: I'll reveal to you the meaning of that incomparable expression as soon as you are kind enough to inform me why you are Ernest in town and Jack in the country.

JACK: Well, produce my cigarette case first.

ALGERNON: Here it is. (*Hands cigarette case.*) Now produce your explanation, and pray make it improbable. (*Sits on sofa.*)

JACK: My dear fellow, there is nothing improbable about my explanation at all. In fact, it's perfectly ordinary. Old Mr. Thomas Cardew, who adopted me when I was a little boy, under rather peculiar circumstances, and left me all the money I possess, made me in his will guardian to his grand-daughter, Miss Cecily Cardew. Cecily, who addresses me as her uncle from motives of respect that you could not possibly appreciate, lives at my place in the country under the charge of her admirable governess, Miss Prism.

ALGERNON: Where is that place in the country, by the way?

JACK: That is nothing to you, dear boy. You are not going to be invited. . . . I may tell you candidly that the place is not in Shropshire.

ALGERNON: I suspected that, my dear fellow! I have Bunburyed all over Shropshire on two separate occasions. Now, go on. Why are you Ernest in town and Jack in the country?

JACK: My dear Algy, I don't know whether you will be able to understand my real motives. You are hardly serious enough. When one is placed in the position of guardian, one has to adopt a very high moral tone on all subjects. It's one's duty to do so. And as a high moral tone can hardly be said to conduce very much to either one's health or one's happiness if carried to excess, in order to get up to town I have always pretended to have a younger brother of the name of Ernest, who lives in the Albany, and gets into the most dreadful scrapes. That, my dear Algy, is the whole truth pure and simple.

ALGERNON: The truth is rarely pure and never simple. Modern life would be very tedious if it were either, and modern literature a complete impossibility!

JACK: That wouldn't be at all a bad thing.

ALGERNON: Literary criticism is not your forte, my dear fellow. Don't try it. You should leave that to people who haven't been at a University. They do it so well in the daily papers. What you really are is a Bunburyist. I was quite right in saying you were a Bunburyist. You are one of the most advanced Bunburyists I know.

JACK: What on earth do you mean?

ALGERNON: You have invented a very useful younger brother called Ernest, in order that you may be able to come up to town as often as you like. I have invented an invaluable permanent invalid called Bunbury, in order that I may be able to go down into the country whenever I choose.

JACK: What nonsense.

ALGERNON: It isn't nonsense. Bunbury is perfectly invaluable. If it wasn't for Bunbury's extraordinary bad health, for instance, I wouldn't be able to dine with you at the Savoy to-night, for I have been really engaged to Aunt Augusta for more than a week.

JACK: I haven't asked you to dine with me anywhere to-night.

ALGERNON: I know. You are absurdly careless about sending out invitations. It is very foolish of you. Nothing annoys people so much as not receiving invitations.

JACK: Well, I can't dine at the Savoy. I owe them about £700.* They are always getting judgments and things against me. They bother my life out.

ALGERNON: Why on earth don't you pay them? You have got heaps of money.

JACK: Yes, but Ernest hasn't, and I must keep up Ernest's reputation. Ernest is one of those chaps who never pays a bill. He gets writted about once a week.

ALGERNON: Well, let us dine at Willis's.

JACK: You had much better dine with your Aunt Augusta.

ALGERNON: I haven't the smallest intention of doing anything of the kind. To begin with, I dined there on Monday, and once a week is quite enough to dine with one's own relations. In the second place, whenever I do dine there I am always treated as a member

---

*The dining room of the Savoy Hotel was one of London's finest and most fashionable restaurants; Jack's memory of exactly what he owes is rather vague, as we later learn.

of the family, and sent down with either no woman at all, or two. In the third place, I know perfectly well whom she will place me next to, to-night. She will place me next Mary Farquhar, who always flirts with her own husband across the dinner-table. That is not very pleasant. Indeed, it is not even decent . . . and that sort of thing is enormously on the increase. The amount of women in London who flirt with their own husbands is perfectly scandalous. It looks so bad. It is simply washing one's clean linen in public. Besides, now that I know you to be a confirmed Bunburyist I naturally want to talk to you about Bunburying. I want to tell you the rules.

JACK: I'm not a Bunburyist at all. If Gwendolen accepts me, I am going to kill my brother, indeed I think I'll kill him in any case. Cecily is a little too much interested in him. She is always asking me to forgive him, and that sort of thing. It is rather a bore. So I am going to get rid of Ernest. And I strongly advise you to do the same with Mr. . . . with your invalid friend who has the absurd name.

ALGERNON: Nothing will induce me to part with Bunbury, and if you ever get married, which seems to me extremely problematic, you will be very glad to know Bunbury. A man who marries without knowing Bunbury has a very tedious time of it.

JACK: That is nonsense. If I marry a charming girl like Gwendolen, and she is the only girl I ever saw in my life that I would marry, I certainly won't want to know Bunbury.

ALGERNON: Then your wife will. You don't seem to realise, that in married life three is company and two is none.

JACK (*sententiously*): That, my dear young friend, is the theory that the corrupt French Drama has been propounding for the last fifty years.

ALGERNON: Yes; and that the happy English home has proved in half the time.

JACK: For heaven's sake, don't try to be cynical. It's perfectly easy to be cynical.

ALGERNON: My dear fellow, it isn't easy to be anything nowadays. There's such a lot of beastly competition about. (*The sound of an electric bell is heard.*) Ah! that must be Aunt Augusta. Only relatives, or creditors, ever ring in that Wagnerian manner. Now, if I get her out of the way for ten minutes, so that you can have an opportunity for proposing to Gwendolen, may I dine with you to-night at Willis's?

JACK: I suppose so, if you want to.

ALGERNON: Yes, but you must be serious about it. I hate people who are not serious about meals. It is so shallow of them.

Enter LANE.

LANE: Lady Bracknell and Miss Fairfax.

ALGERNON *goes forward to meet them. Enter* LADY BRACKNELL *and* GWENDOLEN.

LADY BRACKNELL: Good-afternoon, dear Algernon, I hope you are behaving very well.

ALGERNON: I'm feeling very well, Aunt Augusta.

LADY BRACKNELL: That's not quite the same thing. In fact the two things rarely go together. (*Sees* JACK *and bows to him with icy coldness.*)

ALGERNON (*to* GWENDOLEN): Dear me, you are smart!

GWENDOLEN: I am always smart! Am I not, Mr. Worthing?

JACK: You're quite perfect, Miss Fairfax.

GWENDOLEN: Oh! I hope I am not that. It would leave no room for developments, and I intend to develop in many directions. (GWENDOLEN *and* JACK *sit down together in the corner.*)

LADY BRACKNELL: I'm sorry if we are a little late, Algernon, but I was obliged to call on dear Lady Harbury. I hadn't been there since her poor husband's death. I never saw a woman so altered; she looks quite twenty years younger. And now I'll have a cup of tea, and one of those nice cucumber sandwiches you promised me.

ALGERNON: Certainly, Aunt Augusta. (*Goes over to tea table.*)

LADY BRACKNELL: Won't you come and sit here, Gwendolen?

GWENDOLEN: Thanks, mamma, I'm quite comfortable where I am.

ALGERNON (*picking up empty plate in horror*): Good heavens! Lane! Why are there no cucumber sandwiches? I ordered them specially.

LANE (*gravely*): There were no cucumbers in the market this morning, sir. I went down twice.

ALGERNON: No cucumbers!

LANE: No, sir. Not even for ready money.*

ALGERNON: That will do, Lane, thank you.

LANE: Thank you, sir. (*Goes out.*)

ALGERNON: I am greatly distressed, Aunt Augusta, about there being no cucumbers, not even for ready money.

LADY BRACKNELL: It really makes no matter, Algernon. I had some crumpets with Lady Harbury, who seems to me to be living entirely for pleasure now.

ALGERNON: I hear her hair has turned quite gold from grief.

LADY BRACKNELL: It certainly has changed its colour. From what cause I, of course, cannot say. (ALGERNON *crosses and hands tea.*) Thank you. I've quite a treat for you to-night, Algernon. I am going to send you down with Mary Farquhar. She is such a nice woman, and so attentive to her husband. It's delightful to watch them.

ALGERNON: I am afraid, Aunt Augusta, I shall have to give up the pleasure of dining with you to-night after all.

LADY BRACKNELL (*frowning*): I hope not, Algernon. It would put my table completely out. Your uncle would have to dine upstairs. Fortunately he is accustomed to that.

ALGERNON: It is a great bore, and, I need hardly say, a terrible disappointment to me, but the fact is I have just had a telegram to say that my poor friend Bunbury is very ill again. (*Exchanges glances with* JACK.) They seem to think I should be with him.

LADY BRACKNELL: It is very strange. This Mr. Bunbury seems to suffer from curiously bad health.

ALGERNON: Yes; poor Bunbury is a dreadful invalid.

LADY BRACKNELL: Well, I must say, Algernon, that I think it is high time that Mr. Bunbury made up his mind whether he was going to live or to die. This shilly-shallying with the question is absurd. Nor do I in any way approve of the modern sympathy with invalids. I consider it morbid. Illness of any kind is hardly a thing

---

*Lane's dig (for which Algernon quickly dismisses him) suggests that Algernon usually relies on credit at the greengrocer's.

to be encouraged in others. Health is the primary duty of life. I am always telling that to your poor uncle, but he never seems to take much notice . . . as far as any improvement in his ailment goes. Well, Algernon, of course if you are obliged to be beside the bed-side of Mr. Bunbury, I have nothing more to say. But I would be much obliged if you would ask Mr. Bunbury, from me, to be kind enough not to have a relapse on Saturday, for I rely on you to arrange my music for me. It is my last reception, and one wants something that will encourage conversation, particularly at the end of the season when every one has practically said whatever they had to say, which, in most cases, was probably not much.

ALGERNON: I'll speak to Bunbury, Aunt Augusta, if he is still conscious, and I think I can promise you he'll be all right by Saturday. Of course the music is a great difficulty. You see, if one plays good music, people don't listen, and if one plays bad music people don't talk. But I'll run over the programme I've drawn out, if you will kindly come into the next room for a moment.

LADY BRACKNELL: Thank you, Algernon. It is very thoughtful of you. (*Rising and following* ALGERNON.) I'm sure the programme will be delightful, after a few expurgations. French songs I cannot possibly allow. People always seem to think that they are improper, and either look shocked, which is vulgar, or laugh, which is worse. But German sounds a thoroughly respectable language, and indeed, I believe is so. Gwendolen, you will accompany me.

GWENDOLEN: Certainly, mamma.

LADY BRACKNELL *and* ALGERNON *go into the music-room,* GWENDOLEN *remains behind.*

JACK: Charming day it has been, Miss Fairfax.

GWENDOLEN: Pray don't talk to me about the weather, Mr. Worthing. Whenever people talk to me about the weather, I always feel quite certain that they mean something else. And that makes me so nervous.

JACK: I do mean something else.

GWENDOLEN: I thought so. In fact, I am never wrong.

JACK: And I would like to be allowed to take advantage of Lady Bracknell's temporary absence . . .

GWENDOLEN: I would certainly advise you to do so. Mamma has a way of coming back suddenly into a room that I have often had to speak to her about.

JACK (*nervously*): Miss Fairfax, ever since I met you I have admired you more than any girl . . . I have ever met since . . . I met you.

GWENDOLEN: Yes, I am quite well aware of the fact. And I often wish that in public, at any rate, you had been more demonstrative. For me you have always had an irresistible fascination. Even before I met you I was far from indifferent to you. (JACK *looks at her in amazement.*) We live, as I hope you know, Mr. Worthing, in an age of ideals. The fact is constantly mentioned in the more expensive monthly magazines, and has now reached the provincial pulpits, I am told; and my ideal has always been to love some one of the name of Ernest. There is something in that name that inspires absolute confidence. The moment Algernon first mentioned to me that he had a friend called Ernest, I knew I was destined to love you. The name, fortunately for my peace of mind, is, as far as my own experience goes, extremely rare.

JACK: You really love me, Gwendolen?

GWENDOLEN: Passionately!

JACK: Darling! You don't know how happy you've made me.

GWENDOLEN: My own Ernest! (*They embrace.*)

JACK: But you don't really mean to say that you couldn't love me if my name wasn't Ernest?

GWENDOLEN: But your name is Ernest.

JACK: Yes, I know it is. But supposing it was something else? Do you mean to say you couldn't love me then?

GWENDOLEN (*glibly*): Ah! that is clearly a metaphysical speculation, and like most metaphysical speculations has very little reference at all to the actual facts of real life, as we know them.

JACK: Personally, darling, to speak quite candidly, I don't much care about the name of Ernest. . . . I don't think the name suits me at all.

GWENDOLEN: It suits you perfectly. It is a divine name. It has a music of its own. It produces vibrations.

JACK: Well, really, Gwendolen, I must say that I think there are lots of other much nicer names. I think Jack, for instance, a charming name.

GWENDOLEN: Jack? . . . No, there is very little music in the name Jack, if any at all, indeed. It does not thrill. It produces absolutely no vibrations. . . . I have known several Jacks, and they all, without exception, were more than usually plain. Besides, Jack is a notorious domesticity for John! And I pity any woman who is married to a man called John. She would have a very tedious life with him. She would probably never be allowed to know the entrancing pleasure of a single moment's solitude. The only really safe name is Ernest.

JACK: Gwendolen, I must get christened at once—I mean we must get married at once. There is no time to be lost.

GWENDOLEN: Married, Mr. Worthing?

JACK (*astounded*): Well . . . surely. You know that I love you, and you led me to believe, Miss Fairfax, that you were not absolutely indifferent to me.

GWENDOLEN: I adore you. But you haven't proposed to me yet. Nothing has been said at all about marriage. The subject has not even been touched on.

JACK: Well . . . may I propose to you now?

GWENDOLEN: I think it would be an admirable opportunity. And to spare you any possible disappointment, Mr. Worthing, I think it only fair to tell you quite frankly beforehand that I am fully determined to accept you.

JACK: Gwendolen!

GWENDOLEN: Yes, Mr. Worthing, what have you got to say to me?

JACK: You know what I have got to say to you.

GWENDOLEN: Yes, but you don't say it.

JACK: Gwendolen, will you marry me? (*Goes on his knees.*)

GWENDOLEN: Of course I will, darling. How long you have been about it! I am afraid you have had very little experience in how to propose.

JACK: My own one, I have never loved anyone in the world but you.

GWENDOLEN: Yes, but men often propose for practice. I know my brother Gerald does. All my girl-friends tell me so. What wonderfully blue eyes you have, Ernest! They are quite, quite blue. I hope you will always look at me just like that, especially when there are other people present.

Enter LADY BRACKNELL.

LADY BRACKNELL: Mr. Worthing! Rise, sir, from this semi-recumbent posture. It is most indecorous.

GWENDOLEN: Mamma! (*He tries to rise; she restrains him.*) I must beg you to retire. This is no place for you. Besides, Mr. Worthing has not quite finished yet.

LADY BRACKNELL: Finished what, may I ask?

GWENDOLEN: I am engaged to Mr. Worthing, mamma. (*They rise together.*)

LADY BRACKNELL: Pardon me, you are not engaged to any one. When you do become engaged to some one, I, or your father, should his health permit him, will inform you of the fact. An engagement should come on a young girl as a surprise, pleasant or unpleasant, as the case may be. It is hardly a matter that she could be allowed to arrange for herself. . . . And now I have a few questions to put to you, Mr. Worthing!

JACK: I shall be charmed to reply to any questions, Lady Bracknell.

GWENDOLEN: You mean if you know the answers to them. Mamma's questions are sometimes peculiarly inquisitorial.

LADY BRACKNELL: I intend to make them very inquisitorial. And while I am making these inquiries, you, Gwendolen, will wait for me below in the carriage.

GWENDOLEN (*reproachfully*): Mamma!

LADY BRACKNELL: In the carriage, Gwendolen!

GWENDOLEN *goes to the door. She and* JACK *blow kisses to each other behind* LADY BRACKNELL'S *back.* LADY BRACKNELL *looks vaguely about as if she could not understand what the noise was. Finally turns round.*

Gwendolen, the carriage!

GWENDOLEN: Yes, mamma. (*Goes out, looking back at* JACK.)

LADY BRACKNELL (*sitting down*): You can take a seat, Mr. Worthing.

Looks in her pocket for note-book and pencil.

JACK: Thank you, Lady Bracknell, I prefer standing.

LADY BRACKNELL (*pencil and note-book in hand*): I feel bound to tell you that you are not down on my list of eligible young men, although I have the same list as the dear Duchess of Bolton has. We work together, in fact. However, I am quite ready to enter your name, should your answers be what a really affectionate mother requires. Do you smoke?

JACK: Well, yes, I must admit I smoke.

LADY BRACKNELL: I am glad to hear it. A man should always have an occupation of some kind. There are far too many idle men in London as it is. How old are you?

JACK: Twenty-nine.

LADY BRACKNELL: A very good age to be married at. I have always been of opinion that a man who desires to get married should know either everything or nothing. Which do you know?

JACK (*after some hesitation*): I know nothing, Lady Bracknell.

LADY BRACKNELL: I am pleased to hear it. I do not approve of anything that tampers with natural ignorance. Ignorance is like a delicate exotic fruit; touch it and the bloom is gone. The whole theory of modern education is radically unsound. Fortunately in England, at any rate, education produces no effect whatsoever. If it did, it would prove a serious danger to the upper classes, and probably lead to acts of violence in Grosvenor Square. What is your income?

JACK: Between seven and eight thousand a year.

LADY BRACKNELL (*makes a note in her book*): In land, or in investments?

JACK: In investments, chiefly.

LADY BRACKNELL: That is satisfactory. What between the duties expected of one during one's lifetime, and the duties exacted from one after one's death, land has ceased to be either a profit or a pleasure. It gives one position, and prevents one from keeping it up. That's all that can be said about land.

JACK: I have a country house with some land, of course, attached to it, about fifteen hundred acres, I believe; but I don't depend on that for my real income. In fact, as far as I can make out, the poachers are the only people who make anything out of it.

LADY BRACKNELL: A country house! How many bedrooms?

Well, that point can be cleared up afterwards. You have a town house, I hope? A girl with a simple, unspoiled nature, like Gwendolen, could hardly be expected to reside in the country.

JACK: Well, I own a house in Belgrave Square,* but it is let by the year to Lady Bloxham. Of course, I can get it back whenever I like, at six months' notice.

LADY BRACKNELL: Lady Bloxham? I don't know her.

JACK: Oh, she goes about very little. She is a lady considerably advanced in years.

LADY BRACKNELL: Ah, nowadays that is no guarantee of respectability of character. What number in Belgrave Square?

JACK: 149.

LADY BRACKNELL (*shaking her head*): The unfashionable side. I thought there was something. However, that could easily be altered.

JACK: Do you mean the fashion, or the side?

LADY BRACKNELL (*sternly*): Both, if necessary, I presume. What are your politics?

JACK: Well, I am afraid I really have none. I am a Liberal Unionist.

LADY BRACKNELL: Oh, they count as Tories. They dine with us. Or come in the evening at any rate. You have, of course, no sympathy of any kind with the Radical Party?

JACK: Oh! I don't want to put the asses against the classes, if that is what you mean, Lady Bracknell.

LADY BRACKNELL: That is exactly what I do mean . . . ahem! . . . Are your parents living?

JACK: I have lost both my parents.

LADY BRACKNELL: Both? . . . To lose one parent may be regarded as a misfortune . . . to lose both seems like carelessness. Who was your father? He was evidently a man of some wealth. Was he born in what the Radical papers call the purple of commerce, or did he rise from the ranks of the aristocracy?

JACK: I am afraid I really don't know. The fact is, Lady Bracknell, I said I had lost my parents. It would be nearer the truth to say that

---

*Very fashionable residential area in London; Jack indicates in act four that this house will go to Cecily.

my parents seemed to have lost me. . . . I don't actually know who I am by birth. I was . . . well, I was found.

LADY BRACKNELL: Found!

JACK: The late Mr. Thomas Cardew, an old gentleman of a very charitable and kindly disposition, found me, and gave me the name of Worthing, because he happened to have a first-class ticket for Worthing in his pocket at the time. Worthing is a place in Sussex. It is a seaside resort.

LADY BRACKNELL: Where did the charitable gentleman who had a first-class ticket for this seaside resort find you?

JACK (*gravely*): In a hand-bag.

LADY BRACKNELL: A hand-bag?

JACK (*very seriously*): Yes, Lady Bracknell. I was in a hand-bag—a somewhat large, black leather hand-bag, with handles to it—an ordinary hand-bag in fact.

LADY BRACKNELL: In what locality did this Mr. James, or Thomas, Cardew come across this ordinary hand-bag?

JACK: In the cloak-room at Victoria Station.* It was given to him in mistake for his own.

LADY BRACKNELL: The cloak-room at Victoria Station?

JACK: Yes. The Brighton line.

LADY BRACKNELL: The line is immaterial. Mr. Worthing, I confess I feel somewhat bewildered by what you have just told me. To be born, or at any rate bred, in a hand-bag, whether it had handles or not, seems to me to display a contempt for the ordinary decencies of family life that reminds one of the worst excesses of the French Revolution. And I presume you know what that unfortunate movement led to? As for the particular locality in which the hand-bag was found, a cloak-room at a railway station might serve to conceal a social indiscretion—has probably, indeed, been used for that purpose before now—but it could hardly be regarded as an assured basis for a recognised position in good society.

JACK: May I ask you then what you would advise me to do? I need hardly say I would do anything in the world to ensure Gwendolen's happiness.

---

*One of London's major transportation hubs; trains heading south (for places such as Brighton and Worthing) leave from Victoria.

LADY BRACKNELL: I would strongly advise you, Mr. Worthing, to try and acquire some relations as soon as possible, and to make a definite effort to produce at any rate one parent, of either sex, before the season is quite over.

JACK: Well, I don't see how I could possibly manage to do that. I can produce the hand-bag at any moment. It is in my dressing-room at home. I really think that should satisfy you, Lady Bracknell.

LADY BRACKNELL: Me, sir! What has it to do with me? You can hardly imagine that I and Lord Bracknell would dream of allowing our only daughter—a girl brought up with the utmost care—to marry into a cloak-room, and form an alliance with a parcel. (JACK *starts indignantly.*) Kindly open the door for me sir. You will of course understand that for the future there is to be no communication of any kind between you and Miss Fairfax.

LADY BRACKNELL *sweeps out in majestic indignation.* ALGERNON, *from the other room, strikes up the Wedding March.* JACK *looks perfectly furious, and goes to the door.*

JACK: For goodness' sake don't play that ghastly tune, Algy! How idiotic you are!

The music stops and ALGERNON *enters cheerily.*

ALGERNON: Didn't it go off all right, old boy? You don't mean to say Gwendolen refused you? I know it is a way she has. She is always refusing people. I think it is most ill-natured of her.

JACK: Oh, Gwendolen is as right as a trivet. As far as she is concerned, we are engaged. Her mother is perfectly unbearable. Never met such a Gorgon.* . . . I don't really know what a Gorgon is like, but I am quite sure that Lady Bracknell is one. In any case, she is a monster, without being a myth, which is rather unfair. . . . I beg your pardon, Algy, I suppose I shouldn't talk about your own aunt in that way before you.

---

*A mythical monster, the gorgon Medusa was described as a beautiful woman, albeit with snakes as hair, whose gaze could turn men to stone.

ALGERNON: My dear boy, I love hearing my relations abused. It is the only thing that makes me put up with them at all. Relations are simply a tedious pack of people, who haven't got the remotest knowledge of how to live, nor the smallest instinct about when to die.

JACK: Ah! I haven't got any relations. Don't know anything about relations.

ALGERNON: You are a lucky fellow. Relations never lend one any money, and won't give one credit, even for genius. They are a sort of aggravated form of the public.

JACK: And after all, what does it matter whether a man ever had a father and mother or not? Mothers, of course, are all right. They pay a chap's bills and don't bother him. But fathers bother a chap and never pay his bills. I don't know a single chap at the club who speaks to his father.

ALGERNON: Yes! Fathers are certainly not popular just at present. (*Takes up the evening newspaper.*)

JACK: Popular! I bet you anything you like that there is not a single chap, of all the chaps that you and I know, who would be seen walking down St. James' Street with his own father. (*A pause.*) Anything in the papers?

ALGERNON (*still reading*): Nothing.

JACK: What a comfort.

ALGERNON: There is never anything in the papers, as far as I can see.

JACK: I think there is usually a great deal too much in them. They are always bothering one about people one doesn't know, one has never met, and one doesn't care twopence about. Brutes!

ALGERNON: I think people one hasn't met are charming. I'm very much interested at present in a girl I have never met; very much interested indeed.

JACK: Oh, that is nonsense!

ALGERNON: It isn't!

JACK: Well, I won't argue about the matter. You always want to argue about things.

ALGERNON: That is exactly what things were originally made for.

JACK: Upon my word, if I thought that, I'd shoot myself. . . . (*A pause.*) You don't think there is any chance of Gwendolen becoming like her mother in about a hundred and fifty years, do you, Algy?

ALGERNON: All women become like their mothers. That is their tragedy. No man does. That's his.

JACK: Is that clever?

ALGERNON: It is perfectly phrased! And quite as true as any observation in civilised life should be.

JACK: I am sick to death of cleverness. Everybody is clever nowadays. You can't go anywhere without meeting clever people. The thing has become an absolute public nuisance. I wish to goodness we had a few fools left.

ALGERNON: We have.

JACK: I should extremely like to meet them. What do they talk about?

ALGERNON: The fools? Oh! about the clever people of course.

JACK: What fools.

ALGERNON: By the way, did you tell Gwendolen the truth about your being Ernest in town, and Jack in the country?

JACK (*in a very patronising manner*): My dear fellow, the truth isn't quite the sort of thing one tells to a nice, sweet, refined girl. What extraordinary ideas you have about the way to behave to a woman!

ALGERNON: The only way to behave to a woman is to make love to her, if she is pretty, and to some one else, if she is plain.

JACK: Oh, that is nonsense.

ALGERNON: What about the young lady whose guardian you are! Miss Cardew? What about your brother? What about the profligate Ernest?

JACK: Oh! Cecily is all right. Before the end of the week I shall have got rid of my brother . . . I think I'll probably kill him in Paris.

ALGERNON: Why Paris?

JACK: Oh! Less trouble: no nonsense about a funeral and that sort of thing—yes, I'll kill him in Paris. . . . Apoplexy will do perfectly well. Lots of people die of apoplexy, quite suddenly, don't they?

ALGERNON: Yes, but it's hereditary, my dear fellow. It's a sort of thing that runs in families.

JACK: Good heavens! Then I certainly won't choose that. What can I say?

ALGERNON: Oh! Say influenza.

JACK: Oh, no! that wouldn't sound probable at all. Far too many people have had it.

ALGERNON: Oh well! Say anything you choose. Say a severe chill. That's all right.

JACK: You are sure a severe chill isn't hereditary, or anything dreadful of that kind?

ALGERNON: Of course it isn't.

JACK: Very well then. That is settled.

ALGERNON: But I thought you said that . . . Miss Cardew was a little too much interested in your poor brother Ernest? Won't she feel his loss a good deal?

JACK: Oh! that is all right. Cecily is not a silly romantic girl, I am glad to say. She has got a capital appetite, goes long walks, and pays no attention at all to her lessons.

ALGERNON: I would rather like to see Cecily.

JACK: I will take very good care you never do. And you are not to speak of her as Cecily.

ALGERNON: Ah! I believe she is plain. Yes: I know perfectly well what she is like. She is one of those dull, intellectual girls one meets all over the place. Girls who have got large minds and large feet. I am sure she is more than usually plain, and I expect she is about thirty-nine, and looks it.

JACK: She happens to be excessively pretty, and she is only just eighteen.

ALGERNON: Have you told Gwendolen yet that you have an excessively pretty ward who is only just eighteen?

JACK: Oh! one doesn't blurt these things out to people. Life is a question of tact. One leads up to the thing gradually. Cecily and Gwendolen are perfectly certain to be extremely great friends. I'll bet you anything you like that half an hour after they have met, they will be calling each other sister.

ALGERNON: Women only do that when they have called each other a lot of other things first. Now, my dear boy, if we want to get a good table at Willis's, we really must go and dress. Do you know it is nearly seven?

JACK (*irritably*): Oh! it always is nearly seven.

ALGERNON: Well, I'm hungry.

JACK: I never knew you when you weren't. . . . However, all right. I'll go round to the Albany and meet you at Willis's at eight. You can call for me on your way, if you like.

ALGERNON: What shall we do after dinner? Go to a theatre?

JACK: Oh, no! I loathe listening.

ALGERNON: Well, let us go to the Club?

JACK: Oh, no! I hate talking.

ALGERNON: Well, we might trot round to the Empire at ten?

JACK: Oh, no! I can't bear looking at things. It is so silly.

ALGERNON: Well, what shall we do?

JACK: Nothing!

ALGERNON: It is awfully hard work doing nothing. However, I don't mind hard work where there is no definite object of any kind . . .

Enter LANE.

LANE: Miss Fairfax.

Enter GWENDOLEN. LANE *goes out.*

ALGERNON: Gwendolen, upon my word!

GWENDOLEN: Algy, kindly turn your back. I have something very particular to say to Mr. Worthing. As it is somewhat of a private matter, you will of course listen.

ALGERNON: Really, Gwendolen, I don't think I can allow this at all.

GWENDOLEN: Algy, you always adopt a strictly immoral attitude towards life. You are not quite old enough to do that. (ALGERNON *retires to the fireplace.*)

JACK: My own darling.

GWENDOLEN: Ernest, we may never be married. From the expression on mamma's face I fear we never shall. Few parents nowadays pay any regard to what their children say to them. The old-fashioned respect for the young is fast dying out. Whatever influence I ever had over mamma, I lost at the age of three. But although she may prevent us from becoming man and wife, and I may marry some one else, and marry often, nothing that she can possibly do can alter my eternal devotion to you.

JACK: Dear Gwendolen!

GWENDOLEN: The story of your romantic origin, as related to me by mamma, with unpleasing comments, has naturally stirred the deeper fibres of my nature. Your Christian name has an irresistible fascination. The simplicity of your character makes you exquisitely incomprehensible to me. Your town address at the Albany I have. What is your address in the country?

JACK: The Manor House, Woolton, Hertfordshire.

ALGERNON, *who has been carefully listening, smiles to himself, and writes the address on his shirt-cuff. Then picks up the Railway Guide.*

GWENDOLEN: There is a good postal service, I suppose? It may be necessary to do something desperate. That, of course, will require serious consideration. I will communicate with you daily.

JACK: My own one!

GWENDOLEN: How long do you remain in town?

JACK: Till Monday.

GWENDOLEN: Good! Algy, you may turn round now.

ALGERNON: Thanks, I've turned round already.

GWENDOLEN: You may also ring the bell.

JACK: You will let me see you to your carriage, my own darling?

GWENDOLEN: Certainly.

JACK (*to* LANE, *who now enters*): I will see Miss Fairfax out.

LANE: Yes, sir.

JACK *and* GWENDOLEN *go off.*

LANE *presents several letters on a salver to* ALGERNON. *It is to be surmised that they are bills, as* ALGERNON, *after looking at the envelopes, tears them up.*

ALGERNON: A glass of sherry, Lane.

LANE: Yes, sir.

ALGERNON: To-morrow, Lane, I'm going Bunburying.

LANE: Yes, sir.

ALGERNON: I shall probably not be back till Monday. You can put up my dress clothes, my smoking jacket, and all the Bunbury suits . . .

LANE: Yes, sir. (*Handing sherry.*)

ALGERNON: I hope to-morrow will be a fine day, Lane.

LANE: It never is, sir.

ALGERNON: Lane, you're a perfect pessimist.

LANE: I do my best to give satisfaction, sir.

Enter JACK. LANE *goes off.*

JACK: There's a sensible, intellectual girl! the only girl I ever cared for in my life. (ALGERNON *is laughing immoderately.*) What on earth are you so amused at?

ALGERNON: Oh, I'm a little anxious about poor Bunbury, that is all.

JACK: If you don't take care, your friend Bunbury will get you into a serious scrape some day.

ALGERNON: I love scrapes. They are the only things that are never serious.

JACK: Oh, that's nonsense, Algy. You never talk anything but nonsense.

ALGERNON: Nobody ever does.

JACK *looks indignantly at him and leaves the room.* ALGERNON *lights a cigarette, reads his shirt-cuff, and smiles.*

Act Drop

ACT TWO

SCENE: *Garden at the Manor House, Woolton. A flight of grey stone steps leads up to the house. The garden, an old-fashioned one, full of roses. Time of year, July. Basket chairs, and a table covered with books, are set under a large yew-tree.*

MISS PRISM *discovered seated at the table.* CECILY *is at the back watering flowers.*

MISS PRISM (*calling*): Cecily, Cecily! Surely such a utilitarian occupation as the watering of flowers is rather Moulton's duty than yours? Especially at a moment when intellectual pleasures await you. Your German grammar is on the table. Pray open it at page fifteen. We will repeat yesterday's lesson.

CECILY: Oh! I wish you would give Moulton* the German lesson instead of me. Moulton!

MOULTON (*looking out from behind a hedge, with a broad grin on his face*): Eh, Miss Cecily?

CECILY: Wouldn't you like to know German, Moulton? German is the language talked by people who live in Germany.

MOULTON (*shaking his head*): I don't hold with them furrin tongues, miss. (*Bowing to* MISS PRISM.) No offence to you, ma'am. (*Disappears behind hedge.*)

MISS PRISM: Cecily, this will never do. Pray open your Schiller† at once.

CECILY (*coming over very slowly*): But I don't like German. It isn't at

---

* Moulton is mentioned in the revised version of the play (see endnote 1), but otherwise this character is cut from that version.

†Friedrich von Schiller (1759–1805), German playwright and poet; in his play *Wilhelm Tell* (1804) he dramatized the legend of the Swiss hero who used bow and arrow to shoot an apple from his son's head.

all a becoming language. I know perfectly well that I look quite plain after my German lesson.

MISS PRISM: Child, you know how anxious your guardian is that you should improve yourself in every way. He laid particular stress on your German, as he was leaving for town yesterday. Indeed, he always lays stress on your German when he is leaving for town.

CECILY: Dear Uncle Jack is so very serious! Sometimes he is so serious that I think he cannot be quite well.

MISS PRISM (*drawing herself up*): Your guardian enjoys the best of health, and his gravity of demeanour is especially to be commended in one so comparatively young as he is. I know no one who has a higher sense of duty and responsibility.

CECILY: I suppose that is why he often looks a little bored when we three are together.

MISS PRISM: Cecily! I am surprised at you. Mr. Worthing has many troubles in his life. Idle merriment and triviality would be out of place in his conversation. You must remember his constant anxiety about that unfortunate young man his brother.

CECILY: I wish Uncle Jack would allow that unfortunate young man, his brother, to come down here sometimes. We might have a good influence over him, Miss Prism. I am sure you certainly would. You know German, and geology, and things of that kind influence a man very much.

CECILY *begins to write in her diary.*

MISS PRISM (*shaking her head*): I do not think that even I could produce any effect on a character that according to his own brother's admission is irretrievably weak and vacillating. Indeed I am not sure that I would desire to reclaim him. I am not in favour of this modern mania for turning bad people into good people at a moment's notice. As a man sows so let him reap.

CECILY: But men don't sew, Miss Prism. . . . And if they did, I don't see why they should be punished for it. There is a great deal too much punishment in the world. German is a punishment, certainly, and there is far too much German. You told me yourself yesterday that Germany was over-populated.

MISS PRISM: That is no reason why you should be writing your diary instead of translating "William Tell". You must put away your diary, Cecily. I really don't see why you should keep a diary at all.

CECILY: I keep a diary in order to enter the wonderful secrets of my life. If I didn't write them down, I should probably forget all about them.

MISS PRISM: Memory, my dear Cecily, is the diary that we all carry about with us.

CECILY: Yes, but it usually chronicles the things that have never happened, and couldn't possibly have happened. I believe that Memory is responsible for nearly all the three-volume novels that Mudie* sends us.

MISS PRISM: Do not speak slightingly of the three-volume novel, Cecily. I wrote one myself in earlier days.

CECILY: Did you really, Miss Prism? How wonderfully clever you are! I hope it did not end happily? I don't like novels that end happily. They depress me so much.

MISS PRISM: The good ended happily, and the bad unhappily. That is what Fiction means.

CECILY: I suppose so. But it seems very unfair. And was your novel ever published?

MISS PRISM: Alas! no. The manuscript unfortunately was abandoned. (CECILY *starts.*) I use the word in the sense of lost or mislaid. To your work, child, these speculations are profitless.

CECILY (*smiling*): But I see Dr. Chasuble coming up through the garden.

MISS PRISM (*rising and advancing*): Dr. Chasuble! This is indeed a pleasure.

Enter CANON CHASUBLE.†

CHASUBLE: And how are we this morning? Miss Prism, you are, I trust, well?

CECILY: Miss Prism has just been complaining of a slight headache.

---

*Mudie's was a chain of lending libraries throughout England; for a small fee, one could read the latest (and most sensational) novels.

†The chasuble is a garment worn by an officiating priest.

I think it would do her so much good to have a short stroll with you in the Park, Dr. Chasuble.

MISS PRISM: Cecily, I have not mentioned anything about a headache.

CECILY: No, dear Miss Prism, I know that, but I felt instinctively that you had a headache. Indeed I was thinking about that, and not about my German lesson, when the Rector came in.

CHASUBLE: I hope, Cecily, you are not inattentive.

CECILY: Oh, I am afraid I am.

CHASUBLE: That is strange. Were I fortunate enough to be Miss Prism's pupil, I would hang upon her lips. (MISS PRISM *glares.*) I spoke metaphorically. My metaphor was drawn from bees. Ahem! Mr. Worthing, I suppose, has not returned from town yet?

MISS PRISM: We do not expect him till Monday afternoon.

CHASUBLE: Ah yes, he usually likes to spend his Sunday in London. He is not one of those whose sole aim is enjoyment, as, by all accounts, that unfortunate young man his brother seems to be. But I must not disturb Egeria and her pupil any longer.

MISS PRISM: Egeria? My name is Lætitia,* Doctor.

CHASUBLE (*bowing*): A classical allusion merely, drawn from the Pagan authors. I shall see you both no doubt at Evensong?

MISS PRISM: I think, dear Doctor, I will have a stroll with you. I find I have a headache after all, and a walk might do it good.

CHASUBLE: With pleasure, Miss Prism, with pleasure. We might go as far as the schools and back.

MISS PRISM: That would be delightful. Cecily, you will read your Political Economy in my absence. The chapter on the Fall of the Rupee you may omit. It is somewhat too sensational for a young girl. Even these metallic problems have their melodramatic side.

CHASUBLE: Reading Political Economy, Cecily? It is wonderful how girls are educated nowadays. I suppose you know all about relations between Capital and Labour?

CECILY: I am afraid I am not learned at all. All I know is about the relations between Capital and Idleness—and that is merely from observation. So I don't suppose it is true.

---

*In Roman legend, Egeria was a nymph who advised a king; although Dr. Chasuble uses the name figuratively, Miss Prism thinks he means it literally.

MISS PRISM: Cecily, that sounds like Socialism! And I suppose you know where Socialism leads to?

CECILY: Oh, yes! That leads to Rational Dress,* Miss Prism. And I suppose that when a woman is dressed rationally, she is treated rationally. She certainly deserves to be.

CHASUBLE: A wilful lamb! Dear child!

MISS PRISM (*smiling*): A sad trouble sometimes.

CHASUBLE: I envy you such tribulation.

Goes down the garden with MISS PRISM.

CECILY (*picks up books and throws them back on table*): Horrid Political Economy! Horrid Geography! Horrid, horrid German!

Enter MERRIMAN *with a card on a salver.*

MERRIMAN: Mr. Ernest Worthing has just driven over from the station. He has brought his luggage with him.

CECILY (*takes the card and reads it*): "Mr. Ernest Worthing, B.4, The Albany, W." Uncle Jack's brother! Did you tell him Mr. Worthing was in town?

MERRIMAN: Yes, Miss. He seemed very much disappointed. I mentioned that you and Miss Prism were in the garden. He said he was anxious to speak to you privately for a moment.

CECILY (*to herself*): I don't think Miss Prism would like my being alone with him. So I had better send for him at once, before she comes in. (*To* MERRIMAN.) Ask Mr. Ernest Worthing to come here. I suppose you had better talk to the housekeeper about a room for him.

MERRIMAN: I have already sent his luggage up to the Blue Room, Miss: next to Mr. Worthing's own room.

CECILY: Oh! That is all right.

MERRIMAN *goes off.*

---

*In the late nineteenth century, a number of movements sought to make women's fashions, which included the use of constricting corsets, simpler and less painful.

I have never met any really wicked person before. I feel rather frightened. I am so afraid he will look just like everyone else.

Enter ALGERNON, *very gay and debonair.*

He does!

ALGERNON (*raising his hat*): You are my little cousin Cecily, I'm sure.

CECILY: You are under some strange mistake. I am not little. In fact, I believe I am more than usually tall for my age. (ALGERNON *is rather taken aback.*) But I am your cousin Cecily. You, I see from your card, are Uncle Jack's brother, my cousin Ernest, my wicked cousin Ernest.

ALGERNON: Oh! I am not really wicked at all, cousin Cecily. You musn't think that I am wicked.

CECILY: If you are not, then you have certainly been deceiving us all in a very inexcusable manner. You have made Uncle Jack believe that you are very bad. I hope you have not been leading a double life,* pretending to be wicked and being really good all the time. That would be hypocrisy.

ALGERNON (*looks at her in amazement*): Oh! Of course I have been rather reckless.

CECILY: I am glad to hear it.

ALGERNON: In fact, now you mention the subject, I have been very bad in my own small way.

CECILY: I don't think you should be so proud of that, though I am sure it must have been very pleasant.

ALGERNON: It is much pleasanter being here with you.

CECILY: I can't understand how you are here at all. Uncle Jack telegraphed to you yesterday at the Albany that he would see you for the last time at six o'clock. He lets me read all the telegrams he sends you. I know some of them by heart.

ALGERNON: The fact is I didn't get the telegram till it was too late. Then I missed him at the Club, and the Hall Porter said he thought he had come down here. So, of course, I followed as I knew he wanted to see me.

CECILY: He won't be back till Monday afternoon.

ALGERNON: That is a great disappointment. I am obliged to go up

*Cecily ironically reverses the life that her uncle and Algernon actually lead.

by the first train on Monday morning. I have a business appointment that I am anxious . . . to miss!

CECILY: Couldn't you miss it anywhere but in London?

ALGERNON: No: the appointment is in London.

CECILY: Well, I know, of course, how important it is not to keep a business engagement, if one wants to retain any sense of the beauty of life, but still I think you had better wait till Uncle Jack arrives. I know he wants to speak to you about your emigrating.

ALGERNON: About my what?

CECILY: Your emigrating. He has gone up to buy your outfit.

ALGERNON: I certainly wouldn't let Jack buy my outfit. He has no taste in neckties at all.

CECILY: I don't think you will require neckties. Uncle Jack is sending you to Australia.

ALGERNON: Australia! I'd sooner die.

CECILY: Well, he said at dinner on Wednesday night, that you would have to choose between this world, the next world, and Australia.

ALGERNON: Oh, well! The accounts I have received of Australia and the next world are not particularly encouraging. This world is good enough for me, cousin Cecily.

CECILY: Yes, but are you good enough for it?

ALGERNON: I'm afraid I'm not that. That is why I want you to reform me. You might make that your mission, if you don't mind, cousin Cecily.

CECILY: How dare you suggest that I have a mission?

ALGERNON: I beg your pardon: but I thought that every woman had a mission of some kind, nowadays.

CECILY: Every female has! No woman. Besides, I have no time to reform you this afternoon.

ALGERNON: Well, would you mind my reforming myself this afternoon?

CECILY: It is rather Quixotic of you. But I think you should try.

ALGERNON: I will. I feel better already.

CECILY: You are looking a little worse.

ALGERNON: That is because I am hungry.

CECILY: How thoughtless of me. I should have remembered that when one is going to lead an entirely new life, one requires regular and wholesome meals. Miss Prism and I lunch at two, off some roast mutton.

ALGERNON: I fear that would be too rich for me.

CECILY: Uncle Jack, whose health has been sadly undermined by the late hours you keep in town, has been ordered by his London doctor to have pâté de foie gras sandwiches and 1889 champagne* at twelve. I don't know if such invalid fare would suit you.

ALGERNON: Oh! I will be quite content with '89 champagne.

CECILY: I am glad to see you have such simple tastes. This is the dining-room.

ALGERNON: Thank you. Might I have a buttonhole first? I never have any appetite unless I have a buttonhole first.

CECILY: A Maréchal Niel?† (*Picks up scissors.*)

ALGERNON: No, I'd sooner have a pink rose.

CECILY: Why? (*Cuts a flower.*)

ALGERNON: Because you are like a pink rose, Cousin Cecily.

CECILY: I don't think it can be right for you to talk to me like that. Miss Prism never says such things to me.

ALGERNON: Then Miss Prism is a short-sighted old lady. (CECILY *puts the rose in his buttonhole.*) You are the prettiest girl I ever saw.

CECILY: Miss Prism says that all good looks are a snare.

ALGERNON: They are a snare that every sensible man would like to be caught in.

CECILY: Oh, I don't think I would care to catch a sensible man. I shouldn't know what to talk to him about.

They pass into the house. MISS PRISM *and* DR. CHASUBLE *return.*

MISS PRISM: You are too much alone, dear Dr. Chasuble. You should get married. A misanthrope I can understand—a womanthrope, never!

CHASUBLE (*with a scholar's shudder*): Believe me, I do not deserve

---

*Jack's "prescribed" diet of imported goose liver pâté and sparkling wine is obviously another story he has invented to justify his own pleasure.

†Yellow country garden rose.

so neologistic a phrase. The precept as well as the practice of the Primitive Church was distinctly against matrimony.

MISS PRISM (*sententiously*): That is obviously the reason why the Primitive Church has not lasted up to the present day. And you do not seem to realise, dear Doctor, that by persistently remaining single, a man converts himself into a permanent public temptation. Men should be more careful; this very celibacy leads weaker vessels astray.

CHASUBLE: But is a man not equally attractive when married?

MISS PRISM: No married man is ever attractive except to his wife.

CHASUBLE: And often, I've been told, not even to her.

MISS PRISM: That depends on the intellectual sympathies of the woman. Maturity can always be depended on. Ripeness can be trusted. Young women are green. (DR. CHASUBLE *starts.*) I spoke horticulturally. My metaphor was drawn from fruit. But where is Cecily?

CHASUBLE: Perhaps she followed us to the schools.

Enter JACK *slowly from the back of the garden. He is dressed in the deepest mourning, with crêpe hatband and black gloves.*

MISS PRISM: Mr. Worthing!

CHASUBLE: Mr. Worthing?

MISS PRISM: This is indeed a surprise. We did not look for you till Monday afternoon.

JACK (*shakes* MISS PRISM'S *hand in a tragic manner*): I have returned sooner than I expected. Dr. Chasuble, I hope you are well?

CHASUBLE: Dear Mr. Worthing, I trust this garb of woe does not betoken some terrible calamity?

JACK: My brother.

MISS PRISM: More shameful debts and extravagance?

CHASUBLE: Still leading his life of pleasure?

JACK (*shaking his head*): Dead!

CHASUBLE: Your brother Ernest dead?

JACK: Quite dead.

MISS PRISM: What a lesson for him! I trust he will profit by it.

CHASUBLE: Death is the inheritance of us all, Miss Prism. Nor should we look on it as a special judgment, but rather as a general providence. Life were incomplete without it . . . Mr. Worthing, I offer you my sincere condolence. You have at least the consolation of knowing that you were always the most generous and forgiving of brothers.

JACK: Poor Ernest! He had many faults, but it is a sad, sad blow.

CHASUBLE: Very sad indeed. Were you with him at the end?

JACK: No. He died abroad; in Paris,* in fact. I had a telegram last night from the manager of the Grand Hotel.

CHASUBLE: Was the cause of death mentioned?

JACK: A severe chill, it seems.

MISS PRISM: As a man sows, so shall he reap.

CHASUBLE (*raising his hand*): Charity, dear Miss Prism, charity! None of us are perfect. I myself am peculiarly susceptible to draughts. Will the interment take place here?

JACK: No. He seems to have expressed a desire to be buried in Paris.

CHASUBLE: In Paris! (*Shakes his head.*) I fear that hardly points to any very serious state of mind at the last. You would no doubt wish me to make some slight allusion to this tragic domestic affliction next Sunday. (JACK *presses his hand convulsively.*) My sermon on the meaning of the manna in the wilderness can be adapted to almost any occasion, joyful, or, as in the present case, distressing. (*All sigh.*) I have preached it at harvest celebrations, christenings, confirmations, on days of humiliation and festal days. The last time I delivered it was in the Cathedral, as a charity sermon on behalf of the Society for the Prevention of Discontent among the Upper Orders. The Bishop, who was present, was much struck by some of the analogies I drew.

JACK: Ah! that reminds me, you mentioned christenings, I think, Dr. Chasuble? I suppose you know how to christen all right? (DR. CHASUBLE *looks astounded.*) I mean, of course, you are continually christening, aren't you?

MISS PRISM: It is, I regret to say, one of the Rector's most constant

---

*To many English people, the very name of the French capital signified the supposed morally lax lifestyle British society condemned.

duties in this parish. I have often spoken to the poorer classes on the subject. But they don't seem to know what thrift is.*

CHASUBLE: The Church rejects no babe, Miss Prism. In every child, there is the making of a saint. But is there any particular infant in whom you are interested, Mr. Worthing? Your brother was, I believe, unmarried, was he not?

JACK: Oh yes.

MISS PRISM (*bitterly*): People who live entirely for pleasure usually are.†

JACK: But it is not for any child, dear Doctor. I am very fond of children. No! the fact is, I would like to be christened myself, this afternoon, if you have nothing better to do.

CHASUBLE: But surely, Mr. Worthing, you have been christened already?

JACK: I don't remember anything about it.

CHASUBLE: But have you any grave doubts on the subject?

JACK: I have the very gravest doubts. There are circumstances, unnecessary to mention at present, connected with my birth and early life that make me think I was a good deal neglected. I certainly wasn't properly looked after, at any rate. Of course I don't know if the thing would bother you in any way, or if you think I am a little too old now.

CHASUBLE: Oh! I am not by any means a bigoted Paedobaptist.‡ The sprinkling and, indeed, the immersion of adults was a common practice of the Primitive Church.

JACK: Immersion! You don't mean to say that . . .

CHASUBLE: You need have no apprehensions. Sprinkling is all that is necessary, or indeed I think advisable. Our weather is so changeable. At what hour would you wish the ceremony performed?

JACK: Oh, I might trot round about five if that would suit you.

CHASUBLE: Perfectly, perfectly! In fact, I have two similar ceremonies to perform at that time. A case of twins that occurred

---

*Miss Prism's lack of generosity—here for the poor's inability to not have children—indicates her rather narrow prudishness.

†Miss Prism seems to forget that she, too, is unmarried.

‡Dr. Chasuble denies that he thinks only children should be baptized.

recently in one of the outlying cottages on your own estate. Poor Jenkins the carter, a most hard-working man.

JACK: Oh! I don't see much fun in being christened along with other babies. It would be childish. Would half-past five do?

CHASUBLE: Admirably! Admirably! (*Takes out watch.*) And now, dear Mr. Worthing, I will not intrude any longer into a house of sorrow. I would merely beg you not to be too much bowed down by grief. What seem to us bitter trials are often blessings in disguise.

MISS PRISM: This seems to me a blessing of an extremely obvious kind.

Enter CECILY *from the house.*

CECILY: Uncle Jack! Oh, I am pleased to see you back. But what horrid clothes you have got on! Do go and change them.

MISS PRISM: Cecily!

CHASUBLE: My child! my child!

CECILY *goes towards* JACK; *he kisses her brow in a melancholy manner.*

CECILY: What is the matter, Uncle Jack? Do look happy! You look as if you had toothache, and I have got such a surprise for you. Who do you think is in the dining-room? Your brother!

JACK: Who?

CECILY: Your brother Ernest. He arrived about half an hour ago.

JACK: What nonsense! I haven't got a brother.

CECILY: Oh, don't say that. However badly he may have behaved to you in the past he is still your brother. You couldn't be so heartless as to disown him. I'll tell him to come out. And you will shake hands with him, won't you, Uncle Jack? (*Runs back into the house.*)

CHASUBLE: These are very joyful tidings. That telegram from Paris seems to have been a somewhat heartless jest by one who wished to play upon your feelings.

MISS PRISM: After we had all been resigned to his loss, his sudden return seems to me peculiarly distressing.

JACK: My brother is in the dining-room? I don't know what it all means. I think it is perfectly absurd.

Enter ALGERNON *and* CECILY *hand in hand. They come slowly up to* JACK.

JACK: Good heavens! (*Motions* ALGERNON *away.*)

ALGERNON: Brother John, I have come down from town to tell you that I am very sorry for all the trouble I have given you, and that I intend to lead a better life in the future. (JACK *glares at him and does not take his hand.*)

CHASUBLE (*to* MISS PRISM): There is good in that young man. He seems to be sincerely repentant.

MISS PRISM: These sudden conversions do not please me. They belong to Dissent. They savour of the laxity of the Nonconformist.*

CECILY: Uncle Jack, you are not going to refuse your own brother's hand?

JACK: Nothing will induce me to take his hand. I think his coming down here disgraceful. He knows perfectly well why.

CHASUBLE: Young man, you have had a very narrow escape of your life. I hope it will be a warning to you. We were mourning your demise when you entered.

ALGERNON: Yes, I see Jack has got a new suit of clothes. They don't fit him properly. His necktie is wrong.

CECILY: Uncle Jack, do be nice. There is some good in everyone. Ernest has just been telling me about his poor invalid friend Mr. Bunbury whom he goes to visit so often. And surely there must be some good in one who is kind to an invalid, and leaves the pleasures of London to sit by a bed of pain.

JACK: Oh! he has been talking about Bunbury has he?

CECILY: Yes, he has told me all about poor Mr. Bunbury, and his terrible state of health.

JACK: Bunbury! Well, I won't have him talk to you about Bunbury or about anything else. It is enough to drive one perfectly frantic.

CHASUBLE: Mr. Worthing, your brother has been unexpectedly restored to you by the mysterious dispensations of providence, who seems to desire your reconciliation. And indeed it is good for brothers to dwell together in amity.

---

*Someone who does not conform to an established church or religion.

ALGERNON: Of course I admit that the faults were all on my side. But I must say that I think that Brother John's coldness to me is peculiarly painful. I expected a warmer welcome, especially considering it is the first time I have come here.

CECILY: Uncle Jack, if you don't shake hands with Ernest I will never forgive you.

JACK: Never forgive me?

CECILY: Never, never, never!

JACK: I suppose I must then. (*Shakes hands and glares.*) You young scoundrel! You must get out of this place as soon as possible. I don't allow any Bunburying here.

CHASUBLE: It's pleasant, is it not, to see so perfect a reconciliation? You have done a beautiful action to-day, dear child.

MISS PRISM: We must not be premature in our judgments.

Enter MERRIMAN.

MERRIMAN: I have put Mr. Ernest's things in the room next to yours, sir. I suppose that is all right?

JACK: What?

MERRIMAN: Mr. Ernest's luggage, sir. I have unpacked it and put it in the room next to your own.

JACK: His luggage?

MERRIMAN: Yes, sir. Three portmanteaus,* a dressing case, two hat-boxes, and a large luncheon-basket.

ALGERNON: I am afraid I can't stay more than a week this time.

MERRIMAN (*to* ALGERNON): I beg your pardon, sir, there is an elderly gentleman wishes to see you. He has just come in a cab from the station. (*Hands card on salver.*)

ALGERNON: To see me?

MERRIMAN: Yes, sir.

ALGERNON (*reads card*): Parker and Gribsby, Solicitors. I don't know anything about them. Who are they?

JACK (*takes card*): Parker and Gribsby. I wonder who they can be. I expect, Ernest, they have come about some business for your

---

*Large traveling bags; the following scene, in which Mr. Gribsby presents the Savoy's bill, was deleted from the revised version.

friend Bunbury. Perhaps Bunbury wants to make his will and wishes you to be executor. (*To* MERRIMAN.) Show the gentleman in at once.

MERRIMAN: Very good, sir.

MERRIMAN *goes out.*

JACK: I hope, Ernest, that I may rely on the statement you made to me last week when I finally settled all your bills for you. I hope you have no outstanding accounts of any kind.

ALGERNON: I haven't any debts at all, dear Jack. Thanks to your generosity I don't owe a penny, except for a few neckties, I believe.

JACK: I am sincerely glad to hear it.

Enter MERRIMAN.

MERRIMAN: Mr. Gribsby.

MERRIMAN *goes out. Enter* GRIBSBY.

GRIBSBY (*to* DR. CHASUBLE): Mr. Ernest Worthing?

MISS PRISM: This is Mr. Ernest Worthing.

GRIBSBY: Mr. Ernest Worthing?

ALGERNON: Yes.

GRIBSBY: Of B.4, The Albany?

ALGERNON: Yes, that is my address.

GRIBSBY: I am very sorry, sir, but we have a writ of attachment for twenty days against you at the suit of the Savoy Hotel Co. Limited for £762 14*s.* 2*d.**

ALGERNON: Against me?

GRIBSBY: Yes, sir.

ALGERNON: What perfect nonsense! I never dine at the Savoy at

---

*British currency at this time consisted of pounds (£), shillings (s.) and pence (d.); there were 12 pennies to a shilling and 20 shillings to the pound. The sum Jack owes the Savoy roughly translated into $3,800, an enormous amount.

my own expense. I always dine at Willis's. It is far more expensive. I don't owe a penny to the Savoy.

GRIBSBY: The writ is marked as having been served on you personally at The Albany on May the 27th. Judgment was given in default against you on the fifth of June. Since then we have written to you no less than fifteen times, without receiving any reply. In the interest of our clients we had no option but to obtain an order for committal of your person.

ALGERNON: Committal! What on earth do you mean by committal? I haven't the smallest intention of going away. I am staying here for a week. I am staying with my brother. If you imagine I am going up to town the moment I arrive you are extremely mistaken.

GRIBSBY: I am merely a Solicitor myself. I do not employ personal violence of any kind. The Officer of the Court, whose function it is to seize the person of the debtor, is waiting in the fly outside.* He has considerable experience in these matters. That is why we always employ him. But no doubt you will prefer to pay the bill.

ALGERNON: Pay it? How on earth am I going to do that? You don't suppose I have got any money? How perfectly silly you are. No gentleman ever has any money.

GRIBSBY: My experience is that it is usually relations who pay.

ALGERNON: Jack, you really must settle this bill.

JACK: Kindly allow me to see the particular items, Mr. Gribsby . . . (*turns over immense folio*) . . . £762 14*s.* 2*d.* since last October. I am bound to say I never saw such reckless extravagance in all my life. (*Hands it to* DR. CHASUBLE.)

MISS PRISM: £762 for eating! There can be little good in any young man who eats so much, and so often.

CHASUBLE: We are far away from Wordsworth's† plain living and high thinking.

JACK: Now, Dr. Chasuble, do you consider that I am in any way called upon to pay this monstrous account for my brother?

---

*Small horse-drawn vehicle.

†William Wordsworth (1770–1850), well-known Romantic British poet whose poems on nature remained popular in the 1890s.

CHASUBLE: I am bound to say that I do not think so. It would be encouraging his profligacy.

MISS PRISM: As a man sows, so let him reap. This proposed incarceration might be most salutary. It is to be regretted that it is only for twenty days.

JACK: I am quite of your opinion.

ALGERNON: My dear fellow, how ridiculous you are! You know perfectly well that the bill is really yours.

JACK: Mine?

ALGERNON: Yes, you know it is.

CHASUBLE: Mr. Worthing, if this is a jest, it is out of place.

MISS PRISM: It is gross effrontery. Just what I expected from him.

CECILY: And it is ingratitude. I didn't expect that.

JACK: Never mind what he says. This is the way he always goes on. You mean now to say that you are not Ernest Worthing, residing at B.4., The Albany. I wonder, as you are at it, that you don't deny being my brother at all. Why don't you?

ALGERNON: Oh! I am not going to do that, my dear fellow. It would be absurd. Of course I'm your brother. And that is why you should pay this bill for me.

JACK: I will tell you quite candidly that I have not the smallest intention of doing anything of the kind. Dr. Chasuble, the worthy Rector of this parish, and Miss Prism, in whose admirable and sound judgment I place great reliance, are both of the opinion that incarceration would do you a great deal of good. And I think so, too.

GRIBSBY (*pulls out watch*): I am sorry to disturb this pleasant family meeting, but time presses. We have to be at Holloway* not later than four o'clock; otherwise it is difficult to obtain admission. The rules are very strict.

ALGERNON: Holloway!

GRIBSBY: It is at Holloway that detentions of this character take place always.

ALGERNON: Well, I really am not going to be imprisoned in the suburbs† for having dined in the West End.

---

*Prison located in one of London's suburbs.

†Algernon's remark suggests that those who lived in fashionable London looked down on the suburban middle class.

GRIBSBY: The bill is for suppers, not for dinners.

ALGERNON: I really don't care. All I say is that I am not going to be imprisoned in the suburbs.

GRIBSBY: The surroundings I admit are middle class; but the gaol itself is fashionable and well-aired; and there are ample opportunities of taking exercise at certain stated hours of the day. In the case of a medical certificate, which is always easy to obtain, the hours can be extended.

ALGERNON: Exercise! Good God! No gentleman ever takes exercise. You don't seem to understand what a gentleman is.

GRIBSBY: I have met so many of them, sir, that I am afraid I don't. There are the most curious varieties of them. The result of cultivation, no doubt. Will you kindly come now, sir, if it will not be inconvenient to you.

ALGERNON (*appealingly*): Jack!

MISS PRISM: Pray be firm, Mr. Worthing.

CHASUBLE: This is an occasion on which any weakness would be out of place. It would be a form of self-deception.

JACK: I am quite firm, and I don't know what weakness or deception of any kind is.

CECILY: Uncle Jack! I think you have a little money of mine, haven't you? Let me pay this bill. I wouldn't like your own brother to be in prison.

JACK: Oh! I couldn't possibly let you pay it, Cecily. That would be absurd.

CECILY: Then you will, won't you? I think you would be sorry if you thought your own brother was shut up. Of course, I am quite disappointed with him.

JACK: You won't speak to him again, Cecily, will you?

CECILY: Certainly not, unless, of course, he speaks to me first. It would be very rude not to answer him.

JACK: Well, I'll take care he doesn't speak to you. I'll take care he doesn't speak to anybody in this house. The man should be cut. Mr. Gribsby . . .

GRIBSBY: Yes, sr.

JACK: I'll pay this bill for my brother. It is the last bill I shall ever pay for him, too. How much is it?

GRIBSBY: £762 14*s.* 2*d.* Ah! The cab will be five-and-ninepence extra: hired for the convenience of the client.

JACK: All right.

MISS PRISM: I must say that I think such generosity quite foolish.

CHASUBLE (*with a wave of the hand*): The heart has its wisdom as well as the head, Miss Prism.

JACK: Payable to Parker and Gribsby, I suppose?

GRIBSBY: Yes, sir. Kindly don't cross the cheque. Thank you. (*To* DR. CHASUBLE.) Good day. (DR. CHASUBLE *bows coldly.*) Good Day. (MISS PRISM *bows coldly.*) (*To* ALGERNON.) I hope I shall have the pleasure of meeting you again.

ALGERNON: I sincerely hope not. What ideas you have of the sort of society a gentleman wants to mix in. No gentleman ever wants to know a Solicitor who wants to imprison one in the suburbs.

GRIBSBY: Quite so, quite so.

ALGERNON: By the way, Gribsby: Gribsby, you are not to go back to the station in that cab. That is my cab. It was taken for my convenience. You have got to walk to the station. And a very good thing, too. Solicitors don't walk nearly enough. I don't know any Solicitor who takes sufficient exercise. As a rule they sit in stuffy offices all day long neglecting their business.

JACK: You can take the cab, Mr. Gribsby.

GRIBSBY: Thank you, sir.

GRIBSBY *goes out.*

CECILY: The day is getting very sultry, isn't it, Dr. Chasuble?

CHASUBLE: There is thunder in the air.

MISS PRISM: The atmosphere requires to be cleared.

CHASUBLE: Have you read "The Times" this morning, Mr. Worthing? There is a very interesting article on the growth of religious feeling among the laity.

JACK: I am keeping it for after dinner.

Enter MERRIMAN.

MERRIMAN: Luncheon is on the table, sir.

ALGERNON: Ah! That is good news. I am excessively hungry.

CECILY (*interposing*): But you have lunched already.

JACK: Lunched already?

CECILY: Yes, Uncle Jack. He had some pâté de foie gras sandwiches, and a small bottle of that champagne that your doctor ordered for you.

JACK: My '89 champagne!

CECILY: Yes. I thought you would like him to have the same one as yourself.

JACK: Oh! Well, if he has lunched once, he can't be expected to lunch twice. It would be absurd.

MISS PRISM: To partake of two luncheons in one day would not be liberty. It would be licence.

CHASUBLE: Even the pagan philosophers condemned excess in eating. Aristotle speaks of it with severity. He uses the same terms about it as he does about usury.

JACK: Doctor, will you escort the ladies into luncheon?

CHASUBLE: With pleasure.[2]

He goes into the house with MISS PRISM *and* CECILY.

JACK: Your Bunburying has not been a great success after all, Algy. I don't think it is a good day for Bunburying, myself.

ALGERNON: Oh! There are ups and downs in Bunburying, just as there are in everything else. I'd be all right if you would let me have some lunch. The main thing is that I have seen Cecily and she is a darling.

JACK: You are not to talk of Miss Cardew like that. I don't like it.

ALGERNON: Well, I don't like your clothes. You look perfectly ridiculous in them. Why on earth don't you go up and change? It is perfectly childish to be in deep mourning for a man who is actually staying for a whole week with you in your house as a guest. I call it grotesque.

JACK: You are certainly not staying with me for a whole week as a guest or anything else. You have got to leave . . . by the four-five train.

ALGERNON: I certainly won't leave you so long as you are in mourning. It would be most unfriendly. If I were in mourning you would stay with me, I suppose. I should think it very unkind if you didn't.

JACK: Well, will you go if I change my clothes?

ALGERNON: Yes, if you are not too long. I never saw anybody take so long to dress, and with such little result.

JACK: Well, at any rate, that is better than being always over-dressed as you are.

ALGERNON: If I am occasionally a little over-dressed, I make up for it by being always immensely over-educated.

JACK: Your vanity is ridiculous, your conduct an outrage, and your presence in my garden utterly absurd. However, you have got to catch the four-five, and I hope you will have a pleasant journey back to town. This Bunburying, as you call it, has not been a great success for you. (*Goes into the house.*)

ALGERNON: I think it has been a great success. I'm in love with Cecily, and that is everything. It is all very well, but one can't Bunbury when one is hungry. I think I'll join them at lunch. (*Goes towards door.*)

Enter CECILY.

CECILY: I promised Uncle Jack that I wouldn't speak to you again, unless you asked me a question. I can't understand why you don't ask me a question of some kind. I am afraid you are not quite so intellectual as I thought you were at first.

ALGERNON: Cecily, mayn't I come in to lunch?

CECILY: I wonder you can look me in the face after your conduct.

ALGERNON: I love looking you in the face.

CECILY: But why did you try to put your horrid bill on poor Uncle Jack? I think that was inexcusable of you.

ALGERNON: I know it was; but the fact is I have a most wretched memory. I quite forgot I owed the Savoy £762 14*s.* 2*d.*

CECILY: Well, I admit I am glad to hear that you have a bad memory. Good memories are not a quality that women admire much in men.

ALGERNON: Cecily, I am fearfully hungry.

CECILY: I can't understand your being so hungry, considering all you have had to eat since last October.

ALGERNON: Oh! Those suppers were for poor Bunbury. Late suppers are the only things his doctor allows him to eat.

CECILY: Well, I don't wonder then that Mr. Bunbury is always so ill, if he eats suppers for six or eight people every night of the week.

ALGERNON: That is what I always tell him. But he seems to think his doctors know best. He's perfectly silly about doctors.

CECILY: Of course I don't want you to starve, so I have told the butler to send you out some lunch.

ALGERNON: Cecily, what a perfect angel you are! May I not see you again before I go?

CECILY: Miss Prism and I will be here after lunch. I always have my afternoon lessons under the yew-tree.

ALGERNON: Can't you invent something to get Miss Prism out of the way?

CECILY: Do you mean invent a falsehood?

ALGERNON: Oh! Not a falsehood, of course. Simply something that is not quite true, but should be.

CECILY: I am afraid I couldn't possibly do that. I shouldn't know how. People never think of cultivating a young girl's imagination. It is the great defect of modern education. Of course, if you happened to mention that dear Dr. Chasuble was waiting somewhere to see Miss Prism, she would certainly go to meet him. She never likes to keep him waiting. And she has so few opportunities of doing so.

ALGERNON: What a capital suggestion!

CECILY: I didn't suggest anything, Cousin Ernest. Nothing would induce me to deceive Miss Prism in the smallest detail. I merely pointed out that if you adopted a certain line of conduct, a certain result would follow.

ALGERNON: Of course. I beg your pardon, Cousin Cecily. Then I shall come here at half-past three. I have something very serious to say to you.

CECILY: Serious?

ALGERNON: Yes: very serious.

CECILY: In that case I think we had better meet in the house. I don't like talking seriously in the open air. It looks so artificial.

ALGERNON: Then where shall we meet?

Enter JACK.

JACK: The dog-cart is at the door. You have got to go. Your place is by Bunbury. (*Sees* CECILY.) Cecily! Don't you think, Cecily, that you had better return to Miss Prism and Dr. Chasuble?

CECILY: Yes, Uncle Jack. Good-bye, Cousin Ernest. I am afraid I shan't see you again, as I shall be doing my lessons with Miss Prism in the drawing-room at half-past three.

ALGERNON: Good-bye, Cousin Cecily. You have been very kind to me.

CECILY *goes out.*

JACK: Now look here, Algy. You have got to go, and the sooner you go the better. Bunbury is extremely ill, and your place is by his side.

ALGERNON: I can't go at the present moment. I must first just have my second lunch. And you will be pleased to hear that Bunbury is very much better.

JACK: Well, you will have to go at three-fifty, at any rate. I ordered your things to be packed and the dog-cart to come round.

Act Drop[3]

ACT THREE

The drawing-room at the Manor House. CECILY *and* MISS PRISM *discovered; each writing at a separate table.*

MISS PRISM: Cecily! (CECILY *makes no answer.*) Cecily! You are again making entries in your diary. I think I have had occasion more than once to speak to you about that morbid habit of yours.

CECILY: I am merely, as I always do, taking you for my example, Miss Prism.

MISS PRISM: When one has thoroughly mastered the principles of Bimetallism* one has the right to lead an introspective life. Hardly before. I must beg you to return to your Political Economy.

CECILY: In one moment, dear Miss Prism. The fact is I have only chronicled the events of to-day up till two-fifteen, and it was at two-thirty that the fearful catastrophe occurred.

MISS PRISM: Pardon me, Cecily, it was exactly at two-forty-five that Dr. Chasuble mentioned the very painful views held by the Primitive Church on Marriage.

CECILY: I was not referring to Dr. Chasuble at all. I was alluding to the tragic exposure of poor Mr. Ernest Worthing.

MISS PRISM: I highly disapprove of Mr. Ernest Worthing. He is a thoroughly bad young man.

CECILY: I fear he must be. It is the only explanation I can find of his strange attractiveness.

MISS PRISM (*rising*): Cecily, let me entreat of you not to be led away by whatever superficial qualities this unfortunate young man may possess.

CECILY: Ah! Believe me, dear Miss Prism, it is only the superficial qualities that last. Man's deeper nature is soon found out.

---

*The idea that both gold and silver should be used as a monetary standard; in Britain, the pound was based on silver (hence the phrase "pound sterling").

MISS PRISM: Child! I do not know where you get such ideas. They are certainly not to be found in any of the improving books that I have procured for you.

CECILY: Are there ever any ideas in improving books? I fear not. I get my ideas . . . in the garden.

MISS PRISM: Then you should certainly not be so much in the open air. The fact is, you have fallen lately, Cecily, into a bad habit of thinking for yourself. You should give it up. It is not quite womanly . . . Men don't like it.

Enter ALGERNON.

Mr. Worthing, I thought, I may say I was in hopes that you had already returned to town.

ALGERNON: My departure will not long be delayed. I have come to bid you good-bye, Miss Cardew. I am informed that a dog-cart has been already ordered for me. I have no option but to go back again into the cold world.

CECILY: I hardly know, Mr. Worthing, what you can mean by using such an expression. The day, even for the month of July, is unusually warm.

MISS PRISM: Profligacy is apt to dull the senses.

ALGERNON: No doubt. I am far from defending the weather. I think however that it is only my duty to mention to you, Miss Prism, that Dr. Chasuble is expecting you in the vestry.

MISS PRISM: In the vestry! That sounds serious. It can hardly be for any trivial purpose that the Rector selects for an interview a place of such peculiarly solemn associations. I do not think that it would be right to keep him waiting, Cecily?

CECILY: It would be very, very wrong. The vestry is, I am told, excessively damp.

MISS PRISM: True! I had not thought of that, and Dr. Chasuble is sadly rheumatic. Mr. Worthing, we shall probably not meet again. You will allow me, I trust, to express a sincere hope that you will now turn over a new leaf in life.

ALGERNON: I have already begun an entire volume, Miss Prism.

MISS PRISM: I am delighted to hear it. (*Puts on a large unbecoming hat.*) And do not forget that there is always hope even for the most depraved. Do not be idle, Cecily.

CECILY: I have no intention of being idle. I realise only too strongly that I have a great deal of serious work before me.

MISS PRISM: Ah! that is quite as it should be, dear.

MISS PRISM *goes out.*

ALGERNON: This parting, Miss Cardew, is very painful.

CECILY: It is always painful to part from people whom one has known for a very brief space of time. The absence of old friends one can endure with equanimity. But even a momentary separation from anyone to whom one has just been introduced is almost unbearable.

ALGERNON: Thank you.

Enter MERRIMAN.

MERRIMAN: The dog-cart is at the door, sir.

ALGERNON *looks appealingly at* CECILY.

CECILY: It can wait, Merriman, for five minutes.

MERRIMAN: Yes, Miss.

Exit MERRIMAN.

ALGERNON: I hope, Cecily, I shall not offend you if I state quite frankly and openly that you seem to me to be in every way the visible personification of absolute perfection.

CECILY: I think your frankness does you great credit, Ernest. If you will allow me, I will copy your remarks into my diary. (*Goes over to table and begins writing in diary.*)

ALGERNON: Do you really keep a diary? I'd give anything to look at it. May I?

CECILY: Oh, no. (*Puts her hand over it.*) You see, it is simply a very young girl's record of her own thoughts and impressions, and consequently meant for publication. When it appears in volume form I hope you will order a copy. But pray, Ernest, don't stop. I delight in taking down from dictation. I have reached "absolute perfection". You can go on. I am quite ready for more.

ALGERNON (*somewhat taken aback*): Ahem! Ahem!

CECILY: Oh, don't cough, Ernest. When one is dictating one should speak fluently and not cough. Besides, I don't know how to spell a cough. (*Writes as* ALGERNON *speaks.*)

ALGERNON: (*speaking very rapidly*): Miss Cardew, ever since half-past twelve this afternoon, when I first looked upon your wonderful and incomparable beauty, I have not merely been your abject slave and servant, but, soaring upon the pinions of a possibly monstrous ambition, I have dared to love you wildly, passionately, devotedly, hopelessly.

CECILY (*laying down her pen*): Oh! please say that all over again. You speak far too fast and far too indistinctly. Kindly say it all over again.

ALGERNON: Miss Cardew, ever since you were half-past twelve—I mean ever since it was half-past twelve, this afternoon, when I first looked upon your wonderful and incomparable beauty . . .

CECILY: Yes, I have got that, all right.

ALGERNON (*stammering*): I—I—

CECILY *lays down her pen and looks reproachfully at him.*

(*Desperately.*) I have not merely been your abject slave and servant, but, soaring on the pinions of a possibly monstrous ambition, I have dared to love you wildly, passionately, devotedly, hopelessly. (*Takes out his watch and looks at it.*)

CECILY (*after writing for some time, looks up*): I have not taken down "hopelessly". It doesn't seem to make much sense, does it? (*A slight pause.*)

ALGERNON (*starting back*): Cecily!

CECILY: Is that the beginning of an entirely new paragraph? Or should it be followed by a note of admiration?

ALGERNON (*rapidly and romantically*): It is the beginning of an entirely new existence for me, and it shall be followed by such notes of admiration that my whole life shall be a subtle and sustained symphony of Love, Praise and Adoration combined.

CECILY: Oh, I don't think that makes any sense at all. The fact is that men should never try to dictate to women. They never know how to do it, and when they do do it, they always say something particularly foolish.

ALGERNON: I don't care whether what I say is foolish or not. All that I know is that I love you, Cecily. I love you, I want you. I can't live without you, Cecily! You know I love you. Will you marry me? Will you be my wife? (*Rushes over to her and puts his hand on hers.*)

CECILY (*rising*): Oh, you have made me make a blot! And yours is the only real proposal I have ever had in all my life. I should like to have entered it neatly.

Enter MERRIMAN.

MERRIMAN: The dog-cart is waiting, sir.

ALGERNON: Tell it to come round next week at the same hour.

MERRIMAN (*looks at* CECILY *who makes no sign*): Yes, sir.

CECILY: Uncle Jack would be very much annoyed if he knew you were staying on till next week, at the same hour.

ALGERNON: Oh! I don't care about Jack! I don't care for anybody in the whole world but you. I love you. Cecily! you will marry me, won't you?

CECILY: You silly boy! Of course. Why, we have been engaged for the last three months.

ALGERNON: For the last three months?

CECILY: Three months all but a few days. (*Looks at diary, turns over page.*) Yes; it will be exactly three months on Thursday.

ALGERNON: I didn't know.

CECILY: Very few people nowadays ever realise the position in which they are placed. The age is, as Miss Prism often says, a thoughtless one.

ALGERNON: But how did we become engaged?

CECILY: Well, ever since dear Uncle Jack first confessed to us that he had a younger brother who was very wicked and bad, you of course have formed the chief topic of conversation between myself and Miss Prism. And of course a man who is much talked about is always very attractive. One feels there must be something in him, after all. I dare say it was foolish of me, but I fell in love with you, Ernest.

ALGERNON: Darling! And when was the engagement actually settled?

CECILY: On the 14th of February last. Worn out by your entire ignorance of my existence, I determined to end the matter one way or the other, and after a long struggle with myself I accepted you one evening in the garden. The next day I bought this little ring in your name. You see I always wear it, Ernest, and though it shows that you are sadly extravagant, still I have long ago forgiven you for that. Here in this drawer are all the little presents I have given you from time to time, neatly numbered and labelled. This is the pearl necklace you gave me on my birthday. And this is the box in which I keep all your letters. (*Opens box and produces letters tied up with blue ribbon.*)

ALGERNON: My letters! But my own sweet Cecily, I have never written you any letters.

CECILY: You need hardly remind me of that, Ernest. I remember it only too well. I grew tired of asking the postman every morning if he had a London letter for me. My health began to give way under the strain and anxiety. So I wrote your letters for you, and had them posted to me in the village by my maid. I wrote always three times a week and sometimes oftener.

ALGERNON: Oh, do let me read them, Cecily.

CECILY: Oh, I couldn't possibly. They would make you far too conceited. The three you wrote me after I had broken off the engagement are so beautiful and so badly spelt that even now I can hardly read them without crying a little.

ALGERNON: But was our engagement ever broken off?

CECILY: Of course it was. On the 22nd of last March. You can see the entry if you like. (*Shows diary.*) "Today I broke off my engagement with Ernest. I feel it is better to do so. The weather still continues charming."

ALGERNON: But why on earth did you break it off? What had I done? I had done nothing at all. Cecily, I am very much hurt indeed to hear you broke it off. Particularly when the weather was so charming.

CECILY: Men seem to forget very easily. I should have thought you would have remembered the violent letter you wrote to me because I danced with Lord Kelso at the county ball.

ALGERNON: But I did take it all back, Cecily, didn't I?

CECILY: Of course you did. Otherwise I wouldn't have forgiven you or accepted this little gold bangle with the turquoise and diamond heart, that you sent me the next day. (*Shows bangle.*)

ALGERNON: Did I give you this, Cecily? It's very pretty, isn't it?

CECILY: Yes. You have wonderfully good taste, Ernest. I have always said that of you. It's the excuse I've always given for your leading such a bad life.

ALGERNON: My own one! So we have been engaged for three months, Cecily!

CECILY: Yes; how the time has flown, hasn't it?

ALGERNON: I don't think so. I have found the days very long and very dreary without you.

CECILY: You dear romantic boy . . . (*Puts her fingers through his hair.*) I hope your hair curls naturally. Does it?

ALGERNON: Yes darling, with a little help from others.

CECILY: I am so glad.

ALGERNON: You'll never break off our engagement again, Cecily?

CECILY: I don't think that I could break it off now that I have actually met you. Besides, of course, there is the question of your name.

ALGERNON: Yes, of course. (*Nervously.*)

CECILY: You must not laugh at me, darling, but it had always been a girlish dream of mine to love some one whose name was Ernest.

ALGERNON *rises,* CECILY *also.*

There is something in that name that seems to inspire absolute confidence. I pity any poor married woman whose husband is not called Ernest.

ALGERNON: But, my dear child, do you mean to say you could not love me if I had some other name?

CECILY: But what name?

ALGERNON: Oh, any name you like—Algernon—for instance . . .

CECILY: But I don't like the name of Algernon.

ALGERNON: Well, my own dear, sweet, loving little darling, I really can't see why you should object to the name of Algernon. It is not at all a bad name. In fact, it is rather an aristocratic name. Half of the chaps who get into the Bankruptcy Court are called Algernon. But seriously, Cecily—(*moving to her*)—if my name was Algy, couldn't you love me?

CECILY (*rising*): I might respect you, Ernest, I might admire your character, but I fear that I should not be able to give you my undivided attention.

ALGERNON: Ahem! Cecily! (*Picking up hat.*) Your Rector here is, I suppose, thoroughly experienced in the practice of all the rites and ceremonials of the Church?

CECILY: Oh, yes. Dr. Chasuble is a most learned man. He has never written a single book, so you can imagine how much he knows.

ALGERNON: I must see him at once on a most important christening—I mean on most important business.

CECILY: Oh!

ALGERNON: I shan't be away more than half an hour.

CECILY: Considering that we have been engaged since February the 14th, and that I only met you to-day for the first time, I think it is rather hard that you should leave me for so long a period as half an hour. Couldn't you make it twenty minutes?

ALGERNON: I'll be back in no time. (*Kisses her and rushes out.*)

CECILY: What an impetuous boy he is! I like his hair so much. I must enter his proposal in my diary.

Enter MERRIMAN.

MERRIMAN: A Miss Fairfax has just called to see Mr. Worthing. On very important business, Miss Fairfax states.

CECILY: Isn't Mr. Worthing in his library?

MERRIMAN: Mr. Worthing went over in the direction of the Rectory some time ago.

CECILY: Pray ask the lady to come in here; Mr. Worthing is sure to be back soon. And you can bring tea.

MERRIMAN: Yes, Miss. (*Goes out.*)

CECILY: Miss Fairfax! I suppose one of the many good elderly women who are associated with Uncle Jack in some of his Philanthropic work in London. I don't quite like women who are interested in Philanthropic work. I think it is so forward of them.

Enter MERRIMAN.

MERRIMAN: Miss Fairfax.

Enter GWENDOLEN. *Exit* MERRIMAN.

CECILY (*advancing to meet her*): Pray let me introduce myself to you. My name is Cecily Cardew.

GWENDOLEN: Cecily Cardew? (*Moving to her and shaking hands.*) What a very sweet name! Something tells me that we are going to be great friends. I like you already more than I can say. My first impressions of people are never wrong.

CECILY: How nice of you to like me so much after we have known each other such a comparatively short time. Pray sit down.

GWENDOLEN (*still standing up*): I may call you Cecily, may I not?

CECILY: With pleasure!

GWENDOLEN: And you will always call me Gwendolen, won't you?

CECILY: If you wish.

GWENDOLEN: Then that is all quite settled, is it not?

CECILY: I hope so.

A pause. They both sit down together.

GWENDOLEN: Perhaps this might be a favourable opportunity for my mentioning who I am. My father is Lord Bracknell. You have never heard of papa, I suppose?

CECILY: I don't think so.

GWENDOLEN: Outside the family circle, papa, I am glad to say, is entirely unknown. I think that is quite as it should be. The home seems to me to be the proper sphere for the man. And certainly once a man begins to neglect his domestic duties he becomes painfully effeminate, does he not? And I don't like that. It makes men so very attractive. Cecily, mamma, whose views on education are remarkably strict, has brought me up to be extremely short-sighted; it is part of her system; so do you mind my looking at you through my glasses?

CECILY: Oh! not at all, Gwendolen. I am very fond of being looked at.

GWENDOLEN (*after examining* CECILY *carefully through a lorgnette*): You are here on a short visit, I suppose.

CECILY: Oh no! I live here.

GWENDOLEN (*severely*): Really? Your mother, no doubt, or some female relative of advanced years, resides here also?

CECILY: Oh no! I have no mother, nor, in fact, any relations.

GWENDOLEN: Indeed?

CECILY: My dear guardian, with the assistance of Miss Prism, has the arduous task of looking after me.

GWENDOLEN: Your guardian?

CECILY: Yes, I am Mr. Worthing's ward.

GWENDOLEN: Oh! It is strange he never mentioned to me that he had a ward. How secretive of him! He grows more interesting hourly. I am not sure, however, that the news inspires me with feelings of unmixed delight. (*Rising and going to her*.) I am very fond of you, Cecily; I have liked you ever since I met you! But I am bound to state that now that I know that you are Mr. Worthing's ward, I cannot help expressing a wish you were—well, just a little older than you seem to be—and not quite so very alluring in appearance. In fact, if I may speak candidly——

CECILY: Pray do! I think that whenever one has anything unpleasant to say, one should always be quite candid.

GWENDOLEN: Well, to speak with perfect candour, Cecily, I wish that you were fully forty-two, and more than unusually plain for your age. Ernest has a strong upright nature. He is the very soul of truth and honour. Disloyalty would be as impossible to him as deception. But even men of the noblest possible moral character are extremely susceptible to the influence of the physical charms of others. Modern, no less than Ancient History, supplies us with many most painful examples of what I refer to. If it were not so, indeed, History would be quite unreadable.

CECILY: I beg your pardon, Gwendolen, did you say Ernest?

GWENDOLEN: Yes.

CECILY: Oh, but it is not Mr. Ernest Worthing who is my guardian. It is his brother—his elder brother.

GWENDOLEN (*sitting down again*): Ernest never mentioned to me that he had a brother.

CECILY: I am sorry to say they have not been on good terms for a long time.

GWENDOLEN: Ah! that accounts for it. And now that I think of it I have never heard any man mention his brother. The subject seems distasteful to most men. Cecily, you have lifted a load from my mind. I was growing almost anxious. It would have been terrible if any cloud had come across a friendship like ours, would it not? Of course you are quite, quite sure that it is not Mr. Ernest Worthing who is your guardian?

CECILY: Quite sure. (*A pause.*) In fact, I am going to be his.

GWENDOLEN (*inquiringly*): I beg your pardon?

CECILY (*rather shy and confidingly*): Dearest Gwendolen, there is no reason why I should make a secret of it to you. Our little county newspaper is sure to chronicle the fact next week. Mr. Ernest Worthing and I are engaged to be married.

GWENDOLEN (*quite politely, rising*): My darling Cecily, I think there must be some slight error. Mr. Ernest Worthing is engaged to me. The announcement will appear in the "Morning Post" on Saturday at the latest.

CECILY (*very politely, rising*): I am afraid you must be under some misconception. Ernest proposed to me exactly ten minutes ago. (*Shows diary.*)

GWENDOLEN (*examines diary through her lorgnette carefully*): It is certainly very curious, for he asked me to be his wife yesterday afternoon at 5.30. If you would care to verify the incident, pray do so. (*Produces diary of her own.*) I never travel without my diary. One should always have something sensational to read in the train. I am so sorry, dear Cecily, if it is any disappointment to you, but I am afraid I have the prior claim.

CECILY: It would distress me more than I can tell you, dear Gwendolen, if it caused you any mental or physical anguish, but I feel bound to point out that since Ernest proposed to you he clearly has changed his mind.

GWENDOLEN (*meditatively*): If the poor fellow has been entrapped into any foolish promise I shall consider it my duty to rescue him at once, and with a firm hand.

CECILY (*thoughtfully and sadly*): Whatever unfortunate entanglement my dear boy may have got into, I will never reproach him with it after we are married.

GWENDOLYN: Do you allude to me, Miss Cardew, as an entanglement? You are presumptuous. On an occasion of this kind it becomes more than a moral duty to speak one's mind. It becomes a pleasure.

CECILY: Do you suggest, Miss Fairfax, that I entrapped Ernest into an engagement? How dare you? This is no time for wearing the shallow mask of manners. When I see a spade I call it a spade.

GWENDOLEN (*satirically*): I am glad to say that I have never seen a spade. It is obvious that our social spheres have been widely different.

Enter MERRIMAN, *followed by the footman. He carries a salver, table cloth, and plate stand.* CECILY *is about to retort. The presence of the servants exercises a restraining influence, under which both girls chafe.*

MERRIMAN: Shall I lay tea here as usual, Miss?

CECILY (*sternly, in a calm voice*): Yes, as usual.

MERRIMAN *begins to clear table and lay cloth. A long pause.* CECILY *and* GWENDOLEN *glare at each other.*

GWENDOLEN: Are there many interesting walks in the vicinity, Miss Cardew?

CECILY: Oh! yes! a great many. From the top of one of the hills quite close one can see five counties.

GWENDOLEN: Five counties! I don't think I should like that; I hate crowds.

CECILY (*sweetly*): I suppose that is why you live in town?

GWENDOLEN *bites her lip, and beats her foot nervously with her parasol.*

GWENDOLEN (*looking round*): Quite a charming room this is of yours, Miss Cardew.

CECILY: So glad you like it, Miss Fairfax.

GWENDOLEN: I had no idea there was anything approaching

good taste in the more remote country districts. It is quite a surprise to me.

CECILY: I am afraid you judge of the country from what one sees in town. I believe most London houses are extremely vulgar.

GWENDOLEN: I suppose they do dazzle the rural mind. Personally I cannot understand how anybody manages to exist in the country—if anybody who is anybody does. The country always bores me to death.

CECILY: Ah! This is what the newspapers call agricultural depression, is it not? I believe the aristocracy are suffering very much from it just at present. It is almost an epidemic amongst them, I have been told. May I offer you some tea, Miss Fairfax?

GWENDOLEN (*with elaborate politeness*): Thank you. (*Aside.*) Detestable girl! But I require tea!

CECILY (*sweetly*): Sugar?

GWENDOLEN (*superciliously*): No, thank you. Sugar is not fashionable any more.

CECILY *looks angrily at her, takes up the tongs and puts four lumps of sugar into the cup.*

CECILY (*severely*): Cake or bread and butter?

GWENDOLEN (*in a bored manner*): Bread and butter, please. Cake is rarely seen at the best houses nowadays.

CECILY (*cuts a very large slice of cake and puts it on the tray*): Hand that to Miss Fairfax.

MERRIMAN *does so, and goes out with footman.** GWENDOLEN *drinks the tea and makes a grimace. Puts down cup at once, reaches out her hand to the bread and butter, looks at it, and finds it is cake. Rises in indignation.*

GWENDOLEN: You have filled my tea with lumps of sugar, and though I asked most distinctly for bread and butter, you have given me cake. I am known for the gentleness of my disposition, and the

*With servants onstage, Gwendolen and Cecily are unable to express their true feelings.

extraordinary sweetness of my nature, but I warn you, Miss Cardew, you may go too far.

CECILY (*rising*): To save my poor, innocent, trusting boy from the machinations of any other girl there are no lengths to which I would not go.

GWENDOLEN: From the moment I saw you I distrusted you. I felt that you were false and deceitful. I am never deceived in such matters. My first impressions of people are invariably right.

CECILY: It seems to me, Miss Fairfax, that I am trespassing on your valuable time. No doubt you have many other calls of a similar character to make in the neighbourhood.

Enter JACK.

GWENDOLEN (*catching sight of him*): Ernest! My own Ernest!

JACK: Gwendolen! Darling! (*Offers to kiss her.*)

GWENDOLEN (*drawing back*): A moment! May I ask if you are engaged to be married to this young lady? (*Points to* CECILY.)

JACK (*laughing*): To dear little Cecily! Of course not! What could have put such an idea into your pretty little head?

GWENDOLYN: Thank you. You may! (*Offers her cheek.*)

CECILY (*very sweetly*): I knew there must be some misunderstanding, Miss Fairfax. The gentleman whose arm is at present round your waist is my guardian, Mr. John Worthing.

GWENDOLEN: I beg your pardon?

CECILY: This is Uncle Jack.

GWENDOLEN (*receding*): Jack! Oh!

Enter ALGERNON.

CECILY: Here is Ernest.

ALGERNON (*goes over to* CECILY *without noticing anyone else*): My love. (*Offers to kiss her.*)

CECILY (*drawing back*): A moment, Ernest! May I ask you—are you engaged to be married to this young lady?

ALGERNON (*looking round*): To what young lady? Good heavens! Gwendolen!

CECILY: Yes! to good heavens, Gwendolen, I mean to Gwendolen.

ALGERNON (*laughing*): Of course not! What could have put such an idea into your pretty little head?

CECILY: Thank you. (*Presenting her cheek to be kissed.*) You may. (ALGERNON *kisses her.*)

GWENDOLEN: I felt there was some slight error, Miss Cardew. The gentleman who is now embracing you is my cousin, Mr. Algernon Moncrieff.

CECILY (*breaking away from* ALGERNON): Algernon Moncrieff! Oh!

The two girls move towards each other and put their arms round each other's waists as if for protection.

CECILY: Are you called Algernon?

ALGERNON: I cannot deny it.

CECILY: Oh!

GWENDOLEN: Is your name really John?

JACK (*standing rather proudly*): I could deny it if I liked. I could deny anything if I liked. But my name certainly is John. It has been John for years.

CECILY (*to* GWENDOLEN): A gross deception has been practised on both of us.

GWENDOLEN: My poor wounded Cecily!

CECILY: My sweet wronged Gwendolen!

GWENDOLEN (*slowly and seriously*): You will call me sister, will you not?

They embrace. JACK *and* ALGERNON *groan and walk up and down.*

CECILY (*rather brightly*): There is just one question I would like to be allowed to ask my guardian.

GWENDOLEN: An admirable idea! Mr. Worthing, there is just one question I would like to be permitted to put to you. Where is your brother Ernest? We are both engaged to be married to your brother Ernest, so it is a matter of some importance to us to know where your brother Ernest is at present.

JACK (*slowly and hesitatingly*): Gwendolen—Cecily—it is very painful for me to be forced to speak the truth. It is the first time in my life that I have ever been reduced to such a painful position, and I am really quite inexperienced in doing anything of the kind. However, I will tell you quite frankly that I have no brother Ernest. I have no brother at all. I never had a brother in my life, and I certainly have not the smallest intention of ever having one in the future.

CECILY (*surprised*): No brother at all?

JACK (*cheerily*): None!

GWENDOLEN (*severely*): Had you never a brother of any kind?

JACK (*pleasantly*): Never. Not even of any kind.

GWENDOLEN: I am afraid it is quite clear, Cecily, that neither of us is engaged to be married to any one.

CECILY: It is not a very pleasant position for a young girl suddenly to find herself in. Is it?

GWENDOLEN: Let us go into the garden. They will hardly venture to come after us there.

CECILY: No, men are so cowardly, aren't they?

They retire into the garden with scornful looks.

JACK: Pretty mess you have got me into.

ALGERNON *sits down at tea table and pours out some tea. He seems quite unconcerned.*

What on earth do you mean by coming down here and pretending to be my brother? Perfectly monstrous of you!

ALGERNON (*eating muffin*): What on earth do you mean by pretending to have a brother! It was absolutely disgraceful! (*Eats another muffin.*)

JACK: I told you to go away by the three-fifty. I ordered the dog-cart for you. Why on earth didn't you take it?

ALGERNON: I hadn't had my tea.

JACK: This ghastly state of things is what you call Bunburying, I suppose?

ALGERNON: Yes, and a perfectly wonderful Bunbury it is. The most wonderful Bunbury I have ever had in my life.

JACK: Well, you've no right whatsoever to Bunbury here.

ALGERNON: That is absurd. One has a right to Bunbury anywhere one chooses. Every serious Bunburyist knows that.

JACK: Serious Bunburyist! Good heavens!

ALGERNON: Well, one must be serious about something, if one wants to have any amusement in life. I happen to be serious about Bunburying. What on earth you are serious about I haven't got the remotest idea. About everything, I should fancy. You have such an absolutely trivial nature.

JACK: Well, the only small satisfaction I have in the whole of this wretched business is that your friend Bunbury is quite exploded. You won't be able to run down to the country quite so often as you used to do, dear Algy. And a very good thing too.

ALGERNON: Your brother is a little off colour, isn't he, dear Jack? You won't be able to disappear to London quite so frequently as your wicked custom was. And not a bad thing either.

JACK: As for your conduct towards Miss Cardew, I must say that your taking in a sweet, simple, innocent girl like that is quite inexcusable. To say nothing of the fact that she is my ward.

ALGERNON: I can see no possible defence at all for your deceiving a brilliant, clever, thoroughly experienced young lady like Miss Fairfax. To say nothing of the fact that she is my cousin.

JACK: I wanted to be engaged to Gwendolen, that is all. I love her.

ALGERNON: Well, I simply wanted to be engaged to Cecily. I adore her.

JACK: There is certainly no chance of your marrying Miss Cardew.

ALGERNON: I don't think there is much likelihood, Jack, of you and Miss Fairfax being united.

JACK: Well, that is no business of yours.

ALGERNON: If it was my business, I wouldn't talk about it. It is very vulgar to talk about one's business. Only people like stockbrokers do that, and then merely at dinner parties.

JACK: How can you sit there, calmly eating muffins when we are in this horrible trouble, I can't make out. You seem to me to be perfectly heartless.

ALGERNON: Well, I can't eat muffins in an agitated manner. The butter would probably get on my cuffs. One should always eat muffins quite calmly. It is the only way to eat them.

JACK: I say it's perfectly heartless your eating muffins at all, under the circumstances.

ALGERNON: When I am in trouble, eating is the only thing that consoles me. Indeed, when I am in really great trouble, as any one who knows me intimately will tell you, I refuse everything except food and drink. At the present moment I am eating muffins because I am unhappy. Besides, I am particularly fond of muffins. (*Rising.*)

JACK (*rising*): Well, that is no reason why you should eat them all in that greedy way. (*Takes muffins from* ALGERNON.)

ALGERNON (*offering tea-cake*): I wish you would have tea-cake instead. I don't like tea-cake.

JACK: Good heavens! I suppose a man may eat his own muffins in his own house!

ALGERNON: But you have just said it was perfectly heartless to eat muffins.

JACK: I said it was perfectly heartless of you, under the circumstances. That is a very different thing.

ALGERNON: That may be. But the muffins are the same. (*He seizes the muffin-dish from* JACK.)

JACK: Algy, I wish to goodness you would go.

ALGERNON: You can't possibly ask me to go without having some dinner. It's absurd. I never go without my dinner. No one ever does, except vegetarians and people like that. Besides, I have just made arrangements with Dr. Chasuble to be christened at a quarter to six under the name of Ernest.

JACK: My dear fellow, the sooner you give up that nonsense the better. I made arrangements this morning with Dr. Chasuble to be christened myself at 5.30, and I naturally will take the name of Ernest. Gwendolen would wish it. We can't both be christened Ernest. It's absurd. Besides, I have a perfect right to be christened if I like. There is no evidence at all that I have ever been christened by anybody. I should think it extremely probable I never was, and so does Dr. Chasuble. It is entirely different in your case. You have been christened already.

ALGERNON: Yes, but I have not been christened for years.

JACK: Yes, but you have been christened. That is the important thing.

ALGERNON: Quite so. So I know my constitution can stand it. If you are not quite sure about your ever having been christened, I must say I think it rather dangerous your venturing on it now. It might make you very unwell. You can hardly have forgotten that some one very closely connected with you was very nearly carried off this week in Paris by a severe chill.

JACK: Yes; but you said yourself it was not hereditary, or anything of that kind.

ALGERNON: It usen't to be, I know—but I dare say it is now. Science is always making wonderful improvements in things.

JACK: May I ask, Algy, what on earth do you propose to do?

ALGERNON: Nothing. That is what I have been trying to do for the last ten minutes, and you have kept on doing everything in your power to distract my attention from my work.

JACK: Well, I shall go out into the garden, and see Gwendolen. I feel quite sure she expects me.

ALGERNON: I know from her extremely cold manner that Cecily expects me so I certainly shan't go out into the garden. When a man does exactly what a woman expects him to do she doesn't think much of him. One should always do what a woman doesn't expect, just as one should always say what she doesn't understand. The result is invariably perfect sympathy on both sides.

JACK: Oh, that is nonsense. You are always talking nonsense.

ALGERNON: It is much cleverer to talk nonsense than to listen to it, my dear fellow, and a much rarer thing too, in spite of all the public may say.

JACK: I don't listen to you. I can't listen to you.

ALGERNON: Oh, that is merely false modesty. You know perfectly well you could listen to me if you tried. You always under-rate yourself, an absurd thing to do nowadays when there are such a lot of conceited people about. Jack, you are eating the muffins again! I wish you wouldn't. There are only two left. (*Removes plate.*) I told you I was particularly fond of muffins.

JACK: But I hate tea-cake.

ALGERNON: Why on earth do you allow tea-cake to be served up to your guests, then? What ideas you have of hospitality!

JACK (*irritably*): Oh! that is not the point. We are not discussing tea-cakes. (*Crosses.*) Algy! you are perfectly maddening. You never can stick to the point in any conversation.

ALGERNON (*slowly*): No: it always hurts me.

JACK: Good Heavens! What affectation! I loathe affectation.

ALGERNON: Well, my dear fellow, if you don't like affectation, I really don't see what you can like. Besides, it isn't affectation. The point always does hurt me, and I hate physical pain, of any kind.

JACK (*glares at* ALGERNON; *walks up and down stage. Finally comes up to table*): Algy! I have already told you to go. I don't want you here. Why don't you go?

ALGERNON: I haven't quite finished my tea yet. And there is still one muffin left. (*Takes the last muffin.*)

JACK *groans and sinks down in a chair and buries his face in his hands.*

Act Drop

ACT FOUR[4]

SCENE: *The same.*

JACK *and* ALGERNON *discovered in the same position as at the close of Act Three. Enter behind,* GWENDOLEN *and* CECILY.

GWENDOLEN: The fact that they did not follow us at once into the garden, as any one else would have done, seems to me to show that they have some sense of shame left.

CECILY: They have been eating muffins. That looks like repentance.

GWENDOLEN (*after a pause*): They don't seem to notice us at all. Couldn't you cough?

CECILY: But I haven't got a cough.

GWENDOLEN: They're looking at us. What effrontery!

CECILY: They're approaching. That's very forward of them.

GWENDOLEN: Let us preserve a dignified silence.

CECILY: Certainly. It's the only thing to do now.

JACK *and* ALGERNON *whistle some dreadful popular air from a British Opera.**

GWENDOLEN: This dignified silence seems to produce an unpleasant effect.

CECILY: A most distasteful one.

GWENDOLEN: But we will not be the first to speak.

CECILY: Certainly not.

GWENDOLEN: Mr. Worthing, I have something very particular to ask you. Much depends on your reply.

CECILY: Gwendolen, your common sense is invaluable. Mr. Mon-

---

*No doubt Wilde is referring to something by Gilbert and Sullivan.

crieff, kindly answer me the following question. Why did you pretend to be my guardian's brother?

ALGERNON: In order that I might have an opportunity of meeting you.

CECILY (*to* GWENDOLEN): That certainly seems a satisfactory explanation, does it not?

GWENDOLEN: Yes, dear, if you can believe him.

CECILY: I don't. But that does not affect the wonderful beauty of his answer.*

GWENDOLEN: True. In matters of grave importance, style, not sincerity, is the vital thing. Mr. Worthing, what explanation can you offer to me for pretending to have a brother? Was it in order that you might have an opportunity of coming up to town to see me as often as possible?

JACK: Can you doubt it, Miss Fairfax?

GWENDOLEN: I have the greatest doubts upon the subject. But I intend to crush them. This is not the moment for German scepticism. (*Moving to* CECILY.) Their explanations appear to be quite satisfactory, especially Mr. Worthing's. That seems to me to have the stamp of truth upon it.

CECILY: I am more than content with what Mr. Moncrieff said. His voice alone inspires one with absolute credulity.

GWENDOLEN: Then you think we should forgive them?

CECILY: Yes. I mean no.

GWENDOLEN: True! I had forgotten. There are principles at stake that one cannot surrender. Which of us should tell them? The task is not a pleasant one.

CECILY: Could we not both speak at the same time?

GWENDOLEN: An excellent idea! I always speak at the same time as other people. Will you take the time from me?

CECILY: Certainly.

GWENDOLEN *beats time with uplifted finger.*

---

*A beautifully constructed fiction or lie is much truer, implies Cecily, than the truth.

GWENDOLEN *and* CECILY (*speaking together*): Your Christian names are still an insuperable barrier. That is all!

JACK *and* ALGERNON (*speaking together*): Our Christian names! Is that all? But we are going to be christened this afternoon.

GWENDOLEN (*to* JACK): For my sake you are prepared to do this terrible thing?

JACK: I am.

CECILY (*to* ALGERNON): To please me you are ready to face this fearful ordeal?

ALGERNON: I am!

GWENDOLEN: How absurd to talk of the equality of the sexes! Where questions of self-sacrifice are concerned, men are infinitely beyond us.

JACK: We are. (*Clasps hands with* ALGERNON.)

CECILY: They have moments of physical courage of which we women know absolutely nothing.

GWENDOLEN (*to* JACK): Darling.

ALGERNON (*to* CECILY): Darling!

They fall into each other's arms.

Enter MERRIMAN. *When he enters he coughs loudly, seeing the situation.*

MERRIMAN: Ahem! Ahem! Lady Bracknell!

JACK: Good heavens!

Enter LADY BRACKNELL. *The couples separate in alarm. Exit* MERRIMAN.

LADY BRACKNELL: Gwendolen! What does this mean?

GWENDOLEN: Merely that I am engaged to be married to Mr. Worthing, mamma.

LADY BRACKNELL: Come here. Sit down. Sit down immediately. Hesitation of any kind is a sign of mental decay in the young, of physical weakness in the old. (*Turns to* JACK.) Apprised, sir, of my daughter's sudden flight by her trusty maid, whose confidence I purchased by means of a small coin, I followed her at once by a luggage train. Her unhappy father is, I am glad to say, under the impression that she is attending a more than usually lengthy lecture* by the University Extension Scheme on the Influence of a permanent income on Thought. I do not propose to undeceive him. Indeed I have never undeceived him on any question. I would consider it wrong. But, of course, you will clearly understand that all communication between yourself and my daughter must cease immediately from this moment. On this point, as indeed on all points, I am firm.

JACK: I am engaged to be married to Gwendolen, Lady Bracknell!

LADY BRACKNELL: You are nothing of the kind, sir. And now, as regards Algernon! . . . Algernon!

ALGERNON: Yes, Aunt Augusta.

LADY BRACKNELL: May I ask if it is in this house that your invalid friend Mr. Bunbury resides?

ALGERNON (*stammering*): Oh! No! Bunbury doesn't live here. Bunbury is somewhere else at present. In fact, Bunbury is dead.

LADY BRACKNELL: Dead! When did Mr. Bunbury die? His death must have been extremely sudden.

ALGERNON (*airily*): Oh! I killed Bunbury this afternoon. I mean poor Bunbury died this afternoon.

LADY BRACKNELL: What did he die of?

ALGERNON: Bunbury? Oh, he was quite exploded.

LADY BRACKNELL: Exploded! Was he the victim of a revolutionary outrage?[5] I was not aware that Mr. Bunbury was interested in social legislation. If so, he is well punished for his morbidity.

ALGERNON: My dear Aunt Augusta, I mean he was found out! The doctors found out that Bunbury could not live, that is what I mean—so Bunbury died.

LADY BRACKNELL: He seems to have had great confidence in the opinion of his physicians. I am glad, however, that he made up his mind at the last to some definite course of action, and acted under proper medical advice. And now that we have finally got rid of this Mr. Bunbury, may I ask, Mr. Worthing, who is that young

---

*The topic—that having a permanent income without working affects the way one thinks—is especially appropriate to Gwendolen and the other young people in this play.

person whose hand my nephew Algernon is now holding in what seems to me a peculiarly unnecessary manner?

JACK: That lady is Miss Cecily Cardew, my ward.

LADY BRACKNELL *bows coldly to* CECILY.

ALGERNON: I am engaged to be married to Cecily, Aunt Augusta.

LADY BRACKNELL: I beg your pardon?

CECILY: Mr. Moncrieff and I are engaged to be married, Lady Bracknell.

LADY BRACKNELL (*with a shiver, crossing to the sofa and sitting down*): I do not know whether there is anything peculiarly exciting in the air of this particular part of Hertfordshire, but the number of engagements that go on seems to me considerably above the proper average that statistics have laid down for our guidance. I think some preliminary inquiry on my part would not be out of place. Mr. Worthing, is Miss Cardew at all connected with any of the larger railway stations in London? I merely desire information. Until yesterday I had no idea that there were any families or persons whose origin was a Terminus.

JACK *looks perfectly furious, but restrains himself.*

JACK (*in a clear, cold voice*): Miss Cardew is the grand-daughter of the late Mr. Thomas Cardew of 149 Belgrave Square, S.W.; Gervase Park, Dorking, Surrey; and the Sporran, Fifeshire, N.B.

LADY BRACKNELL: That sounds not unsatisfactory. Three addresses always inspire confidence, even in tradesmen. But what proof have I of their authenticity?

JACK: I have carefully preserved the Court Guides of the period. They are open to your inspection, Lady Bracknell.

LADY BRACKNELL (*grimly*): I have known strange errors in that publication.

JACK: Miss Cardew's family solicitors are Messrs. Markby, Markby, and Markby of 149a Lincoln's Inn Fields, Western Central District, London. I have no doubt they will be happy to supply you with any further information. Their office hours are from ten till four.

LADY BRACKNELL: Markby, Markby, and Markby? A firm of the very highest position in their profession. Indeed I am told that one of the Mr. Markbys is occasionally to be seen at dinner parties. So far I am satisfied.

JACK (*very irritably*): How extremely kind of you, Lady Bracknell! I have also in my possession, you will be pleased to hear, certificates of Miss Cardew's birth, baptism, whooping cough, registration, vaccination, confirmation, and the measles; both the German and the English variety.

LADY BRACKNELL: Ah! A life crowded with incident, I see; though perhaps somewhat too exciting for a young girl. I am not myself in favour of premature experiences. (*Rises, looks at her watch.*) Gwendolen! the time approaches for our departure. We have not a moment to lose. As a matter of form, Mr. Worthing, I had better ask you if Miss Cardew has any little fortune?

JACK: Oh! about a hundred and thirty thousand pounds in the Funds. That is all. Good-bye, Lady Bracknell. So pleased to have seen you.

LADY BRACKNELL (*sitting down again*): A moment, Mr. Worthing. A hundred and thirty thousand pounds! And in the Funds! Miss Cardew seems to me a most attractive young lady, now that I look at her. Few girls of the present day have any really solid qualities, any of the qualities that last, and improve with time. We live, I regret to say, in an age of surfaces. (*To* CECILY): Come over here, dear. (CECILY *goes across.*) Pretty child! your dress is sadly simple, and your hair seems almost as Nature might have left it. But we can soon alter all that. A thoroughly experienced French maid produces a really marvellous result in a very brief space of time. I remember recommending one to young Lady Lancing, and after three months her own husband did not know her.

JACK: And after six months nobody knew her.

LADY BRACKNELL (*glares at* JACK *for a few moments. Then bends, with a practised smile, to* CECILY): Kindly turn round, sweet child. (CECILY *turns completely round.*) No, the side view is what I want. (CECILY *presents her profile.*) Yes, quite as I expected. There are distinct social possibilities in your profile. The two weak points in our age are its want of principle and its want of profile. The chin a little higher, dear. Style largely depends on the way the chin is worn. They are worn very high, just at present. Algernon!

ALGERNON: Yes, Aunt Augusta!

LADY BRACKNELL: There are distinct social possibilities in Miss Cardew's profile.

ALGERNON: Cecily is the sweetest, dearest, prettiest girl in the whole world. And I don't care twopence about social possibilities.

LADY BRACKNELL: Never speak disrespectfully of Society, Algernon. Only people who can't get into it do that. (*To* CECILY): Dear child, of course you know that Algernon has nothing but his debts to depend upon. But I do not approve of mercenary marriages. When I married Lord Bracknell I had no fortune of any kind. But I never dreamed for a moment of allowing that to stand in my way. Well, I suppose I must give my consent.

ALGERNON: Thank you, Aunt Augusta.

LADY BRACKNELL: Cecily, you may kiss me!

CECILY (*kisses her*): Thank you, Lady Bracknell.

LADY BRACKNELL: You may also address me as Aunt Augusta for the future.

CECILY: Thank you, Aunt Augusta.

LADY BRACKNELL: The marriage, I think, had better take place quite soon.

ALGERNON: Thank you, Aunt Augusta.

CECILY: Thank you, Aunt Augusta.

LADY BRACKNELL: To speak frankly, I am not in favour of long engagements. They give people the opportunity of finding out each other's character before marriage, which I think is never advisable.

JACK: I beg your pardon for interrupting you, Lady Bracknell, but this engagement is quite out of the question. I am Miss Cardew's guardian, and she cannot marry without my consent until she comes of age. That consent I absolutely decline to give.

LADY BRACKNELL: Upon what grounds, may I ask? Algernon is an extremely, I may almost say an ostentatiously, eligible young man. He has nothing, but he looks everything. What more can one desire?

JACK: It pains me very much to have to speak frankly to you, Lady

Bracknell, about your nephew, but the fact is that I do not approve at all of his moral character. I suspect him of being untruthful.

ALGERNON *and* CECILY *look at him in indignant amazement.*

LADY BRACKNELL: Untruthful! My nephew Algernon? Impossible! He is an Oxonian.[6]

JACK: I fear there can be no possible doubt about the matter. This afternoon during my temporary absence in London on an important question of romance, he obtained admission to my house by means of the false pretence of being my brother. Under an assumed name he drank, I've just been informed by my butler, an entire pint bottle of my Perrier-Jouet, Brut, '89;* wine I was specially reserving for myself. Continuing his disgraceful deception, he succeeded in the course of the afternoon in alienating the affections of my only ward. He subsequently stayed to tea, and devoured every single muffin. And what makes his conduct all the more heartless is, that he was perfectly well aware from the first that I have no brother, that I never had a brother, and that I don't intend to have a brother, not even of any kind. I distinctly told him so myself yesterday afternoon.

CECILY: But, dear Uncle Jack, for the last year you have been telling us all that you had a brother. You dwelt continually on the subject. Algy merely corroborated your statement. It was noble of him.

JACK: Pardon me, Cecily, you are a little too young to understand these matters. To invent anything at all is an act of sheer genius, and, in a commercial age like ours, shows considerable physical courage. Few of our modern novelists dare to invent a single thing. It is an open secret that they don't know how to do it. Upon the other hand, to corroborate a falsehood is a distinctly cowardly action. I know it is a thing that the newspapers do one for the other, every day. But it is not the act of a gentleman. No gentleman ever corroborates anything.

ALGERNON (*furiously*): Upon my word Jack!

---

*One of the most respected brands of champagne, in its finest vintage; Perrier-Jouët is still manufactured.

LADY BRACKNELL: Ahem! Mr. Worthing, after careful consideration I have decided entirely to overlook my nephew's conduct to you.

JACK: That is very generous of you, Lady Bracknell. My own decision, however, is unalterable. I decline to give my consent.

LADY BRACKNELL (*to* CECILY): Come here, sweet child. (CECILY *goes over*). How old are you, dear?

CECILY: Well, I am really only eighteen, but I always admit to twenty when I go to evening parties.

LADY BRACKNELL: You are perfectly right in making some slight alteration. Indeed, no woman should ever be quite accurate about her age. It looks so calculating. . . . (*In a meditative manner.*) Eighteen, but admitting to twenty at evening parties. Well, it will not be very long before you are of age and free from the restraints of tutelage. So I don't think your guardian's consent is, after all, a matter of any importance.

JACK: Pray excuse me, Lady Bracknell, for interrupting you again, but it is only fair to tell you that according to the terms of her grandfather's will Miss Cardew does not come legally of age till she is thirty-five.

LADY BRACKNELL: That does not seem to me to be a grave objection. Thirty-five is a very attractive age. London society is full of women of the very highest birth who have, of their own free choice, remained thirty-five for years. Lady Dumbleton is an instance in point. To my own knowledge she has been thirty-five ever since she arrived at the age of forty, which was many years ago now. I see no reason why our dear Cecily should not be even still more attractive at the age you mention than she is at present. There will be a large accumulation of property.

CECILY (*to* JACK): You are quite sure that I can't marry without your consent till I am thirty-five?

JACK: That is the wise provision of your grandfather's will, Cecily. He undoubtedly foresaw the sort of difficulty that would be likely to occur.

CECILY: Then grandpapa must have had a very extraordinary imagination. Algy . . . could you wait for me till I was thirty-five? Don't speak hastily. It is a very serious question, and much of my future happiness, as well as all of yours, depends on your answer.

ALGERNON: Of course I could, Cecily. How can you ask me such a question? I could wait for ever for you. You know I could.

CECILY: Yes, I felt it instinctively, but I couldn't wait all that time. I hate waiting even five minutes for anybody. It always makes me rather cross. I am not punctual myself, I know, but I do like punctuality in others, and waiting, even to be married, is quite out of the question.

ALGERNON: Then what is to be done, Cecily?

CECILY: I don't know, Mr. Moncrieff.

LADY BRACKNELL: My dear Mr. Worthing, as Miss Cecily states positively that she cannot wait till she is thirty-five—a remark which I am bound to say seems to me to show a somewhat impatient nature—I would beg of you to reconsider your decision.

JACK: But my dear Lady Bracknell, the matter is entirely in your own hands. The moment you consent to my marriage with Gwendolen, I will most gladly allow your nephew to form an alliance with my ward.

LADY BRACKNELL (*rising and drawing herself up*): You must be quite aware that what you propose is out of the question.

JACK: Then a passionate celibacy is all that any of us can look forward to.

LADY BRACKNELL: That is not the destiny I propose for Gwendolen. Algernon, of course, can choose for himself. (*Pulls out her watch.*) Come, dear—(GWENDOLEN *rises*)—we have already missed five, if not six, trains. To miss any more might expose us to comment on the platform.

Enter DR. CHASUBLE.

CHASUBLE: Everything is quite ready for the christenings.

LADY BRACKNELL: The christenings, sir! Is not that somewhat premature?

CHASUBLE (*looking rather puzzled, and pointing to* JACK *and* ALGERNON): Both these gentleman have expressed a desire for immediate baptism.

LADY BRACKNELL: At their age? The idea is grotesque and irreligious! Algernon, I forbid you to be baptized. I will not hear of such excess. Lord Bracknell would be highly displeased if he learned that that was the way in which you wasted your time and money.

CHASUBLE: Am I to understand then that there are to be no christenings at all this afternoon?

JACK: I don't think that, as things are now, it would be of much practical value to either of us, Dr. Chasuble.

CHASUBLE: I am grieved to hear such sentiments from you, Mr. Worthing. They savour of the heretical views of the Anabaptists, views that I have completely refuted in four of my unpublished sermons. Baptismal regeneration is not to be lightly spoken of. Indeed, by the unanimous opinion of the fathers, baptism is a form of new birth. However, where adults are concerned, compulsory christening, except in the case of savage tribes, is, I regret to say, uncanonical, so I shall return to the church at once. Indeed, I have just been informed by the pew-opener that for the last hour and a half Miss Prism has been waiting for me in the vestry.

LADY BRACKNELL (*starting*): Miss Prism! Did I hear you mention a Miss Prism?

CHASUBLE: Yes, Lady Bracknell. I am on my way to join her.

LADY BRACKNELL: Pray allow me to detain you for a moment. This matter may prove to be one of vital importance to Lord Bracknell and myself. Is this Miss Prism a female of repellent aspect, remotely connected with education?

CHASUBLE (*somewhat indignantly*): She is the most cultivated of ladies, and the very picture of respectability.

LADY BRACKNELL: It is obviously the same person. May I ask what position she holds in your household?

CHASUBLE (*severely*): I am a celibate, madam.

JACK (*interposing*): Lady Bracknell, Miss Prism has been for the last three years Miss Cardew's esteemed governess and valued companion.

LADY BRACKNELL: In spite of what I hear of her, I must see her at once. Let her be sent for.

CHASUBLE (*looking off*): She approaches; she is nigh.

Enter MISS PRISM *hurriedly.*

MISS PRISM: I was told you expected me in the vestry, dear

Canon. I have been waiting for you there for an hour and three-quarters. (*Catches sight of* LADY BRACKNELL, *who has fixed her with a stony glare.* MISS PRISM *grows pale and quails. She looks anxiously round as if desirous to escape.*)

LADY BRACKNELL (*in a severe, judicial voice*): Prism! (MISS PRISM *bows her head in shame.*) Come here, Prism! (MISS PRISM *approaches in a humble manner.*) Prism! Where is that baby? (*General consternation. The* CANON *starts back in horror.* ALGERNON *and* JACK *pretend to be anxious to shield* CECILY *and* GWENDOLEN *from hearing the details of a terrible public scandal.*) Twenty-eight years ago, Prism, you left Lord Bracknell's house, Number 104, Upper Grosvenor Street, in charge of a perambulator that contained a baby of the male sex. You never returned. A few weeks later, through the elaborate investigations of the Metropolitan police, the perambulator was discovered at midnight standing by itself in a remote corner of Bayswater. It contained the manuscript of a three-volume novel of more than usually revolting sentimentality. (MISS PRISM *starts in involuntary indignation.*) But the baby was not there. (*Every one looks at* MISS PRISM.) Prism! Where is that baby? (*A pause.*)

MISS PRISM: Lady Bracknell, I admit with shame that I do not know. I only wish I did. The plain facts of the case are these. On the morning of the day you mention, a day that is for ever branded on my memory, I prepared as usual to take the baby out in its perambulator. I had also with me a somewhat old, capacious hand-bag in which I had intended to place the manuscript of a work of fiction that I had written during my few unoccupied hours. In a moment of mental abstraction, for which I never can forgive myself, I deposited the manuscript in the basinette, and placed the baby in the hand-bag.

JACK (*who has been listening attentively*): But where did you deposit the hand-bag?

MISS PRISM: Do not ask me, Mr. Worthing.

JACK: Miss Prism, this is a matter of no small importance to me. I insist on knowing where you deposited the hand-bag that contained that infant.

MISS PRISM: I left it in the cloak-room of one of the larger railway stations in London.

JACK: What railway station?

MISS PRISM (*quite crushed*): Victoria. The Brighton line. (*Sinks into a chair.*)

LADY BRACKNELL (*looking at Jack*): I sincerely hope nothing improbable is going to happen. The improbable is always in bad, or at any rate, questionable taste.

JACK: I must retire to my room for a moment.

CHASUBLE: This news seems to have upset you, Mr. Worthing. I trust your indisposition is merely temporary.

JACK: I will be back in a few moments, dear Canon. Gwendolen! Wait here for me!

GWENDOLEN: If you are not too long, I will wait here for you all my life.

Exit JACK *in great excitement.*

CHASUBLE: What do you think this means, Lady Bracknell?

LADY BRACKNELL: I dare not even suspect, Dr. Chasuble. I need hardly tell you that in families of high position strange coincidences are not supposed to occur. They are hardly considered the thing.

Noises heard overhead as if some one was throwing trunks about. Every one looks up.

CECILY: Uncle Jack seems strangely agitated.

CHASUBLE: Your guardian has a very emotional nature.

LADY BRACKNELL: This noise is extremely unpleasant. It sounds as if he was having an argument with the furniture. I dislike arguments of any kind. They are always vulgar, and often convincing.

CHASUBLE (*looking up*): It has stopped now. (*The noise is redoubled.*)

LADY BRACKNELL: I wish he would arrive at some conclusion.

GWENDOLEN: This suspense is terrible. I hope it will last.

Enter JACK *with a hand-bag of black leather in his hand.*

JACK (*rushing over to* MISS PRISM): Is this the hand-bag, Miss Prism? Examine it carefully before you speak. The happiness of more than one life depends on your answer.

MISS PRISM (*calmly*): It seems to be mine. Yes, here is the injury it received through the upsetting of a Gower Street omnibus in younger and happier days. Here is the stain on the lining caused by the explosion of a temperance beverage, an incident that occurred at Leamington.[7] And here, on the lock, are my initials. I had forgotten that in an extravagant mood I had had them placed there. The bag is undoubtedly mine. I am delighted to have it so unexpectedly restored to me. It has been a great inconvenience being without it all these years.

JACK (*in a pathetic voice*): Miss Prism, more is restored to you than this hand-bag. I was the baby you placed in it.

MISS PRISM (*amazed*): You?

JACK (*embracing her*): Yes . . . mother!

MISS PRISM (*recoiling in indignant astonishment*): Mr. Worthing, I am unmarried!

JACK: Unmarried! I do not deny that is a serious blow. But after all, who has the right to cast a stone against one who has suffered? Cannot repentance wipe out an act of folly? Why should there be one law for men, and another for women. Mother, I forgive you. (*Tries to embrace her again.*)

MISS PRISM (*still more indignant*): But Mr. Worthing, there is some error. Maternity has never been an incident in my life. The suggestion, if it were not made before such a large number of people, would be almost indelicate. (*Pointing to* LADY BRACKNELL.) There stands the lady who can tell you who you really are. (*Retires to back of stage.*)

JACK (*after a pause*): Lady Bracknell, I hate to seem inquisitive, but would you kindly inform me who I am?

LADY BRACKNELL: I am afraid that the news I have to give you will not altogether please you. You are the son of my poor sister, Mrs. Moncrieff, and consequently Algernon's elder brother.

JACK: Algy's elder brother! Then I have a brother after all. I knew I had a brother! I always said I had a brother! Cecily,—how could you have ever doubted that I had a brother! (*Seizes hold of* ALGERNON.) Dr. Chasuble, my unfortunate brother. Miss Prism, my unfortunate brother. Gwendolen, my unfortunate brother. Algy, you young scoundrel, you will have to treat me with more respect in the future. You have never behaved to me like a brother in all your life.

ALGERNON: Well, not till to-day, old boy, I admit. (*Shakes hands.*) I did my best, however, though I was out of practice.

GWENDOLEN (*to* JACK): Darling!

JACK: Darling!

LADY BRACKNELL: Under these strange and unforeseen circumstances you can kiss your Aunt Augusta.

JACK (*staying where he is*): I am dazed with happiness. (*Kisses* GWENDOLEN.) I hardly know who I am kissing.

ALGERNON *takes the opportunity to kiss* CECILY.

GWENDOLEN: I hope that will be the last time I shall ever hear you make such an observation.

JACK: It will, darling.

MISS PRISM (*advancing, after coughing slightly*): Mr. Worthing,— Mr. Moncrieff as I should call you now—after what has just occurred I feel it my duty to resign my position in this household. Any inconvenience I may have caused you in your infancy through placing you inadvertently in this hand-bag I sincerely apologise for.

JACK: Don't mention it, dear Miss Prism. Don't mention anything. I am sure I had a very pleasant time in your nice hand-bag in spite of the slight damage it received through the overturning of an omnibus in your happier days. As for leaving us, the suggestion is absurd.

MISS PRISM: It is my duty to leave. I have really nothing more to teach dear Cecily. In the very difficult accomplishment of getting married I fear my sweet and clever pupil has far outstripped her teacher.

CHASUBLE: A moment—Lætitia!

MISS PRISM: Dr. Chasuble!

CHASUBLE: Lætitia, I have come to the conclusion that the Primitive Church was in error on certain points. Corrupt readings seem to have crept into the text. I beg to solicit the honour of your hand.

MISS PRISM: Frederick, at the present moment words fail me to express my feelings. But I will forward you, this evening, the three last volumes of my diary. In these you will be able to peruse a full account of the sentiments that I have entertained towards you for the last eighteen months.

Enter MERRIMAN.

MERRIMAN: Lady Bracknell's flyman says he cannot wait any longer.

LADY BRACKNELL (*rising*): True! I must return to town at once. (*Pulls out watch.*) I see I have now missed no less than nine trains. There is only one more.

MERRIMAN *goes out.* LADY BRACKNELL *moves towards the door.* Prism, from your last observation to Dr. Chasuble, I learn with regret that you have not yet given up your passion for fiction in three volumes. And, if you really are going to enter into the state of matrimony which at your age seems to me, I feel bound to say, rather like flying in the face of an all-wise Providence, I trust you will be more careful of your husband than you were of your infant charge, and not leave poor Dr. Chasuble lying about at railway stations in hand-bags or receptacles of any kind. Cloak-rooms are notoriously draughty places. (MISS PRISM *bows her head meekly.*) Dr. Chasuble, you have my sincere good wishes, and if baptism be, as you say it is, a form of new birth, I would strongly advise you to have Miss Prism baptised without delay. To be born again would be of considerable advantage to her. Whether such a procedure be in accordance with the practice of the Primitive Church I do not know. But it is hardly probable, I should fancy, that they had to grapple with such extremely advanced problems. (*Turning sweetly to* CECILY *and patting her cheek.*) Sweet child! We will expect you at Upper Grosvenor Street in a few days.

CECILY: Thank you, Aunt Augusta!

LADY BRACKNELL: Come, Gwendolen.

GWENDOLEN (*to* JACK): My own! But what own are you? What is your Christian name, now that you have become some one else?

JACK: Good heavens! . . . I had quite forgotten that point. Your decision on the subject of my name is irrevocable, I suppose?

GWENDOLEN: I never change, except in my affections.

CECILY: What a noble nature you have, Gwendolen!

JACK: Then the question had better be cleared up at once. Aunt Augusta, a moment. At the time when Miss Prism left me in the hand-bag, had I been christened already? Pray be calm, Aunt Augusta. This is a terrible crisis and much depends on your answer.

LADY BRACKNELL (*quite calmly*): Every luxury that money could buy, including christening, had been lavished on you by your fond and doting parents.

JACK: Then I was christened! That is settled. Now, what name was I given? Let me know the worst.

LADY BRACKNELL (*after a pause*): Being the eldest son you were naturally christened after your father.

JACK (*irritably*): Yes, but what was my father's Christian name? Pray don't be so calm, Aunt Augusta. This is a terrible crisis and everything hangs on the nature of your reply. What was my father's Christian name?

LADY BRACKNELL (*meditatively*): I cannot at the present moment recall what the General's Christian name was. Your poor dear mother always addressed him as "General". That I remember perfectly. Indeed, I don't think she would have dared to have called him by his Christian name. But I have no doubt he had one. He was violent in his manner, but there was nothing eccentric about him in any way. That was rather the result of the Indian climate, and marriage, and indigestion, and other things of that kind. In fact he was rather a martinet about the little details of daily life. Too much so, I used to tell my sister.

JACK: Algy! Can't you recollect what our father's Christian name was?

ALGERNON: My dear boy, we were never even on speaking terms. He died before I was a year old.

JACK: His name would appear in the Army Lists of the period, I suppose, Aunt Augusta?

LADY BRACKNELL: The General was essentially a man of peace, except in his domestic life. But I have no doubt his name would appear in any military directory.

JACK: The Army Lists for the last forty years are here. (*Rushes to the bookcase*[8] *and tears the books out. Distributes them rapidly.*) Here, Dr. Chasuble—Miss Prism, two for you—Cecily, Cecily, an Army List. Make a précis of it at once. Algernon, pray search English history for our father's Christian name if you have the smallest filial affection left. Aunt Augusta, I beg you to bring your masculine mind to bear on this subject. Gwendolen—no, it would agitate you too much. Leave these researches to less philosophic natures like ours.

GWENDOLEN (*heroically*): Give me six copies of any period, this century or the last. I do not care which!

JACK: Noble girl! Here are a dozen. More might be an inconvenience to you. (*Brings her a pile of Army Lists—rushes through them himself, taking each one from her hands as she tries to examine it.*) No, just let me look. No, allow me, dear. Darling, I think I can find it out sooner. Just allow me, my love.

CHASUBLE: What station, Mr. Moncrieff, did you say you wished to go to?

JACK (*pausing in despair*): Station! Who on earth is talking about a station? I merely want to find out my father's Christian name.

CHASUBLE: But you have handed me a Bradshaw. (*Looks at it.*) Of 1869, I observe. A book of considerable antiquarian interest: but not in any way bearing on the question of the names usually conferred on Generals at baptism.

CECILY: I am so sorry, Uncle Jack. But Generals don't seem to be even alluded to in the "History of our own times", although it is the best edition. The one written in collaboration with the typewriting machine.

MISS PRISM: To me, Mr. Moncrieff, you have given two copies of the Price Lists of the Civil Service Stores. I do not find Generals marked anywhere. There seems to be either no demand or no supply.

LADY BRACKNELL: This treatise, "The Green Carnation",* as I see it is called, seems to be a book about the culture of exotics. It contains no reference to Generals in it. It seems a morbid and middle-class affair.

JACK (*very irritable indeed*): Good Heavens! and what nonsense are you reading, Algy? (*Takes book from him.*) The Army List? Well, I don't suppose you knew it was the Army List. And you have got it

---

*Scandalous novel, attributed incorrectly to Wilde.

open at the wrong page. Besides, there is the thing staring you in the face. M. Generals . . . Malam—what ghastly names they have—Markby, Migsby, Mobbs, Moncrieff, Moncrieff! Lieutenant 1840, Captain, Lieutenant-Colonel, Colonel, General 1860. Christian names, Ernest John. (*Puts book quietly down and speaks quite calmly.*) I always told you Gwendolen, my name was Ernest, didn't I? Well, it is Ernest after all. I mean it naturally is Ernest.

LADY BRACKNELL: Yes, I remember now that the General was called Ernest. I knew I had some particular reason for disliking the name. Come, Gwendolen. (*Goes out.*)

GWENDOLEN: Ernest! My own Ernest! I felt from the first that you could have no other name!

JACK: Gwendolen, it is a terrible thing for a man to find out suddenly that all his life he has been speaking nothing but the truth. Can you forgive me?

GWENDOLEN: I can. For I feel that you are sure to change.

JACK: My own one!

CHASUBLE (*to* MISS PRISM): Lætitia! (*Embraces her.*)

MISS PRISM (*enthusiastically*): Frederick! At last!

ALGERNON: Cecily! (*Embraces her.*) At last!

JACK: Gwendolen! (*Embraces her.*) At last!

Enter LADY BRACKNELL.

LADY BRACKNELL: I have missed the last train!—My nephew, you seem to be displaying signs of triviality.

JACK: On the contrary, Aunt Augusta, I've now realised for the first time in my life the vital Importance of Being Earnest.

Tableau*

Curtain

---

*The restatement of the play's title and the frozen tableau before the final curtain were common conventions for ending a play in the late nineteenth century.

LADY WINDERMERE'S FAN

THE PERSONS OF THE PLAY

LORD WINDERMERE
LORD DARLINGTON
LORD AUGUSTUS LORTON
MR. DUMBY
MR. CECIL GRAHAM
MR. HOPPER
PARKER, Butler
LADY WINDERMERE
THE DUCHESS OF BERWICK
LADY AGATHA CARLISLE
LADY PLYMDALE
LADY STUTFIELD
LADY JEDBURGH
MRS. COWPER-COWPER
MRS. ERLYNNE
ROSALIE, Maid

ACT ONE

SCENE: *Morning-room of Lord Windermere's house in Carlton House Terrace,* London. The action of the play takes place within twenty-four hours, beginning on a Tuesday afternoon at five o'clock, and ending the next day at 1.30 p.m.* TIME: *The present. Doors C. and R. Bureau with books and papers R. Sofa with small tea-table L. Window opening on to terrace L. Table R.*

LADY WINDERMERE *is at table R., arranging roses in a blue bowl.*†

Enter PARKER.

PARKER: Is your ladyship at home this afternoon?
LADY WINDERMERE: Yes—who has called?
PARKER: Lord Darlington, my lady.
LADY WINDERMERE (*hesitates for a moment*): Show him up—and I'm at home to any one who calls.
PARKER: Yes, my lady. (*Exit C.*)
LADY WINDERMERE: It's best for me to see him before to-night. I'm glad he's come.

Enter PARKER *C.*

PARKER: Lord Darlington.

Enter LORD DARLINGTON *C. Exit* PARKER.

LORD DARLINGTON: How do you do, Lady Windermere?
LADY WINDERMERE: How do you do, Lord Darlington? No, I

---

*Posh Mayfair address near St. James's Palace.
†Wilde was especially attracted to blue china.

can't shake hands with you. My hands are all wet with these roses. Aren't they lovely? They came up from Selby* this morning.

LORD DARLINGTON: They are quite perfect. (*Sees a fan lying on the table.*) And what a wonderful fan! May I look at it?

LADY WINDERMERE: Do. Pretty, isn't it? It's got my name on it, and everything. I have only just seen it myself. It's my husband's birthday present to me. You know to-day is my birthday?

LORD DARLINGTON: No? Is it really?

LADY WINDERMERE: Yes, I'm of age to-day. Quite an important day in my life, isn't it? That is why I am giving this party to-night. Do sit down. (*Still arranging flowers.*)

LORD DARLINGTON (*sitting down*): I wish I had known it was your birthday, Lady Windermere. I would have covered the whole street in front of your house with flowers for you to walk on. They are made for you. (*A short pause.*)

LADY WINDERMERE: Lord Darlington, you annoyed me last night at the Foreign Office. I am afraid you are going to annoy me again.

LORD DARLINGTON: I, Lady Windermere?

Enter PARKER *and* FOOTMAN *C., with tray and tea things.*

LADY WINDERMERE: Put it there, Parker. That will do. (*Wipes her hands with her pocket-handkerchief, goes to tea-table L., and sits down.*) Won't you come over, Lord Darlington?

Exit PARKER *C.*

LORD DARLINGTON (*takes chair and goes across L.C.*): I am quite miserable, Lady Windermere. You must tell me what I did. (*Sits down at table L.*)

LADY WINDERMERE: Well, you kept paying me elaborate compliments the whole evening.

LORD DARLINGTON (*smiling*): Ah, nowadays we are all of us so hard up, that the only pleasant things to pay *are* compliments. They're the only things we *can* pay.

---

*We later learn that Selby is the name of the Windermeres' country house.

LADY WINDERMERE (*shaking her head*): No, I am talking very seriously. You mustn't laugh, I am quite serious. I don't like compliments, and I don't see why a man should think he is pleasing a woman enormously when he says to her a whole heap of things that he doesn't mean.

LORD DARLINGTON: Ah, but I did mean them. (*Takes tea which she offers him.*)

LADY WINDERMERE (*gravely*): I hope not. I should be sorry to have to quarrel with you, Lord Darlington. I like you very much, you know that. But I shouldn't like you at all if I thought you were what most other men are. Believe me, you are better than most other men, and I sometimes think you pretend to be worse.

LORD DARLINGTON: We all have our little vanities, Lady Windermere.

LADY WINDERMERE: Why do you make that your special one? (*Still seated at table L.*)

LORD DARLINGTON (*still seated L.C.*): Oh, nowadays so many conceited people go about Society pretending to be good, that I think it shows rather a sweet and modest disposition to pretend to be bad. Besides, there is this to be said. If you pretend to be good, the world takes you very seriously. If you pretend to be bad, it doesn't. Such is the astounding stupidity of optimism.

LADY WINDERMERE: Don't you *want* the world to take you seriously then, Lord Darlington?

LORD DARLINGTON: No, not the world. Who are the people the world takes seriously? All the dull people one can think of, from the Bishops down to the bores. I should like *you* to take me very seriously, Lady Windermere, *you* more than any one else in life.

LADY WINDERMERE: Why—why me?

LORD DARLINGTON (*after a slight hesitation*): Because I think we might be great friends. Let us be great friends. You may want a friend some day.

LADY WINDERMERE: Why do you say that?

LORD DARLINGTON: Oh!—we all want friends at times.

LADY WINDERMERE: I think we're very good friends already, Lord Darlington. We can always remain so as long as you don't——

LORD DARLINGTON: Don't what?

LADY WINDERMERE: Don't spoil it by saying extravagant silly things to me. You think I am a Puritan, I suppose? Well, I have something of the Puritan in me. I was brought up like that. I am glad of it. My mother died when I was a mere child. I lived always with Lady Julia, my father's elder sister, you know. She was stern to me, but she taught me what the world is forgetting, the difference that there is between what is right and what is wrong. *She* allowed of no compromise. *I* allow of none.

LORD DARLINGTON: My dear Lady Windermere!

LADY WINDERMERE (*leaning back on the sofa*): You look on me as being behind the age.—Well, I am! I should be sorry to be on the same level as an age like this.

LORD DARLINGTON: You think the age very bad?

LADY WINDERMERE: Yes. Nowadays people seem to look on life as a speculation. It is not a speculation. It is a sacrament. Its ideal is Love. Its purification is Sacrifice.

LORD DARLINGTON (*smiling*): Oh, anything is better than being sacrificed!

LADY WINDERMERE (*leaning forward*): Don't say that.

LORD DARLINGTON: I do say it. I felt it—I know it.

Enter PARKER *C.*

PARKER: The men want to know if they are to put the carpets on the terrace for to-night, my lady?

LADY WINDERMERE: You don't think it will rain, Lord Darlington, do you?

LORD DARLINGTON: I won't hear of its raining on your birthday.

LADY WINDERMERE: Tell them to do it at once, Parker.

Exit PARKER *C.*

LORD DARLINGTON (*still seated*): Do you think then—of course I am only putting an imaginary instance—do you think that in the case of a young married couple, say about two years married, if the husband suddenly becomes the intimate friend of a woman of—well, more than doubtful character—is always calling upon her, lunching with her, and probably paying her bills—do you think that the wife should not console herself?

LADY WINDERMERE (*frowning*): Consols herself?

LORD DARLINGTON: Yes, I think she should—I think she has the right.

LADY WINDERMERE: Because the husband is vile—should the wife be vile also?

LORD DARLINGTON: Vileness is a terrible word, Lady Windermere.

LADY WINDERMERE: It is a terrible thing, Lord Darlington.

LORD DARLINGTON: Do you know I am afraid that good people do a great deal of harm in this world. Certainly the greatest harm they do is that they make badness of such extraordinary importance. It is absurd to divide people into good and bad. People are either charming or tedious. I take the side of the charming, and you, Lady Windermere, can't help belonging to them.

LADY WINDERMERE: Now, Lord Darlington. (*Rising and crossing R., front of him.*) Don't stir, I am merely going to finish my flowers. (*Goes to table R.C.*)

LORD DARLINGTON (*rising and moving chair*): And I must say I think you are very hard on modern life, Lady Windermere. Of course there is much against it, I admit. Most women, for instance, nowadays, are rather mercenary.

LADY WINDERMERE: Don't talk about such people.

LORD DARLINGTON: Well then, setting mercenary people aside, who, of course, are dreadful, do you think seriously that women who have committed what the world calls a fault should never be forgiven?

LADY WINDERMERE (*standing at table*): I think they should never be forgiven.

LORD DARLINGTON: And men? Do you think that there should be the same laws for men as there are for women?*

LADY WINDERMERE: Certainly!

LORD DARLINGTON: I think life too complex a thing to be settled by these hard and fast rules.

---

*Darlington raises the issue of the hypocritical Victorian double standard, which held that men should be forgiven for acts for which women should be punished.

LADY WINDERMERE: If we had "these hard and fast rules," we should find life much more simple.

LORD DARLINGTON: You allow of no exceptions?

LADY WINDERMERE: None!

LORD DARLINGTON: Ah, what a fascinating Puritan you are, Lady Windermere!

LADY WINDERMERE: The adjective was unnecessary, Lord Darlington.

LORD DARLINGTON: I couldn't help it. I can resist everything except temptation.

LADY WINDERMERE: You have the modern affectation of weakness.

LORD DARLINGTON (*looking at her*): It's only an affectation, Lady Windermere.

Enter PARKER *C.*

PARKER: The Duchess of Berwick and Lady Agatha Carlisle.

Enter the DUCHESS OF BERWICK *and* LADY AGATHA CARLISLE *C.*

Exit PARKER *C.*

DUCHESS OF BERWICK (*coming down C. and shaking hands*): Dear Margaret, I am so pleased to see you. You remember Agatha, don't you? (*Crossing L.C.*) How do you do, Lord Darlington? I won't let you know my daughter, you are far too wicked.

LORD DARLINGTON: Don't say that, Duchess. As a wicked man I am a complete failure. Why, there are lots of people who say I have never really done anything wrong in the whole course of my life. Of course they only say it behind my back.

DUCHESS OF BERWICK: Isn't he dreadful? Agatha, this is Lord Darlington. Mind you don't believe a word he says. (LORD DARLINGTON *crosses R.C.*) No, no tea, thank you, dear. (*Crosses and sits on sofa.*) We have just had tea at Lady Markby's. Such bad tea, too. It was quite undrinkable. I wasn't at all surprised. Her own son-in-law supplies it. Agatha is looking forward so much to your ball to-night, dear Margaret.

LADY WINDERMERE (*seated L.C.*): Oh, you mustn't think it is going to be a ball, Duchess. It is only a dance in honour of my birthday. A small and early.

LORD DARLINGTON (*standing L.C.*): Very small, very early, and very select, Duchess.

DUCHESS OF BERWICK (*on sofa L.*): Of course it's going to be select. But we know *that*, dear Margaret, about *your* house. It is really one of the few houses in London where I can take Agatha, and where I feel perfectly secure about dear Berwick. I don't know what society is coming to. The most dreadful people seem to go everywhere. They certainly come to my parties—the men get furious if one doesn't ask them. Really, some one should make a stand against it.

LADY WINDERMERE: I will, Duchess. I will have no one in my house about whom there is any scandal.

LORD DARLINGTON (*R.C.*): Oh, don't say that, Lady Windermere. I should never be admitted! (*Sitting.*)

DUCHESS OF BERWICK: Oh, men don't matter. With women it is different. We're good. Some of us are, at least. But we are positively getting elbowed into the corner. Our husbands would really forget our existence if we didn't nag at them from time to time, just to remind them that we have a perfect legal right to do so.

LORD DARLINGTON: It's a curious thing, Duchess, about the game of marriage—a game, by the way, that is going out of fashion—the wives hold all the honours, and invariably lose the odd trick.

DUCHESS OF BERWICK: The odd trick? Is that the husband, Lord Darlington?

LORD DARLINGTON: It would be rather a good name for the modern husband.

DUCHESS OF BERWICK: Dear Lord Darlington, how thoroughly depraved you are!

LADY WINDERMERE: Lord Darlington is trivial.

LORD DARLINGTON: Ah, don't say that, Lady Windermere.

LADY WINDERMERE: Why do you *talk* so trivially about life, then?

LORD DARLINGTON: Because I think that life is far too important a thing ever to talk seriously about it. (*Moves up C.*)

DUCHESS OF BERWICK: What does he mean? Do, as a concession to my poor wits, Lord Darlington, just explain to me what you really mean.

LORD DARLINGTON (*coming down back of table*): I think I had better not, Duchess. Nowadays to be intelligible is to be found out. Good-bye! (*Shakes hands with* DUCHESS.) And now—(*goes up stage*)—Lady Windermere, good-bye. I may come to-night, mayn't I? Do let me come.

LADY WINDERMERE (*standing up stage with* LORD DARLINGTON): Yes, certainly. But you are not to say foolish, insincere things to people.

LORD DARLINGTON (*smiling*): Ah! you are beginning to reform me. It is a dangerous thing to reform any one, Lady Windermere. (*Bows, and exit C.*)

DUCHESS OF BERWICK (*who has risen, goes C.*): What a charming, wicked creature! I like him so much. I'm quite delighted he's gone! How sweet you're looking! Where *do* you get your gowns? And now I must tell you how sorry I am for you, dear Margaret. (*Crosses to sofa and sits with* LADY WINDERMERE.) Agatha, darling!

LADY AGATHA: Yes, mamma. (*Rises.*)

DUCHESS OF BERWICK: Will you go and look over the photograph album that I see there?

LADY AGATHA: Yes, mamma. (*Goes to table up L.*)

DUCHESS OF BERWICK: Dear girl! She is so fond of photographs of Switzerland. Such a pure taste, I think. But I really am so sorry for you, Margaret.

LADY WINDERMERE (*smiling*): Why, Duchess?

DUCHESS OF BERWICK: Oh, on account of that horrid woman. She dresses so well, too, which makes it much worse, sets such a dreadful example. Augustus—you know my disreputable brother—such a trial to us all—well, Augustus is completely infatuated about her. It is quite scandalous, for she is absolutely inadmissible into society. Many a woman has a past, but I am told that she has at least a dozen, and that they all fit.

LADY WINDERMERE: Whom are you talking about, Duchess?

DUCHESS OF BERWICK: About Mrs. Erlynne.

LADY WINDERMERE: Mrs. Erlynne? I never heard of her, Duchess. And what has she to do with me?

DUCHESS OF BERWICK: My poor child! Agatha, darling!

LADY AGATHA: Yes, mamma.

DUCHESS OF BERWICK: Will you go out on the terrace and look at the sunset?

LADY AGATHA: Yes, mamma. (*Exit through window L.*)

DUCHESS OF BERWICK: Sweet girl! So devoted to sunsets! Shows such refinement of feeling, does it not? After all, there is nothing like Nature, is there?

LADY WINDERMERE: But what is it, Duchess? Why do you talk to me about this person?

DUCHESS OF BERWICK: Don't you really know? I assure you we're all so distressed about it. Only last night at dear Lady Jansen's every one was saying how extraordinary it was that, of all men in London, Windermere should behave in such a way.

LADY WINDERMERE: My husband—what has *he* got to do with any woman of that kind?

DUCHESS OF BERWICK: Ah, what indeed, dear? That is the point. He goes to see her continually, and stops for hours at a time, and while he is there she is not at home to any one. Not that many ladies call on her, dear, but she has a great many disreputable men friends—my own brother particularly, as I told you—and that is what makes it so dreadful about Windermere. We looked upon *him* as being such a model husband, but I am afraid there is no doubt about it. My dear nieces—you know the Saville girls, don't you?—such nice domestic creatures—plain, dreadfully plain,—but so good—well, they're always at the window doing fancy work, and making ugly things for the poor, which I think so useful of them in these dreadful socialistic days, and this terrible woman has taken a house in Curzon Street,* right opposite them—such a respectable street, too! I don't know what we're coming to! And they tell me that Windermere goes there four and five times a week—they *see* him. They can't help it—and although they never talk scandal, they—well, of course—they remark on it to every one. And the worst of it all is that I have been told that this woman

* Fashionable street located near Hyde Park.

has got a great deal of money out of somebody, for it seems that she came to London six months ago without anything at all to speak of, and now she has this charming house in Mayfair,* drives her ponies in the Park every afternoon and all—well, all—since she has known poor dear Windermere.

LADY WINDERMERE: Oh, I can't believe it!

DUCHESS OF BERWICK: But it's quite true, my dear. The whole of London knows it. That is why I felt it was better to come and talk to you, and advise you to take Windermere away at once to Homburg or to Aix,† where he'll have something to amuse him, and where you can watch him all day long. I assure you, my dear, that on several occasions after I was first married, I had to pretend to be very ill, and was obliged to drink the most unpleasant mineral waters, merely to get Berwick out of town. He was so extremely susceptible. Though I am bound to say he never gave away any large sums of money to anybody. He is far too high-principled for that!

LADY WINDERMERE (*interrupting*): Duchess, Duchess, it's impossible! (*Rising and crossing stage to C.*) We are only married two years. Our child is but six months old. (*Sits in chair R. of L. table.*)

DUCHESS OF BERWICK: Ah, the dear pretty baby! How is the little darling? Is it a boy or a girl? I hope a girl—ah, no, I remember it's a boy! I'm so sorry. Boys are so wicked. My boy is excessively immoral. You wouldn't believe at what hours he comes home. And he's only left Oxford a few months—I really don't know what they teach them there.

LADY WINDERMERE: Are *all* men bad?

DUCHESS OF BERWICK: Oh, all of them, my dear, all of them, without any exception. And they never grow any better. Men become old, but they never become good.

LADY WINDERMERE: Windermere and I married for love.

DUCHESS OF BERWICK: Yes, we begin like that. It was only Berwick's brutal and incessant threats of suicide that made me accept him at all, and before the year was out, he was running after all kinds of petticoats, every colour, every shape, every material.

---

*The most fashionable district in London, located near Hyde Park.

†Two European spas, the first in Germany, the second in France.

In fact, before the honeymoon was over, I caught him winking at my maid, a most pretty, respectable girl. I dismissed her at once without a character.—No, I remember I passed her on to my sister; poor dear Sir George is so short-sighted, I thought it wouldn't matter. But it did, though—it was most unfortunate. (*Rises.*) And now, my dear child, I must go, as we are dining out. And mind you don't take this little aberration of Windermere's too much to heart. Just take him abroad, and he'll come back to you all right.

LADY WINDERMERE: Come back to me? (*C.*)

DUCHESS OF BERWICK (*L.C.*): Yes, dear, these wicked women get our husbands away from us, but they always come back, slightly damaged, of course. And don't make scenes, men hate them!

LADY WINDERMERE: It is very kind of you, Duchess, to come and tell all this. But I can't believe that my husband is untrue to me.

DUCHESS OF BERWICK: Pretty child! I was like that once. Now I know that all men are monsters. (LADY WINDERMERE *rings bell.*) The only thing to do is to feed the wretches well. A good cook does wonders, and that I know you have. My dear Margaret, you are not going to cry?

LADY WINDERMERE: You needn't be afraid, Duchess, I never cry.

DUCHESS OF BERWICK: That's quite right, dear. Crying is the refuge of plain women but the ruin of pretty ones. Agatha, darling!

LADY AGATHA (*entering L.*): Yes, mamma. (*Stands back of table L.C.*)

DUCHESS OF BERWICK: Come and bid good-bye to Lady Windermere, and thank her for your charming visit. (*Coming down again.*): And by the way, I must thank you for sending a card to Mr. Hopper—he's that rich young Australian people are taking such notice of just at present. His father made a great fortune by selling some kind of food in circular tins—most palatable, I believe—I fancy it is the thing the servants always refuse to eat. But the son is quite interesting. I think he's attracted by dear Agatha's clever talk. Of course, we should be very sorry to lose her, but I think that a mother who doesn't part with a daughter every season has no real affection. We're coming to-night, dear. (PARKER *opens C. doors.*) And remember my advice, take the poor fellow out of town at once, it is the only thing to do. Good-bye, once more; come, Agatha.

Exeunt DUCHESS *and* LADY AGATHA *C.*

LADY WINDERMERE: How horrible! I understand now what Lord Darlington meant by the imaginary instance of the couple not two years married. Oh! it can't be true—she spoke of enormous sums of money paid to this woman. I know where Arthur keeps his bank book—in one of the drawers of that desk. I might find out by that. I *will* find out. (*Opens drawer.*) No, it is some hideous mistake. (*Rises and goes C.*) Some silly scandal! He loves *me*! He loves *me*! But why should I not look? I am his wife, I have a right to look! (*Returns to bureau, takes out book and examines it page by page, smiles and gives a sigh of relief.*) I knew it! there is not a word of truth in this stupid story. (*Puts book back in drawer. As she does so, starts and takes out another book.*) A second book—private—locked! (*Tries to open it, but fails. Sees paper knife on bureau, and with it cuts cover from book. Begins to start at the first page.*) "Mrs. Erlynne—£600—Mrs. Erlynne—£700—Mrs. Erlynne—£400."* Oh! it is true! It is true! How horrible! (*Throws book on floor.*)

Enter LORD WINDERMERE *C.*

LORD WINDERMERE: Well, dear, has the fan been sent home yet? (*Going R.C. Sees book.*) Margaret, you have cut my bank book. You have no right to do such a thing!

LADY WINDERMERE: You think it wrong that you are found out, don't you?

LORD WINDERMERE: I think it wrong that a wife should spy on her husband.

LADY WINDERMERE: I did not spy on you. I never knew of this woman's existence till half an hour ago. Some one who pitied me was kind enough to tell me what every one in London knows al-

---

*These amounts added up to the equivalent of about $8,500, a fabulous sum of money at the time.

ready—your daily visits to Curzon Street, your mad infatuation, the monstrous sums of money you squander on this infamous woman! (*Crossing L.*)

LORD WINDERMERE: Margaret! don't talk like that of Mrs. Erlynne, you don't know how unjust it is!

LADY WINDERMERE (*turning to him*): You are very jealous of Mrs. Erlynne's honour. I wish you had been as jealous of mine.

LORD WINDERMERE: Your honour is untouched, Margaret. You don't think for a moment that—— (*Puts book back into desk.*)

LADY WINDERMERE: I think that you spend your money strangely. That is all. Oh, don't imagine I mind about the money. As far as I am concerned, you may squander everything we have. But what I *do* mind is that you have loved me, you who have taught me to love you, should pass from the love that is given to the love that is bought. Oh, it's horrible! (*Sits on sofa.*) And it is I who feel degraded! *you* don't feel anything. I feel stained, utterly stained. You can't realise how hideous the last six months seems to me now—every kiss you have given me is tainted in my memory.

LORD WINDERMERE (*crossing to her*): Don't say that, Margaret. I never loved any one in the whole world but you.

LADY WINDERMERE (*rises*): Who is this woman, then? Why do you take a house for her?

LORD WINDERMERE: I did not take a house for her.

LADY WINDERMERE: You gave her the money to do it, which is the same thing.

LORD WINDERMERE: Margaret, as far as I have known Mrs. Erlynne——

LADY WINDERMERE: Is there a Mr. Erlynne—or is he a myth?

LORD WINDERMERE: Her husband died many years ago. She is alone in the world.

LADY WINDERMERE: No relations? (*A pause.*)

LORD WINDERMERE: None.

LADY WINDERMERE: Rather curious, isn't it? (*L.*)

LORD WINDERMERE (*L.C.*): Margaret, I was saying to you—and I beg you to listen to me—that as far as I have known Mrs. Erlynne, she has conducted herself well. If years ago——

LADY WINDERMERE: Oh! (*Crossing R.C.*) I don't want details about her life!

LORD WINDERMERE (*C.*): I am not going to give you any details about her life. I tell you simply this—Mrs. Erlynne was once honoured, loved, respected. She was well born, she had position—she lost everything—threw it away, if you like. That makes it all the more bitter. Misfortunes one can endure—they come from outside, they are accidents. But to suffer for one's own faults—ah!—there is the sting of life. It was twenty years ago, too. She was little more than a girl then. She had been a wife for even less time than you have.

LADY WINDERMERE: I am not interested in her—and—you should not mention this woman and me in the same breath. It is an error of taste. (*Sitting R. at desk.*)

LORD WINDERMERE: Margaret, you could save this woman. She wants to get back into society, and she wants you to help her. (*Crossing to her.*)

LADY WINDERMERE: Me!

LORD WINDERMERE: Yes, you.

LADY WINDERMERE: How impertinent of her! (*A pause.*)

LORD WINDERMERE: Margaret, I came to ask you a great favour, and I still ask it of you, though you have discovered what I had intended you should never have known, that I have given Mrs. Erlynne a large sum of money. I want you to send her an invitation for our party to-night. (*Standing L. of her.*)

LADY WINDERMERE: You are mad! (*Rises.*)

LORD WINDERMERE: I entreat you. People may chatter about her, do chatter about her, of course, but they don't know anything definite against her. She has been to several houses—not to houses where you would go, I admit, but still to houses where women who are in what is called Society nowadays do go. That does not content her. She wants you to receive her once.

LADY WINDERMERE: As a triumph for her, I suppose?

LORD WINDERMERE: No; but because she knows that you are a good woman—and that if she comes here once she will have a chance of a happier, a surer life than she has had. She will make no further effort to know you. Won't you help a woman who is trying to get back?

LADY WINDERMERE: No! If a woman really repents, she never wishes to return to the society that has made or seen her ruin.

LORD WINDERMERE: I beg of you.

LADY WINDERMERE (*crossing to door R.*): I am going to dress for dinner, and don't mention the subject again this evening. Arthur—(*going to him C.*)—you fancy because I have no father or mother that I am alone in the world, and that you can treat me as you choose. You are wrong, I have friends, many friends.

LORD WINDERMERE (*L.C.*): Margaret, you are talking foolishly, recklessly. I won't argue with you, but I insist upon your asking Mrs. Erlynne to-night.

LADY WINDERMERE (*R.C.*): I shall do nothing of the kind. (*Crossing L.C.*)

LORD WINDERMERE: You refuse? (*C.*)

LADY WINDERMERE: Absolutely!

LORD WINDERMERE: Ah, Margaret, do this for my sake; it is her last chance.

LADY WINDERMERE: What has that to do with me?

LORD WINDERMERE: How hard good women are!

LADY WINDERMERE: How weak bad men are!

LORD WINDERMERE: Margaret, none of us men may be good enough for the women we marry—that is quite true—but you don't imagine I would ever—oh, the suggestion is monstrous!

LADY WINDERMERE: Why should *you* be different from other men? I am told that there is hardly a husband in London who does not waste his life over *some* shameful passion.

LORD WINDERMERE: I am not one of them.

LADY WINDERMERE: I am not sure of that!

LORD WINDERMERE: You are sure in your heart. But don't make chasm after chasm between us. God knows the last few minutes have thrust us wide enough apart. Sit down and write the card.

LADY WINDERMERE: Nothing in the whole world would induce me.

LORD WINDERMERE (*crossing to bureau*): Then I will! (*Rings electric bell, sits and writes card.*)

LADY WINDERMERE: You are going to invite this woman? (*Crossing to him.*)

LORD WINDERMERE: Yes.

Pause. Enter PARKER.

Parker!

PARKER: Yes, my lord. (*Comes down L.C.*)

LORD WINDERMERE: Have this note sent to Mrs. Erlynne at No. 84A Curzon Street. (*Crossing to L.C. and giving note to* PARKER.) There is no answer!

Exit PARKER *C.*

LADY WINDERMERE: Arthur, if that woman comes here, I shall insult her.

LORD WINDERMERE: Margaret, don't say that.

LADY WINDERMERE: I mean it.

LORD WINDERMERE: Child, if you did such a thing, there's not a woman in London who wouldn't pity you.

LADY WINDERMERE: There is not a *good* woman in London who would not applaud me. We have been too lax. We must make an example. I propose to begin to-night. (*Picking up fan.*) Yes, you gave me this fan to-day; it was your birthday present. If that woman crosses my threshold, I shall strike her across the face with it.

LORD WINDERMERE: Margaret, you couldn't do such a thing.

LADY WINDERMERE: You don't know me! (*Moves R.*)

Enter PARKER.

Parker!

PARKER: Yes, my lady.

LADY WINDERMERE: I shall dine in my own room. I don't want dinner, in fact. See that everything is ready by half-past ten. And, Parker, be sure you pronounce the names of the guests very distinctly to-night. Sometimes you speak so fast that I miss them. I am particularly anxious to hear the names quite clearly, so as to make no mistake. You understand, Parker?

PARKER: Yes, my lady.

LADY WINDERMERE: That will do!

Exit PARKER *C.*

(*Speaking to* LORD WINDERMERE): Arthur, if that woman comes here—I warn you——

LORD WINDERMERE: Margaret, you'll ruin us!

LADY WINDERMERE: Us! From this moment my life is separate

from yours. But if you wish to avoid a public scandal, write at once to this woman, and tell her that I forbid her to come here!

LORD WINDERMERE: I will not—I cannot—she must come!

LADY WINDERMERE: Then I shall do exactly as I have said. (*Goes R.*) You leave me no choice. (*Exit R.*)

LORD WINDERMERE (*calling after her*): Margaret! Margaret! (*A pause.*) My God! What shall I do? I dare not tell her who this woman really is. The shame would kill her. (*Sinks down into a chair and buries his face in his hands.*)

Act Drop

ACT TWO

SCENE: *Drawing-room in Lord Windermere's house. Door R.U. opening into ballroom, where band is playing. Door L. through which guests are entering. Door L.U. opens on to illuminated terrace. Palms, flowers, and brilliant lights. Room crowded with guests. Lady Windermere is receiving them.*

DUCHESS OF BERWICK (*up C.*): So strange Lord Windermere isn't here. Mr. Hopper is very late, too. You have kept those five dances for him, Agatha? (*Comes down.*)

LADY AGATHA: Yes, mamma.

DUCHESS OF BERWICK (*sitting on sofa*): Just let me see your card. I'm so glad Lady Windermere has revived cards.—They're a mother's only safeguard. You dear simple little thing! (*Scratches out two names.*) No nice girl should ever waltz with such particularly younger sons! It looks so fast! The last two dances you might pass on the terrace with Mr. Hopper.

Enter MR. DUMBY *and* LADY PLYMDALE *from the ballroom.*

LADY AGATHA: Yes, mamma.

DUCHESS OF BERWICK (*fanning herself*): The air is so pleasant there.

PARKER: Mrs. Cowper-Cowper. Lady Stutfield. Sir James Royston. Mr. Guy Berkeley.

These people enter as announced.

DUMBY: Good evening, Lady Stutfield. I suppose this will be the last ball of the season?

LADY STUTFIELD: I suppose so, Mr. Dumby. It's been a delightful season, hasn't it?

DUMBY: Quite delightful! Good evening, Duchess. I suppose this will be the last ball of the season?

DUCHESS OF BERWICK: I suppose so, Mr. Dumby. It has been a very dull season, hasn't it?

DUMBY: Dreadfully dull! Dreadfully dull!

MRS. COWPER-COWPER: Good evening, Mr. Dumby. I suppose this will be the last ball of the season?

DUMBY: Oh, I think not. There'll probably be two more. (*Wanders back to* LADY PLYMDALE.)

PARKER: Mr. Rufford. Lady Jedburgh and Miss Graham. Mr. Hopper.

These people enter as announced.

HOPPER: How do you do, Lady Windermere? How do you do, Duchess? (*Bows to* LADY AGATHA.)

DUCHESS OF BERWICK: Dear Mr. Hopper, how nice of you to come so early. We all know how you are run after in London.

HOPPER: Capital place, London! They are not nearly so exclusive in London as they are in Sydney.

DUCHESS OF BERWICK: Ah! we know your value, Mr. Hopper. We wish there were more like you. It would make life so much easier. Do you know, Mr. Hopper, dear Agatha and I are so much interested in Australia. It must be so pretty with all the dear little kangaroos flying about. Agatha has found it on the map. What a curious shape it is! Just like a large packing case. However, it is a very young country, isn't it?

HOPPER: Wasn't it made at the same time as the others, Duchess?

DUCHESS OF BERWICK: How clever you are, Mr. Hopper. You have a cleverness quite of your own. Now I mustn't keep you.

HOPPER: But I should like to dance with Lady Agatha, Duchess.

DUCHESS OF BERWICK: Well, I *hope* she has a dance left. Have you a dance left, Agatha?

LADY AGATHA: Yes, mamma.

DUCHESS OF BERWICK: The next one?

LADY AGATHA: Yes, mamma.

HOPPER: May I have the pleasure? (LADY AGATHA *bows.*)

DUCHESS OF BERWICK: Mind you take great care of my little chatter-box, Mr. Hopper.

LADY AGATHA *and* MR. HOPPER *pass into ballroom.*

Enter LORD WINDERMERE *L.*

LORD WINDERMERE: Margaret, I want to speak to you.
LADY WINDERMERE: In a moment. (*The music stops.*)
PARKER: Lord Augustus Lorton.

Enter LORD AUGUSTUS.

LORD AUGUSTUS: Good evening, Lady Windermere.
DUCHESS OF BERWICK: Sir James, will you take me into the ballroom? Augustus has been dining with us to-night. I really have had quite enough of dear Augustus for the moment.

SIR JAMES ROYSTON *gives the* DUCHESS *his arm and escorts her into the ballroom.*

PARKER: Mr. and Mrs. Arthur Bowden. Lord and Lady Paisley. Lord Darlington.

These people enter as announced.

LORD AUGUSTUS (*coming up to* LORD WINDERMERE): Want to speak to you particularly, dear boy. I'm worn to a shadow. Know I don't look it. None of us men do look what we really are. Demmed good thing, too. What I want to know is this. Who is she? Where does she come from? Why hasn't she got any demmed relations! Demmed nuisance, relations! But they make one so demmed respectable.
LORD WINDERMERE: You are talking of Mrs. Erlynne, I suppose? I only met her six months ago. Till then, I never knew of her existence.
LORD AUGUSTUS: You have seen a good deal of her since then.

LORD WINDERMERE (*coldly*): Yes, I have seen a good deal of her since then. I have just seen her.

LORD AUGUSTUS: Egad! the women are very down on her. I have been dining with Arabella this evening! By Jove! you should have heard what she said about Mrs. Erlynne. She didn't leave a rag on her. . . . (*Aside.*) Berwick and I told her that didn't matter much, as the lady in question must have an extremely fine figure. You should have seen Arabella's expression. . . . But, look here, dear boy. I don't know what to do about Mrs. Erlynne. Egad! I might be married to her; she treats me with such demmed indifference. She's deuced clever, too! She explains everything. Egad! she explains you. She has got any amount of explanations for you—and all of them different.

LORD WINDERMERE: No explanations are necessary about my friendship with Mrs. Erlynne.

LORD AUGUSTUS: Hem! Well, look here, dear old fellow. Do you think she will ever get into this demmed thing called Society? Would you introduce her to your wife? No use beating about the confounded bush. Would you do that?

LORD WINDERMERE: Mrs. Erlynne is coming here to-night.

LORD AUGUSTUS: Your wife has sent her a card?

LORD WINDERMERE: Mrs. Erlynne has received a card.

LORD AUGUSTUS: Then she's all right, dear boy. But why didn't you tell me that before? It would have saved me a heap of worry and demmed misunderstandings!

LADY AGATHA *and* MR. HOPPER *cross and exit on terrace L.U.E.*

PARKER: Mr. Cecil Graham!

Enter MR. CECIL GRAHAM.

CECIL GRAHAM (*bows to* LADY WINDERMERE, *passes over and shakes hands with* LORD WINDERMERE): Good evening, Arthur. Why don't you ask me how I am? I like people to ask me how I am. It shows a wide-spread interest in my health. Now, to-night I am not at all well. Been dining with my people. Wonder why it is one's people are always so tedious? My father would talk morality after dinner. I told him he was old enough to know better. But my experience is that as soon as people are old enough to know better, they don't know anything at all. Hullo, Tuppy! Hear you're going to be married again; thought you were tired of that game.

LORD AUGUSTUS: You're excessively trivial, my dear boy, excessively trivial!

CECIL GRAHAM: By the way, Tuppy, which is it? Have you been twice married and once divorced, or twice divorced and once married? I say you've been twice divorced and once married. It seems so much more probable.

LORD AUGUSTUS: I have a very bad memory. I really don't remember which. (*Moves away R.*)

LADY PLYMDALE: Lord Windermere, I've something most particular to ask you.

LORD WINDERMERE: I am afraid—if you will excuse me—I must join my wife.

LADY PLYMDALE: Oh, you mustn't dream of such a thing. It's most dangerous nowadays for a husband to pay any attention to his wife in public. It always makes people think that he beats her when they're alone. The world has grown so suspicious of anything that looks like a happy married life. But I'll tell you what it is at supper. (*Moves towards door of ballroom.*)

LORD WINDERMERE (*C.*): Margaret! I must speak to you.

LADY WINDERMERE: Will you hold my fan for me, Lord Darlington? Thanks. (*Comes down to him.*)

LORD WINDERMERE (*crossing to her*): Margaret, what you said before dinner was, of course, impossible?

LADY WINDERMERE: That woman is not coming here to-night.

LORD WINDERMERE (*R.C.*): Mrs. Erlynne is coming here, and if you in any way annoy or wound her, you will bring shame and sorrow on us both. Remember that! Ah, Margaret, only trust me! A wife should trust her husband!

LADY WINDERMERE (*C.*): London is full of women who trust their husbands. One can always recognise them. They look so thoroughly unhappy. I am not going to be one of them. (*Moves up.*) Lord Darlington, will you give me back my fan, please?

Thanks. . . . A useful thing a fan, isn't it? . . . I want a friend to-night, Lord Darlington; I didn't know I would want one so soon.

LORD DARLINGTON: Lady Windermere! I knew the time would come some day; but why to-night?

LORD WINDERMERE: I *will* tell her. I must. It would be terrible if there were any scene. Margaret . . .

PARKER: Mrs. Erlynne!

LORD WINDERMERE *starts.* MRS. ERLYNNE *enters, very beautifully dressed and very dignified.* LADY WINDERMERE *clutches at her fan, then lets it drop on the floor. She bows coldly to* MRS. ERLYNNE, *who bows to her sweetly in turn, and sails into the room.*

LORD DARLINGTON: You have dropped your fan, Lady Windermere. (*Picks it up and hands it to her.*)

MRS. ERLYNNE (*C.*): How do you do, again, Lord Windermere? How charming your sweet wife looks! Quite a picture!

LORD WINDERMERE (*in a low voice*): It was terribly rash of you to come!

MRS. ERLYNNE (*smiling*): The wisest thing I ever did in my life. And, by the way, you must pay me a good deal of attention this evening. I am afraid of the women. You must introduce me to some of them. The men I can always manage. How do you do, Lord Augustus? You have quite neglected me lately. I have not seen you since yesterday. I am afraid you're faithless. Every one told me so.

LORD AUGUSTUS (*R.*): Now really, Mrs. Erlynne, allow me to explain.

MRS. ERLYNNE (*R.C.*): No, dear Lord Augustus, you can't explain anything. It is your chief charm.

LORD AUGUSTUS: Ah! if you find charms in me, Mrs. Erlynne——

They converse together. LORD WINDERMERE *moves uneasily about the room watching* MRS. ERLYNNE.

LORD DARLINGTON (*to* LADY WINDERMERE): How pale you are!

LADY WINDERMERE: Cowards are always pale!

LORD DARLINGTON: You look faint. Come out on the terrace.

LADY WINDERMERE: Yes. (*To* PARKER): Parker, send my cloak out.

MRS. ERLYNNE (*crossing to her*): Lady Windermere, how beautifully your terrace is illuminated. Reminds me of Prince Doria's at Rome.

LADY WINDERMERE *bows coldly,** *and goes off with* LORD DARLINGTON.

Oh, how do you do, Mr. Graham? Isn't that your aunt, Lady Jedburgh? I should so much like to know her.

CECIL GRAHAM (*after a moment's hesitation and embarrassment*): Oh, certainly, if you wish it. Aunt Caroline, allow me to introduce Mrs. Erlynne.

MRS. ERLYNNE: So pleased to meet you, Lady Jedburgh. (*Sits beside her on the sofa.*) Your nephew and I are great friends. I am so much interested in his political career. I think he's sure to be a wonderful success. He thinks like a Tory, and talks like a Radical, and that's so important nowadays. He's such a brilliant talker, too. But we all know from whom he inherits that. Lord Allandale was saying to me only yesterday, in the Park, that Mr. Graham talks almost as well as his aunt.

LADY JEDBURGH (*R.*): Most kind of you to say these charming things to me! (MRS. ERLYNNE *smiles, and continues conversation.*)

DUMBY (*to* CECIL GRAHAM): Did you introduce Mrs. Erlynne to Lady Jedburgh?

CECIL GRAHAM: Had to, my dear fellow. Couldn't help it! That woman can make one do anything she wants. How, I don't know.

DUMBY: Hope to goodness she won't speak to me! (*Saunters towards* LADY PLYMDALE.)

MRS. ERLYNNE (*C. To* LADY JEDBURGH): On Thursday? With great pleasure. (*Rises, and speaks to* LORD WINDERMERE, *laughing.*) What a bore it is to have to be civil to these old dowagers! But they always insist on it!

---

*The nonverbal greeting speaks far louder than any dialogue.

LADY PLYMDALE (*to* MR. DUMBY): Who is that well-dressed woman talking to Windermere?

DUMBY: Haven't got the slightest idea! Looks like an *édition de luxe* of a wicked French novel, meant specially for the English market.

MRS. ERLYNNE: So that is poor Dumby with Lady Plymdale? I hear she is frightfully jealous of him. He doesn't seem anxious to speak to me to-night. I suppose he is afraid of her. Those straw-coloured women have dreadful tempers. Do you know, I think I'll dance with you first, Windermere. (LORD WINDERMERE *bites his lip and frowns.*) It will make Lord Augustus so jealous! Lord Augustus! (LORD AUGUSTUS *comes down.*) Lord Windermere insists on my dancing with him first; as it's his own house, I can't well refuse. You know I would much sooner dance with you.

LORD AUGUSTUS (*with a low bow*): I wish I could think so, Mrs. Erlynne.

MRS. ERLYNNE: You know it far too well. I can fancy a person dancing through life with you and finding it charming.

LORD AUGUSTUS (*placing his hand on his white waistcoat*): Oh, thank you, thank you. You are the most adorable of all ladies!

MRS. ERLYNNE: What a nice speech! So simple and so sincere! Just the sort of speech I like. Well, you shall hold my bouquet. (*Goes towards ballroom on* LORD WINDERMERE'S *arm.*) Ah, Mr. Dumby, how are you? I am so sorry I have been out the last three times you have called. Come and lunch on Friday.

DUMBY (*with perfect nonchalance*): Delighted!

LADY PLYMDALE *glares with indignation at* MR. DUMBY. LORD AUGUSTUS *follows* MRS. ERLYNNE *and* LORD WINDERMERE *into the ballroom holding bouquet.*

LADY PLYMDALE (*to* MR. DUMBY): What an absolute brute you are! I never can believe a word you say! Why did you tell me you didn't know her? What do you mean by calling on her three times running? You are not to go to lunch there; of course you understand that?

DUMBY: My dear Laura, I wouldn't dream of going!

LADY PLYMDALE: You haven't told me her name yet! Who is she?

DUMBY (*coughs slightly and smooths his hair*): She's a Mrs. Erlynne.
LADY PLYMDALE: That woman!
DUMBY: Yes; that is what every one calls her.
LADY PLYMDALE: How very interesting! How intensely interesting! I really must have a good stare at her. (*Goes to door of ballroom and looks in.*) I have heard the most shocking things about her. They say she is ruining poor Windermere. And Lady Windermere, who goes in for being so proper, invites her! How extremely amusing! It takes a thoroughly good woman to do a thoroughly stupid thing. You are to lunch there on Friday!
DUMBY: Why?
LADY PLYMDALE: Because I want you to take my husband with you. He has been so attentive lately, that he has become a perfect nuisance. Now, this woman's just the thing for him. He'll dance attendance upon her as long as she lets him, and won't bother me. I assure you, women of that kind are most useful. They form the basis of other people's marriages.*
DUMBY: What a mystery you are!
LADY PLYMDALE (*looking at him*): I wish *you* were!
DUMBY: I am—to myself. I am the only person in the world I should like to know thoroughly; but I don't see any chance of it just at present.

They pass into the ballroom, and LADY WINDERMERE *and* LORD DARLINGTON *enter from the terrace.*

LADY WINDERMERE: Yes. Yes. Her coming here is monstrous, unbearable. I know now what you meant to-day at tea time. Why didn't you tell me right out? You should have!
LORD DARLINGTON: I couldn't! A man can't tell these things about another man! But if I had known he was going to make you ask her here to-night, I think I would have told you. That insult, at any rate, you would have been spared.
LADY WINDERMERE: I did not ask her. He insisted on her coming—against my entreaties—against my commands. Oh! the

---

*Lady Plymdale implies not only that she would like to get rid of her husband for a while but also that she is on very intimate terms with Dumby.

house is tainted for me! I feel that every woman here sneers at me as she dances by with my husband. What have I done to deserve this? I gave him all my life. He took it—used it—spoiled it! I am degraded in my own eyes, and I lack courage—I am a coward! (*Sits down on sofa.*)

LORD DARLINGTON: If I know you at all, I know that you can't live with a man who treats you like this! What sort of life would you have with him? You would feel that he was lying to you every moment of the day. You would feel that the look in his eyes was false, his voice false, his touch false, his passion false. He would come to you when he was weary of others; you would have to comfort him. He would come to you when he was devoted to others; you would have to charm him. You would have to be to him the mask of his real life, the cloak to hide his secret.

LADY WINDERMERE: You are right—you are terribly right. But where am I to turn? You said you would be my friend, Lord Darlington.—Tell me, what am I to do? Be my friend now.

LORD DARLINGTON: Between men and women there is no friendship possible. There is passion, enmity, worship, love, but no friendship. I love you——

LADY WINDERMERE: No, no! (*Rises.*)

LORD DARLINGTON: Yes, I love you! You are more to me than anything in the whole world. What does your husband give you? Nothing. Whatever is in him he gives to this wretched woman, whom he has thrust into your society, into your home, to shame you before every one. I offer you my life——

LADY WINDERMERE: Lord Darlington!

LORD DARLINGTON: My life—my whole life. Take it, and do with it what you will. . . . I love you—love you as I have never loved any living thing. From the moment I met you I loved you, loved you blindly, adoringly, madly! You did not know it then—you know it now! Leave this house to-night. I won't tell you that the world matters nothing, or the world's voice, or the voice of society. They matter a great deal. They matter far too much. But there are moments when one has to choose between living one's own life, fully, entirely, completely—or dragging out some false, shallow, degrading existence that the world in its hypocrisy demands. You have that moment now. Choose! Oh, my love, choose.

LADY WINDERMERE (*moving slowly away from him, and looking at him with startled eyes*): I have not the courage.

LORD DARLINGTON (*following her*): Yes; you have the courage. There may be six months of pain, of disgrace even, but when you no longer bear his name, when you bear mine, all will be well. Margaret, my love, my wife that shall be some day—yes, my wife! You know it! What are you now? This woman has the place that belongs by right to you. Oh! go—go out of this house, with head erect, with a smile upon your lips, with courage in your eyes. All London will know why you did it; and who will blame you? No one. If they do, what matter? Wrong? What is wrong? It's wrong for a man to abandon his wife for a shameless woman. It is wrong for a wife to remain with a man who so dishonours her. You said once you would make no compromise with things. Make none now. Be brave! Be yourself!

LADY WINDERMERE: I am afraid of being myself. Let me think. Let me wait! My husband may return to me. (*Sits down on sofa.*)

LORD DARLINGTON: And you would take him back! You are not what I thought you were. You are just the same as every other woman. You would stand anything rather than face the censure of a world whose praise you would despise. In a week you will be driving with this woman in the Park. She will be your constant guest—your dearest friend. You would endure anything rather than break with one blow this monstrous tie. You are right. You have no courage; none!

LADY WINDERMERE: Ah, give me time to think. I cannot answer you now. (*Passes her hand nervously over her brow.*)

LORD DARLINGTON: It must be now or not at all.

LADY WINDERMERE (*rising from the sofa*): Then, not at all! (*A pause.*)

LORD DARLINGTON: You break my heart!

LADY WINDERMERE: Mine is already broken. (*A pause.*)

LORD DARLINGTON: To-morrow I leave England. This is the last time I shall ever look on you. You will never see me again. For one moment our lives met—our souls touched. They must never meet or touch again. Good-bye, Margaret. (*Exit.*)

LADY WINDERMERE: How alone I am in life. How terribly alone!

The music stops. Enter the DUCHESS OF BERWICK *and* LORD PAISLEY *laughing and talking. Other guests come in from ballroom.*

DUCHESS OF BERWICK: Dear Margaret, I've just been having such a delightful chat with Mrs. Erlynne. I am so sorry for what I said to you this afternoon about her. Of course, she must be all right if *you* invite her. A most attractive woman, and has such sensible views on life. Told me she entirely disapproved of people marrying more than once, so I feel quite safe about poor Augustus. Can't imagine why people speak against her. It's those horrid nieces of mine—the Saville girls—they're always talking scandal. Still, I should go to Homburg, dear, I really should. She is just a little too attractive. But where is Agatha? Oh, there she is. (LADY AGATHA *and* MR. HOPPER *enter from terrace L.U.E.*) Mr. Hopper, I am very, very angry with you. You have taken Agatha out on the terrace, and she is so delicate.

HOPPER (*L.C.*): Awfully sorry, Duchess. We went out for a moment and then got chatting together.

DUCHESS OF BERWICK (*C.*): Ah, about dear Australia, I suppose?

HOPPER: Yes!

DUCHESS OF BERWICK: Agatha, darling! (*Beckons her over.*)

LADY AGATHA: Yes, mamma!

DUCHESS OF BERWICK (*aside*): Did Mr. Hopper definitely——

LADY AGATHA: Yes, mamma.

DUCHESS OF BERWICK: And what answer did you give him, dear child?

LADY AGATHA: Yes, mamma.

DUCHESS OF BERWICK (*affectionately*): My dear one! You always say the right thing. Mr. Hopper! James! Agatha has told me everything. How cleverly you have both kept your secret.

HOPPER: You don't mind my taking Agatha off to Australia, then, Duchess?

DUCHESS OF BERWICK (*indignantly*): To Australia? Oh, don't mention that dreadful vulgar place.

HOPPER: But she said she'd like to come with me.

DUCHESS OF BERWICK (*severely*): Did you say that, Agatha?

LADY AGATHA: Yes, mamma.

DUCHESS OF BERWICK: Agatha, you say the most silly things

possible. I think on the whole that Grosvenor Square would be a more healthy place to reside in. There are lots of vulgar people live in Grosvenor Square, but at any rate there are no horrid kangaroos crawling about. But we'll talk about that to-morrow. James, you can take Agatha down. You'll come to lunch, of course, James. At half-past one, instead of two. The Duke will wish to say a few words to you, I am sure.

HOPPER: I should like to have a chat with the Duke, Duchess. He has not said a single word to me yet.

DUCHESS OF BERWICK: I think you'll find he will have a great deal to say to you to-morrow. (*Exit* LADY AGATHA *with* MR. HOPPER.) And now good-night, Margaret. I'm afraid it's the old, old story, dear. Love—well, not love at first sight, but love at the end of the season, which is so much more satisfactory.

LADY WINDERMERE: Good-night, Duchess.

Exit the DUCHESS OF BERWICK *on* LORD PAISLEY'S *arm.*

LADY PLYMDALE: My dear Margaret, what a handsome woman your husband has been dancing with! I should be quite jealous if I were you! Is she a great friend of yours?

LADY WINDERMERE: No!

LADY PLYMDALE: Really? Good-night, dear. (*Looks at* MR. DUMBY *and exit.*)

DUMBY: Awful manners young Hopper has!

CECIL GRAHAM: Ah! Hopper is one of Nature's gentlemen, the worst type of gentleman I know.

DUMBY: Sensible woman, Lady Windermere. Lots of wives would have objected to Mrs. Erlynne coming. But Lady Windermere has that uncommon thing called common sense.

CECIL GRAHAM: And Windermere knows that nothing looks so like innocence as an indiscretion.

DUMBY: Yes; dear Windermere is becoming almost modern. Never thought he would. (*Bows to* LADY WINDERMERE *and exit.*)

LADY JEDBURGH: Good-night, Lady Windermere. What a fascinating woman Mrs. Erlynne is! She is coming to lunch on Thursday, won't you come too? I expect the Bishop and dear Lady Merton.

LADY WINDERMERE: I am afraid I am engaged, Lady Jedburgh.

LADY JEDBURGH: So sorry. Come, dear.

Exeunt LADY JEDBURGH *and* MISS GRAHAM.

Enter MRS. ERLYNNE *and* LORD WINDERMERE.

MRS. ERLYNNE: Charming ball it has been! Quite reminds me of old days. (*Sits on sofa.*) And I see that there are just as many fools in society as there used to be. So pleased to find that nothing has altered! Except Margaret. She's grown quite pretty. The last time I saw her—twenty years ago, she was a fright in flannel. Positive fright, I assure you. The dear Duchess! and that sweet Lady Agatha! Just the type of girl I like! Well, really, Windermere, if I am to be the Duchess's sister-in-law——

LORD WINDERMERE (*sitting L. of her*): But are you——?

Exit MR. CECIL GRAHAM *with rest of guests.* LADY WINDERMERE *watches, with a look of scorn and pain,* MRS. ERLYNNE *and her husband. They are unconscious of her presence.*

MRS. ERLYNNE: Oh, yes! He's to call to-morrow at twelve o'clock. He wanted to propose to-night. In fact he did. He kept on proposing. Poor Augustus; you know how he repeats himself. Such a bad habit! But I told him I wouldn't give him an answer till to-morrow. Of course I am going to take him. And I dare say I'll make him an admirable wife, as wives go. And there is a great deal of good in Lord Augustus. Fortunately it is all on the surface. Just where good qualities should be. Of course you must help me in this matter.

LORD WINDERMERE: I am not called on to encourage Lord Augustus, I suppose?

MRS. ERLYNNE: Oh, no! I do the encouraging. But you will make me a handsome settlement, Windermere, won't you?

LORD WINDERMERE (*frowning*): Is that what you want to talk to me about to-night?

MRS. ERLYNNE: Yes.

LORD WINDERMERE (*with a gesture of impatience*): I will not talk of it here.

MRS. ERLYNNE (*laughing*): Then we will talk of it on the terrace. Even business should have a picturesque background. Should it not, Windermere? With a proper background women can do anything.

LORD WINDERMERE: Won't to-morrow do as well?

MRS. ERLYNNE: No; you see, to-morrow I am going to accept him. And I think it would be a good thing if I was able to tell him that I had—well, what shall I say?—£2000 a year left to me by a third cousin—or a second husband—or some distant relative of that kind. It would be an additional attraction, wouldn't it? You have a delightful opportunity now of paying me a compliment, Windermere. But you are not very clever at paying compliments. I am afraid Margaret doesn't encourage you in that excellent habit. It's a great mistake on her part. When men give up saying what is charming, they give up thinking what is charming. But seriously, what do you say to £2000? £2500,* I think. In modern life margin is everything. Windermere, don't you think the world an intensely amusing place? I do!

Exit on terrace with LORD WINDERMERE. *Music strikes up in ballroom.*

LADY WINDERMERE: To stay in this house any longer is impossible. To-night a man who loves me offered me his whole life. I refused it. It was foolish of me. I will offer him mine now. I will give him mine. I will go to him! (*Puts on cloak and goes to the door, then turns back. Sits down at table and writes a letter, puts it into an envelope, and leaves it on table.*) Arthur has never understood me. When he reads this, he will. He may do as he chooses now with his life. I have done with mine as I think best, as I think right. It is he who has broken the bond of marriage—not I. I only break its bondage. (*Exit.*)

PARKER *enters L. and crosses towards the ballroom R. Enter* MRS. ERLYNNE.

MRS. ERLYNNE: Is Lady Windermere in the ballroom?

---

*About $10,000 and $12,500, respectively.

PARKER: Her ladyship has just gone out.

MRS. ERLYNNE: Gone out? She's not on the terrace?

PARKER: No, madam. Her ladyship has just gone out of the house.

MRS. ERLYNNE (*starts, and looks at the servant with a puzzled expression in her face*): Out of the house?

PARKER: Yes, madam—her ladyship told me she had left a letter for his lordship on the table.

MRS. ERLYNNE: A letter for Lord Windermere?

PARKER: Yes, madam.

MRS. ERLYNNE: Thank you.

Exit PARKER. *The music in the ballroom stops.*

Gone out of her house! A letter addressed to her husband! (*Goes over to bureau and looks at letter. Takes it up and lays it down again with a shudder of fear.*) No, no! It would be impossible! Life doesn't repeat its tragedies like that! Oh, why does this horrible fancy come across me? Why do I remember now the one moment of my life I most wish to forget? Does life repeat its tragedies? (*Tears letter open and reads it, then sinks down into a chair with a gesture of anguish.*) Oh, how terrible! The same words that twenty years ago I wrote to her father! and how bitterly I have been punished for it! No; my punishment, my real punishment is tonight, is now! (*Still seated R.*)

Enter LORD WINDERMERE *L.U.E.*

LORD WINDERMERE: Have you said good-night to my wife? (*Comes C.*)

MRS. ERLYNNE (*crushing letter in her hand*): Yes.

LORD WINDERMERE: Where is she?

MRS. ERLYNNE: She is very tired. She has gone to bed. She said she had a headache.

LORD WINDERMERE: I must go to her. You'll excuse me?

MRS. ERLYNNE (*rising hurriedly*): Oh, no! It's nothing serious. She's only very tired, that is all. Besides, there are people still in the supper-room. She wants you to make her apologies to them. She said she didn't wish to be disturbed. (*Drops letter.*) She asked me to tell you!

LORD WINDERMERE (*picks up letter*): You have dropped something.

MRS. ERLYNNE: Oh yes, thank you, that is mine. (*Puts out her hand to take it.*)

LORD WINDERMERE (*still looking at letter*): But it's my wife's handwriting, isn't it?

MRS. ERLYNNE (*takes the letter quickly*): Yes, it's—an address. Will you ask them to call my carriage, please?

LORD WINDERMERE: Certainly. (*Goes L. and exit.*)

MRS. ERLYNNE: Thanks! What can I do? What can I do? I feel a passion awakening within me that I never felt before. What can it mean? The daughter must not be like the mother—that would be terrible. How can I save her? How can I save my child? A moment may ruin a life. Who knows that better than I? Windermere must be got out of the house; that is absolutely necessary. (*Goes L.*) But how shall I do it? It must be done somehow. Ah!

Enter LORD AUGUSTUS *R.U.E. carrying bouquet.*

LORD AUGUSTUS: Dear lady, I am in such suspense! May I not have an answer to my request?

MRS. ERLYNNE: Lord Augustus, listen to me. You are to take Lord Windermere down to your club at once, and keep him there as long as possible. You understand?

LORD AUGUSTUS: But you said you wished me to keep early hours!

MRS. ERLYNNE (*nervously*): Do what I tell you. Do what I tell you.

LORD AUGUSTUS: And my reward?

MRS. ERLYNNE: Your reward? Your reward? Oh! ask me that to-morrow. But don't let Windermere out of your sight to-night. If you do I will never forgive you. I will never speak to you again. I'll have nothing to do with you. Remember you are to keep Windermere at your club, and don't let him come back to-night. (*Exit L.*)

LORD AUGUSTUS: Well, really, I might be her husband already. Positively I might. (*Follows her in a bewildered manner.*)

Act Drop

ACT THREE

SCENE: *Lord Darlington's rooms. A large sofa is in front of fireplace R. At the back of the stage a curtain is drawn across the window. Doors L. and R. Table R. with writing materials. Table C. with syphons, glasses, and Tantalus frame. Table L. with cigar and cigarette box. Lamps lit.*

LADY WINDERMERE (*standing by the fireplace*): Why doesn't he come? This waiting is horrible. He should be here. Why is he not here, to wake by passionate words some fire within me? I am cold—cold as a loveless thing. Arthur must have read my letter by this time. If he cared for me, he would have come after me, would have taken me back by force. But he doesn't care. He's entrammelled* by this woman—fascinated by her—dominated by her. If a woman wants to hold a man, she has merely to appeal to what is worst in him. We make gods of men and they leave us. Others make brutes of them and they fawn and are faithful. How hideous life is! . . . Oh! it was mad of me to come here, horribly mad. And yet, which is the worst, I wonder, to be at the mercy of a man who loves one, or the wife of a man who in one's own house dishonours one? What woman knows? What woman in the whole world? But will he love me always, this man to whom I am giving my life? What do I bring him? Lips that have lost the note of joy, eyes that are blinded by tears, chill hands and icy heart. I bring him nothing. I must go back—no; I can't go back, my letter has put me in their power—Arthur would not take me back! That fatal letter! No! Lord Darlington leaves England to-morrow. I will go with him—I have no choice. (*Sits down for a few moments. Then starts up and puts on her cloak.*) No, no! I will go back, let Arthur do with me what he pleases. I can't wait here. It has been madness my coming. I must go at once. As for Lord Darlington.—Oh! here he is! What

*Caught in or captured by a net.

shall I do? What can I say to him? Will he let me go away at all? I have heard that men are brutal, horrible. . . . Oh! (*Hides her face in her hands.*)

Enter MRS. ERLYNNE *L.*

MRS. ERLYNNE: Lady Windermere! (LADY WINDERMERE *starts and looks up. Then recoils in contempt.*) Thank Heaven I am in time. You must go back to your husband's house immediately.

LADY WINDERMERE: Must?

MRS. ERLYNNE (*authoritatively*): Yes, you must! There is not a second to be lost. Lord Darlington may return at any moment.

LADY WINDERMERE: Don't come near me!

MRS. ERYLYNNE: Oh! You are on the brink of ruin, you are on the brink of a hideous precipice. You must leave this place at once; my carriage is waiting at the corner of the street. You must come with me and drive straight home.

LADY WINDERMERE *throws off her cloak and flings it on the sofa.* What are you doing?

LADY WINDERMERE: Mrs. Erlynne—if you had not come here, I would have gone back. But now that I see you, I feel that nothing in the whole world would induce me to live under the same roof as Lord Windermere. You fill me with horror. There is something about you that stirs the wildest—rage within me. And I know why you are here. My husband sent you to lure me back that I might serve as a blind to whatever relations exist between you and him.

MRS. ERLYNNE: Oh! You don't think that—you can't.

LADY WINDERMERE: Go back to my husband, Mrs. Erlynne. He belongs to you and not to me. I suppose he is afraid of a scandal. Men are such cowards. They outrage every law of the world, and are afraid of the world's tongue. But he had better prepare himself. He shall have a scandal. He shall have the worst scandal there has been in London for years. He shall see his name in every vile paper, mine on every hideous placard.

MRS. ERLYNNE: No—no——

LADY WINDERMERE: Yes! he shall. Had he come himself, I admit I would have gone back to the life of degradation you and he had prepared for me—I was going back—but to stay himself at home, and to send you as his messenger—oh! it was infamous—infamous.

MRS. ERLYNNE (*C.*): Lady Windermere, you wrong me horribly—you wrong your husband horribly. He doesn't know you are here—he thinks you are safe in your own house. He thinks you are asleep in your own room. He never read the mad letter you wrote to him!

LADY WINDERMERE (*R.*): Never read it!

MRS. ERLYNNE: No—he knows nothing about it.

LADY WINDERMERE: How simple you think me! (*Going to her.*) You are lying to me!

MRS. ERLYNNE (*restraining herself*): I am not. I am telling you the truth.

LADY WINDERMERE: If my husband didn't read my letter, how is it that you are here? Who told you I had left the house you were shameless enough to enter? Who told you where I had gone to? My husband told you, and sent you to decoy me back. (*Crosses L.*)

MRS. ERLYNNE (*R.C.*): Your husband has never seen the letter. I—saw it, I opened it. I—read it.

LADY WINDERMERE (*turning to her*): You opened a letter of mine to my husband? You wouldn't dare!

MRS. ERLYNNE: Dare! Oh! to save you from the abyss into which you are falling, there is nothing in the world I would not dare, nothing in the whole world. Here is the letter. Your husband has never read it. He never shall read it. (*Going to fireplace.*) It should never have been written. (*Tears it and throws it into the fire.*)

LADY WINDERMERE (*with infinite contempt in her voice and look*): How do I know that that was my letter after all? You seem to think that commonest device can take me in!

MRS. ERLYNNE: Oh! why do you disbelieve everything I tell you? What object do you think I have in coming here, except to save you from utter ruin, to save you from the consequence of a hideous mistake? That letter that is burnt now *was* your letter. I swear it to you!

LADY WINDERMERE (*slowly*): You took good care to burn it before I had examined it. I cannot trust you. You, whose whole life is a lie, how could you speak the truth about anything? (*Sits down.*)

MRS. ERLYNNE (*hurriedly*): Think as you like about me—say what you choose against me, but go back, go back to the husband you love.

LADY WINDERMERE (*sullenly*): I do *not* love him!

MRS. ERLYNNE: You do, and you know that he loves you.

LADY WINDERMERE: He does not understand what love is. He understands it as little as you do—but I see what you want. It would be a great advantage for you to get me back. Dear Heaven! what a life I would have then! Living at the mercy of a woman who has neither mercy nor pity in her, a woman whom it is an infamy to meet, a degradation to know, a vile woman, a woman who comes between husband and wife!

MRS. ERLYNNE (*with a gesture of despair*): Lady Windermere, Lady Windermere, don't say such terrible things. You don't know how terrible they are, how terrible and how unjust. Listen, you must listen! Only go back to your husband, and I promise you never to communicate with him again on any pretext—never to see him—never to have anything to do with his life or yours. The money that he gave me, he gave me not through love, but through hatred, not in worship, but in contempt. The hold I have over him——

LADY WINDERMERE (*rising*): Ah! you admit you have a hold!

MRS. ERLYNNE: Yes, and I will tell you what it is. It is his love for you, Lady Windermere.

LADY WINDERMERE: You expect me to believe that?

MRS. ERYLYNNE: You must believe it! it is true. It is his love for you that has made him submit to—oh! call it what you like, tyranny, threats, anything you choose. But it is his love for you. His desire to spare you—shame, yes, shame and disgrace.

LADY WINDERMERE: What do you mean? You are insolent! What have I to do with you?

MRS. ERLYNNE (*humbly*): Nothing. I know it—but I tell you that your husband loves you—that you may never meet with such love again in your whole life—that such love you will never meet—and that if you throw it away, the day may come when you will starve for love and it will not be given to you, beg for love and it will be denied you.—Oh! Arthur loves you!

LADY WINDERMERE: Arthur? And you tell me there is nothing between you?

MRS. ERLYNNE: Lady Windermere, before Heaven your husband

is guiltless of all offence towards you! And I—I tell you that had it ever occurred to me that such a monstrous suspicion would have entered your mind, I would have died rather than have crossed your life or his—oh! died, gladly died! (*Moves away to sofa R.*)

LADY WINDERMERE: You talk as if you had a heart. Women like you have no hearts. Heart is not in you. You are bought and sold. (*Sits L.C.*)

MRS. ERLYNNE (*starts, with a gesture of pain. Then restrains herself, and comes over to where* LADY WINDERMERE *is sitting. As she speaks, she stretches out her hands towards her, but does not dare to touch her*): Believe what you choose about me. I am not worth a moment's sorrow. But don't spoil your beautiful young life on my account! You don't know what may be in store for you, unless you leave this house at once. You don't know what it is to fall into the pit, to be despised, mocked, abandoned, sneered at—to be an outcast! to find the door shut against one, to have to creep in by hideous byways, afraid every moment lest the mask should be stripped from one's face, and all the while to hear the laughter, the horrible laughter of the world, a thing more tragic than all the tears the world has ever shed. You don't know what it is. One pays for one's sin, and then one pays again, and all one's life one pays. You must never know that.—As for me, if suffering be an expiation, then at this moment I have expiated all my faults, whatever they have been; for to-night you have made a heart in one who had it not, made it and broken it.—But let that pass. I may have wrecked my own life, but I will not let you wreck yours. You—why, you are a mere girl, you would be lost. You haven't got the kind of brains that enables a woman to get back. You have neither the wit nor the courage. You couldn't stand dishonour! No! Go back, Lady Windermere, to the husband who loves you, whom you love. You have a child, Lady Windermere. Go back to that child who even now, in pain or in joy, may be calling to you. (LADY WINDERMERE *rises.*) God gave you that child. He will require from you that you make his life fine, that you watch over him. What answer will you make to God if his life is ruined through you? Back to your house, Lady Windermere—your husband loves you! He has never swerved for a moment from the love he bears you. But even if he had a thousand loves, you must stay with your child. If he was harsh to you, you must stay with your child. If he ill-treated you, you must stay with your child. If he abandoned you, your place is with your child.

LADY WINDERMERE *bursts into tears and buries her face in her hands.*

(*Rushing to her*): Lady Windermere!

LADY WINDERMERE (*holding out her hands to her, helplessly, as a child might do*): Take me home. Take me home.

MRS. ERLYNNE (*is about to embrace her. Then restrains herself. There is a look of wonderful joy in her face*): Come! Where is your cloak? (*Getting it from sofa.*) Here. Put it on. Come at once!

They go to the door.

LADY WINDERMERE: Stop! Don't you hear voices?

MRS. ERLYNNE: No, no! There is no one!

LADY WINDERMERE: Yes, there is! Listen! Oh! that is my husband's voice! He is coming in! Save me! Oh, it's some plot! You have sent for him.

Voices outside.

MRS. ERLYNNE: Silence! I'm here to save you, if I can. But I fear it is too late! There! (*Points to the curtain across the window.*) The first chance you have slip out, if you ever get a chance!

LADY WINDERMERE: But you?

MRS. ERLYNNE: Oh! never mind me. I'll face them.

LADY WINDERMERE *hides herself behind the curtain.*

LORD AUGUSTUS (*outside*): Nonsense, dear Windermere, you must not leave me!

MRS. ERLYNNE: Lord Augustus! Then it is I who am lost! (*Hesitates for a moment, then looks round and sees door R., and exit through it.*)

Enter LORD DARLINGTON, MR. DUMBY, LORD WINDERMERE, LORD AUGUSTUS LORTON, *and* MR. CECIL GRAHAM.

DUMBY: What a nuisance their turning us out of the club at this hour! It's only two o'clock. (*Sinks into a chair.*) The lively part of the evening is only just beginning. (*Yawns and closes his eyes.*)

LORD WINDERMERE: It is very good of you, Lord Darlington, allowing Augustus to force our company on you, but I'm afraid I can't stay long.

LORD DARLINGTON: Really! I am so sorry! You'll take a cigar, won't you?

LORD WINDERMERE: Thanks! (*Sits down.*)

LORD AUGUSTUS (*to* LORD WINDERMERE): My dear boy, you must not dream of going. I have a great deal to talk to you about, of demmed importance, too. (*Sits down with him at L. table.*)

CECIL GRAHAM: Oh! We all know what that is! Tuppy can't talk about anything but Mrs. Erlynne.

LORD WINDERMERE: Well, that is no business of yours, is it, Cecil?

CECIL GRAHAM: None! That is why it interests me. My own business always bores me to death. I prefer other people's.

LORD DARLINGTON: Have something to drink, you fellows. Cecil, you'll have a whisky and soda?

CECIL GRAHAM: Thanks. (*Goes to table with* LORD DARLINGTON) Mrs. Erlynne looked very handsome to-night, didn't she?

LORD DARLINGTON: I am not one of her admirers.

CECIL GRAHAM: I usen't to be, but I am now. Why! she actually made me introduce her to poor dear Aunt Caroline. I believe she is going to lunch there.

LORD DARLINGTON (*in surprise*): No?

CECIL GRAHAM: She is, really.

LORD DARLINGTON: Excuse me, you fellows. I'm going away to-morrow. And I have to write a few letters. (*Goes to writing-table and sits down.*)

DUMBY: Clever woman, Mrs. Erlynne.

CECIL GRAHAM: Hallo, Dumby! I thought you were asleep.

DUMBY: I am, I usually am!

LORD AUGUSTUS: A very clever woman. Knows perfectly well what a demmed fool I am—knows it as well as I do myself.

CECIL GRAHAM *comes towards him laughing.*

Ah, you may laugh, my boy, but it is a great thing to come across a woman who thoroughly understands one.

DUMBY: It is an awfully dangerous thing. They always end by marrying one.

CECIL GRAHAM: But I thought, Tuppy, you were never going to see her again! Yes! you told me so yesterday evening at the club. You said you'd heard——

Whispering to him.

LORD AUGUSTUS: Oh, she's explained that.

CECIL GRAHAM: And the Wiesbaden* affair?

LORD AUGUSTUS: She's explained that too.

DUMBY: And her income, Tuppy? Has she explained that?

LORD AUGUSTUS (*in a very serious voice*): She's going to explain that to-morrow.

CECIL GRAHAM *goes back to C. table.*

DUMBY: Awfully commercial, women nowadays. Our grandmothers threw their caps over the mills, of course, but, by Jove, their grand-daughters only throw their caps over mills that can raise the wind for them.

LORD AUGUSTUS: You want to make her out a wicked woman. She is not!

CECIL GRAHAM: Oh! Wicked women bother one. Good women bore one. That is the only difference between them.

LORD AUGUSTUS (*puffing a cigar*): Mrs. Erlynne has a future before her.

DUMBY: Mrs. Erlynne has a past before her.

LORD AUGUSTUS: I prefer women with a past. They're always so demmed amusing to talk to.

CECIL GRAHAM: Well, you'll have lots of topics of conversation with *her*, Tuppy. (*Rising and going to him.*)

LORD AUGUSTUS: You're getting annoying, dear boy; you're getting demmed annoying.

---

*Popular European spa.

CECIL GRAHAM (*puts his hands on his shoulders*): Now, Tuppy, you've lost your figure and you've lost your character. Don't lose your temper; you have only got one.

LORD AUGUSTUS: My dear boy, if I wasn't the most good-natured man in London——

CECIL GRAHAM: We'd treat you with more respect, wouldn't we, Tuppy? (*Strolls away.*)

DUMBY: The youth of the present day are quite monstrous. They have absolutely no respect for dyed hair.

LORD AUGUSTUS *looks round angrily.*

CECIL GRAHAM: Mrs. Erlynne has a very great respect for dear Tuppy.

DUMBY: Then Mrs. Erlynne sets an admirable example to the rest of her sex. It is perfectly brutal the way most women nowadays behave to men who are not their husbands.

LORD WINDERMERE: Dumby, you are ridiculous, and Cecil, you let your tongue run away with you. You must leave Mrs. Erlynne alone. You don't really know anything about her, and you're always talking scandal against her.

CECIL GRAHAM (*coming towards him L.C.*): My dear Arthur, I never talk scandal. *I* only talk gossip.

LORD WINDERMERE: What is the difference between scandal and gossip?

CECIL GRAHAM: Oh! gossip is charming! History is merely gossip. But scandal is gossip made tedious by morality. Now, I never moralise. A man who moralises is usually a hypocrite, and a woman who moralises is invariably plain. There is nothing in the whole world so unbecoming to a woman as a Nonconformist conscience. And most women know it, I'm glad to say.

LORD AUGUSTUS: Just my sentiments, dear boy, just my sentiments.

CECIL GRAHAM: Sorry to hear it, Tuppy; whenever people agree with me, I always feel I must be wrong.

LORD AUGUSTUS: My dear boy, when I was your age——

CECIL GRAHAM: But you never were, Tuppy, and you never will

be. (*Goes up to C.*) I say, Darlington, let us have some cards. You'll play, Arthur, won't you?

LORD WINDERMERE: No, thanks, Cecil.

DUMBY (*with a sigh*): Good heavens! how marriage ruins a man! It's as demoralising as cigarettes, and far more expensive.

CECIL GRAHAM: You'll play, of course, Tuppy?

LORD AUGUSTUS (*pouring himself out a brandy and soda at table*)*: Can't, dear boy. Promised Mrs. Erlynne never to play or drink again.

CECIL GRAHAM: Now, my dear Tuppy, don't be led astray into the paths of virtue. Reformed, you would be perfectly tedious. That is the worst of women. They always want one to be good. And if we are good, when they meet us, they don't love us at all. They like to find us quite irretrievably bad, and to leave us quite unattractively good.

LORD DARLINGTON (*rising from R. table, where he has been writing letters*): They always do find us bad!

DUMBY: I don't think we are bad. I think we are all good, except Tuppy.

LORD DARLINGTON: No, we are all in the gutter, but some of us are looking at the stars. (*Sits down at C. table.*)

DUMBY: We are all in the gutter, but some of us are looking at the stars? Upon my word, you are very romantic to-night, Darlington.

CECIL GRAHAM: Too romantic! You must be in love. Who is the girl?

LORD DARLINGTON: The woman I love is not free, or thinks she isn't. (*Glances instinctively at* LORD WINDERMERE *while he speaks.*)

CECIL GRAHAM: A married woman, then! Well, there's nothing in the world like the devotion of a married woman. It's a thing no married man knows anything about.

LORD DARLINGTON: Oh! she doesn't love me. She is a good woman. She is the only woman I have ever met in my life.

CECIL GRAHAM: The only good woman you have ever met in your life.

LORD DARLINGTON: Yes!

---

*Lord Augustus's actions speak louder than his words.

CECIL GRAHAM (*lighting a cigarette*): Well, you are a lucky fellow! Why, I have met hundreds of good women. I never seem to meet any but good women. The world is perfectly packed with good women. To know them is a middle-class education.

LORD DARLINGTON: This woman has purity and innocence. She has everything we men have lost.

CECIL GRAHAM: My dear fellow, what on earth should we men do going about with purity and innocence? A carefully thought-out buttonhole is much more effective.

DUMBY: She doesn't really love you then?

LORD DARLINGTON: No, she does not!

DUMBY: I congratulate you, my dear fellow. In this world there are only two tragedies. One is not getting what one wants, and the other is getting it. The last is much the worst; the last is a real tragedy! But I am interested to hear she does not love you. How long could you love a woman who didn't love you, Cecil?

CECIL GRAHAM: A woman who didn't love me? Oh, all my life!

DUMBY: So could I. But it's so difficult to meet one.

LORD DARLINGTON: How can you be so conceited, Dumby?

DUMBY: I didn't say it as a matter of conceit. I said it as a matter of regret. I have been wildly, madly adored. I am sorry I have. It has been an immense nuisance. I should like to be allowed a little time to myself now and then.

LORD AUGUSTUS (*looking round*): Time to educate yourself, I suppose.

DUMBY: No, time to forget all I have learned. That is much more important, dear Tuppy.

LORD AUGUSTUS *moves uneasily in his chair.*

LORD DARLINGTON: What cynics you fellows are!

CECIL GRAHAM: What is a cynic? (*Sitting on the back of the sofa.*)

LORD DARLINGTON: A man who knows the price of everything and the value of nothing.

CECIL GRAHAM: And a sentimentalist, my dear Darlington, is a man who sees an absurd value in everything, and doesn't know the market price of any single thing.

LORD DARLINGTON: You always amuse me, Cecil. You talk as if you were a man of experience.

CECIL GRAHAM: I am. (*Moves up to front of fireplace.*)

LORD DARLINGTON: You are far too young!

CECIL GRAHAM: That is a great error. Experience is a question of instinct about life. I have got it. Tuppy hasn't. Experience is the name Tuppy gives to his mistakes. That is all.

LORD AUGUSTUS *looks round indignantly.*

DUMBY: Experience is the name every one gives to their mistakes.

CECIL GRAHAM (*standing with his back to the fireplace*): One shouldn't commit any. (*Sees* LADY WINDERMERE'S *fan on sofa.*)*

DUMBY: Life would be very dull without them.

CECIL GRAHAM: Of course you are quite faithful to this woman you are in love with, Darlington, to this good woman?

LORD DARLINGTON: Cecil, if one really loves a woman, all other women in the world become absolutely meaningless to one. Love changes one—I am changed.

CECIL GRAHAM: Dear me! How very interesting! Tuppy, I want to talk to you.

LORD AUGUSTUS *takes no notice.*

DUMBY: It's no use talking to Tuppy. You might just as well talk to a brick wall.

CECIL GRAHAM: But I like talking to a brick wall—it's the only thing in the world that never contradicts me! Tuppy!

LORD AUGUSTUS: Well, what is it? What is it? (*Rising and going over to* CECIL GRAHAM.)

CECIL GRAHAM: Come over here. I want you particularly. (*Aside.*) Darlington has been moralising and talking about the purity of love, and that sort of thing, and he has got some woman in his rooms all the time.

LORD AUGUSTUS: No, really! really!

---

*The fan has been on the sofa since early in the act; the audience has been waiting for its discovery.

CECIL GRAHAM (*in a low voice*): Yes, here is her fan. (*Points to the fan.*)

LORD AUGUSTUS (*chuckling*): By Jove! By Jove!

LORD WINDERMERE (*up by door*): I am really off now, Lord Darlington. I am sorry you are leaving England so soon. Pray call on us when you come back! My wife and I will be charmed to see you!

LORD DARLINGTON (*up stage with* LORD WINDERMERE): I am afraid I shall be away for many years. Good-night!

CECIL GRAHAM: Arthur!

LORD WINDERMERE: What?

CECIL GRAHAM: I want to speak to you for a moment. No, do come!

LORD WINDERMERE (*putting on his coat*): I can't—I'm off.

CECIL GRAHAM: It is something very particular. It will interest you enormously.

LORD WINDERMERE (*smiling*): It is some of your nonsense, Cecil.

CECIL: It isn't! It isn't really.

LORD AUGUSTUS (*going to him*): My dear fellow, you mustn't go yet. I have a lot to talk to you about. And Cecil has something to show you.

LORD WINDERMERE (*walking over*): Well, what is it?

CECIL GRAHAM: Darlington has got a woman here in his rooms. Here is her fan. Amusing, isn't it? (*A pause.*)

LORD WINDERMERE: Good God! (*Seizes the fan*—DUMBY *rises.*)

CECIL GRAHAM: What is the matter?

LORD WINDERMERE: Lord Darlington!

LORD DARLINGTON (*turning round*): Yes!

LORD WINDERMERE: What is my wife's fan doing here in your rooms? Hands off, Cecil. Don't touch me.

LORD DARLINGTON: Your wife's fan?

LORD WINDERMERE: Yes, here it is!

LORD DARLINGTON (*walking towards him*): I don't know!

LORD WINDERMERE: You must know. I demand an explanation. Don't hold me, you fool. (*To* CECIL GRAHAM.)

LORD DARLINGTON (*aside*): She is here after all!

LORD WINDERMERE: Speak, sir! Why is my wife's fan here? Answer me! By God! I'll search your rooms, and if my wife's here, I'll—— (*Moves.*)

LORD DARLINGTON: You shall not search my rooms. You have no right to do so. I forbid you!

LORD WINDERMERE: You scoundrel! I'll not leave your room till I have searched every corner of it! What moves behind that curtain? (*Rushes towards the curtain C.*)

MRS ERLYNNE (*enters behind R.*): Lord Windermere!

LORD WINDERMERE: Mrs. Erlynne!

Every one starts and turns round. LADY WINDERMERE *slips out from behind the curtain and glides from the room L.*

MRS. ERLYNNE: I am afraid I took your wife's fan in mistake for my own, when I was leaving your house to-night. I am so sorry. (*Takes fan from him.* LORD WINDERMERE *looks at her in contempt.* LORD DARLINGTON *in mingled astonishment and anger.* LORD AUGUSTUS *turns away. The other men smile at each other.*)

Act Drop

ACT FOUR

SCENE: *Same as in Act One.*

LADY WINDERMERE (*lying on sofa*): How can I tell him? I can't tell him. It would kill me. I wonder what happened after I escaped from that horrible room. Perhaps she told them the true reason of her being there, and the real meaning of that—fatal fan of mine. Oh, if he knows—how can I look him in the face again? He would never forgive me. (*Touches bell.*) How securely one thinks one lives—out of reach of temptation, sin, folly. And then suddenly—Oh! Life is terrible. It rules us, we do not rule it.

Enter ROSALIE *R.*

ROSALIE: Did your ladyship ring for me?

LADY WINDERMERE: Yes. Have you found out at what time Lord Windermere came in last night?

ROSALIE: His lordship did not come in till five o'clock.

LADY WINDERMERE: Five o'clock? He knocked at my door this morning, didn't he?

ROSALIE: Yes, my lady—at half-past nine. I told him your ladyship was not awake yet.

LADY WINDERMERE: Did he say anything?

ROSALIE: Something about your ladyship's fan. I didn't quite catch what his lordship said. Has the fan been lost, my lady? I can't find it, and Parker says it was not left in any of the rooms. He has looked in all of them and on the terrace as well.

LADY WINDERMERE: It doesn't matter. Tell Parker not to trouble. That will do.

Exit ROSALIE.

LADY WINDERMERE (*rising*): She is sure to tell him. I can fancy a person doing a wonderful act of self-sacrifice, doing it spontaneously, recklessly, nobly—and afterwards finding out that it costs too much. Why should she hesitate between her ruin and mine? . . . How strange! I would have publicly disgraced her in my own house. She accepts public disgrace in the house of another to save me. . . . There is a bitter irony in things, a bitter irony in the way we talk of good and bad women*. . . . Oh, what a lesson! and what a pity that in life we only get our lessons when they are of no use to us! For even if she doesn't tell, I must. Oh! the shame of it, the shame of it. To tell it is to live through it all again. Actions are the first tragedy in life, words are the second. Words are perhaps the worst. Words are merciless. . . . Oh! (*Starts as* LORD WINDERMERE *enters.*)

LORD WINDERMERE (*kisses her*): Margaret—how pale you look!

LADY WINDERMERE: I slept very badly.

LORD WINDERMERE (*sitting on sofa with her*): I am so sorry. I came in dreadfully late, and didn't like to wake you. You are crying, dear.

LADY WINDERMERE: Yes, I am crying, for I have something to tell you, Arthur.

LORD WINDERMERE: My dear child, you are not well. You've been doing too much. Let us go away to the country. You'll be all right at Selby. The season is almost over. There is no use staying on. Poor darling! We'll go away to-day, if you like. (*Rises.*) We can easily catch the 3.40. I'll send a wire to Fannen. (*Crosses and sits down at table to write a telegram.*)

LADY WINDERMERE: Yes; let us go away to-day. No; I can't go to-day, Arthur. There is some one I must see before I leave town—some one who has been kind to me.

LORD WINDERMERE (*rising and leaning over sofa*): Kind to you?

LADY WINDERMERE: Far more than that. (*Rises and goes to him.*) I will tell you, Arthur, but only love me, love me as you used to love me.

LORD WINDERMERE: Used to? You are not thinking of that

---

*Lady Windermere has moved from her rigid morality (which she asserts in act one) to a more understanding and tolerant view.

wretched woman who came here last night? (*Coming round and sitting R. of her.*): You don't still imagine—no, you couldn't.

LADY WINDERMERE: I don't. I know now I was wrong and foolish.

LORD WINDERMERE: It was very good of you to receive her last night—but you are never to see her again.

LADY WINDERMERE: Why do you say that? (*A pause.*)

LORD WINDERMERE (*holding her hand*): Margaret, I thought Mrs. Erlynne was a woman more sinned against than sinning, as the phrase goes. I thought she wanted to be good, to get back into a place that she had lost by a moment's folly, to lead again a decent life. I believed what she told me—I was mistaken in her. She is bad—as bad as a woman can be.

LADY WINDERMERE: Arthur, Arthur, don't talk so bitterly about any woman.* I don't think now that people can be divided into the good and the bad as though they were two separate races or creations. What are called good women may have terrible things in them, mad moods of recklessness, assertion, jealousy, sin. Bad women, as they are termed, may have in them sorrow, repentance, pity, sacrifice. And I don't think Mrs. Erlynne a bad woman—I know she's not.

LORD WINDERMERE: My dear child, the woman's impossible. No matter what harm she tries to do us, you must never see her again. She is inadmissible anywhere.

LADY WINDERMERE: But I want to see her. I want her to come here.

LORD WINDERMERE: Never!

LADY WINDERMERE: She came here once as *your* guest. She must come now as *mine*. That is but fair.

LORD WINDERMERE: She should never have come here.

LADY WINDERMERE (*rising*): It is too late, Arthur, to say that now. (*Moves away.*)

LORD WINDERMERE (*rising*): Margaret, if you knew where Mrs. Erlynne went last night, after she left this house, you would not sit in the same room with her. It was absolutely shameless, the whole thing.

---

*Another indication of Lady Windermere's growing maturity.

LADY WINDERMERE: Arthur, I can't bear it any longer. I must tell you. Last night——

Enter PARKER *with a tray on which lie* LADY WINDERMERE'S *fan and a card.*

PARKER: Mrs. Erlynne has called to return your ladyship's fan which she took away by mistake last night. Mrs. Erlynne has written a message on the card.

LADY WINDERMERE: Oh, ask Mrs. Erlynne to be kind enough to come up. (*Reads card.*) Say I shall be very glad to see her.
Exit PARKER.
She wants to see me, Arthur.

LORD WINDERMERE (*takes card and looks at it*): Margaret, I *beg* you not to. Let me see her first, at any rate. She's a dangerous woman. She is the most dangerous woman I know. You don't realise what you're doing.

LADY WINDERMERE: It is right that I should see her.

LORD WINDERMERE: My child, you may be on the brink of a great sorrow. Don't go to meet it. It is absolutely necessary that I should see her before you do.

LADY WINDERMERE: Why should it be necessary?

Enter PARKER.

PARKER: Mrs. Erlynne.

Enter MRS. ERYLNNE. *Exit* PARKER.

MRS. ERLYNNE: How do you do, Lady Windermere? (*To* LORD WINDERMERE): How do you do? Do you know, Lady Windermere, I am so sorry about your fan. I can't imagine how I made such a silly mistake. Most stupid of me. And as I was driving in your direction, I thought I would take the opportunity of returning your property in person with many apologies for my carelessness, and of bidding you good-bye.

LADY WINDERMERE: Good-bye? (*Moves towards sofa with* MRS.

ERLYNNE *and sits down beside her.*) Are you going away, then, Mrs. Erlynne?

MRS. ERLYNNE: Yes; I am going to live abroad again. The English climate doesn't suit me. My—heart is affected here, and that I don't like. I prefer living in the south. London is too full of fogs and—and serious people, Lord Windermere. Whether the fogs produce the serious people or whether the serious people produce the fogs, I don't know, but the whole thing rather gets on my nerves, and so I'm leaving this afternoon by the Club Train.*

LADY WINDERMERE: This afternoon? But I wanted so much to come and see you.

MRS. ERLYNNE: How kind of you! But I am afraid I have to go.

LADY WINDERMERE: Shall I never see you again, Mrs. Erlynne?

MRS. ERLYNNE: I am afraid not. Our lives lie too far apart. But there is a little thing I would like you to do for me. I want a photograph of you, Lady Windermere—would you give me one? You don't know how gratified I should be.

LADY WINDERMERE: Oh, with pleasure. There is one on that table. I'll show it to you. (*Goes across to the table.*)

LORD WINDERMERE (*coming up to* MRS. ERLYNNE *and speaking in a low voice*): It is monstrous your intruding yourself here after your conduct last night.

MRS. ERLYNNE (*with an amused smile*): My dear Windermere, manners before morals!

LADY WINDERMERE (*returning*): I'm afraid it is very flattering—I am not so pretty as that. (*Showing photograph.*)

MRS. ERLYNNE: You are much prettier. But haven't you got one of yourself with your little boy?

LADY WINDERMERE: I have. Would you prefer one of those?

MRS ERLYNNE: Yes.

LADY WINDERMERE: I'll go and get it for you, if you'll excuse me for a moment. I have one upstairs.

MRS ERLYNNE: So sorry, Lady Windermere, to give you so much trouble.

---

*Luxurious train that served food.

LADY WINDERMERE (*moves to door R.*): No trouble at all, Mrs. Erlynne.

MRS. ERLYNNE: Thanks so much.

Exit LADY WINDERMERE *R.*

You seem rather out of temper this morning, Windermere. Why should you be? Margaret and I get on charmingly together.

LORD WINDERMERE: I can't bear to see you with her. Besides, you have not told me the truth, Mrs. Erlynne.

MRS. ERLYNNE: I have not told *her* the truth, you mean.

LORD WINDERMERE (*standing C.*): I sometimes wish you had. I should have been spared then the misery, the anxiety, the annoyance of the last six months. But rather than my wife should know—that the mother whom she was taught to consider as dead, the mother whom she has mourned as dead, is living—a divorced woman, going about under an assumed name, a bad woman preying upon life, as I know you now to be—rather than that, I was ready to supply you with money to pay bill after bill, extravagance after extravagance, to risk what occurred yesterday, the first quarrel I have ever had with my wife. You don't understand what that means to me. How could you? But I tell you that the only bitter words that ever came from those sweet lips of hers were on your account, and I hate to see you next her. You sully the innocence that is in her. (*Moves L.C.*) And then I used to think that with all your faults you were frank and honest. You are not.

MRS. ERLYNNE: Why do you say that?

LORD WINDERMERE: You made me get you an invitation to my wife's ball.

MRS. ERLYNNE: For my daughter's ball—yes.

LORD WINDERMERE: You came, and within an hour of your leaving the house you are found in a man's rooms—you are disgraced before every one. (*Goes up stage C.*)

MRS. ERLYNNE: Yes.

LORD WINDERMERE (*turning round on her*): Therefore I have a right to look upon you as what you are—a worthless, vicious woman. I have the right to tell you never to enter this house, never to attempt to come near my wife——

MRS. ERLYNNE (*coldly*): My daughter, you mean.

LORD WINDERMERE: You have no right to claim her as your

daughter. You left her, abandoned her when she was but a child in the cradle, abandoned her for your lover, who abandoned you in turn.

MRS. ERLYNNE (*rising*): Do you count that to his credit, Lord Windermere—or to mine?

LORD WINDERMERE: To his, now that I know you.

MRS. ERLYNNE: Take care—you had better be careful.

LORD WINDERMERE: Oh, I am not going to mince words for you. I know you thoroughly.

MRS. ERLYNNE (*looking steadily at him*): I question that.

LORD WINDERMERE: I *do* know you. For twenty years of your life you lived without your child, without a thought of your child. One day you read in the papers that she had married a rich man. You saw your hideous chance. You knew that to spare her the ignominy of learning that a woman like you was her mother, I would endure anything. You began your blackmailing.

MRS. ERLYNNE (*shrugging her shoulders*): Don't use ugly words, Windermere. They are vulgar. I saw my chance, it is true, and took it.

LORD WINDERMERE: Yes, you took it—and spoiled it all last night by being found out.

MRS. ERLYNNE (*with a strange smile*): You are quite right, I spoiled it all last night.

LORD WINDERMERE: And as for your blunder in taking my wife's fan from here and then leaving it about in Darlington's rooms, it is unpardonable. I can't bear the sight of it now. I shall never let my wife use it again. The thing is soiled for me. You should have kept it and not brought it back.

MRS. ERLYNNE: I think I *shall* keep it. (*Goes up.*) It's extremely pretty. (*Takes up fan.*) I shall ask Margaret to give it to me.

LORD WINDERMERE: I hope my wife will give it to you.

MRS. ERLYNNE: Oh, I'm sure she will have no objection.

LORD WINDERMERE: I wish that at the same time she would give you a miniature she kisses every night before she prays.—It's the miniature of a young innocent-looking girl with beautiful *dark* hair.

MRS. ERLYNNE: Ah, yes, I remember. How long ago that seems! (*Goes to sofa and sits down.*) It was done before I was married. Dark hair and an innocent expression were the fashion then, Windermere! (*A pause.*)

LORD WINDERMERE: What do you mean by coming here this morning? What is your object? (*Crossing L.C. and sitting.*)

MRS. ERLYNNE (*with a note of irony in her voice*): To bid good-bye to my dear daughter, of course.

LORD WINDERMERE *bites his under lip in anger.* MRS. ERLYNNE *looks at him, and her voice and manner become serious. In her accents as she talks there is a note of deep tragedy. For a moment she reveals herself.*

Oh, don't imagine I am going to have a pathetic scene with her, weep on her neck and tell her who I am, and all that kind of thing. I have no ambition to play the part of a mother. Only once in my life have I known a mother's feelings. That was last night. They were terrible—they made me suffer—they made me suffer too much. For twenty years, as you say, I have lived childless—I want to live childless still. (*Hiding her feelings with a trivial laugh.*) Besides, my dear Windermere, how on earth could I pose as a mother with a grown-up daughter? Margaret is twenty-one, and I have never admitted that I am more than twenty-nine, or thirty at the most. Twenty-nine when there are pink shades, thirty when there are not. So you see what difficulties it would involve. No, as far as I am concerned, let your wife cherish the memory of this dead, stainless mother. Why should I interfere with her illusions? I find it hard enough to keep my own. I lost one illusion last night. I thought I had no heart. I find I have, and a heart doesn't suit me, Windermere. Somehow it doesn't go with modern dress. It makes one look old. (*Takes up hand-mirror from table and looks into it.*) And it spoils one's career at critical moments.

LORD WINDERMERE: You fill me with horror—with absolute horror.

MRS. ERLYNNE (*rising*): I suppose, Windermere, you would like me to retire into a convent, or become a hospital nurse, or something of that kind, as people do in silly modern novels. That is stupid of you, Arthur; in real life we don't do such things—not as long as we have any good looks left, at any rate. No—what consoles one nowadays is not repentance, but pleasure. Repentance is quite out of date. And besides, if a woman really repents, she has to go to a bad dressmaker, otherwise no one believes in her. And nothing in the world would induce me to do that. No; I am going to pass entirely out of your two lives. My coming into them has been a mistake—I discovered that last night.

LORD WINDERMERE: A fatal mistake.

MRS. ERLYNNE (*smiling*): Almost fatal.

LORD WINDERMERE: I am sorry now I did not tell my wife the whole thing at once.

MRS. ERLYNNE: I regret my bad actions. You regret your good ones—that is the difference between us.

LORD WINDERMERE: I don't trust you. I *will* tell my wife. It's better for her to know, and from me. It will cause her infinite pain—it will humiliate her terribly, but it's right that she should know.

MRS. ERLYNNE: You propose to tell her?

LORD WINDERMERE: I am going to tell her.

MRS. ERLYNNE (*going up to him*): If you do, I will make my name so infamous that it will mar every moment of her life. It will ruin her, and make her wretched. If you dare to tell her, there is no depth of degradation I will not sink to, no pit of shame I will not enter. You shall not tell her—I forbid you.

LORD WINDERMERE: Why?

MRS. ERLYNNE (*after a pause*): If I said to you that I cared for her, perhaps loved her even—you would sneer at me, wouldn't you?

LORD WINDERMERE: I should feel it was not true. A mother's love means devotion, unselfishness, sacrifice. What could you know of such things?

MRS. ERLYNNE: You are right. What could I know of such things? Don't let us talk any more about it—as for telling my daughter who I am, that I do not allow. It is my secret, it is not yours. If I make up my mind to tell her, and I think I will, I shall tell her before I leave the house—if not, I shall never tell her.

LORD WINDERMERE (*angrily*): Then let me beg of you to leave our house at once. I will make your excuses to Margaret.

Enter LADY WINDERMERE *R. She goes over to* MRS. ERLYNNE *with the photograph in her hand.* LORD WINDERMERE *moves to back of sofa, and anxiously watches* MRS. ERLYNNE *as the scene progresses.*

LADY WINDERMERE: I am so sorry, Mrs. Erlynne, to have kept you waiting. I couldn't find the photograph anywhere. At last I discovered it in my husband's dressing-room—he had stolen it.

MRS. ERLYNNE (*takes the photograph from her and looks at it*): I am not surprised—it is charming. (*Goes over to sofa with* LADY WINDERMERE, *and sits down beside her. Looks again at the photograph.*) And so that is your little boy! What is he called?

LADY WINDERMERE: Gerard, after my dear father.*

MRS. ERLYNNE (*laying the photograph down*): Really?

LADY WINDERMERE: Yes. If it had been a girl, I would have called it after my mother. My mother had the same name as myself, Margaret.

MRS. ERLYNNE: My name is Margaret too.

LADY WINDERMERE: Indeed!

MRS. ERLYNNE: Yes. (*Pause.*) You are devoted to your mother's memory, Lady Windermere, your husband tells me.

LADY WINDERMERE: We all have ideals in life. At least we all should have. Mine is my mother.

MRS. ERLYNNE: Ideals are dangerous things. Realities are better. They wound, but they're better.

LADY WINDERMERE (*shaking her head*): If I lost my ideals, I should lose everything.

MRS. ERLYNNE: Everything?

LADY WINDERMERE: Yes. (*Pause.*)

MRS. ERLYNNE: Did your father often speak to you of your mother?

LADY WINDERMERE: No, it gave him too much pain. He told me how my mother had died a few months after I was born. His eyes filled with tears as he spoke. Then he begged me never to mention her name to him again. It made him suffer even to hear it. My father—my father really died of a broken heart. His was the most ruined life I know.

MRS. ERLYNNE (*rising*): I am afraid I must go now, Lady Windermere.

LADY WINDERMERE (*rising*): Oh no, don't.

---

*The following scene is heavy with irony; the tension between the two is shortly broken when Mrs. Erlynne rises.

MRS. ERLYNNE: I think I had better. My carriage must have come back by this time. I sent it to Lady Jedburgh's with a note.

LADY WINDERMERE: Arthur, would you mind seeing if Mrs. Erlynne's carriage has come back?

MRS. ERLYNNE: Pray don't trouble, Lord Windermere.

LADY WINDERMERE: Yes, Arthur, do go, please.

LORD WINDERMERE *hesitates for a moment and looks at* MRS. ERLYNNE. *She remains quite impassive. He leaves the room.*

(*To* MRS. ERLYNNE): Oh! What am I to say to you? You saved me last night. (*Goes towards her.*)

MRS. ERLYNNE: Hush—don't speak of it.

LADY WINDERMERE: I must speak of it. I can't let you think that I am going to accept this sacrifice. I am not. It is too great. I am going to tell my husband everything. It is my duty.

MRS. ERLYNNE: It is not your duty—at least you have duties to others besides him. You say you owe me something?

LADY WINDERMERE: I owe you everything.

MRS. ERLYNNE: Then pay your debt by silence. That is the only way in which it can be paid. Don't spoil the one good thing I have done in my life by telling it to any one. Promise me that what passed last night will remain a secret between us. You must not bring misery into your husband's life. Why spoil his love? You must not spoil it. Love is easily killed. Oh! how easily love is killed. Pledge me your word, Lady Windermere, that you will *never* tell him. I insist upon it.

LADY WINDERMERE (*with bowed head*): It is your will, not mine.

MRS. ERLYNNE: Yes, it is my will. And never forget your child—I like to think of you as a mother. I like you to think of yourself as one.

LADY WINDERMERE (*looking up*): I always will now. Only once in my life I have forgotten my own mother—that was last night. Oh, if I had remembered her I should not have been so foolish, so wicked.

MRS. ERLYNNE (*with a slight shudder*): Hush, last night is quite over.

Enter LORD WINDERMERE.

LORD WINDERMERE: Your carriage has not come back yet, Mrs. Erlynne.

MRS. ERLYNNE: It makes no matter. I'll take a hansom. There is nothing in the world so respectable as a good Shrewsbury and Talbot.* And now, dear Lady Windermere, I am afraid it is really good-bye. (*Moves up C.*) Oh, I remember. You'll think me absurd, but do you know I've taken a great fancy to this fan that I was silly enough to run away with last night from your ball. Now, I wonder would you give it to me? Lord Windermere says you may. I know it is his present.

LADY WINDERMERE: Oh, certainly, if it will give you any pleasure. But it has my name on it. It has "Margaret" on it.

MRS. ERLYNNE: But we have the same Christian name.

LADY WINDERMERE: Oh, I forgot. Of course, do have it. What a wonderful chance our names being the same!

MRS. ERLYNNE: Quite wonderful. Thanks—it will always remind me of you. (*Shakes hands with her.*)

Enter PARKER.

PARKER: Lord Augustus Lorton. Mrs. Erlynne's carriage has come.

Enter LORD AUGUSTUS.

LORD AUGUSTUS: Good-morning, dear boy. Good-morning, Lady Windermere. (*Sees* MRS. ERLYNNE.) Mrs. Erlynne!

MRS. ERLYNNE: How do you do, Lord Augustus? Are you quite well this morning?

LORD AUGUSTUS (*coldly*): Quite well, thank you, Mrs. Erlynne.

MRS. ERLYNNE: You don't look at all well, Lord Augustus. You stop up too late—it is so bad for you. You really should take more care of yourself. Good-bye, Lord Windermere. (*Goes towards door with a bow to* LORD AUGUSTUS. *Suddenly smiles and looks back at*

---

*Manufacturers of carriages used as taxis in London; people referred to their vehicles by their brand names just as we refer to automobiles.

him.) Lord Augustus! Won't you see me to my carriage? You might carry the fan.

LORD WINDERMERE: Allow me!

MRS. ERLYNNE: No; I want Lord Augustus. I have a special message for the dear Duchess. Won't you carry the fan, Lord Augustus?

LORD AUGUSTUS: If you really desire it, Mrs. Erlynne.

MRS. ERLYNNE (*laughing*): Of course I do. You'll carry it so gracefully. You would carry off anything gracefully, dear Lord Augustus. (*When she reaches the door she looks back for a moment at* LADY WINDERMERE. *Their eyes meet. Then she turns, and exit C. followed by* LORD AUGUSTUS.)

LADY WINDERMERE: You will never speak against Mrs. Erlynne again, Arthur, will you?

LORD WINDERMERE (*gravely*): She is better than one thought her.

LADY WINDERMERE: She is better than I am.

LORD WINDERMERE (*smiling as he strokes her hair*): Child, you and she belong to different worlds. Into your world evil has never entered.

LADY WINDERMERE: Don't say that, Arthur. There is the same world for all of us, and good and evil, sin and innocence, go through it hand in hand. To shut one's eyes to half of life that one may live securely is as though one blinded oneself that one might walk with more safety in a land of pit and precipice.

LORD WINDERMERE (*moves down with her*): Darling, why do you say that?

LADY WINDERMERE (*sits on sofa*): Because I, who had shut my eyes to life, came to the brink. And one who had separated us——

LORD WINDERMERE: We were never separated.

LADY WINDERMERE: We never must be again. O Arthur, don't love me less, and I will trust you more. I will trust you absolutely. Let us go to Selby. In the Rose Garden at Selby the roses are white and red.

Enter LORD AUGUSTUS *C.*

LORD AUGUSTUS: Arthur, she has explained everything!

LADY WINDERMERE *looks horribly frightened at this.* LORD WINDERMERE *starts.* LORD AUGUSTUS *takes* WINDERMERE *by the arm and brings him to front of stage. He talks rapidly and in a low voice.* LADY WINDERMERE *stands watching them in terror.*
My dear fellow, she has explained every demmed thing. We all wronged her immensely. It was entirely for my sake she went to Darlington's rooms. Called first at the Club—fact is, wanted to put me out of suspense—and being told I had gone on—followed—naturally frightened when she heard a lot of us coming in—retired to another room—I assure you, most gratifying to me, the whole thing. We all behaved brutally to her. She is just the woman for me. Suits me down to the ground. All the conditions she makes are that we live entirely out of England. A very good thing too. Demmed clubs, demmed climate, demmed cooks, demmed everything. Sick of it all!

LADY WINDERMERE (*frightened*): Has Mrs. Erlynne——?

LORD AUGUSTUS (*advancing towards her with a low bow*): Yes, Lady Windermere—Mrs. Erlynne has done me the honour of accepting my hand.

LORD WINDERMERE: Well, you are certainly marrying a very clever woman!

LADY WINDERMERE (*taking her husband's hand*): Ah, you're marrying a very good woman!

Curtain

A WOMAN OF NO IMPORTANCE

THE PERSONS OF THE PLAY

LORD ILLINGWORTH
SIR JOHN PONTEFRACT
LORD ALFRED RUFFORD
MR. KELVIL, M.P.
THE VEN. ARCHDEACON
DAUBENY, D.D.
GERALD ARBUTHNOT
FARQUHAR, Butler
FRANCIS, Footman
LADY HUNSTANTON
LADY CAROLINE PONTEFRACT
LADY STUTFIELD
MRS. ALLONBY
MISS HESTER WORSLEY
ALICE, Maid
MRS. ARBUTHNOT

ACT ONE

SCENE: *Lawn in front of the terrace at Hunstanton Chase. The action of the play takes place within twenty-four hours.* TIME: *The present.*

SIR JOHN *and* LADY CAROLINE PONTEFRACT, MISS WORSLEY, *on chairs under large yew tree.*

LADY CAROLINE: I believe this is the first English country house you have stayed at, Miss Worsley?

HESTER: Yes, Lady Caroline.

LADY CAROLINE: You have no country houses, I am told, in America?

HESTER: We have not many.

LADY CAROLINE: Have you any country? What we should call country?

HESTER (*smiling*): We have the largest country in the world, Lady Caroline. They used to tell us at school that some of our states are as big as France and England put together.

LADY CAROLINE: Ah! you must find it very draughty, I should fancy. (*To* SIR JOHN): John, you should have your muffler. What is the use of my always knitting mufflers for you if you won't wear them?

SIR JOHN: I am quite warm, Caroline, I assure you.

LADY CAROLINE: I think not, John. Well, you couldn't come to a more charming place than this, Miss Worsley, though the house is excessively damp, quite unpardonably damp, and dear Lady Hunstanton is sometimes a little lax about the people she asks down here. (*To* SIR JOHN): Jane mixes too much. Lord Illingworth, of course, is a man of high distinction. It is a privilege to meet him. And that member of Parliament, Mr. Kettle——

SIR JOHN: Kelvil, my love, Kelvil.

LADY CAROLINE: He must be quite respectable. One has never

heard his name before in the whole course of one's life, which speaks volumes for a man, nowadays. But Mrs. Allonby is hardly a very suitable person.

HESTER: I dislike Mrs. Allonby. I dislike her more than I can say.

LADY CAROLINE: I am not sure, Miss Worsley, that foreigners like yourself should cultivate likes or dislikes about the people they are invited to meet. Mrs. Allonby is very well born. She is a niece of Lord Brancaster's. It is said, of course, that she ran away twice before she was married. But you know how unfair people often are. I myself don't believe she ran away more than once.

HESTER: Mr. Arbuthnot is very charming.

LADY CAROLINE: Ah, yes! the young man who has a post in a bank. Lady Hunstanton is most kind in asking him here, and Lord Illingworth seems to have taken quite a fancy to him. I am not sure, however, that Jane is right in taking him out of his position. In my young days, Miss Worsley, one never met any one in society who worked for their living. It was not considered the thing.

HESTER: In America those are the people we respect most.

LADY CAROLINE: I have no doubt of it.

HESTER: Mr. Arbuthnot has a beautiful nature! He is so simple, so sincere. He has one of the most beautiful natures I have ever come across. It is a privilege to meet *him*.

LADY CAROLINE: It is not customary in England, Miss Worsley, for a young lady to speak with such enthusiasm of any person of the opposite sex. English women conceal their feelings till after they are married. They show them then.

HESTER: Do you, in England, allow no friendship to exist between a young man and a young girl?

Enter LADY HUNSTANTON, *followed by* FOOTMAN *with shawls and a cushion.*

LADY CAROLINE: We think it very inadvisable. Jane, I was just saying what a pleasant party you have asked us to meet. You have a wonderful power of selection. It is quite a gift.

LADY HUNSTANTON: Dear Caroline, how kind of you! I think we all do fit in very nicely together. And I hope our charming American visitor will carry back pleasant recollections of our English country life. (*To Footman*): The cushion, there, Francis. And my shawl. The Shetland. Get the Shetland.

Exit Footman for shawl. Enter GERALD ARBUTHNOT.

GERALD: Lady Hunstanton, I have such good news to tell you. Lord Illingworth has just offered to make me his secretary.

LADY HUNSTANTON: His secretary? That is good news indeed, Gerald. It means a very brilliant future in store for you. Your dear mother will be delighted. I really must try and induce her to come up here to-night. Do you think she would, Gerald? I know how difficult it is to get her to go anywhere.

GERALD: Oh! I am sure she would, Lady Hunstanton, if she knew Lord Illingworth had made me such an offer.

Enter Footman with shawl.

LADY HUNSTANTON: I will write and tell her about it, and ask her to come up and meet him. (*To Footman*): Just wait, Francis. (*Writes letter.*)

LADY CAROLINE: That is a very wonderful opening for so young a man as you are, Mr. Arbuthnot.

GERALD: It is indeed, Lady Caroline. I trust I shall be able to show myself worthy of it.

LADY CAROLINE: I trust so.

GERALD (*to* HESTER): *You* have not congratulated me yet, Miss Worsley.

HESTER: Are you very pleased about it?

GERALD: Of course I am. It means everything to me—things that were out of the reach of hope before may be within hope's reach now.

HESTER: Nothing should be out of the reach of hope. Life is a hope.

LADY HUNSTANTON: I fancy, Caroline, that Diplomacy is what Lord Illingworth is aiming at. I heard that he was offered Vienna. But that may not be true.

LADY CAROLINE: I don't think that England should be represented abroad by an unmarried man, Jane. It might lead to complications.

LADY HUNSTANTON: You are too nervous, Caroline. Believe me, you are too nervous. Besides, Lord Illingworth may marry any day. I was in hopes he would have married Lady Kelso. But I believe he said her family was too large. Or was it her feet? I forget which. I regret it very much. She was made to be an ambassador's wife.

LADY CAROLINE: She certainly has a wonderful faculty of remembering people's names, and forgetting their faces.

LADY HUNSTANTON: Well, that is very natural, Caroline, is it not? (*To Footman*): Tell Henry to wait for an answer. I have written a line to your dear mother, Gerald, to tell her your good news, and to say she really must come to dinner.

Exit Footman.

GERALD: That is awfully kind of you, Lady Hunstanton. (*To* HESTER): Will you come for a stroll, Miss Worsley?

HESTER: With pleasure. (*Exit with* GERALD.)

LADY HUNSTANTON: I am very much gratified at Gerald Arbuthnot's good fortune. He is quite a *protégé* of mine. And I am particularly pleased that Lord Illingworth should have made the offer of his own accord without my suggesting anything. Nobody likes to be asked favours. I remember poor Charlotte Pagden making herself quite unpopular one season, because she had a French governess she wanted to recommend to every one.

LADY CAROLINE: I saw the governess, Jane. Lady Pagden sent her to me. It was before Eleanor came out. She was far too good-looking to be in any respectable household. I don't wonder Lady Pagden was so anxious to get rid of her.

LADY HUNSTANTON: Ah, that explains it.

LADY CAROLINE: John, the grass is too damp for you. You had better go and put on your overshoes at once.

SIR JOHN: I am quite comfortable, Caroline, I assure you.

LADY CAROLINE: You must allow me to be the best judge of that, John. Pray do as I tell you.

SIR JOHN *gets up and goes off.*

LADY HUNSTANTON: You spoil him, Caroline, you do indeed!
Enter MRS. ALLONBY *and* LADY STUTFIELD.
(*To* MRS. ALLONBY): Well, dear, I hope you like the park. It is said to be well timbered.

MRS. ALLONBY: The trees are wonderful, Lady Hunstanton.

LADY STUTFIELD: Quite, quite wonderful.

MRS. ALLONBY: But somehow, I feel sure that if I lived in the country for six months, I should become so unsophisticated that no one would take the slightest notice of me.

LADY HUNSTANTON: I assure you, dear, that the country has not that effect at all. Why, it was from Melthorpe, which is only two miles from here, that Lady Belton eloped with Lord Fethersdale. I remember the occurrence perfectly. Poor Lord Belton died three days afterwards of joy, or gout. I forget which. We had a large party staying here at the time, so we were all very much interested in the whole affair.

MRS. ALLONBY: I think to elope is cowardly. It's running away from danger. And danger has become so rare in modern life.

LADY CAROLINE: As far as I can make out, the young women of the present day seem to make it the sole object of their lives to be always playing with fire.

MRS. ALLONBY: The one advantage of playing with fire, Lady Caroline, is that one never gets even singed. It is the people who don't know how to play with it who get burned up.

LADY STUTFIELD: Yes; I see that. It is very, very helpful.

LADY HUNSTANTON: I don't know how the world would get on with such a theory as that, dear Mrs. Allonby.

LADY STUTFIELD: Ah! The world was made for men and not for women.

MRS. ALLONBY: Oh, don't say that, Lady Stutfield. We have a much better time than they have. There are far more things forbidden to us than are forbidden to them.

LADY STUTFIELD: Yes; that is quite, quite true. I had not thought of that.

Enter SIR JOHN *and* MR. KELVIL.

LADY HUNSTANTON: Well, Mr. Kelvil, have you got through your work?

KELVIL: I have finished my writing for the day, Lady Hunstanton. It has been an arduous task. The demands on the time of a public man are very heavy nowadays, very heavy indeed. And I don't think they meet with adequate recognition.

LADY CAROLINE: John, have you got your overshoes on?

SIR JOHN: Yes, my love.

LADY CAROLINE: I think you had better come over here, John. It is more sheltered.

SIR JOHN: I am quite comfortable, Caroline.

LADY CAROLINE: I think not, John. You had better sit beside me.

SIR JOHN *rises and goes across.*

LADY STUTFIELD: And what have you been writing about this morning, Mr. Kelvil?

KELVIL: On the usual subject, Lady Stutfield. On Purity.

LADY STUTFIELD: That must be such a very, very interesting thing to write about.

KELVIL: It is the one subject of really national importance, nowadays, Lady Stutfield. I purpose addressing my constituents on the question before Parliament meets. I find that the poorer classes of this country display a marked desire for a higher ethical standard.

LADY STUTFIELD: How quite, quite nice of them.

LADY CAROLINE: Are you in favour of women taking part in politics, Mr. Kettle?

SIR JOHN: Kelvil, my love, Kelvil.

KELVIL: The growing influence of women is the one reassuring thing in our political life, Lady Caroline. Women are always on the side of morality, public and private.

LADY STUTFIELD: It is so very, very gratifying to hear you say that.

LADY HUNSTANTON: Ah, yes!—the moral qualities in women—that is the important thing. I am afraid, Caroline, that dear Lord Illingworth doesn't value the moral qualities in women as much as he should.

Enter LORD ILLINGWORTH.

LADY STUTFIELD: The world says that Lord Illingworth is very, very wicked.

LORD ILLINGWORTH: But what world says that, Lady Stutfield? It must be the next world. This world and I are on excellent terms. (*Sits down beside* MRS. ALLONBY.)

LADY STUTFIELD: Every one *I* know says you are very, very wicked.

LORD ILLINGWORTH: It is perfectly monstrous the way people go about, nowadays, saying things against one behind one's back that are absolutely and entirely true.

LADY HUNSTANTON: Dear Lord Illingworth is quite hopeless, Lady Stutfield. I have given up trying to reform him. It would take a Public Company with a Board of Directors and a paid Secretary to do that. But you have the secretary already, Lord Illingworth, haven't you? Gerald Arbuthnot has told us of his good fortune; it is really most kind of you.

LORD ILLINGWORTH: Oh, don't say that, Lady Hunstanton. Kind is a dreadful word. I took a great fancy to young Arbuthnot the moment I met him, and he'll be of considerable use to me in something I am foolish enough to think of doing.

LADY HUNSTANTON: He is an admirable young man. And his mother is one of my dearest friends. He has just gone for a walk with our pretty American. She is very pretty, is she not?

LADY CAROLINE: Far too pretty. These American girls carry off all the good matches. Why can't they stay in their own country? They are always telling us it is the Paradise of women.

LORD ILLINGWORTH: It is, Lady Caroline. That is why, like Eve, they are so extremely anxious to get out of it.

LADY CAROLINE: Who are Miss Worsley's parents?

LORD ILLINGWORTH: American women are wonderfully clever in concealing their parents.

LADY HUNSTANTON: My dear Lord Illingworth, what do you mean? Miss Worsley, Caroline, is an orphan. Her father was a very wealthy millionaire or philanthropist, or both, I believe, who entertained my son quite hospitably, when he visited Boston. I don't know how he made his money, originally.

KELVIL: I fancy in American dry goods.

LADY HUNSTANTON: What are American dry goods?

LORD ILLINGWORTH: American novels.

LADY HUNSTANTON: How very singular! . . . Well, from whatever source her large fortune came, I have a great esteem for Miss Worsley. She dresses exceedingly well. All Americans do dress well. They get their clothes in Paris.

MRS. ALLONBY: They say, Lady Hunstanton, that when good Americans die they go to Paris.

LADY HUNSTANTON: Indeed? And when bad Americans die, where do they go to?

LORD ILLINGWORTH: Oh, they go to America.

KELVIL: I am afraid you don't appreciate America, Lord Illingworth. It is a very remarkable country, especially considering its youth.

LORD ILLINGWORTH: The youth of America is their oldest tradition. It has been going on now for three hundred years. To hear them talk one would imagine they were in their first childhood. As far as civilisation goes they are in their second.

KELVIL: There is undoubtedly a great deal of corruption in American politics. I suppose you allude to that?

LORD ILLINGWORTH: I wonder.

LADY HUNSTANTON: Politics are in a sad way, everywhere, I am told. They certainly are in England. Dear Mr. Cardew is ruining the country. I wonder Mrs. Cardew allows him. I am sure, Lord Illingworth, you don't think that uneducated people should be allowed to have votes?

LORD ILLINGWORTH: I think they are the only people who should.

KELVIL: Do you take no side then in modern politics, Lord Illingworth?

LORD ILLINGWORTH: One should never take sides in anything, Mr. Kelvil. Taking sides is the beginning of sincerity, and earnestness follows shortly afterwards, and the human being becomes a bore. However, the House of Commons* really does very little harm. You can't make people good by Act of Parliament—that is something.

KELVIL: You cannot deny that the House of Commons has always shown great sympathy with the sufferings of the poor.

LORD ILLINGWORTH: That is its special vice. That is the special vice of the age. One should sympathise with the joy, the beauty, the colour of life. The less said about life's sores the better, Mr. Kelvil.

KELVIL: Still our East End is a very important problem.

LORD ILLINGWORTH: Quite so. It is the problem of slavery. And we are trying to solve it by amusing the slaves.

LADY HUNSTANTON: Certainly, a great deal may be done by means of cheap entertainments, as you say, Lord Illingworth. Dear Dr. Daubeny, our rector here, provides, with the assistance of his curates, really admirable recreations for the poor during the winter. And much good may be done by means of a magic lantern, or a missionary, or some popular amusement of that kind.

LADY CAROLINE: I am not at all in favour of amusements for the poor, Jane. Blankets and coals are sufficient. There is too much love of pleasure amongst the upper classes as it is. Health is what we want in modem life. The tone is not healthy, not healthy at all.

KELVIL: You are quite right, Lady Caroline.

LADY CAROLINE: I believe I am usually right.

MRS. ALLONBY: Horrid word "health."

LORD ILLINGWORTH: Silliest word in our language, and one knows so well the popular idea of health. The English country gentleman galloping after a fox—the unspeakable in full pursuit of the uneatable.

KELVIL: May I ask, Lord Illingworth, if you regard the House of Lords as a better institution than the House of Commons?

LORD ILLINGWORTH: A much better institution, of course.

---

*In the English Parliament, the lower house, to which members were elected; the upper house is the House of Lords, whose members consist of peers (nobility) and Anglican prelates.

We in the House of Lords are never in touch with public opinion. That makes us a civilised body.

KELVIL: Are you serious in putting forward such a view?

LORD ILLINGWORTH: Quite serious, Mr. Kelvil. (*To* MRS. ALLONBY): Vulgar habit that is people have nowadays of asking one, after one has given them an idea, whether one is serious or not. Nothing is serious except passion. The intellect is not a serious thing, and never has been. It is an instrument on which one plays, that is all. The only serious form of intellect I know is the British intellect. And on the British intellect the illiterates play the drum.

LADY HUNSTANTON: What are you saying, Lord Illingworth, about the drum?

LORD ILLINGWORTH: I was merely talking to Mrs. Allonby about the leading articles in the London newspapers.

LADY HUNSTANTON: But do you believe all that is written in the newspapers?

LORD ILLINGWORTH: I do. Nowadays it is only the unreadable that occurs. (*Rises with* MRS. ALLONBY.)

LADY HUNSTANTON: Are you going, Mrs. Allonby?

MRS. ALLONBY: Just as far as the conservatory. Lord Illingworth told me this morning that there was an orchid there as beautiful as the seven deadly sins.

LADY HUNSTANTON: My dear, I hope there is nothing of the kind. I will certainly speak to the gardener.

Exit MRS. ALLONBY *and* LORD ILLINGWORTH.

LADY CAROLINE: Remarkable type, Mrs. Allonby.

LADY HUNSTANTON: She lets her clever tongue run away with her sometimes.

LADY CAROLINE: Is that the only thing, Jane, Mrs. Allonby allows to run away with her?

LADY HUNSTANTON: I hope so, Caroline, I am sure.
Enter LORD ALFRED.
Dear Lord Alfred, do join us.

LORD ALFRED *sits down beside* LADY STUTFIELD.

LADY CAROLINE: You believe good of every one, Jane. It is a great fault.

LADY STUTFIELD: Do you really, really think, Lady Caroline, that one should believe evil of every one?

LADY CAROLINE: I think it is much safer to do so, Lady Stutfield. Until, of course, people are found out to be good. But that requires a great deal of investigation nowadays.

LADY STUTFIELD: But there is so much unkind scandal in modern life.

LADY CAROLINE: Lord Illingworth remarked to me last night at dinner that the basis of every scandal is an absolutely immoral certainty.

KELVIL: Lord Illingworth is, of course, a very brilliant man, but he seems to me to be lacking in that fine faith in the nobility and purity of life which is so important in this century.

LADY STUTFIELD: Yes, quite, quite important, is it not?

KELVIL: He gives me the impression of a man who does not appreciate the beauty of our English home-life. I would say that he was tainted with foreign ideas on the subject.

LADY STUTFIELD: There is nothing, nothing like the beauty of home-life, is there?

KELVIL: It is the mainstay of our moral system in England, Lady Stutfield. Without it we would become like our neighbours.

LADY STUTFIELD: That would be so, so sad, would it not?

KELVIL: I am afraid, too, that Lord Illingworth regards woman simply as a toy. Now, I have never regarded woman as a toy. Woman is the intellectual helpmeet of man in public as in private life. Without her we should forget the true ideals. (*Sits down beside* LADY STUTFIELD.)

LADY STUTFIELD: I am so very, very glad to hear you say that.

LADY CAROLINE: You are a married man, Mr. Kettle?

SIR JOHN: Kelvil, dear, Kelvil.

KELVIL: I am married, Lady Caroline.

LADY CAROLINE: Family?

KELVIL: Yes.

LADY CAROLINE: How many?

KELVIL: Eight.

LADY STUTFIELD *turns her attention to* LORD ALFRED.

LADY CAROLINE: Mrs. Kettle and the children are, I suppose, at the seaside?

SIR JOHN *shrugs his shoulders.*

KELVIL: My wife is at the seaside with the children, Lady Caroline.

LADY CAROLINE: You will join them later on, no doubt?

KELVIL: If my public engagements permit me.

LADY CAROLINE: Your public life must be a great source of gratification to Mrs. Kettle.

SIR JOHN: Kelvil, my love, Kelvil.

LADY STUTFIELD (*to* LORD ALFRED): How very, very charming those gold-tipped cigarettes of yours are, Lord Alfred.

LORD ALFRED: They are awfully expensive. I can only afford them when I'm in debt.

LADY STUTFIELD: It must be terribly, terribly distressing to be in debt.

LORD ALFRED: One must have some occupation nowadays. If I hadn't my debts I shouldn't have anything to think about. All the chaps I know are in debt.

LADY STUTFIELD: But don't the people to whom you owe the money give you a great, great deal of annoyance?

Enter Footman.

LORD ALFRED: Oh, no, they write; I don't.

LADY STUTFIELD: How very, very strange.

LADY HUNSTANTON: Ah, here is a letter, Caroline, from dear Mrs. Arbuthnot. She won't dine. I am so sorry. But she will come in the evening. I am very pleased, indeed. She is one of the sweetest of women. Writes a beautiful hand, too, so large, so firm. (*Hands letter to* LADY CAROLINE.)

LADY CAROLINE (*looking at it*): A little lacking in femininity, Jane. Femininity is the quality I admire most in women.

LADY HUNSTANTON (*taking back letter and leaving it on table*): Oh! she is very feminine, Caroline, and so good, too. You should hear what the Archdeacon says of her. He regards her as his right hand in the parish. (*Footman speaks to her.*) In the Yellow Drawing-room. Shall we all go in? Lady Stutfield, shall we go in to tea?

LADY STUTFIELD: With pleasure, Lady Hunstanton.

They rise and proceed to go off. SIR JOHN *offers to carry* LADY STUTFIELD'S *cloak.*

LADY CAROLINE: John! If you would allow your nephew to look after Lady Stutfield's cloak, you might help me with my work-basket.

Enter LORD ILLINGWORTH *and* MRS. ALLONBY.

SIR JOHN: Certainly, my love.

Exeunt.

MRS. ALLONBY: Curious thing, plain women are always jealous of their husbands, beautiful women never are!

LORD ILLINGWORTH: Beautiful women never have time. They are always so occupied in being jealous of other people's husbands.

MRS. ALLONBY: I should have thought Lady Caroline would have grown tired of conjugal anxiety by this time! Sir John is her fourth!

LORD ILLINGWORTH: So much marriage is certainly not becoming. Twenty years of romance make a woman look like a ruin; but twenty years of marriage make her something like a public building.

MRS. ALLONBY: Twenty years of romance! Is there such a thing?

LORD ILLINGWORTH: Not in our day. Women have become too brilliant. Nothing spoils a romance so much as a sense of humour in the woman.

MRS. ALLONBY: Or the want of it in the man.

LORD ILLINGWORTH: You are quite right. In a Temple every one should be serious, except the thing that is worshipped.

MRS. ALLONBY: And that should be man?

LORD ILLINGWORTH: Women kneel so gracefully; men don't.

MRS. ALLONBY: You are thinking of Lady Stutfield!

LORD ILLINGWORTH: I assure you I have not thought of Lady Stutfield for the last quarter of an hour.

MRS. ALLONBY: Is she such a mystery?

LORD ILLINGWORTH: She is more than a mystery—she is a mood.

MRS. ALLONBY: Moods don't last.

LORD ILLINGWORTH: It is their chief charm.

Enter HESTER *and* GERALD.

GERALD: Lord Illingworth, every one has been congratulating me, Lady Hunstanton and Lady Caroline, and . . . every one. I hope I shall make a good secretary.

LORD ILLINGWORTH: You will be the pattern secretary, Gerald. (*Talks to him.*)

MRS. ALLONBY: You enjoy country life, Miss Worsley?

HESTER: Very much, indeed.

MRS. ALLONBY: Don't find yourself longing for a London dinner-party?

HESTER: I dislike London dinner-parties.

MRS. ALLONBY: I adore them. The clever people never listen, and the stupid people never talk.

HESTER: I think the stupid people talk a great deal.

MRS. ALLONBY: Ah, I never listen!

LORD ILLINGWORTH: My dear boy, if I didn't like you I wouldn't have made you the offer. It is because I like you so much that I want to have you with me.

Exit HESTER *with* GERALD.

Charming fellow, Gerald Arbuthnot!

MRS. ALLONBY: He is very nice; very nice indeed. But I can't stand the American young lady.

LORD ILLINGWORTH: Why?

MRS. ALLONBY: She told me yesterday, and in quite a loud voice too, that she was only eighteen. It was most annoying.

LORD ILLINGWORTH: One should never trust a woman who tells one her real age. A woman who would tell one that, would tell one anything.

MRS. ALLONBY: She is a Puritan besides——

LORD ILLINGWORTH: Ah, that is inexcusable. I don't mind plain women being Puritans. It is the only excuse they have for being plain. But she is decidedly pretty. I admire her immensely. (*Looks steadfastly at* MRS. ALLONBY.)

MRS. ALLONBY: What a thoroughly bad man you must be!

LORD ILLINGWORTH: What do you call a bad man?

MRS. ALLONBY: The sort of man who admires innocence.

LORD ILLINGWORTH: And a bad woman?

MRS. ALLONBY: Oh! the sort of woman a man never gets tired of.

LORD ILLINGWORTH: You are severe—on yourself.

MRS. ALLONBY: Define us as a sex.

LORD ILLINGWORTH: Sphinxes without secrets.

MRS. ALLONBY: Does that include the Puritan women?

LORD ILLINGWORTH: Do you know, I don't believe in the existence of Puritan women? I don't think there is a woman in the world who would not be a little flattered if one made love to her. It is that which makes women so irresistibly adorable.

MRS. ALLONBY: You think there is no woman in the world who would object to being kissed?

LORD ILLINGWORTH: Very few.

MRS. ALLONBY: Miss Worsley would not let you kiss her.

LORD ILLINGWORTH: Are you sure?

MRS. ALLONBY: Quite.

LORD ILLINGWORTH: What do you think she'd do if I kissed her?

MRS. ALLONBY: Either marry you, or strike you across the face with her glove. What would you do if she struck you across the face with her glove?

LORD ILLINGWORTH: Fall in love with her, probably.

MRS. ALLONBY: Then it is lucky you are not going to kiss her!

LORD ILLINGWORTH: Is that a challenge?

MRS. ALLONBY: It is an arrow shot into the air.

LORD ILLINGWORTH: Don't you know that I always succeed in whatever I try?

MRS. ALLONBY: I am sorry to hear it. We women adore failures. They lean on us.

LORD ILLINGWORTH: You worship successes. You cling to them.

MRS. ALLONBY: We are the laurels to hide their baldness.

LORD ILLINGWORTH: And they need you always, except at the moment of triumph.

MRS. ALLONBY: They are uninteresting then.

LORD ILLINGWORTH: How tantalising you are! (*A pause.*)

MRS. ALLONBY: Lord Illingworth, there is one thing I shall always like you for.

LORD ILLINGWORTH: Only one thing? And I have so many bad qualities.

MRS. ALLONBY: Ah, don't be too conceited about them. You may lose them as you grow old.

LORD ILLINGWORTH: I never intend to grow old. The soul is born old but grows young. That is the comedy of life.

MRS. ALLONBY: And the body is born young and grows old. That is life's tragedy.

LORD ILLINGWORTH: Its comedy also, sometimes. But what is the mysterious reason why you will always like me?

MRS. ALLONBY: It is that you have never made love to me.

LORD ILLINGWORTH: I have never done anything else.

MRS. ALLONBY: Really? I have not noticed it.

LORD ILLINGWORTH: How unfortunate! It might have been a tragedy for both of us.

MRS. ALLONBY: We should each have survived.

LORD ILLINGWORTH: One can survive everything nowadays, except death, and live down anything except a good reputation.

MRS. ALLONBY: Have you tried a good reputation?

LORD ILLINGWORTH: It is one of the many annoyances to which I have never been subjected.

MRS. ALLONBY: It may come.

LORD ILLINGWORTH: Why do you threaten me?

MRS. ALLONBY: I will tell you when you have kissed the Puritan.

Enter Footman.

FRANCIS: Tea is served in the Yellow Drawing-room, my lord.

LORD ILLINGWORTH: Tell her ladyship we are coming in.

FRANCIS: Yes, my lord. (*Exit.*)

LORD ILLINGWORTH: Shall we go in to tea?

MRS. ALLONBY: Do you like such simple pleasures?

LORD ILLINGWORTH: I adore simple pleasures. They are the last refuge of the complex. But, if you wish, let us stay here. Yes, let us stay here. The Book of Life begins with a man and a woman in a garden.

MRS. ALLONBY: It ends with Revelations.

LORD ILLINGWORTH: You fence divinely. But the button has come off your foil.

MRS. ALLONBY: I have still the mask.

LORD ILLINGWORTH: It makes your eyes lovelier.

MRS. ALLONBY: Thank you. Come.

LORD ILLINGWORTH (*sees* MRS. ARBUTHNOT'S *letter on table, and takes it up and looks at envelope*): What a curious handwriting! It reminds me of the handwriting of a woman I used to know years ago.

MRS. ALLONBY: Who?

LORD ILLINGWORTH: Oh! no one. No one in particular. A woman of no importance.* (*Throws letter down, and passes up the steps of the terrace with* MRS. ALLONBY. *They smile at each other.*)

Act Drop

---

*Here, Wilde uses the title of the play to bring down the curtain on act one; in *Earnest*, he does so to end the play.

ACT TWO

SCENE: *Drawing-room at Hunstanton Chase, after dinner, lamps lit.** *Door L.C. Door R.C. Ladies seated on sofa.*

MRS. ALLONBY: What a comfort it is to have got rid of the men for a little!

LADY STUTFIELD: Yes; men persecute us dreadfully, don't they?

MRS. ALLONBY: Persecute us? I wish they did.

LADY HUNSTANTON: My dear!

MRS. ALLONBY: The annoying thing is that the wretches can be perfectly happy without us. That is why I think it is every woman's duty never to leave them alone for a single moment, except during this short breathing space after dinner; without which, I believe, we poor women would be absolutely worn to shadows.

Enter Servants with coffee.

LADY HUNSTANTON: Worn to shadows, dear?

MRS. ALLONBY: Yes, Lady Hunstanton. It is such a strain keeping men up to the mark. They are always trying to escape from us.

LADY STUTFIELD: It seems to me that it is we who are always trying to escape from them. Men are so very, very heartless. They know their power and use it.

LADY CAROLINE (*takes coffee from Servant*): What stuff and nonsense all this about men is! The thing to do is to keep men in their proper place.

MRS. ALLONBY: But what is their proper place, Lady Caroline?

LADY CAROLINE: Looking after their wives, Mrs. Allonby.

---

*After dinner, which was served at 8:00 P.M., women withdrew (hence the name of the room—drawing, for withdrawing).

MRS. ALLONBY (*takes coffee from Servant*): Really? And if they're not married?

LADY CAROLINE: If they are not married, they would be looking after a wife. It's perfectly scandalous the amount of bachelors who are going about society. There should be a law passed to compel them all to marry within twelve months.

LADY STUTFIELD (*refuses coffee*): But if they're in love with some one who, perhaps, is tied to another?

LADY CAROLINE: In that case, Lady Stutfield, they would be married off in a week to some plain respectable girl, in order to teach them not to meddle with other people's property.

MRS. ALLONBY: I don't think that we should ever be spoken of as other people's property. All men are married women's property. That is the only true definition of what married women's property really is. But we don't belong to any one.

LADY STUTFIELD: Oh, I am so very, very glad to hear you say so.

LADY HUNSTANTON: But do you really think, dear Caroline, that legislation would improve matters in any way? I am told that, nowadays, all the married men live like bachelors, and all the bachelors like married men.

MRS. ALLONBY: I certainly never know one from the other.

LADY STUTFIELD: Oh, I think one can always know at once whether a man has home claims upon his life or not. I have noticed a very, very sad expression in the eyes of so many married men.

MRS. ALLONBY: Ah, all that I have noticed is that they are horribly tedious when they are good husbands, and abominably conceited when they are not.

LADY HUNSTANTON: Well, I suppose the type of husband has completely changed since my young days, but I'm bound to state that poor dear Hunstanton was the most delightful of creatures, and as good as gold.

MRS. ALLONBY: Ah, my husband is a sort of promissory note; I'm tired of meeting him.

LADY CAROLINE: But you renew him from time to time, don't you?

MRS. ALLONBY: Oh no, Lady Caroline. I have only had one husband as yet. I suppose you look upon me as quite an amateur.

LADY CAROLINE: With your views on life I wonder you married at all.

MRS. ALLONBY: So do I.

LADY HUNSTANTON: My dear child, I believe you are really very happy in your married life, but that you like to hide your happiness from others.

MRS. ALLONBY: I assure you I was horribly deceived in Ernest.

LADY HUNSTANTON: Oh, I hope not, dear. I knew his mother quite well. She was a Stratton, Caroline, one of Lord Crowland's daughters.

LADY CAROLINE: Victoria Stratton? I remember her perfectly. A silly, fair-haired woman with no chin.

MRS. ALLONBY: Ah, Ernest has a chin. He has a very strong chin, a square chin. Ernest's chin is far too square.

LADY STUTFIELD: But do you really think a man's chin can be too square? I think a man should look very, very strong, and that his chin should be quite, quite square.

MRS. ALLONBY: Then you should certainly know Ernest, Lady Stutfield. It is only fair to tell you beforehand he has got no conversation at all.

LADY STUTFIELD: I adore silent men.

MRS. ALLONBY: Oh, Ernest isn't silent. He talks the whole time. But he has got no conversation. What he talks about I don't know. I haven't listened to him for years.

LADY STUTFIELD: Have you never forgiven him then? How sad that seems! But all life is very, very sad, is it not?

MRS. ALLONBY: Life, Lady Stutfield, is simply a *mauvais quart d'heure** made up of exquisite moments.

LADY STUTFIELD: Yes, there are moments, certainly. But was it something very, very wrong that Mr. Allonby did? Did he become angry with you, and say anything that was unkind or true?

MRS. ALLONBY: Oh, dear, no. Ernest is invariably calm. That is one of the reasons he always gets on my nerves. Nothing is so aggravating as calmness. There is something positively brutal about

---

*A bad quarter of an hour.

the good temper of most modern men. I wonder we women stand it as well as we do.

LADY STUTFIELD: Yes; men's good temper shows they are not so sensitive as we are, not so finely strung. It makes a great barrier often between husband and wife, does it not? But I would so much like to know what was the wrong thing Mr. Allonby did.

MRS. ALLONBY: Well, I will tell you, if you solemnly promise to tell everybody else.

LADY STUTFIELD: Thank you, thank you. I will make a point of repeating it.

MRS. ALLONBY: When Ernest and I were engaged, he swore to me positively on his knees that he had never loved any one before in the whole course of his life. I was very young at the time, so I didn't believe him, I needn't tell you. Unfortunately, however, I made no inquiries of any kind till after I had been actually married four or five months. I found out then that what he had told me was perfectly true. And that sort of thing makes a man so absolutely uninteresting.

LADY HUNSTANTON: My dear!

MRS. ALLONBY: Men always want to be a woman's first love. That is their clumsy vanity. We women have a more subtle instinct about things. What we like is to be a man's last romance.

LADY STUTFIELD: I see what you mean. It's very, very beautiful.

LADY HUNSTANTON: My dear child, you don't mean to tell me that you won't forgive your husband because he never loved any one else? Did you ever hear such a thing, Caroline? I am quite surprised.

LADY CAROLINE: Oh, women have become so highly educated, Jane, that nothing should surprise us nowadays, except happy marriages. They apparently are getting remarkably rare.

MRS. ALLONBY: Oh, they're quite out of date.

LADY STUTFIELD: Except amongst the middle classes, I have been told.

MRS. ALLONBY: How like the middle classes!

LADY STUTFIELD: Yes—is it not?—very, very like them.

LADY CAROLINE: If what you tell us about the middle classes is true, Lady Stutfield, it redounds greatly to their credit. It is much to be regretted that in our rank of life the wife should be so persistently frivolous, under the impression apparently that it is the proper thing to be. It is to that I attribute the unhappiness of so many marriages we all know of in society.

MRS. ALLONBY: Do you know, Lady Caroline, I don't think the frivolity of the wife has ever anything to do with it. More marriages are ruined nowadays by the common sense of the husband than by anything else. How can a woman be expected to be happy with a man who insists on treating her as if she was a perfectly rational being?

LADY HUNSTANTON: My dear!

MRS. ALLONBY: Man, poor, awkward, reliable, necessary man belongs to a sex that has been rational for millions and millions of years. He can't help himself. It is in his race. The History of Woman is very different. We have always been picturesque protests against the mere existence of common sense. We saw its dangers from the first.

LADY STUTFIELD: Yes, the common sense of husbands is certainly most, most trying. Do tell me your conception of the Ideal Husband.* I think it would be so very, very helpful.

MRS. ALLONBY: The Ideal Husband? There couldn't be such a thing. The institution is wrong.

LADY STUTFIELD: The Ideal Man, then, in his relations to *us*.

LADY CAROLINE: He would probably be extremely realistic.

MRS. ALLONBY: The Ideal Man! Oh, the Ideal Man should talk to us as if we were goddesses, and treat us as if we were children. He should refuse all our serious requests, and gratify every one of our whims. He should encourage us to have caprices, and forbid us to have missions. He should always say much more than he means, and always mean much more than he says.

LADY HUNSTANTON: But how could he do both, dear?

MRS. ALLONBY: He should never run down other pretty women. That would show he had no taste, or make one suspect that he had too much. No; he should be nice about them all, but say that somehow they don't attract him.

LADY STUTFIELD: Yes, that is always very, very pleasant to hear about other women.

---

*Perhaps a cleverly placed advertisement for Wilde's next play.

MRS. ALLONBY: If we ask him a question about anything, he should give us an answer all about ourselves. He should invariably praise us for whatever qualities he knows we haven't got. But he should be pitiless, quite pitiless, in reproaching us for the virtues that we have never dreamed of possessing. He should never believe that we know the use of useful things. That would be unforgivable. But he should shower on us everything we don't want.

LADY CAROLINE: As far as I can see, he is to do nothing but pay bills and compliments.

MRS. ALLONBY: He should persistently compromise us in public, and treat us with absolute respect when we are alone. And yet he should be always ready to have a perfectly terrible scene, whenever we want one, and to become miserable, absolutely miserable, at a moment's notice, and to overwhelm us with just reproaches in less than twenty minutes, and to be positively violent at the end of half an hour, and to leave us for ever at a quarter to eight, when we have to go and dress for dinner. And when, after that, one has seen him for really the last time, and he has refused to take back the little things he has given one, and promised never to communicate with one again, or to write one any foolish letters, he should be perfectly broken-hearted, and telegraph to one all day long, and send one little notes every half-hour by a private hansom, and dine quite alone at the club, so that every one should know how unhappy he was. And after a whole dreadful week, during which one has gone about everywhere with one's husband, just to show how absolutely lonely one was, he may be given a third last parting, in the evening, and then, if his conduct has been quite irreproachable, and one has behaved really badly to him, he should be allowed to admit that he has been entirely in the wrong, and when he has admitted that, it becomes a woman's duty to forgive, and one can do it all over again from the beginning, with variations.

LADY HUNSTANTON: How clever you are, my dear! You never mean a single word you say.

LADY STUTFIELD: Thank you, thank you. It has been quite, quite entrancing. I must try and remember it all. There are such a number of details that are so very, very important.

LADY CAROLINE: But you have not told us yet what the reward of the Ideal Man is to be.

MRS. ALLONBY: His reward? Oh, infinite expectation. That is quite enough for him.

LADY STUTFIELD: But men are so terribly, terribly exacting, are they not?

MRS. ALLONBY: That makes no matter. One should never surrender.

LADY STUTFIELD: Not even to the Ideal Man?

MRS. ALLONBY: Certainly not to him. Unless, of course, one wants to grow tired of him.

LADY STUTFIELD: Oh! . . . Yes. I see that. It is very, very helpful. Do you think, Mrs. Allonby, I shall ever meet the Ideal Man? Or are there more than one?

MRS. ALLONBY: There are just four in London, Lady Stutfield.

LADY HUNSTANTON: Oh, my dear!

MRS. ALLONBY (*going over to her*): What has happened? Do tell me.

LADY HUNSTANTON (*in a low voice*): I had completely forgotten that the American young lady has been in the room all the time. I am afraid some of this clever talk may have shocked her a little.

MRS. ALLONBY: Ah, that will do her so much good!

LADY HUNSTANTON: Let us hope she didn't understand much. I think I had better go over and talk to her. (*Rises and goes across to* HESTER WORSLEY.) Well, dear Miss Worsley. (*Sitting down beside her.*) How quiet you have been in your nice little corner all this time! I suppose you have been reading a book? There are so many books here in the library.

HESTER: No, I have been listening to the conversation.

LADY HUNSTANTON: You mustn't believe everything that was said, you know, dear.

HESTER: I didn't believe any of it.

LADY HUNSTANTON: That is quite right, dear.

HESTER (*continuing*): I couldn't believe that any women could really hold such views of life as I have heard to-night from some of your guests. (*An awkward pause.*)

LADY HUNSTANTON: I hear you have such pleasant society in America. Quite like our own in places, my son wrote to me.

HESTER: There are cliques in America as elsewhere, Lady Hunstanton. But true American society consists simply of all the good women and good men we have in our country.

LADY HUNSTANTON: What a sensible system, and I dare say quite pleasant, too. I am afraid in England we have too many artificial social barriers. We don't see as much as we should of the middle and lower classes.

HESTER: In America we have no lower classes.

LADY HUNSTANTON: Really? What a very strange arrangement!

MRS. ALLONBY: What is that dreadful girl talking about?

LADY STUTFIELD: She is painfully natural, is she not?

LADY CAROLINE: There are a great many things you haven't got in America, I am told, Miss Worsley. They say you have no ruins, and no curiosities.

MRS. ALLONBY (*to* LADY STUTFIELD): What nonsense! They have their mothers and their manners.

HESTER: The English aristocracy supply us with our curiosities, Lady Caroline. They are sent over to us every summer, regularly, in the steamers, and propose to us the day after they land. As for ruins, we are trying to build up something that will last longer than brick or stone. (*Gets up to take her fan from table.*)

LADY HUNSTANTON: What is that, dear? Ah, yes, an iron Exhibition, is it not, at that place that has the curious name?[1]

HESTER (*standing by table*): We are trying to build up life, Lady Hunstanton, on a better, truer, purer basis than life rests on here. This sounds strange to you all, no doubt. How could it sound other than strange? You rich people in England, you don't know how you are living. How could you know? You shut out from your society the gentle and the good. You laugh at the simple and the pure. Living, as you all do, on others and by them, you sneer at self-sacrifice, and if you throw bread to the poor, it is merely to keep them quiet for a season. With all your pomp and wealth and art you don't know how to live—you don't even know that. You love the beauty that you can see and touch and handle, the beauty that you can destroy, and do destroy, but of the unseen beauty of life, of the unseen beauty of a higher life, you know nothing. You have lost life's secret. Oh, your English society seems to me shallow, selfish, foolish. It has blinded its eyes, and stopped its ears. It lies like a leper in purple. It sits like a dead thing smeared with gold. It is all wrong, all wrong.

LADY STUTFIELD: I don't think one should know of these things. It is not very, very nice, is it?

LADY HUNSTANTON: My dear Miss Worsley, I thought you liked English society so much. You were such a success in it. And you were so much admired by the best people. I quite forget what Lord Henry Weston said of you—but it was most complimentary, and you know what an authority he is on beauty.

HESTER: Lord Henry Weston! I remember him, Lady Hunstanton. A man with a hideous smile and a hideous past. He is asked everywhere. No dinner-party is complete without him. What of those whose ruin is due to him? They are outcasts. They are nameless. If you met them in the street you would turn your head away. I don't complain of their punishment. Let all women who have sinned be punished.

MRS. ARBUTHNOT *enters from terrace behind in a cloak with a lace veil over her head. She hears the last words and starts.*

LADY HUNSTANTON: My dear young lady!

HESTER: It is right that they should be punished, but don't let them be the only ones to suffer. If a man and woman have sinned, let them both go forth into the desert to love or loathe each other there. Let them both be branded. Set a mark, if you wish, on each, but don't punish the one and let the other go free. Don't have one law for men and another for women. You are unjust to women in England. And till you count what is a shame in a woman to be infamy in a man, you will always be unjust, and Right, that pillar of fire, and Wrong, that pillar of cloud, will be made dim to your eyes, or be not seen at all, or if seen, not regarded.

LADY CAROLINE: Might I, dear Miss Worsley, as you are standing up, ask you for my cotton that is just behind you? Thank you.

LADY HUNSTANTON: My dear Mrs. Arbuthnot! I am so pleased you have come up. But I didn't hear you announced.

MRS. ARBUTHNOT: Oh, I came straight in from the terrace, Lady Hunstanton, just as I was. You didn't tell me you had a party.

LADY HUNSTANTON: Not a party. Only a few guests who are staying in the house, and whom you must know. Allow me. (*Tries to help her. Rings bell.*) Caroline, this is Mrs. Arbuthnot, one of my sweetest friends. Lady Caroline Pontefract, Lady Stutfield, Mrs. Allonby, and my young American friend, Miss Worsley, who has just been telling us all how wicked we are.

HESTER: I am afraid you think I spoke too strongly, Lady Hunstanton. But there are some things in England——

LADY HUNSTANTON: My dear young lady, there was a great deal of truth, I dare say, in what you said, and you looked very pretty while you said it, which is much more important, Lord Illingworth would tell us. The only point where I thought you were a little hard was about Lady Caroline's brother, about poor Lord Henry. He is really such good company.

Enter Footman.

Take Mrs. Arbuthnot's things.

Exit Footman with wraps.

HESTER: Lady Caroline, I had no idea it was your brother. I am sorry for the pain I must have caused you—I——

LADY CAROLINE: My dear Miss Worsley, the only part of your little speech, if I may so term it, with which I thoroughly agreed, was the part about my brother. Nothing that you could possibly say could be too bad for him. I regard Henry as infamous, absolutely infamous. But I am bound to state, as you were remarking, Jane, that he is excellent company, and he has one of the best cooks in London, and after a good dinner one can forgive anybody, even one's own relations.

LADY HUNSTANTON (*to* Miss WORSLEY): Now, do come, dear, and make friends with Mrs. Arbuthnot. She is one of the good, sweet, simple people you told us we never admitted into society. I am sorry to say Mrs. Arbuthnot comes very rarely to me. But that is not my fault.

MRS. ALLONBY: What a bore it is the men staying so long after dinner! I expect they are saying the most dreadful things about us.

LADY STUTFIELD: Do you really think so?

MRS. ALLONBY: I am sure of it.

LADY STUTFIELD: How very, very horrid of them! Shall we go on to the terrace?

MRS. ALLONBY: Oh, anything to get away from the dowagers and the dowdies. (*Rises and goes with* LADY STUTFIELD *to door L.C.*) We are only going to look at the stars, Lady Hunstanton.

LADY HUNSTANTON: You will find a great many, dear, a great many. But don't catch cold. (*To* MRS. ARBUTHNOT): We shall all miss Gerald so much, dear Mrs. Arbuthnot.

MRS. ARBUTHNOT: But has Lord Illingworth really offered to make Gerald his secretary?

LADY HUNSTANTON: Oh, yes! He has been most charming about it. He has the highest possible opinion of your boy. You don't know Lord Illingworth, I believe, dear.

MRS. ARBUTHNOT: I have never met him.

LADY HUNSTANTON: You know him by name, no doubt?

MRS. ARBUTHNOT: I am afraid I don't. I live so much out of the world, and see so few people. I remember hearing years ago of an old Lord Illingworth who lived in Yorkshire, I think.

LADY HUNSTANTON: Ah, yes. That would be the last Earl but one. He was a very curious man. He wanted to marry beneath him. Or wouldn't, I believe. There was some scandal about it. The present Lord Illingworth is quite different. He is very distinguished. He does—well, he does nothing, which I am afraid our pretty American visitor here thinks very wrong of anybody, and I don't know that he cares much for the subjects in which you are so interested, dear Mrs. Arbuthnot. Do you think, Caroline, that Lord Illingworth is interested in the Housing of the Poor?

LADY CAROLINE: I should fancy not at all, Jane.

LADY HUNSTANTON: We all have our different tastes, have we not? But Lord Illingworth has a very high position, and there is nothing he couldn't get if he chose to ask for it. Of course, he is comparatively a young man still, and he has only come to his title within—how long exactly is it, Caroline, since Lord Illingworth succeeded?

LADY CAROLINE: About four years, I think, Jane. I know it was the same year in which my brother had his last exposure in the evening newspapers.

LADY HUNSTANTON: Ah, I remember. That would be about

four years ago. Of course, there were a great many people between the present Lord Illingworth and the title, Mrs. Arbuthnot. There was—who was there, Caroline?

LADY CAROLINE: There was poor Margaret's baby. You remember how anxious she was to have a boy, and it was a boy, but it died, and her husband died shortly afterwards, and she married almost immediately, one of Lord Ascot's sons, who, I am told, beats her.

LADY HUNSTANTON: Ah, that is in the family, dear, that is in the family. And there was also, I remember, a clergyman who wanted to be a lunatic, or a lunatic who wanted to be a clergyman, I forget which, but I know the Court of Chancery investigated the matter, and decided that he was quite sane. And I saw him afterwards at poor Lord Plumstead's with straws in his hair, or something very odd about him. I can't recall what. I often regret, Lady Caroline, that dear Lady Cecilia never lived to see her son get the title.

MRS. ARBUTHNOT: Lady Cecilia?

LADY HUNSTANTON: Lord Illingworth's mother, dear Mrs. Arbuthnot, was one of the Duchess of Jerningham's pretty daughters, and she married Sir Thomas Harford, who wasn't considered a very good match for her at the time, though he was said to be the handsomest man in London. I knew them all quite intimately, and both the sons, Arthur and George.

MRS. ARBUTHNOT: It was the eldest son who succeeded, of course, Lady Hunstanton?

LADY HUNSTANTON: No, dear, he was killed in the hunting field. Or was it fishing, Caroline? I forget. But George came in for everything. I always tell him that no younger son has ever had such good luck as he has had.

MRS. ARBUTHNOT: Lady Hunstanton, I want to speak to Gerald at once. Might I see him? Can he be sent for?

LADY HUNSTANTON: Certainly, dear. I will send one of the servants into the dining-room to fetch him.* I don't know what keeps the gentlemen so long. (*Rings bell.*) When I knew Lord Illingworth first as plain George Harford, he was simply a very brilliant young

*While women went to the drawing room after dinner, men might remain in the dining room (as here) or go to a smoking or billiards room.

man about town, with not a penny of money except what poor dear Lady Cecilia gave him. She was quite devoted to him. Chiefly, I fancy, because he was on bad terms with his father. Oh, here is the dear Archdeacon. (*To Servant*): It doesn't matter.

Enter SIR JOHN *and* DOCTOR DAUBENY. SIR JOHN *goes over to* LADY STUTFIELD, DOCTOR DAUBENY *to* LADY HUNSTANTON.

THE ARCHDEACON: Lord Illingworth has been most entertaining. I have never enjoyed myself more. (*Sees* MRS. ARBUTHNOT.) Ah, Mrs. Arbuthnot.

LADY HUNSTANTON (*to* DOCTOR DAUBENY): You see I have got Mrs. Arbuthnot to come to me at last.

THE ARCHDEACON: That is a great honour, Lady Hunstanton. Mrs. Daubeny will be quite jealous of you.

LADY HUNSTANTON: Ah, I am so sorry Mrs. Daubeny could not come with you to-night. Headache as usual, I suppose.

THE ARCHDEACON: Yes, Lady Hunstanton; a perfect martyr. But she is happiest alone. She is happiest alone.

LADY CAROLINE (*to her husband*): John!

SIR JOHN *goes over to his wife.* DOCTOR DAUBENY *talks to* LADY HUNSTANTON *and* MRS. ARBUTHNOT.

MRS. ARBUTHNOT *watches* LORD ILLINGWORTH *the whole time. He has passed across the room without noticing her, and approaches* MRS. ALLONBY, *who with* LADY STUTFIELD *is standing by the door looking on to the terrace.*

LORD ILLINGWORTH: How is the most charming woman in the world?

MRS. ALLONBY (*taking* LADY STUTFIELD *by the hand*): We are both quite well, thank you, Lord Illingworth. But what a short time you have been in the dining-room! It seems as if we had only just left.

LORD ILLINGWORTH: I was bored to death. Never opened my lips the whole time. Absolutely longing to come in to you.

MRS. ALLONBY: You should have. The American girl has been giving us a lecture.

LORD ILLINGWORTH: Really? All Americans lecture, I believe. I suppose it is something in their climate. What did she lecture about?

MRS. ALLONBY: Oh, Puritanism, of course.

LORD ILLINGWORTH: I am going to convert her, am I not? How long do you give me?

MRS. ALLONBY: A week.

LORD ILLINGWORTH: A week is more than enough.

Enter GERALD *and* LORD ALFRED.

GERALD (*going to* Mrs. ARBUTHNOT): Dear mother!

MRS. ARBUTHNOT: Gerald, I don't feel at all well. See me home, Gerald. I shouldn't have come.

GERALD: I am so sorry, mother. Certainly. But you must know Lord Illingworth first. (*Goes across room.*)

MRS. ARBUTHNOT: Not to-night, Gerald.

GERALD: Lord Illingworth, I want you so much to know my mother.

LORD ILLINGWORTH: With the greatest pleasure. (*To* MRS. ALLONBY): I'll be back in a moment. People's mothers always bore me to death. All women become like their mothers. That is their tragedy.

MRS. ALLONBY: No man does. That is his.

LORD ILLINGWORTH: What a delightful mood you are in to-night! (*Turns round and goes across with* GERALD *to* MRS. ARBUTHNOT. *When he sees her, he starts back in wonder. Then slowly his eyes turn towards* GERALD.)

GERALD: Mother, this is Lord Illingworth, who has offered to take me as his private secretary.

MRS. ARBUTHNOT *bows coldly.*

It is a wonderful opening for me, isn't it? I hope he won't be disappointed in me, that is all. You'll thank Lord Illingworth, mother, won't you?

MRS. ARBUTHNOT: Lord Illingworth is very good, I am sure, to interest himself in you for the moment.

LORD ILLINGWORTH (*putting his hand on* GERALD'S *shoulder*): Oh, Gerald and I are great friends already, Mrs. . . . Arbuthnot.

MRS. ARBUTHNOT: There can be nothing in common between you and my son, Lord Illingworth.

GERALD: Dear mother, how can you say so? Of course, Lord Illingworth is awfully clever and that sort of thing. There is nothing Lord Illingworth doesn't know.

LORD ILLINGWORTH: My dear boy!

GERALD: He knows more about life than any one I have ever met. I feel an awful duffer when I am with you, Lord Illingworth. Of course, I have had so few advantages. I have not been to Eton or Oxford like other chaps. But Lord Illingworth doesn't seem to mind that. He had been awfully good to me, mother.

MRS. ARBUTHNOT: Lord Illingworth may change his mind. He may not really want you as his secretary.

GERALD: Mother!

MRS. ARBUTHNOT: You must remember, as you said yourself, you have had so few advantages.

MRS. ALLONBY: Lord Illingworth, I want to speak to you for a moment. Do come over.

LORD ILLINGWORTH: Will you excuse me, Mrs. Arbuthnot? Now, don't let your charming mother make any more difficulties, Gerald. The thing is quite settled, isn't it?

GERALD: I hope so.

LORD ILLINGWORTH *goes across to* MRS. ALLONBY.

MRS. ALLONBY: I thought you were never going to leave the lady in black velvet.

LORD ILLINGWORTH: She is excessively handsome. (*Looks at* MRS. ARBUTHNOT.)

LADY HUNSTANTON: Caroline, shall we all make a move to the music-room? Miss Worsley is going to play. You'll come too, dear Mrs. Arbuthnot, won't you? You don't know what a treat is in store for you. (*To* DOCTOR DAUBENY): I must really take Miss Worsley down some afternoon to the rectory. I should so much like dear Mrs. Daubeny to hear her on the violin. Ah, I forgot. Dear Mrs. Daubeny's hearing is a little defective, is it not?

THE ARCHDEACON: Her deafness is a great privation to her. She can't even hear my sermons now. She reads them at home. But she has many resources in herself, many resources.

LADY HUNSTANTON: She reads a good deal, I suppose?

THE ARCHDEACON: Just the very largest print. The eyesight is rapidly going. But she's never morbid, never morbid.

GERALD (*to* LORD ILLINGWORTH): Do speak to my mother, Lord Illingworth, before you go into the music-room. She seems to think, somehow, you don't mean what you said to me.

MRS. ALLONBY: Aren't you coming?

LORD ILLINGWORTH: In a few moments. Lady Hunstanton, if Mrs. Arbuthnot would allow me, I would like to say a few words to her, and we will join you later on.

LADY HUNSTANTON: Ah, of course. You will have a great deal to say to her, and she will have a great deal to thank you for. It is not every son who gets such an offer, Mrs. Arbuthnot. But I know you appreciate that, dear.

LADY CAROLINE: John!

LADY HUNSTANTON: Now, don't keep Mrs. Arbuthnot too long, Lord Illingworth. We can't spare her.

Exit following the other guests. Sound of violin heard from music-room.

LORD ILLINGWORTH: So that is our son, Rachel! Well, I am very proud of him. He is a Harford, every inch of him. By the way, why Arbuthnot, Rachel?

MRS. ARBUTHNOT: One name is as good as another, when one has no right to any name.

LORD ILLINGWORTH: I suppose so—but why Gerald?

MRS. ARBUTHNOT: After a man whose heart I broke—after my father.

LORD ILLINGWORTH: Well, Rachel, what is over is over. All I have got to say now is that I am very, very much pleased with our boy. The world will know him merely as my private secretary, but to me he will be something very near, and very dear. It is a curious thing, Rachel; my life seemed to be quite complete. It was not so. It lacked something, it lacked a son. I have found my son now. I am glad I have found him.

MRS. ARBUTHNOT: You have no right to claim him, or the smallest part of him. The boy is entirely mine, and shall remain mine.

LORD ILLINGWORTH: My dear Rachel, you have had him to yourself for over twenty years. Why not let me have him for a little now? He is quite as much mine as yours.

MRS. ARBUTHNOT: Are you talking of the child you abandoned? Of the child who, as far as you are concerned, might have died of hunger and of want?

LORD ILLINGWORTH: You forget, Rachel, it was you who left me. It was not I who left you.

MRS. ARBUTHNOT: I left you because you refused to give the child a name. Before my son was born, I implored you to marry me.

LORD ILLINGWORTH: I had no expectations then. And besides, Rachel, I wasn't much older than you were. I was only twenty-two. I was twenty-one, I believe, when the whole thing began in your father's garden.

MRS. ARBUTHNOT: When a man is old enough to do wrong he should be old enough to do right also.

LORD ILLINGWORTH: My dear Rachel, intellectual generalities are always interesting, but generalities in morals mean absolutely nothing. As for saying I left our child to starve, that, of course, is untrue and silly. My mother offered you six hundred a year. But you wouldn't take anything. You simply disappeared, and carried the child away with you.

MRS. ARBUTHNOT: I wouldn't have accepted a penny from her. Your father was different. He told you, in my presence, when we were in Paris, that it was your duty to marry me.

LORD ILLINGWORTH: Oh, duty is what one expects from others, it is not what one does oneself. Of course, I was influenced by my mother. Every man is when he is young.

MRS. ARBUTHNOT: I am glad to hear you say so. Gerald shall certainly not go away with you.

LORD ILLINGWORTH: What nonsense, Rachel!

MRS. ARBUTHNOT: Do you think I would allow my son——

LORD ILLINGWORTH: Our son.

MRS. ARBUTHNOT: My son—(LORD ILLINGWORTH *shrugs*

his shoulders)—to go away with the man who spoiled my youth, who ruined my life, who has tainted every moment of my days? You don't realise what my past has been in suffering and in shame.

LORD ILLINGWORTH: My dear Rachel, I must candidly say that I think Gerald's future considerably more important than your past.

MRS. ARBUTHNOT: Gerald cannot separate his future from my past.

LORD ILLINGWORTH: That is exactly what he should do. That is exactly what you should help him to do. What a typical woman you are! You talk sentimentally and you are thoroughly selfish the whole time. But don't let us have a scene. Rachel, I want you to look at this matter from the common-sense point of view, from the point of view of what is best for our son, leaving you and me out of the question. What is our son at present? An underpaid clerk in a small Provincial Bank in a third-rate English town. If you imagine he is quite happy in such a position, you are mistaken. He is thoroughly discontented.

MRS. ARBUTHNOT: He was not discontented till he met you. You have made him so.

LORD ILLINGWORTH: Of course I made him so. Discontent is the first step in the progress of a man or a nation. But I did not leave him with a mere longing for things he could not get. No, I made him a charming offer. He jumped at it, I need hardly say. Any young man would. And now, simply because it turns out that I am the boy's own father and he my own son, you propose practically to ruin his career. That is to say, if I were a perfect stranger, you would allow Gerald to go away with me, but as he is my own flesh and blood you won't. How utterly illogical you are!

MRS. ARBUTHNOT: I will not allow him to go.

LORD ILLINGWORTH: How can you prevent it? What excuse can you give to him for making him decline such an offer as mine? I won't tell him in what relations I stand to him, I need hardly say. But you daren't tell him. You know that. Look how you have brought him up.

MRS. ARBUTHNOT: I have brought him up to be a good man.

LORD ILLINGWORTH: Quite so. And what is the result? You have educated him to be your judge if he ever finds you out. And a bitter, an unjust judge he will be to you. Don't be deceived, Rachel. Children begin by loving their parents. After a time they judge them. Rarely, if ever, do they forgive them.*

MRS. ARBUTHNOT: George, don't take my son away from me. I have had twenty years of sorrow, and I have only had one thing to love me, only one thing to love. You have had a life of joy, and pleasure, and success. You have been quite happy, you have never thought of us. There was no reason, according to your views of life, why you should have remembered us at all. Your meeting us was a mere accident, a horrible accident. Forget it. Don't come now, and rob me of—of all I have in the whole world. You are so rich in other things. Leave me the little vineyard of my life; leave me the walled-in garden and the well of water; the ewe-lamb God sent me, in pity or in wrath, oh! leave me that. George, don't take Gerald from me.

LORD ILLINGWORTH: Rachel, at the present moment you are not necessary to Gerald's career; I am. There is nothing more to be said on the subject.

MRS. ARBUTHNOT: I will not let him go.

LORD ILLINGWORTH: Here is Gerald. He has a right to decide for himself.

Enter GERALD.

GERALD: Well, dear mother, I hope you have settled it all with Lord Illingworth?

MRS. ARBUTHNOT: I have not, Gerald.

LORD ILLINGWORTH: Your mother seems not to like your coming with me, for some reason.

GERALD: Why, mother?

MRS. ARBUTHNOT: I thought you were quite happy here with me, Gerald. I didn't know you were so anxious to leave me.

GERALD: Mother, how can you talk like that? Of course I have been quite happy with you. But a man can't stay always with his mother. No chap does. I want to make myself a position, to do

---

*This beautifully phrased description will come back to haunt Illingworth.

something. I thought you would have been proud to see me Lord Illingworth's secretary.

MRS. ARBUTHNOT: I do not think you would be suitable as a private secretary to Lord Illingworth. You have no qualifications.

LORD ILLINGWORTH: I don't wish to seem to interfere for a moment, Mrs. Arbuthnot, but as far as your last objection is concerned, I surely am the best judge. And I can only tell you that your son has all the qualifications I had hoped for. He has more, in fact, than I had even thought of. Far more. (MRS. ARBUTHNOT *remains silent.*) Have you any other reason, Mrs. Arbuthnot, why you don't wish your son to accept this post?

GERALD: Have you, mother? Do answer.

LORD ILLINGWORTH: If you have, Mrs. Arbuthnot, pray, pray say it. We are quite by ourselves here. Whatever it is, I need not say I will not repeat it.

GERALD: Mother?

LORD ILLINGWORTH: If you would like to be alone with your son, I will leave you. You may have some other reason you don't wish me to hear.

MRS. ARBUTHNOT: I have no other reason.

LORD ILLINGWORTH: Then, my dear boy, we may look on the thing as settled. Come, you and I will smoke a cigarette on the terrace together. And Mrs. Arbuthnot, pray let me tell you, that I think you have acted very, very wisely.

Exit with GERALD. MRS. ARBUTHNOT *is left alone. She stands immobile with a look of unutterable sorrow on her face.*

Act Drop

ACT THREE

SCENE: *The Picture Gallery at Hunstanton Chase. Door at back leading on to terrace.*

LORD ILLINGWORTH *and* GERALD, *R.C.* LORD ILLINGWORTH *lolling on a sofa.* GERALD *in a chair.*

LORD ILLINGWORTH: Thoroughly sensible woman, your mother, Gerald. I knew she would come round in the end.

GERALD: My mother is awfully conscientious, Lord Illingworth, and I know she doesn't think I am educated enough to be your secretary. She is perfectly right, too. I was fearfully idle when I was at school, and I couldn't pass an examination now to save my life.

LORD ILLINGWORTH: My dear Gerald, examinations are of no value whatsoever. If a man is a gentleman, he knows quite enough, and if he is not a gentleman, whatever he knows is bad for him.

GERALD: But I am so ignorant of the world, Lord Illingworth.

LORD ILLINGWORTH: Don't be afraid, Gerald. Remember that you've got on your side the most wonderful thing in the world—youth! There is nothing like youth. The middle-aged are mortgaged to Life. The old are in life's lumber-room. But youth is the Lord of Life. Youth has a kingdom waiting for it. Every one is born a king, and most people die in exile, like most kings. To win back my youth, Gerald, there is nothing I wouldn't do—except take exercise, get up early, or be a useful member of the community.

GERALD: But you don't call yourself old, Lord Illingworth?

LORD ILLINGWORTH: I am old enough to be your father, Gerald.

GERALD: I don't remember my father; he died years ago.

LORD ILLINGWORTH: So Lady Hunstanton told me.

GERALD: It is very curious, my mother never talks to me about my father. I sometimes think she must have married beneath her.

LORD ILLINGWORTH (*winces slightly*): Really? (*Goes over and puts his hand on* GERALD'S *shoulder.*) You have missed not having a father, I suppose, Gerald?

GERALD: Oh, no; my mother has been so good to me. No one ever had such a mother as I have had.

LORD ILLINGWORTH: I am quite sure of that. Still I should imagine that most mothers don't quite understand their sons. Don't realise, I mean, that a son has ambitions, a desire to see life, to make himself a name. After all, Gerald, you couldn't be expected to pass all your life in such a hole as Wrockley, could you?

GERALD: Oh, no! It would be dreadful!

LORD ILLINGWORTH: A mother's love is very touching, of course, but it is often curiously selfish. I mean, there is a good deal of selfishness in it.

GERALD (*slowly*): I suppose there is.

LORD ILLINGWORTH: Your mother is a thoroughly good woman. But good women have such limited views of life, their horizon is so small, their interests are so petty, aren't they?

GERALD: They are awfully interested, certainly, in things we don't care much about.

LORD ILLINGWORTH: I suppose your mother is very religious, and that sort of thing.

GERALD: Oh, yes, she's always going to church.

LORD ILLINGWORTH: Ah! she is not modern, and to be modern is the only thing worth being nowadays. You want to be modern, don't you, Gerald? You want to know life as it really is. Not to be put off with any old-fashioned theories about life. Well, what you have to do at present is simply to fit yourself for the best society. A man who can dominate a London dinner-table can dominate the world. The future belongs to the dandy. It is the exquisites who are going to rule.*

GERALD: I should like to wear nice things awfully, but I have always been told that a man should not think so much about his clothes.

LORD ILLINGWORTH: People nowadays are so absolutely superficial that they don't understand the philosophy of the superfi-

---

*Illingworth articulates his own distorted version of Aestheticism.

cial. By the way, Gerald, you should learn how to tie your tie better. Sentiment is all very well for the buttonhole. But the essential thing for a necktie is style. A well-tied tie is the first serious step in life.

GERALD (*laughing*): I might be able to learn how to tie a tie, Lord Illingworth, but I should never be able to talk as you do. I don't know how to talk.

LORD ILLINGWORTH: Oh! talk to every woman as if you loved her, and to every man as if he bored you, and at the end of your first season you will have the reputation of possessing the most perfect social tact.

GERALD: But it is very difficult to get into society, isn't it?

LORD ILLINGWORTH: To get into the best society, nowadays, one has either to feed people, amuse people, or shock people—that is all!

GERALD: I suppose society is wonderfully delightful!

LORD ILLINGWORTH: To be in it is merely a bore. But to be out of it simply a tragedy. Society is a necessary thing. No man has any real success in this world unless he has got women to back him, and women rule society. If you have not got women on your side you are quite over. You might just as well be a barrister or a stockbroker, or a journalist at once.

GERALD: It is very difficult to understand women, is it not?

LORD ILLINGWORTH: You should never try to understand them. Women are pictures. Men are problems. If you want to know what a woman really means—which, by the way, is always a dangerous thing to do—look at her, don't listen to her.

GERALD: But women are awfully clever, aren't they?

LORD ILLINGWORTH: One should always tell them so. But, to the philosopher, my dear Gerald, women represent the triumph of matter over mind—just as men represent the triumph of mind over morals.

GERALD: How then can women have so much power as you say they have?

LORD ILLINGWORTH: The history of women is the history of the worst form of tyranny the world has ever known. The tyranny of the weak over the strong. It is the only tyranny that lasts.

GERALD: But haven't women got a refining influence?

LORD ILLINGWORTH: Nothing refines but the intellect.

GERALD: Still, there are many different kinds of women, aren't there?

LORD ILLINGWORTH: Only two kinds in society: the plain and the coloured.

GERALD: But there are good women in society, aren't there?

LORD ILLINGWORTH: Far too many.

GERALD: But do you think women shouldn't be good?

LORD ILLINGWORTH: One should never tell them so, they'd all become good at once. Women are a fascinatingly wilful sex. Every woman is a rebel, and usually in wild revolt against herself.

GERALD: You have never been married, Lord Illingworth, have you?

LORD ILLINGWORTH: Men marry because they are tired; women because they are curious. Both are disappointed.

GERALD: But don't you think one can be happy when one is married?

LORD ILLINGWORTH: Perfectly happy. But the happiness of a married man, my dear Gerald, depends on the people he has not married.

GERALD: But if one is in love?

LORD ILLINGWORTH: One should always be in love. That is the reason one should never marry.

GERALD: Love is a very wonderful thing, isn't it?

LORD ILLINGWORTH: When one is in love one begins by deceiving oneself. And one ends by deceiving others. That is what the world calls a romance. But a really *grande passion* is comparatively rare nowadays. It is the privilege of people who have nothing to do. That is the one use of the idle classes in a country, and the only possible explanation of us Harfords.

GERALD: Harfords, Lord Illingworth?

LORD ILLINGWORTH: That is my family name. You should study the Peerage, Gerald. It is the one book a young man about town should know thoroughly, and it is the best thing in fiction the English have ever done. And now, Gerald, you are going into a perfectly new life with me, and I want you to know how to live.

MRS. ARBUTHNOT *appears on terrace behind.*

For the world has been made by fools that wise men should live in it!

Enter L.C. LADY HUNSTANTON *and* DOCTOR DAUBENY.

LADY HUNSTANTON: Ah! here you are, dear Lord Illingworth. Well, I suppose you have been telling our young friend, Gerald, what his new duties are to be, and giving him a great deal of good advice over a pleasant cigarette.

LORD ILLINGWORTH: I have been giving him the best of advice, Lady Hunstanton, and the best of cigarettes.

LADY HUNSTANTON: I am so sorry I was not here to listen to you, but I suppose I am too old now to learn. Except from you, dear Archdeacon, when you are in your nice pulpit. But then I always know what you are going to say, so I don't feel alarmed. (*Sees* MRS. ARBUTHNOT.) Ah! dear Mrs. Arbuthnot, do come and join us. Come, dear.

Enter MRS. ARBUTHNOT.

Gerald has been having such a long talk with Lord Illingworth; I am sure you must feel very much flattered at the pleasant way in which everything has turned out for him. Let us sit down. (*They sit down.*) And how is your beautiful embroidery going on?

MRS. ARBUTHNOT: I am always at work, Lady Hunstanton.

LADY HUNSTANTON: Mrs. Daubeny embroiders a little, too, doesn't she?

THE ARCHDEACON: She was very deft with her needle once, quite a Dorcas.* But the gout has crippled her fingers a good deal. She has not touched the tambour frame for nine or ten years. But she has many other amusements. She is very much interested in her own health.

LADY HUNSTANTON: Ah! that is always a nice distraction, is it not? Now, what are you talking about, Lord Illingworth? Do tell us.

LORD ILLINGWORTH: I was on the point of explaining to Gerald that the world has always laughed at its own tragedies, that

*Woman who, in the early days of Christianity, sewed clothes for the poor.

being the only way in which it has been able to bear them. And that, consequently, whatever the world has treated seriously belongs to the comedy side of things.

LADY HUNSTANTON: Now I am quite out of my depth. I usually am when Lord Illingworth says anything. And the Humane Society is most careless. They never rescue me. I am left to sink. I have a dim idea, dear Lord Illingworth, that you are always on the side of the sinners, and I know I always try to be on the side of the saints, but that is as far as I get. And after all, it may be merely the fancy of a drowning person.

LORD ILLINGWORTH: The only difference between the saint and the sinner is that every saint has a past, and every sinner has a future.

LADY HUNSTANTON: Ah! that quite does for me. I haven't a word to say. You and I, dear Mrs. Arbuthnot, are behind the age. We can't follow Lord Illingworth. Too much care was taken with our education, I am afraid. To have been well brought up is a great drawback nowadays. It shuts one out from so much.

MRS. ARBUTHNOT: I should be sorry to follow Lord Illingworth in any of his opinions.

LADY HUNSTANTON: You are quite right, dear.

GERALD *shrugs his shoulders and looks irritably over at his mother. Enter* LADY CAROLINE.

LADY CAROLINE: Jane, have you seen John anywhere?

LADY HUNSTANTON: You needn't be anxious about him, dear. He is with Lady Stutfield; I saw them some time ago, in the Yellow Drawing-room. They seem quite happy together. You are not going, Caroline? Pray sit down.

LADY CAROLINE: I think I had better look after John.

Exit LADY CAROLINE.

LADY HUNSTANTON: It doesn't do to pay men so much attention. And Caroline has really nothing to be anxious about. Lady Stutfield is very sympathetic. She is just as sympathetic about one thing as she is about another. A beautiful nature.

Enter SIR JOHN *and* MRS. ALLONBY.

Ah! here is Sir John! And with Mrs. Allonby too! I suppose it was Mrs. Allonby I saw him with. Sir John, Caroline has been looking everywhere for you.

MRS. ALLONBY: We have been waiting for her in the Music-room, dear Lady Hunstanton.

LADY HUNSTANTON: Ah! the Music-room, of course. I thought it was the Yellow Drawing-room, my memory is getting so defective. (*To the* ARCHDEACON) Mrs. Daubeny has a wonderful memory, hasn't she?

THE ARCHDEACON: She used to be quite remarkable for her memory, but since her last attack she recalls chiefly the events of her early childhood. But she finds great pleasure in such retrospections, great pleasure.

Enter LADY STUTFIELD *and* MR. KELVIL.

LADY HUNSTANTON: Ah! dear Lady Stutfield! and what has Mr. Kelvil been talking to you about?

LADY STUTFIELD: About Bimetallism, as well as I remember.

LADY HUNSTANTON: Bimetallism! Is that quite a nice subject? However, I know people discuss everything very freely nowadays. What did Sir John talk to you about, dear Mrs. Allonby?

MRS. ALLONBY: About Patagonia.

LADY HUNSTANTON: Really? What a remote topic! But very improving, I have no doubt.

MRS. ALLONBY: He has been most interesting on the subject of Patagonia. Savages seem to have quite the same views as cultured people on almost all subjects. They are excessively advanced.

LADY HUNSTANTON: What do they do?

MRS. ALLONBY: Apparently everything.

LADY HUNSTANTON: Well, it is very gratifying, dear Archdeacon, is it not, to find that Human Nature is permanently one.—On the whole, the world is the same world, is it not?

LORD ILLINGWORTH: The world is simply divided into two classes—those who believe the incredible, like the public—and those who do the improbable——

MRS. ALLONBY: Like yourself?

LORD ILLINGWORTH: Yes; I am always astonishing myself. It is the only thing that makes life worth living.

LADY STUTFIELD: And what have you been doing lately that astonishes you?

LORD ILLINGWORTH: I have been discovering all kinds of beautiful qualities in my own nature.

MRS. ALLONBY: Ah! don't become quite perfect all at once. Do it gradually!

LORD ILLINGWORTH: I don't intend to grow perfect at all. At least, I hope I shan't. It would be most inconvenient. Women love us for our defects. If we have enough of them, they will forgive us everything, even our gigantic intellects.

MRS. ALLONBY: It is premature to ask us to forgive analysis. We forgive adoration; that is quite as much as should be expected from us.

Enter LORD ALFRED. *He joins* LADY STUTFIELD.

LADY HUNSTANTON: Ah! we women should forgive everything, shouldn't we, dear Mrs. Arbuthnot? I am sure you agree with me in that.

MRS. ARBUTHNOT: I do not, Lady Hunstanton. I think there are many things women should never forgive.

LADY HUNSTANTON: What sort of things?

MRS. ARBUTHNOT: The ruin of another woman's life. (*Moves slowly away to back of stage.*)

LADY HUNSTANTON: Ah! those things are very sad, no doubt, but I believe there are admirable homes where people of that kind are looked after and reformed, and I think on the whole that the secret of life is to take things very, very easily.

MRS. ALLONBY: The secret of life is never to have an emotion that is unbecoming.

LADY STUTFIELD: The secret of life is to appreciate the pleasure of being terribly, terribly deceived.

KELVIL: The secret of life is to resist temptation, Lady Stutfield.

LORD ILLINGWORTH: There is no secret of life. Life's aim, if it has one, is simply to be always looking for temptations. There are not nearly enough. I sometimes pass a whole day without coming across a single one. It is quite dreadful. It makes one so nervous about the future.

LADY HUNSTANTON (*shakes her fan at him*): I don't know how it is, Lord Illingworth, but everything you have said to-day seems to me excessively immoral. It has been most interesting, listening to you.

LORD ILLINGWORTH: All thought is immoral. Its very essence is destruction. If you think of anything, you kill it. Nothing survives being thought of.

LADY HUNSTANTON: I don't understand a word, Lord Illingworth. But I have no doubt it is all quite true. Personally, I have very little to reproach myself with, on the score of thinking. I don't believe in women thinking too much. Women should think in moderation, as they should do all things in moderation.

LORD ILLINGWORTH: Moderation is a fatal thing, Lady Hunstanton. Nothing succeeds like excess.

LADY HUNSTANTON: I hope I shall remember that. It sounds an admirable maxim. But I'm beginning to forget everything. It's a great misfortune.

LORD ILLINGWORTH: It is one of your most fascinating qualities, Lady Hunstanton. No woman should have a memory. Memory in a woman is the beginning of dowdiness. One can always tell from a woman's bonnet whether she has got a memory or not.

LADY HUNSTANTON: How charming you are, dear Lord Illingworth. You always find out that one's most glaring fault is one's important virtue. You have the most comforting view of life.

Enter FARQUHAR.

FARQUHAR: Doctor Daubeny's carriage!

LADY HUNSTANTON: My dear Archdeacon! It is only half-past ten.

THE ARCHDEACON (*rising*): I am afraid I must go, Lady Hunstanton. Tuesday is always one of Mrs. Daubeny's bad nights.

LADY HUNSTANTON (*rising*): Well, I won't keep you from her. (*Goes with him towards door.*) I have told Farquhar to put a brace of partridge into the carriage. Mrs. Daubeny may fancy them.

THE ARCHDEACON: It is very kind of you, but Mrs. Daubeny

never touches solids now. Lives entirely on jellies. But she is wonderfully cheerful, wonderfully cheerful. She has nothing to complain of.

Exit with LADY HUNSTANTON.

MRS. ALLONBY (*goes over to* LORD ILLINGWORTH): There is a beautiful moon to-night.

LORD ILLINGWORTH: Let us go and look at it. To look at anything that is inconstant is charming nowadays.

MRS. ALLONBY: You have your looking-glass.

LORD ILLINGWORTH: It is unkind. It merely shows me my wrinkles.

MRS. ALLONBY: Mine is better behaved. It never tells me the truth.

LORD ILLINGWORTH: Then it is in love with you.

Exeunt SIR JOHN, LADY STUTFIELD, MR. KELVIL, *and* LORD ALFRED.

GERALD (*to* LORD ILLINGWORTH): May I come too?

LORD ILLINGWORTH: Do, my dear boy. (*Moves towards door with* MRS. ALLONBY *and* GERALD.)

LADY CAROLINE *enters, looks rapidly round and goes out in opposite direction to that taken by* SIR JOHN *and* LADY STUTFIELD.

MRS. ARBUTHNOT: Gerald!

GERALD: What, mother!

Exit LORD ILLINGWORTH *with* MRS. ALLONBY.

MRS. ARBUTHNOT: It is getting late. Let us go home.

GERALD: My dear mother. Do let us wait a little longer. Lord Illingworth is so delightful, and, by the way, mother, I have a great surprise for you. We are starting for India at the end of this month.

MRS. ARBUTHNOT: Let us go home.

GERALD: If you really want to, of course, mother, but I must bid good-bye to Lord Illingworth first. I'll be back in five minutes. (*Exit.*)

MRS. ARBUTHNOT: Let him leave me if he chooses, but not with him—not with him! I couldn't bear it. (*Walks up and down.*)

Enter HESTER.

HESTER: What a lovely night it is, Mrs. Arbuthnot.

MRS. ARBUTHNOT: Is it?

HESTER: Mrs. Arbuthnot, I wish you would let us be friends. You are so different from the other women here. When you came into the Drawing-room this evening, somehow you brought with you a sense of what is good and pure in life. I had been foolish. There are things that are right to say, but that may be said at the wrong time and to the wrong people.

MRS. ARBUTHNOT: I heard what you said. I agree with it, Miss Worsley.

HESTER: I didn't know you had heard it. But I knew you would agree with me. A woman who has sinned should be punished, shouldn't she?

MRS. ARBUTHNOT: Yes.

HESTER: She shouldn't be allowed to come into the society of good men and women?

MRS. ARBUTHNOT: She should not.

HESTER: And the man should be punished in the same way?

MRS. ARBUTHNOT: In the same way. And the children, if there are children, in the same way also?

HESTER: Yes, it is right that the sins of the parents should be visited on the children. It is a just law. It is God's law.*

MRS. ARBUTHNOT: It is one of God's terrible laws. (*Moves away to fireplace.*)

HESTER: You are distressed about your son leaving you, Mrs. Arbuthnot?

MRS. ARBUTHNOT: Yes.

HESTER: Do you like him going away with Lord Illingworth? Of

*Like Lady Windermere, Hester begins as a judgmental prig.

course there is position, no doubt, and money, but position and money are not everything, are they?

MRS. ARBUTHNOT: They are nothing; they bring misery.

HESTER: Then why do you let your son go with him?

MRS. ARBUTHNOT: He wishes it himself.

HESTER: But if you asked him he would stay, would he not?

MRS. ARBUTHNOT: He has set his heart on going.

HESTER: He couldn't refuse you anything. He loves you too much. Ask him to stay. Let me send him to you. He is on the terrace at this moment with Lord Illingworth. I heard them laughing together as I passed through the Music-room.

MRS. ARBUTHNOT: Don't trouble, Miss Worsley, I can wait. It is of no consequence.

HESTER: No, I'll tell him you want him. Do—do ask him to stay.

Exit HESTER.

MRS. ARBUTHNOT: He won't come—I know he won't come.

Enter LADY CAROLINE. *She looks round anxiously. Enter* GERALD.

LADY CAROLINE: Mr. Arbuthnot, may I ask you is Sir John anywhere on the terrace?

GERALD: No, Lady Caroline, he is not on the terrace.

LADY CAROLINE: It is very curious. It is time for him to retire.

Exit LADY CAROLINE.

GERALD: Dear mother, I am afraid I kept you waiting. I forgot all about it. I am so happy to-night, mother; I have never been so happy.

MRS. ARBUTHNOT: At the prospect of going away?

GERALD: Don't put it like that, mother. Of course I am sorry to leave you. Why, you are the best mother in the whole world. But after all, as Lord Illingworth says, it is impossible to live in such a place as Wrockley. You don't mind it. But I'm ambitious; I want something more than that. I want to have a career. I want to do something that will make you proud of me, and Lord Illingworth is going to help me. He is going to do everything for me.

MRS. ARBUTHNOT: Gerald, don't go away with Lord Illingworth. I implore you not to. Gerald, I beg you!

GERALD: Mother, how changeable you are! You don't seem to know your own mind for a single moment. An hour and a half ago in the Drawing-room you agreed to the whole thing; now you turn round and make objections, and try to force me to give up my one chance in life. Yes, my one chance. You don't suppose that men like Lord Illingworth are to be found every day, do you, mother? It is very strange that when I have had such a wonderful piece of good luck, the one person to put difficulties in my way should be my own mother. Besides, you know, mother, I love Hester Worsley. Who could help loving her? I love her more than I ever have told you, far more. And if I had a position, if I had prospects, I could—I could ask her to . . . Don't you understand now, mother, what it means to me to be Lord Illingworth's secretary? To start like that is to find a career ready for one—before one—waiting for one. If I were Lord Illingworth's secretary I could ask Hester to be my wife. As a wretched bank clerk with a hundred a year it would be an impertinence.

MRS. ARBUTHNOT: I fear you need have no hopes of Miss Worsley. I know her views on life. She has just told them to me. (*A pause.*)

GERALD: Then I have my ambition left, at any rate. That is something—I am glad I have that! You have always tried to crush my ambition, mother—haven't you? You have told me that the world is a wicked place, that success is not worth having, that society is shallow, and all that sort of thing—well, I don't believe it, mother. I think the world must be delightful. I think society must be exquisite. I think success is a thing worth having. You have been wrong in all that you taught me, mother, quite wrong. Lord Illingworth is a successful man. He is a fashionable man. He is a man who lives in the world and for it. Well, I would give anything to be just like Lord Illingworth.

MRS. ARBUTHNOT: I would sooner see you dead.

GERALD: Mother, what is your objection to Lord Illingworth? Tell me—tell me right out. What is it?

MRS. ARBUTHNOT: He is a bad man.

GERALD: In what way bad? I don't understand what you mean.

MRS. ARBUTHNOT: I will tell you.

GERALD: I suppose you think him bad, because he doesn't believe the same things as you do. Well, men are different from women, mother. It is natural that they should have different views.

MRS. ARBUTHNOT: It is not what Lord Illingworth believes, or what he does not believe, that makes him bad. It is what he is.

GERALD: Mother, is it something you know of him? Something you actually know?

MRS. ARBUTHNOT: It is something I know.

GERALD: Something you are quite sure of?

MRS. ARBUTHNOT: Quite sure of.

GERALD: How long have you known it?

MRS. ARBUTHNOT: For twenty years.

GERALD: Is it fair to go back twenty years in any man's career? And what have you or I to do with Lord Illingworth's early life? What business is it of ours?

MRS. ARBUTHNOT: What this man has been, he is now, and will be always.

GERALD: Mother, tell me what Lord Illingworth did? If he did anything shameful, I will not go away with him. Surely you know me well enough for that?

MRS. ARBUTHNOT: Gerald, come near to me. Quite close to me, as you used to do when you were a little boy, when you were mother's own boy.

GERALD *sits down beside his mother. She runs her fingers through his hair, and strokes his hands.**

Gerald, there was a girl once, she was very young, she was little over eighteen at the time. George Harford—that was Lord Illingworth's name then—George Harford met her. She knew nothing about life. He—knew everything. He made this girl love him. He

---

*The stage directions, which may seem overly dramatic to modern audiences, reflect the sentimentality of Victorian society.

made her love so much that she left her father's house with him one morning. She loved him so much, and he had promised to marry her! He had solemnly promised to marry her, and she had believed him. She was very young, and—and ignorant of what life really is. But he put the marriage off from week to week, and month to month.—She trusted in him all the while. She loved him.—Before her child was born—for she had a child—she implored him for the child's sake to marry her, that the child might have a name, that her sin might not be visited on the child, who was innocent. He refused. After the child was born she left him, taking the child away, and her life was ruined, and her soul ruined, and all that was sweet, and good, and pure in her ruined also. She suffered terribly—she suffers now. She will always suffer. For her there is no joy, no peace, no atonement. She is a woman who drags a chain like a guilty thing. She is a woman who wears a mask, like a thing that is a leper. The fire cannot purify her. The waters cannot quench her anguish. Nothing can heal her! no anodyne can give her sleep! no poppies forgetfulness! She is lost! She is a lost soul! That is why I call Lord Illingworth a bad man. That is why I don't want my boy to be with him.

GERALD: My dear mother, it all sounds very tragic, of course. But I dare say the girl was just as much to blame as Lord Illingworth was.—After all, would a really nice girl, a girl with any nice feelings at all, go away from her home with a man to whom she was not married, and live with him as his wife? No nice girl would.

MRS. ARBUTHNOT (*after a pause*): Gerald, I withdraw all my objections. You are at liberty to go away with Lord Illingworth, when and where you choose.

GERALD: Dear mother, I knew you wouldn't stand in my way. You are the best woman God ever made. And, as for Lord Illingworth, I don't believe he is capable of anything infamous or base. I can't believe it of him—I can't.

HESTER (*outside*): Let me go! Let me go!

Enter HESTER *in terror, and rushes over to* GERALD *and flings herself in his arms.*

HESTER: Oh! save me—save me from him!
GERALD: From whom?
HESTER: He has insulted me! Horribly insulted me! Save me!
GERALD: Who? Who has dared——?

LORD ILLINGWORTH *enters at back of stage.* HESTER *breaks from* GERALD'S *arms and points to him.*

GERALD (*he is quite beside himself with rage and indignation*): Lord Illingworth, you have insulted the purest thing on God's earth, a thing as pure as my own mother. You have insulted the woman I love most in the world with my own mother. As there is a God in Heaven, I will kill you!

MRS. ARBUTHNOT (*rushing across and catching hold of him*): No! no!

GERALD (*thrusting her back*): Don't hold me, mother. Don't hold me—I'll kill him!

MRS. ARBUTHNOT: Gerald!

GERALD: Let me go, I say!

MRS. ARBUTHNOT: Stop, Gerald, stop! He is your own father!

GERALD *clutches his mother's hands and looks into her face. She sinks slowly on the ground in shame.* HESTER *steals towards the door.* LORD ILLINGWORTH *frowns and bites his lip. After a time* GERALD *raises his mother up, puts his arm round her, and leads her from the room.*

Act Drop

ACT FOUR

SCENE: *Sitting-room at Mrs. Arbuthnot's house at Wrockley. Large open French window at back, looking on to garden. Doors R.C. and L.C.*

GERALD ARBUTHNOT *writing at table.*

Enter ALICE *R.C. followed by* LORD HUNSTANTON *and* MRS. ALLONBY.

ALICE: Lady Hunstanton and Mrs. Allonby. (*Exit L.C.*)
LADY HUNSTANTON: Good-morning, Gerald.
GERALD (*rising*): Good-morning, Lady Hunstanton. Good-morning, Mrs. Allonby.
LADY HUNSTANTON (*sitting down*): We came to inquire for your dear mother, Gerald. I hope she is better?
GERALD: My mother has not come down yet, Lady Hunstanton.
LADY HUNSTANTON: Ah, I am afraid the heat was too much for her last night. I think there must have been thunder in the air. Or perhaps it was the music. Music makes one feel so romantic—at least it always gets on one's nerves.
MRS. ALLONBY: It's the same thing, nowadays.
LADY HUNSTANTON: I am so glad I don't know what you mean, dear. I am afraid you mean something wrong. Ah, I see you're examining Mrs. Arbuthnot's pretty room. Isn't it nice and old-fashioned?
MRS. ALLONBY (*surveying the room through her lorgnette*): It looks quite the happy English home.
LADY HUNSTANTON: That's just the word, dear; that just describes it. One feels your mother's good influence in everything she has about her, Gerald.
MRS. ALLONBY: Lord Illingworth says that all influence is bad, but that a good influence is the worst in the world.

LADY HUNSTANTON: When Lord Illingworth knows Mrs. Arbuthnot better he will change his mind. I must certainly bring him here.

MRS. ALLONBY: I should like to see Lord Illingworth in a happy English home.

LADY HUNSTANTON: It would do him a great deal of good, dear. Most women in London, nowadays, seem to furnish their rooms with nothing but orchids, foreigners, and French novels. But here we have the room of a sweet saint. Fresh natural flowers, books that don't shock one, pictures that one can look at without blushing.

MRS. ALLONBY: But I like blushing.

LADY HUNSTANTON: Well, there *is* a good deal to be said for blushing, if one can do it at the proper moment. Poor dear Hunstanton used to tell me I didn't blush nearly often enough. But then he was so very particular. He wouldn't let me know any of his men friends, except those who were over seventy, like poor Lord Ashton; who afterwards, by the way, was brought into the Divorce Court. A most unfortunate case.

MRS. ALLONBY: I delight in men over seventy. They always offer one the devotion of a lifetime. I think seventy an ideal age for a man.

LADY HUNSTANTON: She is quite incorrigible, Gerald, isn't she? By-the-by, Gerald, I hope your dear mother will come and see me more often now. You and Lord Illingworth start almost immediately, don't you?

GERALD: I have given up my intention of being Lord Illingworth's secretary.

LADY HUNSTANTON: Surely not, Gerald! It would be most unwise of you. What reason can you have?

GERALD: I don't think I should be suitable for the post.

MRS. ALLONBY: I wish Lord Illingworth would ask me to be his secretary. But he says I am not serious enough.

LADY HUNSTANTON: My dear, you really mustn't talk like that in this house. Mrs. Arbuthnot doesn't know anything about the wicked society in which we all live. She won't go into it. She is far too good. I consider it was a great honour her coming to me last night. It gave quite an atmosphere of respectability to the party.

MRS. ALLONBY: Ah, that must have been what you thought was thunder in the air.

LADY HUNSTANTON: My dear, how can you say that? There is no resemblance between the two things at all. But really, Gerald, what do you mean by not being suitable?

GERALD: Lord Illingworth's views of life and mine are too different.

LADY HUNSTANTON: But, my dear Gerald, at your age you shouldn't have any views of life. They are quite out of place. You must be guided by others in this matter. Lord Illingworth has made you the most flattering offer, and travelling with him you would see the world—as much of it, at least, as one should look at—under the best auspices possible, and stay with all the right people, which is so important at this solemn moment in your career.

GERALD: I don't want to see the world; I've seen enough of it.

MRS. ALLONBY: I hope you don't think you have exhausted life, Mr. Arbuthnot. When a man says that, one knows that life has exhausted him.

GERALD: I don't wish to leave my mother.

LADY HUNSTANTON: Now, Gerald, that is pure laziness on your part. Not leave your mother! If I were your mother I would insist on your going.

Enter ALICE *L.C.*

ALICE: Mrs. Arbuthnot's compliments, my lady, but she has a bad headache, and cannot see any one this morning. (*Exit* R.C.)

LADY HUNSTANTON (*rising*): A bad headache! I am so sorry! Perhaps you'll bring her up to Hunstanton this afternoon, if she is better, Gerald.

GERALD: I am afraid not this afternoon, Lady Hunstanton.

LADY HUNSTANTON: Well, to-morrow, then. Ah, if you had a father, Gerald, he wouldn't let you waste your life here. He would send you with Lord Illingworth at once. But mothers are so weak. They give up to their sons in everything. We are all heart, all heart. Come, dear, I must call at the rectory and inquire for Mrs. Daubeny, who, I am afraid, is far from well. It is wonderful how the Archdeacon bears up, quite wonderful. He is the most sympathetic of husbands. Quite a model. Good-bye, Gerald; give my fondest love to your mother.

MRS. ALLONBY: Good-bye, Mr. Arbuthnot.

GERALD: Good-bye.

Exit LADY HUNSTANTON *and* MRS. ALLONBY. GERALD *sits down and reads over his letter.*

GERALD: What name can I sign? I, who have no right to any name. (*Signs name, puts letter into envelope, addresses it, and is about to seal it, when door L.C. opens and* MRS. ARBUTHNOT *enters.* GERALD *lays down sealing-wax. Mother and son look at each other.*)

LADY HUNSTANTON (*through French window at the back*): Good-bye again, Gerald. We are taking the short cut across your pretty garden. Now, remember my advice to you—start at once with Lord Illingworth.

MRS. ALLONBY: *Au revoir*, Mr. Arbuthnot. Mind you bring me back something nice from your travels—not an Indian shawl—on no account an Indian shawl. (*Exeunt.*)

GERALD: Mother, I have just written to him.

MRS. ARBUTHNOT: To whom?

GERALD: To my father. I have written to tell him to come here at four o'clock this afternoon.

MRS. ARBUTHNOT: He shall not come here. He shall not cross the threshold of my house.

GERALD: He must come.

MRS. ARBUTHNOT: Gerald, if you are going away with Lord Illingworth, go at once. Go before it kills me; but don't ask me to meet him.

GERALD: Mother, you don't understand. Nothing in the world would induce me to go away with Lord Illingworth, or to leave you. Surely you know me well enough for that. No; I have written to him to say——

MRS. ARBUTHNOT: What can you have to say to him?

GERALD: Can't you guess, mother, what I have written in this letter?

MRS. ARBUTHNOT: No.

GERALD: Mother, surely you can. Think, think what must be done, now, at once, within the next few days.

MRS. ARBUTHNOT: There is nothing to be done.

GERALD: I have written to Lord Illingworth to tell him that he must marry you.

MRS. ARBUTHNOT: Marry me?

GERALD: Mother, I will force him to do it. The wrong that has been done you must be repaired. Atonement must be made. Justice may be slow, mother, but it comes in the end. In a few days you shall be Lord Illingworth's lawful wife.

MRS. ARBUTHNOT: But, Gerald——

GERALD: I will insist upon his doing it. I will make him do it; he will not dare to refuse.

MRS. ARBUTHNOT: But, Gerald, it is I who refuse. I will not marry Lord Illingworth.

GERALD: Not marry him? Mother!

MRS. ARBUTHNOT: I will not marry him.

GERALD: But you don't understand: it is for your sake I am talking, not for mine. This marriage, this necessary marriage, this marriage which for obvious reasons must inevitably take place, will not help me, will not give me a name that will be really, rightly mine to bear. But surely it will be something for you, that you, my mother, should, however late, become the wife of the man who is my father. Will not that be something?

MRS. ARBUTHNOT: I will not marry him.

GERALD: Mother, you must.

MRS. ARBUTHNOT: I will not. You talk of atonement for a wrong done. What atonement can be made to me? There is no atonement possible. I am disgraced; he is not. That is all. It is the usual history of a man and a woman as it usually happens, as it always happens. And the ending is the ordinary ending. The woman suffers. The man goes free.

GERALD: I don't know if that is the ordinary ending, mother; I hope it is not. But your life, at any rate, shall not end like that. The man shall make whatever reparation is possible. It is not enough. It does not wipe out the past, I know that. But at least it makes the future better, better for you, mother.

MRS. ARBUTHNOT: I refuse to marry Lord Illingworth.

GERALD: If he came to you himself and asked you to be his wife you would give him a different answer. Remember, he is my father.

MRS. ARBUTHNOT: If he came himself, which he will not do, my answer would be the same. Remember, I am your mother.

GERALD: Mother, you make it terribly difficult for me by talking like that; and I can't understand why you won't look at this matter from the right, from the only proper standpoint. It is to take away the bitterness out of your life, to take away the shadow that lies on your name, that this marriage must take place. There is no alternative; and after the marriage you and I can go away together. But the marriage must take place first. It is a duty that you owe, not merely to yourself, but to all other women—yes; to all the other women in the world, lest he betray more.

MRS. ARBUTHNOT: I owe nothing to other women. There is not one of them to help me. There is not one woman in the world to whom I could go for pity, if I would take it, or for sympathy, if I could win it. Women are hard on each other. That girl, last night, good though she is, fled from the room as though I were a tainted thing. She was right. I am a tainted thing. But my wrongs are my own, and I will bear them alone. I must bear them alone. What have women who have not sinned to do with me, or I with them? We do not understand each other.*

Enter HESTER *behind.*

GERALD: I implore you to do what I ask you.

MRS. ARBUTHNOT: What son has ever asked of his mother to make so hideous a sacrifice? None.

GERALD: What mother has ever refused to marry the father of her own child? None.

MRS. ARBUTHNOT: Let me be the first, then. I will not do it.

GERALD: Mother, you believe in religion, and you brought me up to believe in it also. Well, surely your religion, the religion that

---

*Here, as near the end of the play, Mrs. Arbuthnot has internalized the strict views of Victorian society; even without others knowing what she has done, she has made herself a social outcast.

you taught me when I was a boy, mother, must tell you that I am right. You know it, you feel it.

MRS. ARBUTHNOT: I do not know it. I do not feel it, nor will I ever stand before God's altar and ask God's blessing on so hideous a mockery as a marriage between me and George Harford. I will not say the words the Church bids us to say. I will not say them. I dare not. How could I swear to love the man I loathe, to honour him who wrought you dishonour, to obey him who, in his mastery, made me to sin? No; marriage is a sacrament for those who love each other. It is not for such as him, or such as me. Gerald, to save you from the world's sneers and taunts I have lied to the world. For twenty years I have lied to the world. I could not tell the world the truth. Who can ever? But not for my own sake will I lie to God, and in God's presence. No, Gerald, no ceremony, Church-hallowed or State-made, shall ever bind me to George Harford. It may be that I am too bound to him already, who, robbing me, yet left me richer, so that in the mire of my life I found the pearl of price, or what I thought would be so.

GERALD: I don't understand you now.

MRS. ARBUTHNOT: Men don't understand what mothers are. I am no different from other women except in the wrong done me and the wrong I did, and my very heavy punishments and great disgrace. And yet, to bear you I had to look on death. To nurture you I had to wrestle with it. Death fought with me for you. All women have to fight with death to keep their children. Death, being childless, wants our children from us. Gerald, when you were naked I clothed you, when you were hungry I gave you food. Night and day all that long winter I tended you. No office is too mean, no care too lowly for the thing we women love—and oh! how *I* loved *you*. Not Hannah, Samuel more. And you needed love, for you were weakly, and only love could have kept you alive. Only love can keep any one alive. And boys are careless often, and without thinking give pain, and we always fancy that when they come to man's estate and know us better they will repay us. But it is not so. The world draws them from our side, and they make friends with whom they are happier than they are with us, and have amusements from which we are barred, and interests that are not ours; and they are unjust to us often, for when they find life bitter they blame us for it, and when they find it sweet we do not taste its sweetness with them. . . . You made many friends and went into their houses and were glad with them, and I, knowing my secret, did not dare to follow, but stayed at home and closed the door, shut out the sun and sat in darkness. My past was ever with me. . . . And you thought I didn't care for the pleasant things of life. I tell you I longed for them, but did not dare to touch them, feeling I had no right. You thought I was happier working amongst the poor. That was my mission, you imagined. It was not, but where else was I to go? The sick do not ask if the hand that smooths their pillow is pure, nor the dying care if the lips that touch their brow have known the kiss of sin. It was you I thought of all the time; I gave to them the love you did not need; lavished on them a love that was not theirs. . . . And you thought I spent too much of my time in going to Church, and in Church duties. But where else could I turn? God's house is the only house where sinners are made welcome, and you were always in my heart, Gerald, too much in my heart. For, though day after day, at morn or evensong, I have knelt in God's house, I have never repented of my sin. How could I repent of my sin when you, my love, were its fruit. Even now that you are bitter to me I cannot repent. I do not. You are more to me than innocence. I would rather be your mother—oh! much rather!—than have been always pure. . . . Oh, don't you see? don't you understand! It is my dishonour that has made you so dear to me. It is my disgrace that has bound you so closely to me. It is the price I paid for you—the price of soul and body—that makes me love you as I do. Oh, don't ask me to do this horrible thing. Child of my shame, be still the child of my shame!

GERALD: Mother, I didn't know you loved me so much as that. And I will be a better son to you than I have been. And you and I must never leave each other . . . but, mother . . . I can't help it . . . you must become my father's wife. You must marry him. It is your duty.

HESTER (*running forward and embracing* MRS. ARBUTHNOT): No, no; you shall not. That would be real dishonour, the first you have ever known. That would be real disgrace: the first to touch you. Leave him and come with me. There are other countries than England. . . . Oh! other countries over sea, better, wiser, and less unjust lands. The world is very wide and very big.

MRS. ARBUTHNOT: No, not for me. For me the world is shrivelled to a palm's breadth, and where I walk there are thorns.

HESTER: It shall not be so. We shall somewhere find green valleys and fresh waters, and if we weep, well, we shall weep together. Have we not both loved him?

GERALD: Hester!

HESTER (*waving him back*): Don't, don't! You cannot love me at all unless you love her also. You cannot honour me, unless she's holier to you. In her all womanhood is martyred. Not she alone, but all of us are stricken in her house.

GERALD: Hester, Hester, what shall I do?

HESTER: Do you respect the man who is your father?

GERALD: Respect him? I despise him! He is infamous.

HESTER: I thank you for saving me from him last night.

GERALD: Ah, that is nothing. I would die to save you. But you don't tell me what to do now!

HESTER: Have I not thanked you for saving *me*?

GERALD: But what should I do?

HESTER: Ask your own heart, not mine. I never had a mother to save, or shame.

MRS. ARBUTHNOT: He is hard—he is hard. Let me go away.

GERALD (*rushes over and kneels down beside his mother*): Mother, forgive me; I have been to blame.

MRS. ARBUTHNOT: Don't kiss my hands; they are cold. My heart is cold: something has broken it.

HESTER: Ah, don't say that. Hearts live by being wounded. Pleasure may turn a heart to stone, riches may make it callous, but sorrow—oh, sorrow, cannot break it. Besides, what sorrows have you now? Why, at this moment you are more dear to him than ever, *dear* though you have *been*, and oh! how dear you *have* been always. Ah! be kind to him.

GERALD: You are my mother and my father all in one. I need no second parent. It was for you I spoke, for you alone. Oh, say something, mother. Have I but found one love to lose another? Don't tell me that. Oh, mother, you are cruel. (*Gets up and flings himself sobbing on a sofa.*)

MRS. ARBUTHNOT (*to* HESTER): But has he found indeed another love?

HESTER: You know I have loved him always.

MRS. ARBUTHNOT: But we are very poor.

HESTER: Who, being loved, is poor? Oh, no one. I hate my riches. They are a burden. Let him share it with me.

MRS. ARBUTHNOT: But we are disgraced. We rank among the outcasts. Gerald is nameless. The sins of the parents should be visited on the children. It is God's law.

HESTER: I was wrong. God's law is only Love.

MRS. ARBUTHNOT (*rises, and taking* HESTER *by the hand, goes slowly over to where* GERALD *is lying on the sofa with his head buried in his hands. She touches him and he looks up*): Gerald, I cannot give you a father, but I have brought you a wife.

GERALD: Mother, I am not worthy either of her or you.

MRS. ARBUTHNOT: So she comes first, you are worthy. And when you are away, Gerald . . . with . . . her—oh, think of me sometimes. Don't forget me. And when you pray, pray for me. We should pray when we are happiest, and you will be happy, Gerald.

HESTER: Oh, you don't think of leaving us?

GERALD: Mother, you won't leave us?

MRS. ARBUTHNOT: I might bring shame upon you!

GERALD: Mother!

MRS. ARBUTHNOT: For a little then; and if you let me, near you always.

HESTER (*to* MRS. ARBUTHNOT): Come out with us to the garden.

MRS. ARBUTHNOT: Later on, later on.

Exeunt HESTER *and* GERALD.

MRS. ARBUTHNOT *goes towards door L.C. Stops at looking-glass over mantelpiece and looks into it.*

Enter ALICE *R.C.*

ALICE: A gentleman to see you, ma'am.

MRS. ARBUTHNOT: Say I am not at home. Show me the card. (*Takes card from salver and looks at it.*) Say I will not see him.

LORD ILLINGWORTH *enters.* MRS. ARBUTHNOT *sees him in the glass and starts, but does not turn round. Exit* ALICE.

What can you have to say to me to-day, George Harford? You can have nothing to say to me. You must leave this house.

LORD ILLINGWORTH: Rachel, Gerald knows everything about you and me now, so some arrangement must be come to that will suit us all three. I assure you, he will find in me the most charming and generous of fathers.

MRS. ARBUTHNOT: My son may come in at any moment. I saved you last night. I may not be able to save you again. My son feels my dishonour strongly, terribly strongly. I beg you to go.

LORD ILLINGWORTH (*sitting down*): Last night was excessively unfortunate. That silly Puritan girl making a scene merely because I wanted to kiss her. What harm is there in a kiss?

MRS. ARBUTHNOT (*turning round*): A kiss may ruin a human life, George Harford. *I* know that. *I* know that too well.

LORD ILLINGWORTH: We won't discuss that at present. What is of importance to-day, as yesterday, is still our son. I am extremely fond of him, as you know, and odd though it may seem to you, I admired his conduct last night immensely. He took up the cudgels for that pretty prude with wonderful promptitude. He is just what I should have liked a son of mine to be. Except that no son of mine should ever take the side of the Puritans; that is always an error. Now, what I propose is this.

MRS. ARBUTHNOT: Lord Illingworth, no proposition of yours interests me.

LORD ILLINGWORTH: According to our ridiculous English laws, I can't legitimise Gerald. But I can leave him my property. Illingworth is entailed, of course, but it is a tedious barrack of a place. He can have Ashby, which is much prettier, Harborough, which has the best shooting in the north of England, and the house in St. James's Square. What more can a gentleman desire in this world?

MRS. ARBUTHNOT: Nothing more, I am quite sure.

LORD ILLINGWORTH: As for a title, a title is really rather a nuisance in these democratic days. As George Harford I had everything I wanted. Now I have merely everything that other people want, which isn't nearly so pleasant. Well, my proposal is this.

MRS. ARBUTHNOT: I told you I was not interested, and I beg you to go.

LORD ILLINGWORTH: The boy is to be with you for six months in the year, and with me for the other six. That is perfectly fair, is it not? You can have whatever allowance you like, and live where you choose. As for your past, no one knows anything about it except myself and Gerald. There is the Puritan, of course, the Puritan in white muslin, but she doesn't count. She couldn't tell the story without explaining that she objected to being kissed, could she? And all the women would think her a fool and the men think her a bore. And you need not be afraid that Gerald won't be my heir. I needn't tell you I have not the slightest intention of marrying.

MRS. ARBUTHNOT: You come too late. My son has no need of you. You are not necessary.

LORD ILLINGWORTH: What do you mean, Rachel?

MRS. ARBUTHNOT: That you are not necessary to Gerald's career. He does not require you.

LORD ILLINGWORTH: I do not understand you.

MRS. ARBUTHNOT: Look into the garden. (LORD ILLINGWORTH *rises and goes towards window.*) You had better not let them see you; you bring unpleasant memories. (LORD ILLINGWORTH *looks out and starts.*) She loves him. They love each other. We are safe from you, and we are going away.

LORD ILLINGWORTH: Where?

MRS. ARBUTHNOT: We will not tell you, and if you find us we will not know you. You seem surprised. What welcome would you get from the girl whose lips you tried to soil, from the boy whose life you have shamed, from the mother whose dishonour comes from you?

LORD ILLINGWORTH: You have grown hard, Rachel.

MRS. ARBUTHNOT: I was too weak once. It is well for me that I have changed.

LORD ILLINGWORTH: I was very young at the time. We men know life too early.

MRS. ARBUTHNOT: And we women know life too late. That is the difference between men and women. (*A pause.*)

LORD ILLINGWORTH: Rachel, I want my son. My money may be of no use to him now. I may be of no use to him, but I want my son. Bring us together, Rachel. You can do it if you choose. (*Sees letter on table.*)

MRS. ARBUTHNOT: There is no room in my boy's life for *you*. He is not interested in *you*.

LORD ILLINGWORTH: Then why does he write to me?

MRS. ARBUTHNOT: What do you mean?

LORD ILLINGWORTH: What letter is this? (*Takes up letter.*)

MRS. ARBUTHNOT: That—is nothing. Give it to me.

LORD ILLINGWORTH: It is addressed to *me*.

MRS. ARBUTHNOT: You are not to open it. I forbid you to open it.

LORD ILLINGWORTH: And in Gerald's handwriting.

MRS. ARBUTHNOT: It was not to have been sent. It is a letter he wrote to you this morning, before he saw me. But he is sorry now he wrote it, very sorry. You are not to open it. Give it to me.

LORD ILLINGWORTH: It belongs to me. (*Opens it, sits down and reads it slowly.* MRS. ARBUTHNOT *watches him all the time.*) You have read this letter, I suppose, Rachel?

MRS. ARBUTHNOT: No.

LORD ILLINGWORTH: You know what is in it?

MRS. ARBUTHNOT: Yes!

LORD ILLINGWORTH: I don't admit for a moment that the boy is right in what he says. I don't admit that it is any duty of mine to marry you. I deny it entirely. But to get my son back I am ready—yes, I am ready to marry you, Rachel—and to treat you always with the deference and respect due to my wife. I will marry you as soon as you choose. I give you my word of honour.

MRS. ARBUTHNOT: You made that promise to me once before and broke it.

LORD ILLINGWORTH: I will keep it now. And that will show you that I love my son, at least as much as you love him. For when I marry you, Rachel, there are some ambitions I shall have to surrender. High ambitions, too, if any ambition is high.

MRS. ARBUTHNOT: I decline to marry you, Lord Illingworth.

LORD ILLINGWORTH: Are you serious?

MRS. ARBUTHNOT: Yes.

LORD ILLINGWORTH: Do tell me your reasons. They would interest me enormously.

MRS. ARBUTHNOT: I have already explained them to my son.

LORD ILLINGWORTH: I suppose they were intensely sentimental, weren't they? You women live by your emotions and for them. You have no philosophy of life.

MRS. ARBUTHNOT: You are right. We women live by our emotions and for them. By our passions, and for them, if you will. I have two passions, Lord Illingworth: my love of him, my hate of you. You cannot kill those. They feed each other.

LORD ILLINGWORTH: What sort of love is that which needs to have hate as its brother?

MRS. ARBUTHNOT: It is the sort of love I have for Gerald. Do you think that terrible? Well, it is terrible. All love is terrible. All love is a tragedy. I loved you once, Lord Illingworth. Oh, what a tragedy for a woman to have loved you!

LORD ILLINGWORTH: So you really refuse to marry me?

MRS. ARBUTHNOT: Yes.

LORD ILLINGWORTH: Because you hate me?

MRS. ARBUTHNOT: Yes.

LORD ILLINGWORTH: And does my son hate me as you do?

MRS. ARBUTHNOT: No.

LORD ILLINGWORTH: I am glad of that, Rachel.

MRS. ARBUTHNOT: He merely despises you.

LORD ILLINGWORTH: What a pity! What a pity for him, I mean.

MRS. ARBUTHNOT: Don't be deceived, George. Children begin by loving their parents. After a time they judge them. Rarely if ever do they forgive them.*

LORD ILLINGWORTH (*reads letter over again, very slowly*): May I ask by what arguments you made the boy who wrote this letter,

---

*The restatement of this line, this time addressed to Illingworth, embodies high irony.

this beautiful, passionate letter, believe that you should not marry his father, the father of your own child?

MRS. ARBUTHNOT: It was not I who made him see it. It was another.

LORD ILLINGWORTH: What *fin-de-siècle* person?

MRS. ARBUTHNOT: The Puritan, Lord Illingworth. (*A pause.*)

LORD ILLINGWORTH (*winces, then rises slowly and goes over to table where his hat and gloves are.* MRS. ARBUTHNOT *is standing close to the table. He picks up one of the gloves, and begins putting it on*): There is not much then for me to do here, Rachel?

MRS. ARBUTHNOT: Nothing.

LORD ILLINGWORTH: It is good-bye, is it?

MRS. ARBUTHNOT: For ever, I hope, this time, Lord Illingworth.

LORD ILLINGWORTH: How curious! At this moment you look exactly as you looked the night you left me twenty years ago. You have just the same expression in your mouth. Upon my word, Rachel, no woman ever loved me as you did. Why, you gave yourself to me like a flower, to do anything I liked with. You were the prettiest of playthings, the most fascinating of small romances. . . . (*Pulls out watch.*) Quarter to two! Must be strolling back to Hunstanton. Don't suppose I shall see you there again. I'm sorry, I am, really. It's been an amusing experience to have met amongst people of one's own rank, and treated quite seriously too, one's mistress and one's——

MRS. ARBUTHNOT *snatches up glove and strikes* LORD ILLINGWORTH *across the face with it.* LORD ILLINGWORTH *starts. He is dazed by the insult of his punishment. Then he controls himself and goes to window and looks out at his son. Sighs and leaves the room.*

MRS. ARBUTHNOT (*falls sobbing on the sofa*): He would have said it. He would have said it.*

---

*In the nineteenth century, the word "bastard" was considered profanity and could not be spoken onstage.

Enter GERALD *and* HESTER *from the garden.*

GERALD: Well, dear mother. You never came out after all. So we have come in to fetch you. Mother, you have not been crying? (*Kneels down beside her.*)

MRS. ARBUTHNOT: My boy! My boy! My boy! (*Running her fingers through his hair.*)

HESTER (*coming over*): But you have two children now. You'll let me be your daughter?

MRS. ARBUTHNOT (*looking up*): Would you choose me for a mother?

HESTER: You of all women I have ever known.

They move towards the door leading into garden with their arms round each other's waists. GERALD *goes to table L.C. for his hat. On turning round he sees* LORD ILLINGWORTH'S *glove lying on the floor, and picks it up.*

GERALD: Hallo, mother, whose glove is this? You have had a visitor. Who was it?

MRS. ARBUTHNOT (*turning round*): Oh! no one. No one in particular. A man of no importance.*

Curtain

---

*Mrs. Arbuthnot reverses the title line that closes act one. This time, the characters are unaware of the irony, although the audience can savor it.

AN IDEAL HUSBAND

THE PERSONS OF THE PLAY

THE EARL OF CAVERSHAM, K.G.
VISCOUNT GORING, his son
SIR ROBERT CHILTERN, Bart., Under-Secretary for Foreign Affairs
VICOMTE DE NANJAC, Attaché at French Embassy in London
MR. MONTFORD
MASON, Butler to Sir Robert Chiltern
PHIPPS, Lord Goring's servant
JAMES and HAROLD, Footmen
LADY CHILTERN
LADY MARKBY
THE COUNTESS OF BASILDON
MRS. MARCHMONT
MISS MABEL CHILTERN, Sir Robert Chiltern's sister
MRS. CHEVELEY

ACT ONE

SCENE: *The octagon room at Sir Robert Chiltern's house in Grosvenor Square, London. The action of the play is completed within twenty-four hours.* TIME: *The present.*

The room is brilliantly lighted and full of guests.

At the top of the staircase stands LADY CHILTERN, *a woman of grave Greek beauty, about twenty-seven years of age. She receives the guests as they come up. Over the well of the staircase hangs a great chandelier with wax lights, which illumine a large eighteenth-century French tapestry—representing the Triumph of Love, from a design by Boucher—that is stretched on the staircase wall. On the right is the entrance to the music-room. The sound of a string quartette is faintly heard. The entrance on the left leads to other reception-rooms.* MRS. MARCHMONT *and* LADY BASILDON, *two very pretty women, are seated together on a Louis Seize sofa. They are types of exquisite fragility. Their affectation of manner has a delicate charm. Watteau would have loved to paint them.*[1]

MRS. MARCHMONT: Going on to the Hartlocks' to-night, Margaret?

LADY BASILDON: I suppose so. Are you?

MRS. MARCHMONT: Yes. Horribly tedious parties they give, don't they?

LADY BASILDON: Horribly tedious! Never know why I go. Never know why I go anywhere.

MRS. MARCHMONT: I come here to be educated.

LADY BASILDON: Ah! I hate being educated!

MRS. MARCHMONT: So do I. It puts one almost on a level with the commercial classes, doesn't it? But dear Gertrude Chiltern is always telling me that I should have some serious purpose in life. So I come here to try to find one.

LADY BASILDON (*looking round through her lorgnette*): I don't see anybody here to-night whom one could possibly call a serious purpose. The man who took me in to dinner talked to me about his wife the whole time.

MRS. MARCHMONT: How very trivial of him!

LADY BASILDON: Terribly trivial! What did your man talk about?

MRS. MARCHMONT: About myself.

LADY BASILDON (*languidly*): And were you interested?

MRS. MARCHMONT (*shaking her head*): Not in the smallest degree.

LADY BASILDON: What martyrs we are, dear Margaret!

MRS. MARCHMONT (*rising*): And how well it becomes us, Olivia!

They rise and go towards the music-room. The VICOMTE DE NANJAC, *a young attaché known for his neckties and his Anglomania, approaches with a low bow, and enters into conversation.*

MASON (*announcing guests from the top of the staircase*): Mr. and Lady Jane Barford. Lord Caversham.

Enter LORD CAVERSHAM, *an old gentleman of seventy, wearing the riband and star of the Garter. A fine Whig type. Rather like a portrait by Lawrence.*

LORD CAVERSHAM: Good-evening, Lady Chiltern! Has my good-for-nothing young son been here?

LADY CHILTERN (*smiling*): I don't think Lord Goring has arrived yet.

MABEL CHILTERN (*coming up to* LORD CAVERSHAM): Why do you call Lord Goring good-for-nothing?

MABEL CHILTERN *it a perfect example of the English type of prettiness, the apple-blossom type. She has all the fragrance and freedom of a flower. There is ripple after ripple of sunlight in her hair, and the little mouth, with its parted lips, is expectant, like the mouth of a child. She has the fascinating tyranny of youth, and the astonishing courage of innocence. To sane people she is not rem-*

iniscent of any work of art. But she is really like a Tanagra statuette, and would be rather annoyed if she were told so.

LORD CAVERSHAM: Because he leads such an idle life.

MABEL CHILTERN: How can you say such a thing? Why, he rides in the Row at ten o'clock in the morning, goes to the Opera three times a week, changes his clothes at least five times a day, and dines out every night of the season. You don't call that leading an idle life, do you?

LORD CAVERSHAM (*looking at her with a kindly twinkle in his eyes*): You are a very charming young lady!

MABEL CHILTERN: How sweet of you to say that, Lord Caversham! Do come to us more often. You know we are always at home on Wednesdays, and you look so well with your star!

LORD CAVERSHAM: Never go anywhere now. Sick of London Society. Shouldn't mind being introduced to my own tailor; he always votes on the right side. But object strongly to being sent down to dinner with my wife's milliner. Never could stand Lady Caversham's bonnets.

MABEL CHILTERN: Oh, I love London Society! I think it has immensely improved. It is entirely composed now of beautiful idiots and brilliant lunatics. Just what Society should be.

LORD CAVERSHAM: Hum! Which is Goring? Beautiful idiot, or the other thing?

MABEL CHILTERN (*gravely*): I have been obliged for the present to put Lord Goring into a class quite by himself. But he is developing charmingly!

LORD CAVERSHAM: Into what?

MABEL CHILTERN (*with a little curtsey*): I hope to let you know very soon, Lord Caversham!

MASON (*announcing guests*): Lady Markby. Mrs. Cheveley.

Enter LADY MARKBY *and* MRS. CHEVELEY. LADY MARKBY *is a pleasant, kindly, popular woman, with gray hair à la marquise and good lace.* MRS. CHEVELEY, *who accompanies her, is tall and rather slight. Lips very thin and highly-coloured, a line of scarlet on a pallid face. Venetian red hair, aquiline nose, and long throat. Rouge accentuates the natural paleness of her complexion. Gray-green eyes that move restlessly. She is in heliotrope, with dia-*

*monds. She looks rather like an orchid, and makes great demands on one's curiosity. In all her movements she is extremely graceful. A work of art, on the whole, but showing the influence of too many schools.**

LADY MARKBY: Good-evening, dear Gertrude! So kind of you to let me bring my friend, Mrs. Cheveley. Two such charming women should know each other!

LADY CHILTERN (*advances towards* MRS. CHEVELEY *with a sweet smile. Then suddenly stops, and bows rather distantly*): I think Mrs. Cheveley and I have met before. I did not know she had married a second time.

LADY MARKBY (*genially*): Ah, nowadays people marry as often as they can, don't they? It is most fashionable. (*To* DUCHESS OF MARYBOROUGH): Dear Duchess, and how is the Duke? Brain still weak, I suppose? Well, that is only to be expected, is it not? His good father was just the same. There is nothing like race, is there?

MRS. CHEVELEY (*playing with her fan*): But have we really met before, Lady Chiltern? I can't remember where. I have been out of England for so long.

LADY CHILTERN: We were at school together, Mrs. Cheveley.

MRS. CHEVELEY (*superciliously*): Indeed? I have forgotten all about my schooldays. I have a vague impression that they were detestable.

LADY CHILTERN (*coldly*): I am not surprised!

MRS. CHEVELEY (*in her sweetest manner*): Do you know, I am quite looking forward to meeting your clever husband, Lady Chiltern. Since he has been at the Foreign Office, he has been so much talked of in Vienna. They actually succeed in spelling his name right in the newspapers. That in itself is fame, on the continent.

LADY CHILTERN: I hardly think there will be much in common between you and my husband, Mrs. Cheveley! (*Moves away.*)

VICOMTE DE NANJAC: Ah, chère Madame, quelle surprise! I have not seen you since Berlin!

MRS. CHEVELEY: Not since Berlin, Vicomte. Five years ago!

---

*The two ladies are painted with an Aestheticist's eye.

VICOMTE DE NANJAC: And you are younger and more beautiful than ever. How do you manage it?

MRS. CHEVELEY: By making it a rule only to talk to perfectly charming people like yourself.

VICOMTE DE NANJAC: Ah! you flatter me. You butter me, as they say here.

MRS. CHEVELEY: Do they say that here? How dreadful of them!

VICOMTE DE NANJAC: Yes, they have a wonderful language. It should be more widely known.

SIR ROBERT CHILTERN *enters. A man of forty, but looking somewhat younger. Clean-shaven, with finely-cut features, dark-haired and dark-eyed. A personality of mark. Not popular—few personalities are. But intensely admired by the few, and deeply respected by the many. The note of his manner is that of perfect distinction, with a slight touch of pride. One feels that he is conscious of the success he has made in life. A nervous temperament, with a tired look. The firmly-chiselled mouth and chin contrast strikingly with the romantic expression in the deep-set eyes. The variance is suggestive of an almost complete separation of passion and intellect, as though thought and emotion were each isolated in its own sphere through some violence of will-power. There is nervousness in the nostrils, and in the pale, thin, pointed hands. It would be inaccurate to call him picturesque. Picturesqueness cannot survive the House of Commons. But Vandyck would have liked to have painted his head.*[2]

SIR ROBERT CHILTERN: Good-evening, Lady Markby. I hope you have brought Sir John with you?

LADY MARKBY: Oh! I have brought a much more charming person than Sir John. Sir John's temper since he has taken seriously to politics has become quite unbearable. Really, now that the House of Commons is trying to become useful, it does a great deal of harm.

SIR ROBERT CHILTERN: I hope not, Lady Markby. At any rate we do our best to waste the public time, don't we? But who is this charming person you have been kind enough to bring to us?

LADY MARKBY: Her name is Mrs. Cheveley! One of the Dorsetshire Cheveleys, I suppose. But I really don't know. Families are so mixed nowadays. Indeed, as a rule, everybody turns out to be somebody else.

SIR ROBERT CHILTERN: Mrs. Cheveley? I seem to know the name.

LADY MARKBY: She has just arrived from Vienna.

SIR ROBERT CHILTERN: Ah! yes. I think I know whom you mean.

LADY MARKBY: Oh! she goes everywhere there, and has such pleasant scandals about all her friends. I really must go to Vienna next winter. I hope there is a good chef at the Embassy.

SIR ROBERT CHILTERN: If there is not, the Ambassador will certainly have to be recalled. Pray point out Mrs. Cheveley to me. I should like to see her.

LADY MARKBY: Let me introduce you. (*To* MRS. CHEVELEY): My dear, Sir Robert Chiltern is dying to know you!

SIR ROBERT CHILTERN (*bowing*): Every one is dying to know the brilliant Mrs. Cheveley. Our attachés at Vienna write to us about nothing else.

MRS. CHEVELEY: Thank you, Sir Robert. An acquaintance that begins with a compliment is sure to develop into a real friendship. It starts in the right manner. And I find that I know Lady Chiltern already.

SIR ROBERT CHILTERN: Really?

MRS. CHEVELEY: Yes. She has just reminded me that we were at school together. I remember it perfectly now. She always got the good conduct prize. I have a distinct recollection of Lady Chiltern always getting the good conduct prize!

SIR ROBERT CHILTERN (*smiling*): And what prizes did you get, Mrs. Cheveley?

MRS. CHEVELEY: My prizes came a little later on in life. I don't think any of them were for good conduct. I forget!

SIR ROBERT CHILTERN: I am sure they were for something charming!

MRS. CHEVELEY: I don't know that women are always rewarded for being charming. I think they are usually punished for it! Certainly, more women grow old nowadays through the faithfulness of their admirers than through anything else! At least that is the only way I can account for the terribly haggard look of most of your pretty women in London!

SIR ROBERT CHILTERN: What an appalling philosophy that

sounds! To attempt to classify you, Mrs. Cheveley, would be an impertinence. But may I ask, at heart, are you an optimist or a pessimist? Those seem to be the only two fashionable religions left to us nowadays.

MRS. CHEVELEY: Oh, I'm neither. Optimism begins in a broad grin, and Pessimism ends with blue spectacles. Besides, they are both of them merely poses.

SIR ROBERT CHILTERN: You prefer to be natural?

MRS. CHEVELEY: Sometimes. But it is such a very difficult pose to keep up.

SIR ROBERT CHILTERN: What would those modern psychological novelists, of whom we hear so much, say to such a theory as that?

MRS. CHEVELEY: Ah! the strength of women comes from the fact that psychology cannot explain us. Men can be analysed, women . . . merely adored.

SIR ROBERT CHILTERN: You think science cannot grapple with the problem of women?

MRS. CHEVELEY: Science can never grapple with the irrational. That is why it has no future before it, in this world.

SIR ROBERT CHILTERN: And women represent the irrational.

MRS. CHEVELEY: Well-dressed women do.

SIR ROBERT CHILTERN (*with a polite bow*): I fear I could hardly agree with you there. But do sit down. And now tell me, what makes you leave your brilliant Vienna for our gloomy London—or perhaps the question is indiscreet?

MRS. CHEVELEY: Questions are never indiscreet. Answers sometimes are.

SIR ROBERT CHILTERN: Well, at any rate, may I know if it is politics or pleasure?

MRS. CHEVELEY: Politics are my only pleasure. You see, nowadays it is not fashionable to flirt till one is forty, or to be romantic till one is forty-five, so we poor women who are under thirty, or say we are, have nothing open to us but politics or philanthropy. And philanthropy seems to me to have become simply the refuge of people who wish to annoy their fellow-creatures. I prefer politics. I think they are more . . . becoming!

SIR ROBERT CHILTERN: A political life is a noble career!

MRS. CHEVELEY: Sometimes. And sometimes it is a clever game, Sir Robert. And sometimes it is a great nuisance.
SIR ROBERT CHILTERN: Which do you find it?
MRS. CHEVELEY: A combination of all three. (*Drops her fan.*)
SIR ROBERT CHILTERN (*picks up fan*): Allow me!
MRS. CHEVELEY: Thanks.
SIR ROBERT CHILTERN: But you have not told me yet what makes you honour London so suddenly. Our season is almost over.
MRS. CHEVELEY: Oh! I don't care about the London season! It is too matrimonial. People are either hunting for husbands, or hiding from them. I wanted to meet you. It is quite true. You know what a woman's curiosity is. Almost as great as a man's! I wanted immensely to meet you, and . . . to ask you to do something for me.
SIR ROBERT CHILTERN: I hope it is not a little thing, Mrs. Cheveley. I find that little things are so very difficult to do.
MRS. CHEVELEY (*after a moment's reflection*): No, I don't think it is quite a little thing.
SIR ROBERT CHILTERN: I am so glad. Do tell me what it is.
MRS. CHEVELEY: Later on. (*Rises.*) And now may I walk through your beautiful house? I hear your pictures are charming. Poor Baron Arnheim—you remember the Baron?—used to tell me you had some wonderful Corots.*
SIR ROBERT CHILTERN (*with an almost imperceptible start*): Did you know Baron Arnheim well?
MRS. CHEVELEY (*smiling*): Intimately. Did you?
SIR ROBERT CHILTERN: At one time.
MRS. CHEVELEY: Wonderful man, wasn't he?
SIR ROBERT CHILTERN (*after a pause*): He was very remarkable, in many ways.
MRS. CHEVELEY: I often think it such a pity he never wrote his memoirs. They would have been most interesting.
SIR ROBERT CHILTERN: Yes: he knew men and cities well, like the old Greek.†

---

*Mrs. Cheveley is referring to the pioneering French Barbizon School painter Jean Baptiste Camille Corot (1796–1875).

†Chiltern is referring to the classical Greek traveler and writer Herodotus (c.480–c.425 B.C.).

MRS. CHEVELEY: Without the dreadful disadvantage of having a Penelope waiting at home for him.

MASON: Lord Goring.

Enter LORD GORING. *Thirty-four, but always says he is younger. A well-bred, expressionless face. He is clever, but would not like to be thought so. A flawless dandy, he would be annoyed if he were considered romantic. He plays with life, and is on perfectly good terms with the world. He is fond of being misunderstood. It gives him a post of vantage.*

SIR ROBERT CHILTERN: Good-evening, my dear Arthur! Mrs. Cheveley, allow me to introduce to you Lord Goring, the idlest man in London.

MRS. CHEVELEY: I have met Lord Goring before.

LORD GORING (*bowing*): I did not think you would remember me, Mrs. Cheveley.

MRS. CHEVELEY: My memory is under admirable control. And are you still a bachelor?

LORD GORING: I . . . believe so.

MRS. CHEVELEY: How very romantic.

LORD GORING: Oh! I am not at all romantic. I am not old enough. I leave romance to my seniors.

SIR ROBERT CHILTERN: Lord Goring is the result of Boodle's Club,* Mrs. Cheveley.

MRS. CHEVELEY: He reflects every credit on the institution.

LORD GORING: May I ask are you staying in London long?

MRS. CHEVELEY: That depends partly on the weather, partly on the cooking, and partly on Sir Robert.

SIR ROBERT CHILTERN: You are not going to plunge us into a European war, I hope?

MRS. CHEVELEY: There is no danger, at present!

She nods to LORD GORING, *with a look of amusement in her eyes, and goes out with* SIR ROBERT CHILTERN. LORD GORING *saunters over to* MABEL CHILTERN.

---

*Exclusive gentleman's club.

MABEL CHILTERN: You are very late!

LORD GORING: Have you missed me?

MABEL CHILTERN: Awfully!

LORD GORING: Then I am sorry I did not stay away longer. I like being missed.

MABEL CHILTERN: How very selfish of you!

LORD GORING: I am very selfish.

MABEL CHILTERN: You are always telling me of your bad qualities, Lord Goring.

LORD GORING: I have only told you half of them as yet, Miss Mabel!

MABEL CHILTERN: Are the others very bad?

LORD GORING: Quite dreadful! When I think of them at night I go to sleep at once.

MABEL CHILTERN: Well, I delight in your bad qualities. I wouldn't have you part with one of them.

LORD GORING: How very nice of you! But then you are always nice. By the way, I want to ask you a question, Miss Mabel. Who brought Mrs. Cheveley here? That woman in heliotrope, who has just gone out of the room with your brother?

MABEL CHILTERN: Oh, I think Lady Markby brought her. Why do you ask?

LORD GORING: I haven't seen her for years, that is all.

MABEL CHILTERN: What an absurd reason!

LORD GORING: All reasons are absurd.

MABEL CHILTERN: What sort of a woman is she?

LORD GORING: Oh! a genius in the daytime and a beauty at night!

MABEL CHILTERN: I dislike her already.

LORD GORING: That shows your admirable good taste.

VICOMTE DE NANJAC (*approaching*): Ah, the English young lady is the dragon of good taste, is she not? Quite the dragon of good taste.

LORD GORING: So the newspapers are always telling us.

VICOMTE DE NANJAC: I read all your English newspapers. I find them so amusing.

LORD GORING: Then, my dear Nanjac, you must certainly read between the lines.

VICOMTE DE NANJAC: I should like to, but my professor objects. (*To* MABEL CHILTERN): May I have the pleasure of escorting you to the music-room, Mademoiselle?

MABEL CHILTERN (*looking very disappointed*): Delighted, Vicomte, quite delighted! (*Turning to* LORD GORING): Aren't you coming to the music-room?

LORD GORING: Not if there is any music going on, Miss Mabel.

MABEL CHILTERN (*severely*): The music is in German. You would not understand it.

Goes out with the VICOMTE DE NANJAC. LORD CAVERSHAM *comes up to his son.*

LORD CAVERSHAM: Well, sir! what are you doing here? Wasting your life as usual! You should be in bed, sir. You keep too late hours! I heard of you the other night at Lady Rufford's dancing till four o'clock in the morning!

LORD GORING: Only a quarter to four, father.

LORD CAVERSHAM: Can't make out how you stand London Society. The thing has gone to the dogs, a lot of damned nobodies talking about nothing.

LORD GORING: I love talking about nothing, father. It is the only thing I know anything about.

LORD CAVERSHAM: You seem to me to be living entirely for pleasure.

LORD GORING: What else is there to live for, father? Nothing ages like happiness.

LORD CAVERSHAM: You are heartless, sir, very heartless.

LORD GORING: I hope not, father. Good-evening, Lady Basildon!

LADY BASILDON (*arching two pretty eyebrows*): Are you here? I had no idea you ever came to political parties.

LORD GORING: I adore political parties. They are the only place left to us where people don't talk politics.

LADY BASILDON: I delight in talking politics. I talk them all day long. But I can't bear listening to them. I don't know how the unfortunate men in the House stand these long debates.

LORD GORING: By never listening.

LADY BASILDON: Really?

LORD GORING (*in his most serious manner*): Of course. You see, it is a very dangerous thing to listen. If one listens one may be convinced; and a man who allows himself to be convinced by an argument is a thoroughly unreasonable person.

LADY BASILDON: Ah! that accounts for so much in men that I have never understood, and so much in women that their husbands never appreciate in them!

MRS. MARCHMONT (*with a sigh*): Our husbands never appreciate anything in us. We have to go to others for that!

LADY BASILDON (*emphatically*): Yes, always to others, have we not?

LORD GORING (*smiling*): And those are the views of the two ladies who are known to have the most admirable husbands in London.

MRS. MARCHMONT: That is exactly what we can't stand. My Reginald is quite hopelessly faultless. He is really unendurably so, at times! There is not the smallest element of excitement in knowing him.

LORD GORING: How terrible! Really, the thing should be more widely known!

LADY BASILDON: Basildon is quite as bad; he is as domestic as if he was a bachelor.

MRS. MARCHMONT (*pressing* LADY BASILDON'S *hand*): My poor Olivia! We have married perfect husbands, and we are well punished for it.

LORD GORING: I should have thought it was the husbands who were punished.

MRS. MARCHMONT (*drawing herself up*): Oh, dear no! They are as happy as possible! And as for trusting us, it is tragic how much they trust us.

LADY BASILDON: Perfectly tragic!

LORD GORING: Or comic, Lady Basildon?

LADY BASILDON: Certainly not comic, Lord Goring. How unkind of you to suggest such a thing!

MRS. MARCHMONT: I am afraid Lord Goring is in the camp of the enemy, as usual. I saw him talking to that Mrs. Cheveley when he came in.

LORD GORING: Handsome woman, Mrs. Cheveley!

LADY BASILDON (*stiffly*): Please don't praise other women in our presence. You might wait for us to do that!

LORD GORING: I did wait.

MRS. MARCHMONT: Well, we are not going to praise her. I hear she went to the Opera on Monday night, and told Tommy Rufford at supper that, as far as she could see, London Society was entirely made up of dowdies and dandies.

LORD GORING: She is quite right, too. The men are all dowdies and the women are all dandies, aren't they?

MRS. MARCHMONT (*after a pause*): Oh! do you really think that is what Mrs. Cheveley meant?

LORD GORING: Of course. And a very sensible remark for Mrs. Cheveley to make, too.

Enter MABEL CHILTERN. *She joins the group.*

MABEL CHILTERN: Why are you talking about Mrs. Cheveley? Everybody is talking about Mrs. Cheveley! Lord Goring says—what did you say, Lord Goring, about Mrs. Cheveley? Oh! I remember, that she was a genius in the daytime and a beauty at night.

LADY BASILDON: What a horrid combination! So very unnatural!

MRS. MARCHMONT (*in her most dreamy manner*): I like looking at geniuses, and listening to beautiful people!

LORD GORING: Ah! that is morbid of you, Mrs. Marchmont!

MRS. MARCHMONT (*brightening to a look of real pleasure*): I am so glad to hear you say that. Marchmont and I have been married for seven years, and he has never once told me that I was morbid. Men are so painfully unobservant.

LADY BASILDON (*turning to her*): I have always said, dear Margaret, that you were the most morbid person in London.

MRS. MARCHMONT: Ah! but you are always sympathetic, Olivia!

MABEL CHILTERN: Is it morbid to have a desire for food? I have a great desire for food. Lord Goring, will you give me some supper?

LORD GORING: With pleasure, Miss Mabel. (*Moves away with her.*)

MABEL CHILTERN: How horrid you have been! You have never talked to me the whole evening!

LORD GORING: How could I? You went away with the child-diplomatist.

MABEL CHILTERN: You might have followed us. Pursuit would have been only polite. I don't think I like you at all this evening!

LORD GORING: I like you immensely.

MABEL CHILTERN: Well, I wish you'd show it in a more marked way!

They go downstairs.

MRS. MARCHMONT: Olivia, I have a curious feeling of absolute faintness. I think I should like some supper very much. I know I should like some supper.

LADY BASILDON: I am positively dying for supper, Margaret!

MRS. MARCHMONT: Men are so horribly selfish, they never think of these things.

LADY BASILDON: Men are grossly material, grossly material!

The VICOMTE DE NANJAC *enters from the music-room with some other guests. After having carefully examined all the people present, he approaches* LADY BASILDON.

VICOMTE DE NANJAC: May I have the honour of taking you down to supper, Countess?

LADY BASILDON (*coldly*): I never take supper, thank you, Vicomte. (*The* VICOMTE *is about to retire.* LADY BASILDON, *seeing this, rises at once and takes his arm.*) But I will come down with you with pleasure.

VICOMTE DE NANJAC: I am so fond of eating! I am very English in all my tastes.

LADY BASILDON: You look quite English, Vicomte, quite English.

They pass out. MR. MONTFORD, *a perfectly groomed young dandy, approaches* MRS. MARCHMONT.

MR. MONTFORD: Like some supper, Mrs. Marchmont?

MRS. MARCHMONT (*languidly*): Thank you, Mr. Montford, I never touch supper. (*Rises hastily and takes his arm.*) But I will sit beside you, and watch you.

MR. MONTFORD: I don't know that I like being watched when I am eating!

MRS. MARCHMONT: Then I will watch some one else.

MR. MONTFORD: I don't know that I should like that either.

MRS. MARCHMONT (*severely*): Pray, Mr. Montford, do not make these painful scenes of jealousy in public!

They go downstairs with the other guests, passing SIR ROBERT CHILTERN *and* MRS. CHEVELEY, *who now enter.*

SIR ROBERT CHILTERN: And are you going to any of our country houses before you leave England, Mrs. Cheveley?

MRS. CHEVELEY: Oh, no! I can't stand your English house-parties. In England people actually try to be brilliant at breakfast. That is dreadful of them! Only dull people are brilliant at breakfast. And then the family skeleton is always reading family prayers. My stay in England really depends on you, Sir Robert. (*Sits down on the sofa.*)

SIR ROBERT CHILTERN (*taking a seat beside her*): Seriously?

MRS. CHEVELEY: Quite seriously. I want to talk to you about a great political and financial scheme, about this Argentine Canal Company, in fact.

SIR ROBERT CHILTERN: What a tedious, practical subject for you to talk about, Mrs. Cheveley!

MRS. CHEVELEY: Oh, I like tedious, practical subjects. What I don't like are tedious, practical people. There is a wide difference. Besides, you are interested, I know, in International Canal schemes. You were Lord Radley's secretary, weren't you, when the Government bought the Suez Canal shares?

SIR ROBERT CHILTERN: Yes. But the Suez Canal was a very great and splendid undertaking. It gave us our direct route to India. It had imperial value. It was necessary that we should have control. This Argentine scheme is a commonplace Stock Exchange swindle.

MRS. CHEVELEY: A speculation, Sir Robert! A brilliant, daring speculation.

SIR ROBERT CHILTERN: Believe me, Mrs. Cheveley, it is a swindle. Let us call things by their proper names. It makes matters simpler. We have all the information about it at the Foreign Office. In fact, I sent out a special Commission to inquire into the matter privately, and they report that the works are hardly begun, and as for the money already subscribed, no one seems to know what has become of it. The whole thing is a second Panama,* and with not a quarter of the chance of success that miserable affair ever had. I hope you have not invested in it. I am sure you are far too clever to have done that.

MRS. CHEVELEY: I have invested very largely in it.

SIR ROBERT CHILTERN: Who could have advised you to do such a foolish thing?

MRS. CHEVELEY: Your old friend—and mine.

SIR ROBERT CHILTERN: Who?

MRS. CHEVELEY: Baron Arnheim.

SIR ROBERT CHILTERN (*frowning*): Ah! yes. I remember hearing, at the time of his death, that he had been mixed up in the whole affair.

MRS. CHEVELEY: It was his last romance. His last but one, to do him justice.

SIR ROBERT CHILTERN (*rising*): But you have not seen my Corots yet. They are in the music-room. Corots seem to go with music, don't they? May I show them to you?

MRS. CHEVELEY (*shaking her head*): I am not in a mood to-night for silver twilights, or rose-pink dawns. I want to talk business. (*Motions to him with her fan to sit down again beside her.*)

SIR ROBERT CHILTERN: I fear I have no advice to give you, Mrs. Cheveley, except to interest yourself in something less dangerous. The success of the Canal depends, of course, on the attitude of England, and I am going to lay the report of the Commissioners before the House to-morrow night.

---

*There had been several canal schemes, some fraudulent, before the United States dug the Panama Canal.

MRS. CHEVELEY: That you must not do. In your own interests, Sir Robert, to say nothing of mine, you must not do that.

SIR ROBERT CHILTERN (*looking at her in wonder*): In my own interests? My dear Mrs. Cheveley, what do you mean? (*Sits down beside her.*)

MRS. CHEVELEY: Sir Robert, I will be quite frank with you. I want you to withdraw the report that you had intended to lay before the House, on the ground that you have reasons to believe that the Commissioners have been prejudiced or misinformed, or something. Then I want you to say a few words to the effect that the Government is going to reconsider the question, and that you have reason to believe that the Canal, if completed, will be of great international value. You know the sort of things ministers say in cases of this kind. A few ordinary platitudes will do. In modern life nothing produces such an effect as a good platitude. It makes the whole world kin. Will you do that for me?

SIR ROBERT CHILTERN: Mrs. Cheveley, you cannot be serious in making me such a proposition!

MRS. CHEVELEY: I am quite serious.

SIR ROBERT CHILTERN (*coldly*): Pray allow me to believe that you are not.

MRS. CHEVELEY (*speaking with great deliberation and emphasis*): Ah! but I am. And if you do what I ask you, I . . . will pay you very handsomely!

SIR ROBERT CHILTERN: Pay me!

MRS. CHEVELEY: Yes.

SIR ROBERT CHILTERN: I am afraid I don't quite understand what you mean.

MRS. CHEVELEY (*leaning back on the sofa and looking at him*): How very disappointing! And I have come all the way from Vienna in order that you should thoroughly understand me.

SIR ROBERT CHILTERN: I fear I don't.

MRS. CHEVELEY (*in her most nonchalant manner*): My dear Sir Robert, you are a man of the world, and you have your price, I suppose. Everybody has nowadays. The drawback is that most people are so dreadfully expensive. I know I am. I hope you will be more reasonable in your terms.

SIR ROBERT CHILTERN (*rises indignantly*): If you will allow me,

I will call your carriage for you. You have lived so long abroad, Mrs. Cheveley, that you seem to be unable to realise that you are talking to an English gentleman.

MRS. CHEVELEY (*detains him by touching his arm with her fan, and keeping it there while she is talking*): I realise that I am talking to a man who laid the foundation of his fortune by selling to a Stock Exchange speculator a Cabinet secret.

SIR ROBERT CHILTERN (*biting his lip*): What do you mean?

MRS. CHEVELEY (*rising and facing him*): I mean that I know the real origin of your wealth and your career, and I have got your letter, too.

SIR ROBERT CHILTERN: What letter?

MRS. CHEVELEY (*contemptuously*): The letter you wrote to Baron Arnheim, when you were Lord Radley's secretary, telling the Baron to buy Suez Canal shares—a letter written three days before the Government announced its own purchase.

SIR ROBERT CHILTERN (*hoarsely*): It is not true.

MRS. CHEVELEY: You thought that letter had been destroyed. How foolish of you! It is in my possession.

SIR ROBERT CHILTERN: The affair to which you allude was no more than a speculation. The House of Commons had not yet passed the bill; it might have been rejected.

MRS. CHEVELEY: It was a swindle, Sir Robert. Let us call things by their proper names. It makes everything simpler. And now I am going to sell you that letter, and the price I ask for it is your public support of the Argentine scheme. You made your own fortune out of one canal. You must help me and my friends to make our fortunes out of another!

SIR ROBERT CHILTERN: It is infamous, what you propose—infamous!

MRS. CHEVELEY: Oh, no! This is the game of life as we all have to play it, Sir Robert, sooner or later!

SIR ROBERT CHILTERN: I cannot do what you ask me.

MRS CHEVELEY: You mean you cannot help doing it. You know you are standing on the edge of a precipice. And it is not for you to make terms. It is for you to accept them. Supposing you refuse——

SIR ROBERT CHILTERN: What then?

MRS. CHEVELEY: My dear Sir Robert, what then? You are ruined, that is all! Remember to what a point your Puritanism in England has brought you. In old days nobody pretended to be a bit better than his neighbours. In fact, to be a bit better than one's neighbour was considered excessively vulgar and middle-class. Nowadays, with our modern mania for morality, every one has to pose as a paragon of purity, incorruptibility, and all the other seven deadly virtues—and what is the result? You all go over like ninepins—one after the other. Not a year passes in England without somebody disappearing. Scandals used to lend charm, or at least interest, to a man—now they crush him. And yours is a very nasty scandal. You couldn't survive it. If it were known that as a young man, secretary to a great and important minister, you sold a Cabinet secret for a large sum of money, and that was the origin of your wealth and career, you would be hounded out of public life, you would disappear completely. And after all, Sir Robert, why should you sacrifice your entire future rather than deal diplomatically with your enemy? For the moment I am your enemy. I admit it! And I am much stronger than you are. The big battalions are on my side. You have a splendid position, but it is your splendid position that makes you so vulnerable. You can't defend it! And I am in attack. Of course I have not talked morality to you. You must admit in fairness that I have spared you that. Years ago you did a clever, unscrupulous thing; it turned out a great success. You owe to it your fortune and position. And now you have got to pay for it. Sooner or later we have all to pay for what we do. You have to pay now. Before I leave you to-night, you have got to promise me to suppress your report, and to speak in the House in favour of this scheme.

SIR ROBERT CHILTERN: What you ask is impossible.

MRS. CHEVELEY: You must make it possible. You are going to make it possible. Sir Robert, you know what your English newspapers are like. Suppose that when I leave this house I drive down to some newspaper office, and give them this scandal and the proofs of it. Think of their loathsome joy, of the delight they would have in dragging you down, of the mud and mire they would plunge you in. Think of the hypocrite with his greasy smile penning his leading article, and arranging the foulness of the public placard.

SIR ROBERT CHILTERN: Stop! You want me to withdraw the report and to make a short speech stating that I believe there are possibilities in the scheme?

MRS. CHEVELEY (*sitting down on the sofa*): Those are my terms.

SIR ROBERT CHILTERN (*in a low voice*): I will give you any sum of money you want.

MRS. CHEVELEY: Even you are not rich enough, Sir Robert, to buy back your past. No man is.

SIR ROBERT CHILTERN: I will not do what you ask me. I will not.

MRS. CHEVELEY: You have to. If you don't. . . . (*Rises from the sofa.*)

SIR ROBERT CHILTERN (*bewildered and unnerved*): Wait a moment! What did you propose? You said that you would give me back my letter, didn't you?

MRS. CHEVELEY: Yes. That is agreed. I will be in the Ladies' Gallery* to-morrow night at half-past eleven. If by that time—and you will have had heaps of opportunity—you have made an announcement to the House in the terms I wish, I shall hand you back your letter with the prettiest thanks, and the best, or at any rate the most suitable, compliment I can think of. I intend to play quite fairly with you. One should always play fairly . . . when one has the winning cards. The Baron taught me that . . . amongst other things.

SIR ROBERT CHILTERN: You must let me have time to consider your proposal.

MRS. CHEVELEY: No; you must settle now!

SIR ROBERT CHILTERN: Give me a week—three days!

MRS. CHEVELEY: Impossible! I have got to telegraph to Vienna to-night.

SIR ROBERT CHILTERN: My God! what brought you into my life?

MRS. CHEVELEY: Circumstances. (*Moves towards the door.*)

---

*At Parliament women were restricted to a special balcony.

SIR ROBERT CHILTERN: Don't go. I consent. The report shall be withdrawn. I will arrange for a question to be put to me on the subject.

MRS. CHEVELEY: Thank you. I knew we should come to an amicable agreement. I understood your nature from the first. I analysed you, though you did not adore me. And now you can get my carriage for me, Sir Robert. I see the people coming up from supper, and Englishmen always get romantic after a meal, and that bores me dreadfully. (*Exit* SIR ROBERT CHILTERN.)

Enter Guests, LADY CHILTERN, LADY MARKBY, LORD CAVERSHAM, LADY BASILDON, MRS. MARCHMONT, VICOMTE DE NANJAC, MR. MONTFORD.

LADY MARKBY: Well, dear Mrs. Cheveley, I hope you have enjoyed yourself. Sir Robert is very entertaining, is he not?

MRS. CHEVELEY: Most entertaining! I have enjoyed my talk with him immensely.

LADY MARKBY: He has had a very interesting and brilliant career. And he has married a most admirable wife. Lady Chiltern is a woman of the very highest principles, I am glad to say. I am a little too old now, myself, to trouble about setting a good example, but I always admire people who do. And Lady Chiltern has a very ennobling effect on life, though her dinner-parties are rather dull sometimes. But one can't have everything, can one? And now I must go, dear. Shall I call for you to-morrow?

MRS. CHEVELEY: Thanks.

LADY MARKBY: We might drive in the Park at five. Everything looks so fresh in the Park now!

MRS. CHEVELEY: Except the people!

LADY MARKBY: Perhaps the people are a little jaded. I have often observed that the Season as it goes on produces a kind of softening of the brain. However, I think anything is better than high intellectual pressure. That is the most unbecoming thing there is. It makes the noses of the young girls so particularly large. And there is nothing so difficult to marry as a large nose; men don't like them. Good-night, dear! (*To* LADY CHILTERN): Good-night, Gertrude! (*Goes out on* LORD CAVERSHAM'S *arm.*)

MRS. CHEVELEY: What a charming house you have, Lady Chiltern! I have spent a delightful evening. It has been so interesting getting to know your husband.

LADY CHILTERN: Why did you wish to meet my husband, Mrs. Cheveley?

MRS. CHEVELEY: Oh, I will tell you. I wanted to interest him in this Argentine Canal scheme, of which I dare say you have heard. And I found him most susceptible—susceptible to reason, I mean. A rare thing in a man. I converted him in ten minutes. He is going to make a speech in the House to-morrow night in favour of the idea. We must go to the Ladies' Gallery and hear him! It will be a great occasion!

LADY CHILTERN: There must be some mistake. That scheme could never have my husband's support.

MRS. CHEVELEY: Oh, I assure you it's all settled. I don't regret my tedious journey from Vienna now. It has been a great success. But, of course, for the next twenty-four hours the whole thing is a dead secret.

LADY CHILTERN (*gently*): A secret? Between whom?

MRS. CHEVELEY (*with a flash of amusement in her eyes*): Between your husband and myself.

SIR ROBERT CHILTERN (*entering*): Your carriage is here, Mrs. Cheveley!

MRS. CHEVELEY: Thanks! Good-evening, Lady Chiltern! Good-night, Lord Goring! I am at Claridge's.* Don't you think you might leave a card?

LORD GORING: If you wish it, Mrs. Cheveley!

MRS. CHEVELEY: Oh, don't be so solemn about it, or I shall be obliged to leave a card on you. In England I suppose that would hardly be considered *en règle.*† Abroad, we are more civilised. Will you see me down, Sir Robert? Now that we have both the same interests at heart we shall be great friends, I hope!

---

*Fashionable hotel in London, still in operation.

†Correct.

Sails out on SIR ROBERT CHILTERN'S *arm.* LADY CHILTERN *goes to the top of the staircase and looks down at them as they descend. Her expression is troubled. After a little time she is joined by some of the guests, and passes with them into another reception-room.*

MABEL CHILTERN: What a horrid woman!

LORD GORING: You should go to bed, Miss Mabel.

MABEL CHILTERN: Lord Goring!

LORD GORING: My father told me to go to bed an hour ago. I don't see why I shouldn't give you the same advice. I always pass on good advice. It is the only thing to do with it. It is never of any use to oneself.

MABEL CHILTERN: Lord Goring, you are always ordering me out of the room. I think it most courageous of you. Especially as I am not going to bed for hours. (*Goes over to the sofa.*) You can come and sit down if you like, and talk about anything in the world, except the Royal Academy,* Mrs. Cheveley, or novels in Scotch dialect. They are not improving subjects. (*Catches sight of something that is lying on the sofa half-hidden by the cushion.*) What is this? Some one has dropped a diamond brooch! Quite beautiful, isn't it? (*Shows it to him.*) I wish it was mine, but Gertrude won't let me wear anything but pearls, and I am thoroughly sick of pearls. They make one look so plain, so good and so intellectual. I wonder whom the brooch belongs to.

LORD GORING: I wonder who dropped it.

MABEL CHILTERN: It is a beautiful brooch.

LORD GORING: It is a handsome bracelet.

MABEL CHILTERN: It isn't a bracelet. It's a brooch.

LORD GORING: It can be used as a bracelet. (*Takes it from her, and, pulling out a green letter-case, puts the ornament carefully in it, and replaces the whole thing in his breast-pocket with the most perfect sang froid.*†)

MABEL CHILTERN: What are you doing?

---

*The Royal Academy of Arts, which offered painting and sculpture exhibitions (and still does today).

†Literally, "cold blood" in French; the phrase in English denotes self-possession or imperturbability under pressure.

LORD GORING: Miss Mabel, I am going to make a rather strange request to you.

MABEL CHILTERN (*eagerly*): Oh, pray do! I have been waiting for it all the evening.

LORD GORING (*is a little taken aback, but recovers himself*): Don't mention to anybody that I have taken charge of this brooch. Should any one write and claim it, let me know at once.

MABEL CHILTERN: That is a strange request.

LORD GORING: Well, you see I gave this brooch to somebody once, years ago.

MABEL CHILTERN: You did?

LORD GORING: Yes.

LADY CHILTERN *enters alone. The other guests have gone.*

MABEL CHILTERN: Then I shall certainly bid you good-night. Good-night, Gertrude! (*Exit.*)

LADY CHILTERN: Good-night, dear! (*To* LORD GORING): You saw whom Lady Markby brought here to-night?

LORD GORING: Yes. It was an unpleasant surprise. What did she come here for?

LADY CHILTERN: Apparently to try and lure Robert to uphold some fraudulent scheme in which she is interested. The Argentine Canal, in fact.

LORD GORING: She has mistaken her man, hasn't she?

LADY CHILTERN: She is incapable of understanding an upright nature like my husband's!

LORD GORING: Yes. I should fancy she came to grief if she tried to get Robert into her toils. It is extraordinary what astounding mistakes clever women make.

LADY CHILTERN: I don't call women of that kind clever. I call them stupid!

LORD GORING: Same thing often. Good-night, Lady Chiltern!

LADY CHILTERN: Good-night!

Enter SIR ROBERT CHILTERN.

SIR ROBERT CHILTERN: My dear Arthur, you are not going? Do stop a little!

LORD GORING: Afraid I can't, thanks. I have promised to look in at the Hartlocks'. I believe they have got a mauve Hungarian band that plays mauve Hungarian music. See you soon. Good-bye! (*Exit.*)

SIR ROBERT CHILTERN: How beautiful you look to-night, Gertrude!

LADY CHILTERN: Robert, it is not true, is it? You are not going to lend your support to this Argentine speculation? You couldn't!

SIR. ROBERT CHILTERN (*starting*): Who told you I intended to do so?

LADY CHILTERN: That woman who has just gone out, Mrs. Cheveley, as she calls herself now. She seemed to taunt me with it. Robert, I know this woman. You don't. We were at school together. She was untruthful, dishonest, an evil influence on every one whose trust or friendship she could win. I hated, I despised her. She stole things, she was a thief. She was sent away for being a thief. Why do you let her influence you?

SIR ROBERT CHILTERN: Gertrude, what you tell me may be true, but it happened many years ago. It is best forgotten! Mrs. Cheveley may have changed since then. No one should be entirely judged by their past.

LADY CHILTERN (*sadly*): One's past is what one is. It is the only way by which people should be judged.

SIR ROBERT CHILTERN: That is a hard saying, Gertrude!

LADY CHILTERN: It is a true saying, Robert. And what did she mean by boasting that she had got you to lend your support, your name, to a thing I have heard you describe as the most dishonest and fraudulent scheme there has ever been in political life?

SIR ROBERT CHILTERN (*biting his lip*): I was mistaken in the view I took. We all may make mistakes.

LADY CHILTERN: But you told me yesterday that you had received the report from the Commission, and that it entirely condemned the whole thing.

SIR ROBERT CHILTERN (*walking up and down*): I have reasons now to believe that the Commission was prejudiced, or, at any rate, misinformed. Besides, Gertrude, public and private life are different things. They have different laws, and move on different lines.

LADY CHILTERN: They should both represent man at his highest. I see no difference between them.

SIR ROBERT CHILTERN (*stopping*): In the present case, on a matter of practical politics, I have changed my mind. That is all.

LADY CHILTERN: All!

SIR ROBERT CHILTERN (*sternly*): Yes!

LADY CHILTERN: Robert! Oh! it is horrible that I should have to ask you such a question—Robert, are you telling me the whole truth?

SIR ROBERT CHILTERN: Why do you ask me such a question?

LADY CHILTERN (*after a pause*): Why do you not answer it?

SIR ROBERT CHILTERN (*sitting down*): Gertrude, truth is a very complex thing, and politics is a very complex business. There are wheels within wheels. One may be under certain obligations to people that one must pay. Sooner or later in political life one has to compromise. Every one does.

LADY CHILTERN: Compromise? Robert, why do you talk so differently to-night from the way I have always heard you talk? Why are you changed?

SIR ROBERT CHILTERN: I am not changed. But circumstances alter things.

LADY CHILTERN: Circumstances should never alter principles.

SIR ROBERT CHILTERN: But if I told you——

LADY CHILTERN: What?

SIR ROBERT CHILTERN: That it was necessary, vitally necessary?

LADY CHILTERN: It can never be necessary to do what is not honourable. Or if it be necessary, then what is it that I have loved! But it is not, Robert; tell me it is not. Why should it be? What gain would you get? Money? We have no need of that! And money that comes from a tainted source is a degradation. Power? But power is nothing in itself. It is power to do good that is fine—that, and that only. What is it, then? Robert, tell me why you are going to do this dishonourable thing!

SIR ROBERT CHILTERN: Gertrude, you have no right to use

that word. I told you it was a question of rational compromise. It is no more than that.

LADY CHILTERN: Robert, that is all very well for other men, for men who treat life simply as a sordid speculation; but not for you, Robert, not for you. You are different. All your life you have stood apart from others. You have never let the world soil you. To the world, as to myself, you have been an ideal always. Oh! be that ideal still. That great inheritance throw not away—that tower of ivory do not destroy. Robert, men can love what is beneath them—things unworthy, stained, dishonoured. We women worship when we love; and when we lose our worship, we lose everything. Oh! don't kill my love for you, don't kill that!

SIR ROBERT CHILTERN: Gertrude!

LADY CHILTERN: I know that there are men with horrible secrets in their lives—men who have done some shameful thing, and who in some critical moment have to pay for it, by doing some other act of shame—oh! don't tell me you are such as they are! Robert, is there in your life any secret dishonour or disgrace? Tell me, tell me at once, that——

SIR ROBERT CHILTERN: That what?

LADY CHILTERN (*speaking very slowly*): That our lives may drift apart.

SIR ROBERT CHILTERN: Drift apart?

LADY CHILTERN: That they may entirely separate. It would be better for us both.

SIR ROBERT CHILTERN: Gertrude, there is nothing in my past life that you might not know.

LADY CHILTERN: I was sure of it, Robert, I was sure of it. But why did you say those dreadful things, things so unlike your real self? Don't let us ever talk about the subject again. You will write, won't you, to Mrs. Cheveley, and tell her that you cannot support this scandalous scheme of hers? If you have given her any promise you must take it back, that is all!

SIR ROBERT CHILTERN: Must I write and tell her that?

LADY CHILTERN: Surely, Robert! What else is there to do?

SIR ROBERT CHILTERN: I might see her personally. It would be better.

LADY CHILTERN: You must never see her again, Robert. She is

not a woman you should ever speak to. She is not worthy to talk to a man like you. No; you must write to her at once, now, this moment, and let your letter show her that your decision is quite irrevocable!

SIR ROBERT CHILTERN: Write this moment!

LADY CHILTERN: Yes.

SIR ROBERT CHILTERN: But it is so late. It is close on twelve.

LADY CHILTERN: That makes no matter. She must know at once that she has been mistaken in you—and that you are not a man to do anything base or underhand or dishonourable. Write here, Robert. Write that you decline to support this scheme of hers, as you hold it to be a dishonest scheme. Yes—write the word dishonest. She knows what that word means. (SIR ROBERT CHILTERN *sits down and writes a letter. His wife takes it up and reads it.*) Yes; that will do. (*Rings bell.*) And now the envelope. (*He writes the envelope slowly. Enter* MASON.) Have this letter sent at once to Claridge's Hotel. There is no answer. (*Exit* MASON. LADY CHILTERN *kneels down beside her husband and puts her arms around him.*) Robert, love gives one an instinct to things. I feel to-night that I have saved you from something that might have been a danger to you, from something that might have made men honour you less than they do. I don't think you realise sufficiently, Robert, that you have brought into the political life of our time a nobler atmosphere, a finer attitude towards life, a freer air of purer aims and higher ideals—I know it, and for that I love you, Robert.

SIR ROBERT CHILTERN: Oh, love me always, Gertrude, love me always!

LADY CHILTERN: I will love you always, because you will always be worthy of love. We needs must love the highest when we see it! (*Kisses him and rises and goes out.*)

SIR ROBERT CHILTERN *walks up and down for a moment; then sits down and buries his face in his hands. The Servant enters and begins putting out the lights.* SIR ROBERT CHILTERN *looks up.*

SIR ROBERT CHILTERN: Put out the lights, Mason, put out the lights!*

The Servant puts out the lights. The room becomes almost dark. The only light there is comes from the great chandelier that hangs over the staircase and illumines the tapestry of the Triumph of Love.

Act Drop

*Chiltern's final lines in act one echo Othello's words to Desdemona in Shakespeare's *Othello* (act 5, scene 2).

ACT TWO

SCENE: *Morning-room at Sir Robert Chiltern's house.*

LORD GORING, *dressed in the height of fashion, is lounging in an armchair.* SIR ROBERT CHILTERN *is standing in front of the fireplace. He is evidently in a state of great mental excitement and distress. As the scene progresses he paces nervously up and down the room.*

LORD GORING: My dear Robert, it's a very awkward business, very awkward indeed. You should have told your wife the whole thing. Secrets from other people's wives are a necessary luxury in modern life. So, at least, I am always told at the club by people who are bald enough to know better. But no man should have a secret from his own wife. She invariably finds it out. Women have a wonderful instinct about things. They can discover everything except the obvious.

SIR ROBERT CHILTERN: Arthur, I couldn't tell my wife. When could I have told her? Not last night. It would have made a life-long separation between us, and I would have lost the love of the one woman in the world I worship, of the only woman who had ever stirred love within me. Last night it would have been quite impossible. She would have turned from me in horror . . . in horror and in contempt.

LORD GORING: Is Lady Chiltern as perfect as all that?

SIR ROBERT CHILTERN: Yes; my wife is as perfect as all that.

LORD GORING (*taking off his left-hand glove*): What a pity! I beg your pardon, my dear fellow, I didn't quite mean that. But if what you tell me is true, I should like to have a serious talk about life with Lady Chiltern.

SIR ROBERT CHILTERN: It would be quite useless.

LORD GORING: May I try?

SIR ROBERT CHILTERN: Yes; but nothing could make her alter her views.

LORD GORING: Well, at the worst it would simply be a psychological experiment.

SIR ROBERT CHILTERN: All such experiments are terribly dangerous.

LORD GORING: Everything is dangerous, my dear fellow. If it wasn't so, life wouldn't be worth living. . . . Well, I am bound to say that I think you should have told her years ago.

SIR ROBERT CHILTERN: When? When we were engaged? Do you think she would have married me if she had known that the origin of my fortune is such as it is, the basis of my career such as it is, and that I had done a thing that I suppose most men would call shameful and dishonourable?

LORD GORING (*slowly*): Yes; most men would call it ugly names. There is no doubt of that.

SIR ROBERT CHILTERN (*bitterly*): Men who every day do something of the same kind themselves. Men who, each one of them, have worse secrets in their own lives.

LORD GORING: That is the reason they are so pleased to find out other people's secrets. It distracts public attention from their own.

SIR ROBERT CHILTERN: And, after all, whom did I wrong by what I did? No one.

LORD GORING (*looking at him steadily*): Except yourself, Robert.

SIR ROBERT CHILTERN (*after a pause*): Of course I had private information about a certain transaction contemplated by the Government of the day, and I acted on it. Private information is practically the source of every large modern fortune.

LORD GORING (*tapping his boot with his cane*): And public scandal invariably the result.

SIR ROBERT CHILTERN (*pacing up and down the room*): Arthur, do you think that what I did nearly eighteen years ago should be brought up against me now? Do you think it fair that a man's whole career should be ruined for a fault done in one's boyhood almost? I was twenty-two at the time, and I had the double misfortune of being well-born and poor, two unforgivable things nowadays. Is it fair that the folly, the sin of one's youth, if men choose to call it a sin, should wreck a life like mine, should place me in the pillory, should shatter all that I have worked for, all that I have built up? Is it fair, Arthur?

LORD GORING: Life is never fair, Robert. And perhaps it is a good thing for most of us that it is not.

SIR ROBERT CHILTERN: Every man of ambition has to fight his century with its own weapons. What this century worships is wealth. The God of this century is wealth. To succeed one must have wealth. At all costs one must have wealth.

LORD GORING: You underrate yourself, Robert. Believe me, without your wealth you could have succeeded just as well.

SIR ROBERT CHILTERN: When I was old, perhaps. When I had lost my passion for power, or could not use it. When I was tired, worn out, disappointed. I wanted my success when I was young. Youth is the time for success. I couldn't wait.

LORD GORING: Well, you certainly have had your success while you are still young. No one in our day has had such a brilliant success. Under-Secretary for Foreign Affairs at the age of forty—that's good enough for any one, I should think.

SIR ROBERT CHILTERN: And if it is all taken away from me now? If I lose everything over a horrible scandal? If I am hounded from public life?

LORD GORING: Robert, how could you have sold yourself for money?

SIR ROBERT CHILTERN (*excitedly*): I did not sell myself for money. I bought success at a great price. That is all.

LORD GORING (*gravely*): Yes; you certainly paid a great price for it. But what first made you think of doing such a thing?

SIR ROBERT CHILTERN: Baron Arnheim.

LORD GORING: Damned scoundrel!

SIR ROBERT CHILTERN: No; he was a man of a most subtle and refined intellect. A man of culture, charm, and distinction. One of the most intellectual men I ever met.

LORD GORING: Ah! I prefer a gentlemanly fool any day. There is more to be said for stupidity than people imagine. Personally, I have a great admiration for stupidity. It is a sort of fellow-feeling, I suppose. But how did he do it? Tell me the whole thing.

SIR ROBERT CHILTERN (*throws himself into an arm-chair by the writing-table*): One night after dinner at Lord Radley's the Baron began talking about success in modern life as something that one could reduce to an absolutely definite science. With that wonderfully fascinating quiet voice of his he expounded to us the most terrible of all philosophies, the philosophy of power, preached to us the most marvellous of all gospels, the gospel of gold. I think he saw the effect he had produced on me, for some days afterwards he wrote and asked me to come and see him. He was living then in Park Lane,* in the house Lord Woolcomb has now. I remember so well how, with a strange smile on his pale, curved lips, he led me through his wonderful picture gallery, showed me his tapestries, his enamels, his jewels, his carved ivories, made me wonder at the strange loveliness of the luxury in which he lived; and then told me that luxury was nothing but a background, a painted scene in a play, and that power, power over other men, power over the world, was the one thing worth having, the one supreme pleasure worth knowing, the one joy one never tired of, and that in our century only the rich possessed it.

LORD GORING (*with great deliberation*): A thoroughly shallow creed.

SIR ROBERT CHILTERN (*rising*): I didn't think so then. I don't think so now. Wealth has given me enormous power. It gave me at the very outset of my life freedom, and freedom is everything. You have never been poor, and never known what ambition is. You cannot understand what a wonderful chance the Baron gave me. Such a chance as few men get.

LORD GORING: Fortunately for them, if one is to judge by results. But tell me definitely, how did the Baron finally persuade you to—well, to do what you did?

SIR ROBERT CHILTERN: When I was going away he said to me that if I ever could give him any private information of real value he would make me a very rich man. I was dazed at the prospect he held out to me, and my ambition and my desire for power were at that time boundless. Six weeks later certain private documents passed through my hands.

LORD GORING (*keeping his eyes steadily fixed on the carpet*): State documents?

---

*Posh street adjacent to Hyde Park.

SIR ROBERT CHILTERN: Yes.

LORD GORING *sighs, then passes his hand across his forehead and looks up.*

LORD GORING: I had no idea that you, of all men in the world, could have been so weak, Robert, as to yield to such a temptation as Baron Arnheim held out to you.

SIR ROBERT CHILTERN: Weak? Oh, I am sick of hearing that phrase. Sick of using it about others. Weak! Do you really think, Arthur, that it is weakness that yields to temptation? I tell you that there are terrible temptations that it requires strength, strength and courage, to yield to. To stake all one's life on a single moment, to risk everything on one throw, whether the stake be power or pleasure, I care not—there is no weakness in that. There is a horrible, a terrible courage. I had that courage. I sat down the same afternoon and wrote Baron Arnheim the letter this woman now holds. He made three-quarters of a million over the transaction.

LORD GORING: And you?

SIR ROBERT CHILTERN: I received from the Baron £110,000.*

LORD GORING: You were worth more, Robert.

SIR ROBERT CHILTERN: No; that money gave me exactly what I wanted, power over others. I went into the House immediately. The Baron advised me in finance from time to time. Before five years I had almost trebled my fortune. Since then everything that I have touched has turned out a success. In all things connected with money I have had a luck so extraordinary that sometimes it has made me almost afraid. I remember having read somewhere, in some strange book, that when the gods wish to punish us they answer our prayers.

LORD GORING: But tell me, Robert, did you never suffer any regret for what you had done?

SIR ROBERT CHILTERN: No. I felt that I had fought the century with its own weapons, and won.

LORD GORING (*sadly*): You thought you had won.

---

*More than a half-million dollars in American money—a substantial fortune at the time.

SIR ROBERT CHILTERN: I thought so. (*After a long pause*): Arthur, do you despise me for what I have told you?

LORD GORING (*with deep feeling in his voice*): I am very sorry for you, Robert, very sorry indeed.

SIR ROBERT CHILTERN: I don't say that I suffered any remorse. I didn't. Not remorse in the ordinary, rather silly sense of the word. But I have paid conscience money many times. I had a wild hope that I might disarm destiny. The sum Baron Arnheim gave me I have distributed twice over in public charities since then.

LORD GORING (*looking up*): In public charities? Dear me! what a lot of harm you must have done, Robert!

SIR ROBERT CHILTERN: Oh, don't say that, Arthur; don't talk like that!

LORD GORING: Never mind what I say, Robert! I am always saying what I shouldn't say. In fact, I usually say what I really think. A great mistake nowadays. It makes one so liable to be understood. As regards this dreadful business, I will help you in whatever way I can. Of course you know that.

SIR ROBERT CHILTERN: Thank you, Arthur, thank you. But what is to be done? What can be done?

LORD GORING (*leaning back with his hands in his pockets*): Well, the English can't stand a man who is always saying he is in the right, but they are very fond of a man who admits that he has been in the wrong. It is one of the best things in them. However, in your case, Robert, a confession would not do. The money, if you will allow me to say so, is . . . awkward. Besides, if you did make a clean breast of the whole affair, you would never be able to talk morality again. And in England a man who can't talk morality twice a week to a large, popular, immoral audience is quite over as a serious politician. There would be nothing left for him as a profession except Botany or the Church. A confession would be of no use. It would ruin you.

SIR ROBERT CHILTERN: It would ruin me. Arthur, the only thing for me to do now is to fight the thing out.

LORD GORING (*rising from his chair*): I was waiting for you to say that, Robert. It is the only thing to do now. And you must begin by telling your wife the whole story.

SIR ROBERT CHILTERN: That I will not do.

LORD GORING: Robert, believe me, you are wrong.

SIR ROBERT CHILTERN: I couldn't do it. It would kill her love for me. And now about this woman, this Mrs. Cheveley. How can I defend myself against her? You knew her before, Arthur, apparently.

LORD GORING: Yes.

SIR ROBERT CHILTERN: Did you know her well?

LORD GORING (*arranging his necktie*): So little that I got engaged to be married to her once, when I was staying at the Tenbys'. The affair lasted for three days . . . nearly.

SIR ROBERT CHILTERN: Why was it broken off?

LORD GORING (*airily*): Oh, I forget. At least, it makes no matter. By the way, have you tried her with money? She used to be confoundedly fond of money.

SIR ROBERT CHILTERN: I offered her any sum she wanted. She refused.

LORD GORING: Then the marvellous gospel of gold breaks down sometimes. The rich can't do everything, after all.

SIR ROBERT CHILTERN: Not everything. I suppose you are right. Arthur, I feel that public disgrace is in store for me. I feel certain of it. I never knew what terror was before. I know it now. It is as if a hand of ice were laid upon one's heart. It is as if one's heart were beating itself to death in some empty hollow.

LORD GORING (*striking the table*): Robert, you must fight her. You must fight her.

SIR ROBERT CHILTERN: But how?

LORD GORING: I can't tell you how at present. I have not the smallest idea. But every one has some weak point. There is some flaw in each one of us. (*Strolls over to the fireplace and looks at himself in the glass.*) My father tells me that even I have faults. Perhaps I have. I don't know.

SIR ROBERT CHILTERN: In defending myself against Mrs. Cheveley I have a right to use any weapon I can find, have I not?

LORD GORING (*still looking in the glass*): In your place I don't think I should have the smallest scruple in doing so. She is thoroughly well able to take care of herself.

SIR ROBERT CHILTERN (*sits down at the table and takes a pen in his hand*): Well, I shall send a cipher telegram to the Embassy at Vienna, to inquire if there is anything known against her. There may be some secret scandal she might be afraid of.

LORD GORING (*settling his buttonhole*): Oh, I should fancy Mrs. Cheveley is one of those very modern women of our time who find a new scandal as becoming as a new bonnet, and air them both in the Park every afternoon at five-thirty. I am sure she adores scandals, and that the sorrow of her life at present is that she can't manage to have enough of them.

SIR ROBERT CHILTERN (*writing*): Why do you say that?

LORD GORING (*turning round*): Well, she wore far too much rouge last night, and not quite enough clothes. That is always a sign of despair in a woman.

SIR ROBERT CHILTERN (*striking a bell*): But it is worth while my wiring to Vienna, is it not?

LORD GORING: It is always worth while asking a question, though it is not always worth while answering one.

Enter MASON.

SIR ROBERT CHILTERN: Is Mr. Trafford in his room?

MASON: Yes, Sir Robert.

SIR ROBERT CHILTERN (*puts what he has written into an envelope, which he then carefully closes*): Tell him to have this sent off in cipher at once. There must not be a moment's delay.

MASON: Yes, Sir Robert.

SIR ROBERT CHILTERN: Oh! just give that back to me again.

Writes something on the envelope. MASON *then goes out with the letter.*

SIR ROBERT CHILTERN: She must have had some curious hold over Baron Arnheim. I wonder what it was.

LORD GORING (*smiling*): I wonder.

SIR ROBERT CHILTERN: I will fight her to the death, as long as my wife knows nothing.

LORD GORING (*strongly*): Oh, fight in any case—in any case.

SIR ROBERT CHILTERN (*with a gesture of despair*): If my wife found out, there would be little left to fight for. Well, as soon as I hear from Vienna, I shall let you know the result. It is a chance, just a chance, but I believe in it. And as I fought the age with its own weapons, I will fight her with her weapons. It is only fair, and she looks like a woman with a past, doesn't she?

LORD GORING: Most pretty women do. But there is a fashion in pasts just as there is a fashion in frocks. Perhaps Mrs. Cheveley's past is merely a slightly *décolleté** one, and they are excessively popular nowadays. Besides, my dear Robert, I should not build too high hopes on frightening Mrs. Cheveley. I should not fancy Mrs. Cheveley is a woman who would be easily frightened. She has survived all her creditors, and she shows wonderful presence of mind.

SIR ROBERT CHILTERN: Oh! I live on hopes now. I clutch at every chance. I feel like a man on a ship that is sinking. The water is round my feet, and the very air is bitter with storm. Hush! I hear my wife's voice.

Enter LADY CHILTERN *in walking dress.*

LADY CHILTERN: Good-afternoon, Lord Goring.

LORD GORING: Good-afternoon, Lady Chiltern! Have you been in the Park?

LADY CHILTERN: No; I have just come from the Woman's Liberal Association, where, by the way, Robert, your name was received with loud applause, and now I have come in to have my tea. (*To* LORD GORING): You will wait and have some tea, won't you?

LORD GORING: I'll wait for a short time, thanks.

LADY CHILTERN: I will be back in a moment. I am only going to take my hat off.

LORD GORING (*in his most earnest manner*): Oh! please don't. It is so pretty. One of the prettiest hats I ever saw. I hope the Woman's Liberal Association received it with loud applause.

LADY CHILTERN (*with a smile*): We have much more important work to do than look at each other's bonnets, Lord Goring.

LORD GORING: Really? What sort of work?

---

*In using a term that usually refers to a low-cut woman's dress, Goring implies that Mrs. Cheveley's career has been somewhat risqué.

LADY CHILTERN: Oh! dull, useful, delightful things, Factory Acts, Female Inspectors, the Eight Hours' Bill, the Parliamentary Franchise. . . . Everything, in fact, that you would find thoroughly uninteresting.

LORD GORING: And never bonnets?

LADY CHILTERN (*with mock indignation*): Never bonnets, never!

LADY CHILTERN *goes out through the door leading to her boudoir.*

SIR ROBERT CHILTERN (*takes* LORD GORING'S *hand*): You have been a good friend to me, Arthur, a thoroughly good friend.

LORD GORING: I don't know that I have been able to do much for you, Robert, as yet. In fact, I have not been able to do anything for you, as far as I can see. I am thoroughly disappointed with myself.

SIR ROBERT CHILTERN: You have enabled me to tell you the truth. That is something. The truth has always stifled me.

LORD GORING: Ah! the truth is a thing I get rid of as soon as possible! Bad habit, by the way. Makes one very unpopular at the club . . . with the older members. They call it being conceited. Perhaps it is.

SIR ROBERT CHILTERN: I would to God that I had been able to tell the truth . . . to live the truth. Ah! that is the great thing in life, to live the truth. (*Sighs, and goes towards the door.*) I'll see you soon again, Arthur, shan't I?

LORD GORING: Certainly. Whenever you like. I'm going to look in at the Bachelors' Ball to-night, unless I find something better to do. But I'll come round to-morrow morning. If you should want me to-night by any chance, send round a note to Curzon Street.

SIR ROBERT CHILTERN: Thank you.

As he reaches the door, LADY CHILTERN *enters from her boudoir.*

LADY CHILTERN: You are not going, Robert?

SIR ROBERT CHILTERN: I have some letters to write, dear.

LADY CHILTERN (*going to him*): You work too hard, Robert. You seem never to think of yourself; and you are looking so tired.

SIR ROBERT CHILTERN: It is nothing, dear, nothing. (*He kisses her and goes out.*)

LADY CHILTERN (*to* LORD GORING): Do sit down. I am so glad you have called. I want to talk to you about . . . well, not about bonnets, or the Woman's Liberal Association. You take far too much interest in the first subject, and not nearly enough in the second.

LORD GORING: You want to talk to me about Mrs. Cheveley?

LADY CHILTERN: Yes. You have guessed it. After you left last night I found out that what she had said was really true. Of course I made Robert write her a letter at once, withdrawing his promise.

LORD GORING: So he gave me to understand.

LADY CHILTERN: To have kept it would have been the first stain on a career that has been stainless always. Robert must be above reproach. He is not like other men. He cannot afford to do what other men do. (*She looks at* LORD GORING, *who remains silent.*) Don't you agree with me? You are Robert's greatest friend. You are our greatest friend, Lord Goring. No one, except myself, knows Robert better than you do. He has no secrets from me, and I don't think he has any from you.

LORD GORING: He certainly has no secrets from me. At least I don't think so.

LADY CHILTERN: Then am I not right in my estimate of him? I know I am right. But speak to me frankly.

LORD GORING (*looking straight at her*): Quite frankly?

LADY CHILTERN: Surely. You have nothing to conceal, have you?

LORD GORING: Nothing. But, my dear Lady Chiltern, I think, if you will allow me to say so, that in practical life——

LADY CHILTERN (*smiling*): Of which you know so little, Lord Goring——

LORD GORING: Of which I know nothing by experience, though I know something by observation. I think that in practical life there is something about success, actual success, that is a little unscrupulous, something about ambition that is unscrupulous always. Once a man has set his heart and soul on getting to a certain point, if he has to climb the crag, he climbs the crag; if he has to walk in the mire——

LADY CHILTERN: Well?

LORD GORING: He walks in the mire. Of course I am only talking generally about life.

LADY CHILTERN (*gravely*): I hope so. Why do you look at me so strangely, Lord Goring?

LORD GORING: Lady Chiltern, I have sometimes thought that . . . perhaps you are a little hard in some of your views on life. I think that . . . often you don't make sufficient allowances. In every nature there are elements of weakness, or worse than weakness. Supposing, for instance, that—that any public man, my father, or Lord Merton, or Robert, say, had, years ago, written some foolish letter to some one. . . .

LADY CHILTERN: What do you mean by a foolish letter?

LORD GORING: A letter gravely compromising one's position. I am only putting an imaginary case.

LADY CHILTERN: Robert is as incapable of doing a foolish thing as he is of doing a wrong thing.

LORD GORING (*after a long pause*): Nobody is incapable of doing a foolish thing. Nobody is incapable of doing a wrong thing.

LADY CHILTERN: Are you a Pessimist? What will the other dandies say? They will all have to go into mourning.

LORD GORING (*rising*): No, Lady Chiltern, I am not a Pessimist. Indeed I am not sure that I quite know what pessimism really means. All I do know is that life cannot be understood without much charity, cannot be lived without much charity. It is love, and not German philosophy, that is the true explanation of this world, whatever may be the explanation of the next. And if you are ever in trouble, Lady Chiltern, trust me absolutely, and I will help you in every way I can. If you ever want me, come to me for my assistance, and you shall have it. Come at once to me.

LADY CHILTERN (*looking at him in surprise*): Lord Goring, you are talking quite seriously. I don't think I ever heard you talk seriously before.

LORD GORING (*laughing*): You must excuse me, Lady Chiltern. It won't occur again, if I can help it.

LADY CHILTERN: But I like you to be serious.

Enter MABEL CHILTERN, *in the most ravishing frock.*

MABEL CHILTERN: Dear Gertrude, don't say such a dreadful thing to Lord Goring. Seriousness would be very unbecoming to him. Good-afternoon, Lord Goring! Pray be as trivial as you can.

LORD GORING: I should like to, Miss Mabel, but I am afraid I am . . . a little out of practice this morning; and besides, I have to be going now.

MABEL CHILTERN: Just when I have come in! What dreadful manners you have! I am sure you were very badly brought up.*

LORD GORING: I was.

MABEL CHILTERN: I wish I had brought you up!

LORD GORING: I am so sorry you didn't.

MABEL CHILTERN: It is too late now, I suppose?

LORD GORING (*smiling*): I am not so sure.

MABEL CHILTERN: Will you ride to-morrow morning?

LORD GORING: Yes, at ten.

MABEL CHILTERN: Don't forget.

LORD GORING: Of course I shan't. By the way, Lady Chiltern, there is no list of your guests in *The Morning Post* of to-day. It has apparently been crowded out by the County Council, or the Lambeth Conference, or something equally boring. Could you let me have a list? I have a particular reason for asking you.

LADY CHILTERN: I am sure Mr. Trafford will be able to give you one.

LORD GORING: Thanks, so much.

MABEL CHILTERN: Tommy is the most useful person in London.

LORD GORING (*turning to her*): And who is the most ornamental?

MABEL CHILTERN (*triumphantly*): I am.

LORD GORING: How clever of you to guess it! (*Takes up his hat and cane.*) Good-bye, Lady Chiltern! You will remember what I said to you, won't you?

LADY CHILTERN: Yes; but I don't know why you said it to me.

LORD GORING: I hardly know myself. Good-bye, Miss Mabel!

MABEL CHILTERN (*with a little moue of disappointment*): I wish you were not going. I have had four wonderful adventures this morn-

---

*In French these words (*mal élevé*) constitute the ultimate insult; Mabel is referring to Goring's bad manners rather than his upbringing.

ing; four and a half, in fact. You might stop and listen to some of them.

LORD GORING: How very selfish of you to have four and a half! There won't be any left for me.

MABEL CHILTERN: I don't want you to have any. They would not be good for you.

LORD GORING: That is the first unkind thing you have ever said to me. How charmingly you said it! Ten to-morrow.

MABEL CHILTERN: Sharp.

LORD GORING: Quite sharp. But don't bring Mr. Trafford.

MABEL CHILTERN (*with a little toss of her head*): Of course I shan't bring Tommy Trafford. Tommy Trafford is in great disgrace.

LORD GORING: I am delighted to hear it. (*Bows and goes out.*)

MABEL CHILTERN: Gertrude, I wish you would speak to Tommy Trafford.

LADY CHILTERN: What has poor Mr. Trafford done this time? Robert says he is the best secretary he has ever had.

MABEL CHILTERN: Well, Tommy has proposed to me again. Tommy really does nothing but propose to me. He proposed to me last night in the music-room, when I was quite unprotected, as there was an elaborate trio going on. I didn't dare to make the smallest repartee, I need hardly tell you. If I had, it would have stopped the music at once. Musical people are so absurdly unreasonable. They always want one to be perfectly dumb at the very moment when one is longing to be absolutely deaf. Then he proposed to me in broad daylight this morning, in front of that dreadful statue of Achilles. Really, the things that go on in front of that work of art are quite appalling. The police should interfere. At luncheon I saw by the glare in his eye that he was going to propose again, and I just managed to check him in time by assuring him that I was a bimetallist. Fortunately I don't know what bimetallism means. And I don't believe anybody else does either. But the observation crushed Tommy for ten minutes. He looked quite shocked. And then Tommy is so annoying in the way he proposes. If he proposed at the top of his voice, I should not mind so much. That might produce some effect on the public. But he does it in a horrid confidential way. When Tommy wants to be romantic he talks to one just like a doctor. I am very fond of Tommy, but his methods of proposing are quite out of date. I wish, Gertrude, you would speak to him, and tell him that once a week is quite often enough to propose to any one, and that it should always be done in a manner that attracts some attention.

LADY CHILTERN: Dear Mabel, don't talk like that. Besides, Robert thinks very highly of Mr. Trafford. He believes he has a brilliant future before him.

MABEL CHILTERN: Oh! I wouldn't marry a man with a future before him for anything under the sun.

LADY CHILTERN: Mabel!

MABEL CHILTERN: I know, dear. You married a man with a future, didn't you! But then Robert was a genius, and you have a noble, self-sacrificing character. You can stand geniuses. I have no character at all, and Robert is the only genius I could ever bear. As a rule, I think they are quite impossible. Geniuses talk so much, don't they? Such a bad habit! And they are always thinking about themselves, when I want them to be thinking about me. I must go round now and rehearse at Lady Basildon's. You remember, we are having tableaux, don't you? The Triumph of something, I don't know what! I hope it will be triumph of me. Only triumph I am really interested in at present. (*Kisses* LADY CHILTERN *and goes out; then comes running back*). Oh, Gertrude, do you know who is coming to see you? That dreadful Mrs. Cheveley, in a most lovely gown. Did you ask her?

LADY CHILTERN (*rising*): Mrs. Cheveley! Coming to see me? Impossible!

MABEL CHILTERN: I assure you she is coming upstairs, as large as life and not nearly so natural.

LADY CHILTERN: You need not wait, Mabel. Remember, Lady Basildon is expecting you.

MABEL CHILTERN: Oh! I must shake hands with Lady Markby. She is delightful. I love being scolded by her.

Enter MASON.

MASON: Lady Markby. Mrs. Cheveley.

Enter LADY MARKBY *and* MRS. CHEVELEY.

LADY CHILTERN (*advancing to meet them*): Dear Lady Markby, how nice of you to come and see me! (*Shakes hands with her, and bows somewhat distantly to* MRS. CHEVELEY.) Won't you sit down, Mrs. Cheveley?

MRS. CHEVELEY: Thanks. Isn't that Miss Chiltern? I should like so much to know her.

LADY CHILTERN: Mabel, Mrs. Cheveley wishes to know you. (MABEL CHILTERN *gives a little nod.*)

MRS. CHEVELEY (*sitting down*): I thought your frock so charming, last night, Miss Chiltern. So simple and . . . suitable.

MABEL CHILTERN: Really? I must tell my dressmaker. It will be such a surprise to her. Good-bye, Lady Markby!

LADY MARKBY: Going already?

MABEL CHILTERN: I am so sorry but I am obliged to. I am just off to rehearsal. I have got to stand on my head in some tableaux.

LADY MARKBY: On your head, child? Oh! I hope not. I believe it is most unhealthy. (*Takes a seat on the sofa next to* LADY CHILTERN.)

MABEL CHILTERN: But it is for an excellent charity; in aid of the Undeserving, the only people I am really interested in. I am the secretary, and Tommy Trafford is treasurer.

MRS. CHEVELEY: And what is Lord Goring?

MABEL CHILTERN: Oh! Lord Goring is president.

MRS. CHEVELEY: The post should suit him admirably, unless he has deteriorated since I knew him first.

LADY MARKBY (*reflecting*): You are remarkably modern, Mabel. A little too modern, perhaps. Nothing is so dangerous as being too modern. One is apt to grow old-fashioned quite suddenly. I have known many instances of it.

MABEL CHILTERN: What a dreadful prospect!

LADY MARKBY: Ah! my dear, you need not be nervous. You will always be as pretty as possible. That is the best fashion there is, and the only fashion that England succeeds in setting.

MABEL CHILTERN (*with a curtsey*): Thank you so much, Lady Markby, for England . . . and myself. (*Goes out.*)

LADY MARKBY (*turning to* LADY CHILTERN): Dear Gertrude, we just called to know if Mrs. Cheveley's diamond brooch has been found.

LADY CHILTERN: Here?

MRS. CHEVELEY: Yes. I missed it when I got back to Claridge's, and I thought I might possibly have dropped it here.

LADY CHILTERN: I have heard nothing about it. But I will send for the butler and ask. (*Touches the bell.*)

MRS. CHEVELEY: Oh, pray don't trouble, Lady Chiltern. I dare say I lost it at the Opera, before we came on here.

LADY MARKBY: Ah yes, I suppose it must have been at the Opera. The fact is, we all scramble and jostle so much nowadays that I wonder we have anything at all left on us at the end of an evening. I know myself that, when I am coming back from the Drawing room, I always feel as if I hadn't a shred on me, except a small shred of decent reputation, just enough to prevent the lower classes making painful observations through the windows of the carriage. The fact is that our Society is terribly over-populated. Really, some one should arrange a proper scheme of assisted emigration. It would do a great deal of good.

MRS. CHEVELEY: I quite agree with you, Lady Markby. It is nearly six years since I have been in London for the Season, and I must say Society has become dreadfully mixed. One sees the oddest people everywhere.

LADY MARKBY: That is quite true, dear. But one needn't know them. I'm sure I don't know half the people who come to my house. Indeed, from all I hear, I shouldn't like to.

Enter MASON.

LADY CHILTERN: What sort of brooch was it that you lost, Mrs. Cheveley?

MRS. CHEVELEY: A diamond snake-brooch with a ruby, a rather large ruby.

LADY MARKBY: I thought you said there was a sapphire on the head, dear?

MRS. CHEVELEY (*smiling*): No. Lady Markby—a ruby.

LADY MARKBY (*nodding her head*): And very becoming, I am quite sure.

LADY CHILTERN: Has a ruby and diamond brooch been found in any of the rooms this morning, Mason?

MASON: No, my lady.

MRS. CHEVELEY: It really is of no consequence, Lady Chiltern. I am so sorry to have put you to any inconvenience.

LADY CHILTERN (*coldly*): Oh, it has been no inconvenience. That will do, Mason. You can bring tea. (*Exit* MASON.)

LADY MARKBY: Well, I must say it is most annoying to lose anything. I remember once at Bath, years ago, losing in the Pump Room an exceedingly handsome cameo bracelet that Sir John had given me. I don't think he has ever given me anything since, I am sorry to say. He has sadly degenerated. Really, this horrid House of Commons quite ruins our husbands for us. I think the Lower House by far the greatest blow to a happy married life that there has been since that terrible thing called the Higher Education of Women was invented.

LADY CHILTERN: Ah! it is heresy to say that in this house, Lady Markby. Robert is a great champion of the Higher Education of Women, and so, I am afraid, am I.

MRS. CHEVELEY: The higher education of men is what I should like to see. Men need it so sadly.

LADY MARKBY: They do, dear. But I am afraid such a scheme would be quite unpractical. I don't think man has much capacity for development. He has got as far as he can, and that is not far, is it? With regard to women, well, dear Gertrude, you belong to the younger generation, and I am sure it is all right if you approve of it. In my time, of course, we were taught not to understand anything. That was the old system, and wonderfully interesting it was. I assure you that the amount of things I and my poor dear sister were taught not to understand was quite extraordinary. But modern women understand everything, I am told.

MRS. CHEVELEY: Except their husbands. That is the one thing the modern woman never understands.

LADY MARKBY: And a very good thing too, dear, I dare say. It might break up many a happy home if they did. Not yours, I need hardly say, Gertrude. You have married a pattern husband. I wish I could say as much for myself. But since Sir John has taken to attending the debates regularly, which he never used to do in the good old days, his language has become quite impossible. He always seems to think that he is addressing the House, and consequently whenever he discusses the state of the agricultural labourer, or the Welsh Church, or something quite improper of that kind, I am obliged to send all the servants out of the room. It is not pleasant to see one's own butler, who has been with one for twenty-three years, actually blushing at the sideboard, and the footmen making contortions in corners like persons in circuses. I assure you my life will be quite ruined unless they send John at once to the Upper House. He won't take any interest in politics then, will he? The House of Lords is so sensible. An assembly of gentlemen. But in his present state, Sir John is really a great trial. Why, this morning before breakfast was half over, he stood up on the hearth-rug, put his hands in his pockets, and appealed to the country at the top of his voice. I left the table as soon as I had my second cup of tea, I need hardly say. But his violent language could be heard all over the house! I trust, Gertrude, that Sir Robert is not like that?

LADY CHILTERN: But I am very much interested in politics, Lady Markby. I love to hear Robert talk about them.

LADY MARKBY: Well, I hope he is not as devoted to Blue Books as Sir John is. I don't think they can be quite improving reading for any one.

MRS. CHEVELEY (*languidly*): I have never read a Blue Book. I prefer books . . . in yellow covers.[3]

LADY MARKBY (*genially unconscious*): Yellow is a gayer colour, is it not? I used to wear yellow a good deal in my early days, and would do so now if Sir John was not so painfully personal in his observations, and a man on the question of dress is always ridiculous, is he not?

MRS. CHEVELEY: Oh, no! I think men are the only authorities on dress.

LADY MARKBY: Really? One wouldn't say so from the sort of hats they wear? Would one?

The butler enters, followed by the footman. Tea is set on a small table close to LADY CHILTERN.

LADY CHILTERN: May I give you some tea, Mrs. Cheveley?

MRS. CHEVELEY: Thanks. (*The butler hands* MRS. CHEVELEY *a cup of tea on a salver.*)

LADY CHILTERN: Some tea, Lady Markby?

LADY MARKBY: No thanks, dear. (*The servants go out.*) The fact is, I have promised to go round for ten minutes to see poor Lady Brancaster, who is in very great trouble. Her daughter, quite a well-brought-up girl, too, has actually become engaged to be married to a curate in Shropshire. It is very sad, very sad indeed. I can't understand this modern mania for curates. In my time we girls saw them, of course, running about the place like rabbits. But we never took any notice of them, I need hardly say. But I am told that nowadays country society is quite honeycombed with them. I think it most irreligious. And then the eldest son has quarrelled with his father, and it is said that when they meet at the club Lord Brancaster always hides himself behind the money article in *The Times*. However, I believe that is quite a common occurrence nowadays and that they have to take in extra copies of *The Times* at all the clubs in St. James's Street; there are so many sons who won't have anything to do with their fathers, and so many fathers who won't speak to their sons. I think myself, it is very much to be regretted.

MRS. CHEVELEY: So do I. Fathers have so much to learn from their sons nowadays.

LADY MARKBY: Really, dear? What?

MRS. CHEVELEY: The art of living. The only really Fine Art we have produced in modern times.

LADY MARKBY (*shaking her head*): Ah! I am afraid Lord Brancaster knew a good deal about that. More than his poor wife ever did. (*Turning to* LADY CHILTERN): You know Lady Brancaster, don't you, dear?

LADY CHILTERN: Just slightly. She was staying at Langton last autumn, when we were there.

LADY MARKBY: Well, like all stout women, she looks the very picture of happiness, as no doubt you noticed. But there are many tragedies in her family, besides this affair of the curate. Her own sister, Mrs. Jekyll, had a most unhappy life; through no fault of her own, I am sorry to say. She ultimately was so broken-hearted that she went into a convent, or on to the operatic stage, I forget which. No; I think it was decorative art-needlework she took up. I know she had lost all sense of pleasure in life. (*Rising*): And now,

Gertrude, if you will allow me, I shall leave Mrs. Cheveley in your charge and call back for her in a quarter of an hour. Or perhaps, dear Mrs. Cheveley, you wouldn't mind waiting in the carriage while I am with Lady Brancaster. As I intend it to be a visit of condolence, I shan't stay long.

MRS. CHEVELEY (*rising*): I don't mind waiting in the carriage at all, provided there is somebody to look at one.

LADY MARKBY: Well, I hear the curate is always prowling about the house.

MRS. CHEVELEY: I am afraid I am not fond of girl friends.

LADY CHILTERN (*rising*): Oh, I hope Mrs. Cheveley will stay here a little. I should like to have a few minutes' conversation with her.

MRS. CHEVELEY: How very kind of you, Lady Chiltern! Believe me, nothing would give me greater pleasure.

LADY MARKBY: Ah! no doubt you both have many pleasant reminiscences of your schooldays to talk over together. Good-bye, dear Gertrude! Shall I see you at Lady Bonar's to-night? She has discovered a wonderful new genius. He does . . . nothing at all, I believe. That is a great comfort, is it not?

LADY CHILTERN: Robert and I are dining at home by ourselves to-night, and I don't think I shall go anywhere afterwards. Robert, of course, will have to be in the House. But there is nothing interesting on.

LADY MARKBY: Dining at home by yourselves? Is that quite prudent? Ah, I forgot, your husband is an exception. Mine is the general rule, and nothing ages a woman so rapidly as having married the general rule.

Exit LADY MARKBY.

MRS. CHEVELEY: Wonderful woman, Lady Markby, isn't she? Talks more and says less than anybody I ever met. She is made to be a public speaker. Much more so than her husband, though he is a typical Englishman, always dull and usually violent.

LADY CHILTERN (*makes no answer, but remains standing. There is a pause. Then the eyes of the two women meet.* LADY CHILTERN *looks stern and pale.* MRS. CHEVELEY *seems rather amused*): Mrs. Cheveley, I think it is right to tell you quite frankly that, had I known who you really were, I should not have invited you to my house last night.

MRS. CHEVELEY (*with an impertinent smile*): Really?

LADY CHILTERN: I could not have done so.

MRS. CHEVELEY: I see that after all these years you have not changed a bit, Gertrude.

LADY CHILTERN: I never change.

MRS. CHEVELEY (*elevating her eyebrows*): Then life has taught you nothing?

LADY CHILTERN: It has taught me that a person who has once been guilty of a dishonest and dishonourable action may be guilty of it a second time, and should be shunned.

MRS. CHEVELEY: Would you apply that rule to every one?

LADY CHILTERN: Yes, to every one, without exception.

MRS. CHEVELEY: Then I am sorry for you, Gertrude, very sorry for you.

LADY CHILTERN: You see now, I am sure, that for many reasons any further acquaintance between us during your stay in London is quite impossible?

MRS. CHEVELEY (*leaning back in her chair*): Do you know, Gertrude, I don't mind your talking morality a bit. Morality is simply the attitude we adopt towards people whom we personally dislike. You dislike me. I am quite aware of that. And I have always detested you. And yet I have come here to do you a service.

LADY CHILTERN (*contemptuously*): Like the service you wished to render my husband last night, I suppose. Thank heaven, I saved him from that.

MRS. CHEVELEY (*starting to her feet*): It was you who made him write that insolent letter to me? It was you who made him break his promise?

LADY CHILTERN: Yes.

MRS. CHEVELEY: Then you must make him keep it. I give you till to-morrow morning—no more. If by that time your husband does not solemnly bind himself to help me in this great scheme in which I am interested——

LADY CHILTERN: This fraudulent speculation——

MRS. CHEVELEY: Call it what you choose. I hold your husband in the hollow of my hand, and if you are wise you will make him do what I tell him.

LADY CHILTERN (*rising and going towards her*): You are impertinent. What has my husband to do with you? With a woman like you?

MRS. CHEVELEY (*with a bitter laugh*): In this world like meets with like. It is because your husband is himself fraudulent and dishonest that we pair so well together. Between you and him there are chasms. He and I are closer than friends. We are enemies linked together. The same sin binds us.

LADY CHILTERN: How dare you class my husband with yourself? How dare you threaten him or me? Leave my house. You are unfit to enter it.

SIR ROBERT CHILTERN *enters from behind. He hears his wife's last words, and sees to whom they are addressed. He grows deadly pale.*

MRS. CHEVELEY: Your house! A house bought with the price of dishonour. A house, everything in which has been paid for by fraud. (*Turns round and sees* SIR ROBERT CHILTERN.) Ask him what the origin of his fortune is! Get him to tell you how he sold to a stockbroker a Cabinet secret. Learn from him to what you owe your position.

LADY CHILTERN: It is not true! Robert! It is not true!

MRS. CHEVELEY (*pointing at him with outstretched finger*): Look at him! Can he deny it! Does he dare to?

SIR ROBERT CHILTERN: Go! Go at once. You have done your worst now.

MRS. CHEVELEY: My worst? I have not yet finished with you, with either of you. I give you both till to-morrow at noon. If by then you don't do what I bid you to do, the whole world shall know the origin of Robert Chiltern.

SIR ROBERT CHILTERN *strikes the bell. Enter* MASON.

SIR ROBERT CHILTERN: Show Mrs. Cheveley out.

MRS. CHEVELEY *starts; then bows with somewhat exaggerated politeness to* LADY CHILTERN, *who makes no sign of response. As she passes by* SIR ROBERT CHILTERN, *who is standing close to the door, she pauses for a moment and looks him straight in the face. She then goes out, followed by the servant, who closes the door after him. The husband and wife are left alone.* LADY CHILTERN *stands like some one in a dreadful dream. Then she turns round and looks at her husband. She looks at him with strange eyes, as though she was seeing him for the first time.*

LADY CHILTERN: You sold a Cabinet secret for money! You began your life with fraud! You built up your career on dishonour! Oh, tell me it is not true! Lie to me! Lie to me! Tell me it is not true.

SIR ROBERT CHILTERN: What this woman said is quite true. But, Gertrude, listen to me. You don't realise how I was tempted. Let me tell you the whole thing. (*Goes towards her.*)

LADY CHILTERN: Don't come near me. Don't touch me. I feel as if you had soiled me for ever. Oh! what a mask you have been wearing all these years! A horrible painted mask! You sold yourself for money. Oh! a common thief were better. You put yourself up to sale to the highest bidder! You were bought in the market. You lied to the whole world. And yet you will not lie to me.

SIR ROBERT CHILTERN (*rushing towards her*): Gertrude! Gertrude!

LADY CHILTERN (*thrusting him back with outstretched hands*): No, don't speak! Say nothing! Your voice wakes terrible memories—memories of things that made me love you—memories of words that made me love you—memories that now are horrible to me. And how I worshipped you! You were to me something apart from common life, a thing pure, noble, honest, without stain. The world seemed to me finer because you were in it, and goodness more real because you lived. And now—oh, when I think that I made of a man like you my ideal! the ideal of my life!

SIR ROBERT CHILTERN: There was your mistake. There was your error. The error all women commit. Why can't you women love us, faults and all? Why do you place us on monstrous pedestals? We have all feet of clay, women as well as men; but when we men love women, we love them knowing their weaknesses, their follies, their imperfections, love them all the more, it may be, for that reason. It is not the perfect, but the imperfect, who have need of love. It is when we are wounded by our own hands, or by the hands of others, that love should come to cure us—else what use is love at all? All sins, except a sin against itself, Love should forgive. All lives, save loveless lives, true Love should pardon. A man's love is like that. It is wider, larger, more human than a woman's. Women think that they are making ideals of men. What they are making of us are false idols merely. You made your false idol of me, and I had not the courage to come down, show you my wounds, tell you my weaknesses. I was afraid that I might lose your love, as I have lost it now. And so, last night you ruined my life for me—yes, ruined it! What this woman asked of me was nothing compared to what she offered to me. She offered security, peace, stability. The sin of my youth, that I had thought was buried, rose up in front of me, hideous, horrible, with its hands at my throat. I could have killed it for ever, sent it back into its tomb, destroyed its record, burned the one witness against me. You prevented me. No one but you, you know it. And now what is there before me but public disgrace, ruin, terrible shame, the mockery of the world, a lonely dishonoured life, a lonely dishonoured death, it may be, some day? Let women make no more ideals of men! let them not put them on altars and bow before them or they may ruin other lives as completely as you—you whom I have so wildly loved—have ruined mine!

He passes from the room. LADY CHILTERN *rushes towards him, but the door is closed when she reaches it. Pale with anguish, bewildered, helpless, she sways like a plant in the water. Her hands, outstretched, seem to tremble in the air like blossoms in the wind. Then she flings herself down beside a sofa and buries her face. Her sobs are like the sobs of a child.*

Act Drop

ACT THREE

SCENE: *The Library in Lord Goring's house in Curzon Street, London. An Adam room. On the right is the door leading into the hall. On the left, the door of the smoking-room. A pair of folding doors at the back open into the drawing-room. The fire is lit. Phipps, the butler, is arranging some newspapers on the writing-table. The distinction of Phipps is his impassivity. He has been termed by enthusiasts the Ideal Butler. The Sphinx is not so incommunicable. He is a mask with a manner. Of his intellectual or emotional life, history knows nothing. He represents the dominance of form.*

Enter LORD GORING *in evening dress with a buttonhole. He is wearing a silk hat and Inverness cape. White-gloved, he carries a Louis Seize cane. His are all the delicate fopperies of Fashion. One sees that he stands in immediate relation to modern life, makes it indeed, and so masters it. He is the first well-dressed philosopher in the history of thought.*

LORD GORING: Got my second buttonhole for me, Phipps?

PHIPPS: Yes, my lord. (*Takes his hat, cane, and cape, and presents new buttonhole on salver.*)

LORD GORING: Rather distinguished thing, Phipps. I am the only person of the smallest importance in London at present who wears a buttonhole.

PHIPPS: Yes, my lord. I have observed that.

LORD GORING (*taking out old buttonhole*): You see, Phipps, Fashion is what one wears oneself. What is unfashionable is what other people wear.

PHIPPS: Yes, my lord.

LORD GORING: Just as vulgarity is simply the conduct of other people.

PHIPPS: Yes, my lord.

LORD GORING (*putting in new buttonhole*): And falsehoods the truths of other people.

PHIPPS: Yes, my lord.

LORD GORING: Other people are quite dreadful. The only possible society is oneself.

PHIPPS: Yes, my lord.

LORD GORING: To love oneself is the beginning of a lifelong romance, Phipps.

PHIPPS: Yes, my lord.

LORD GORING (*looking at himself in the glass*): Don't think I quite like this buttonhole, Phipps. Makes me look a little too old. Makes me almost in the prime of life, eh, Phipps?

PHIPPS: I don't observe any alteration in your lordship's appearance.

LORD GORING: You don't, Phipps?

PHIPPS: No, my lord.

LORD GORING: I am not quite sure. For the future a more trivial buttonhole, Phipps, on Thursday evenings.

PHIPPS: I will speak to the florist, my lord. She has had a loss in her family lately, which perhaps accounts for the lack of triviality your lordship complains of in the buttonhole.

LORD GORING: Extraordinary thing about the lower classes in England—they are always losing their relations.

PHIPPS: Yes, my lord! They are extremely fortunate in that respect.

LORD GORING (*turns round and looks at him.* PHIPPS *remains impassive*): Hum! Any letters, Phipps?

PHIPPS: Three, my lord. (*Hands letters on a salver.*)

LORD GORING (*takes letters*): Want my cab round in twenty minutes.

PHIPPS: Yes, my lord. (*Goes towards door.*)

LORD GORING (*holds up letter in pink envelope*): Ahem, Phipps, when did this letter arrive?

PHIPPS: It was brought by hand just after your lordship went to the club.

LORD GORING: That will do. (*Exit* PHIPPS.) Lady Chiltern's handwriting on Lady Chiltern's pink notepaper. That is rather curious. I thought Robert was to write. Wonder what Lady Chiltern has got to say to me? (*Sits at bureau and opens letter, and reads it.*) 'I want you. I trust you. I am coming to you. Gertrude.' (*Puts down the letter with a puzzled look. Then takes it up, and reads it again slowly.*) 'I want you. I trust you. I am coming to you.' She has found out everything! Poor woman! Poor woman! (*Pulls out watch and looks at it.*) But what an hour to call! Ten o'clock! I shall have to give up going to the Berkshires. However, it is always nice to be expected, and not to arrive. I am not expected at the Bachelors', so I shall certainly go there. Well, I will make her stand by her husband. That is the only thing for any woman to do. It is the growth of the moral sense of women that makes marriage such a hopeless, one-sided institution. Ten o'clock. She should be here soon. I must tell Phipps I am not in to any one else. (*Goes towards bell.*)

Enter PHIPPS.

PHIPPS: Lord Caversham.

LORD GORING: Oh, why will parents always appear at the wrong time? Some extraordinary mistake in nature, I suppose. (*Enter* LORD CAVERSHAM.) Delighted to see you, my dear father. (*Goes to meet him.*)

LORD CAVERSHAM: Take my cloak off.

LORD GORING: Is it worth while, father?

LORD CAVERSHAM: Of course it is worth while, sir. Which is the most comfortable chair?

LORD GORING: This one, father. It is the chair I use myself, when I have visitors.

LORD CAVERSHAM: Thank ye. No draught, I hope, in this room?

LORD GORING: No, father.

LORD CAVERSHAM (*sitting down*): Glad to hear it. Can't stand draughts. No draughts at home.

LORD GORING: Good many breezes, father.

LORD CAVERSHAM: Eh? Eh? Don't understand what you mean. Want to have a serious conversation with you, sir.

LORD GORING: My dear father! At this hour?

LORD CAVERSHAM: Well, sir, it is only ten o'clock. What is your objection to the hour? I think the hour is an admirable hour!

LORD GORING: Well, the fact is, father, this is not my day for talking seriously. I am very sorry, but it is not my day.

LORD CAVERSHAM: What do you mean, sir?

LORD GORING: During the Season, father, I only talk seriously on the first Tuesday in every month, from four to seven.

LORD CAVERSHAM: Well, make it Tuesday, sir, make it Tuesday.

LORD GORING: But it is after seven, father, and my doctor says I must not have any serious conversation after seven. It makes me talk in my sleep.

LORD CAVERSHAM: Talk in your sleep, sir? What does that matter? You are not married.

LORD GORING: No, father, I am not married.

LORD CAVERSHAM: Hum! That is what I have come to talk to you about, sir. You have got to get married, and at once. Why, when I was your age, sir, I had been an inconsolable widower for three months, and was already paying my addresses to your admirable mother. Damme, sir, it is your duty to get married. You can't be always living for pleasure. Every man of position is married nowadays. Bachelors are not fashionable any more. They are a damaged lot. Too much is known about them. You must get a wife, sir. Look where your friend Robert Chiltern has got to by probity, hard work, and a sensible marriage with a good woman. Why don't you imitate him, sir? Why don't you take him for your model?

LORD GORING: I think I shall, father.

LORD CAVERSHAM: I wish you would, sir. Then I should be happy. At present I make your mother's life miserable on your account. You are heartless, sir, quite heartless.

LORD GORING: I hope not, father.

LORD CAVERSHAM: And it is high time for you to get married. You are thirty-four years of age, sir.

LORD GORING: Yes, father, but I only admit to thirty-two—thirty-one and a half when I have a really good buttonhole. This buttonhole is not . . . trivial enough.

LORD CAVERSHAM: I tell you you are thirty-four, sir. And there is a draught in your room, besides, which makes your conduct worse. Why did you tell me there was no draught, sir? I feel a draught, sir, I feel it distinctly.

LORD GORING: So do I, father. It is a dreadful draught. I will come and see you to-morrow, father. We can talk over anything you like. Let me help you on with your cloak, father.

LORD CAVERSHAM: No, sir; I have called this evening for a definite purpose, and I am going to see it through at all costs to my health or yours. Put down my cloak, sir.

LORD GORING: Certainly, father. But let us go into another room. (*Rings bell.*) There is a dreadful draught here. (*Enter* PHIPPS.) Phipps, is there a good fire in the smoking-room?

PHIPPS: Yes, my lord.

LORD GORING: Come in there, father. Your sneezes are quite heartrending.

LORD CAVERSHAM: Well, sir, I suppose I have a right to sneeze when I choose?

LORD GORING (*apologetically*): Quite so, father. I was merely expressing sympathy.

LORD CAVERSHAM: Oh, damn sympathy. There is a great deal too much of that sort of thing going on nowadays.

LORD GORING: I quite agree with you, father. If there was less sympathy in the world there would be less trouble in the world.

LORD CAVERSHAM (*going towards the smoking-room*): That is a paradox, sir. I hate paradoxes.

LORD GORING: So do I, father. Everybody one meets is a paradox nowadays. It is a great bore. It makes society so obvious.

LORD CAVERSHAM (*turning round, and looking at his son beneath his bushy eyebrows*): Do you always really understand what you say, sir?

LORD GORING (*after some hesitation*): Yes, father, if I listen attentively.

LORD CAVERSHAM (*indignantly*): If you listen attentively! . . . Conceited young puppy!

Goes off grumbling into the smoking-room. PHIPPS *enters.*

LORD GORING: Phipps, there is a lady coming to see me this evening on particular business. Show her into the drawing-room when she arrives. You understand?

PHIPPS: Yes, my lord.

LORD GORING: It is a matter of the gravest importance, Phipps.

PHIPPS: I understand, my lord.

LORD GORING: No one else is to be admitted, under any circumstances.

PHIPPS: I understand, my lord. (*Bell rings.*)

LORD GORING: Ah! that is probably the lady. I shall see her myself.

Just as he is going towards the door LORD CAVERSHAM *enters from the smoking-room.*

LORD CAVERSHAM: Well, sir? am I to wait attendance on you?

LORD GORING (*considerably perplexed*): In a moment, father. Do excuse me. (LORD CAVERSHAM *goes back.*) Well, remember my instructions, Phipps—into that room.

PHIPPS: Yes, my lord.

LORD GORING *goes into the smoking-room.* HAROLD, *the footman, shows* MRS. CHEVELEY *in. Lamia-like, she is in green and silver. She has a cloak of black satin, lined with dead rose-leaf silk.*

HAROLD: What name, madam?

MRS. CHEVELEY (*to* PHIPPS, *who advances towards her*): Is Lord Goring not here? I was told he was at home?

PHIPPS: His lordship is engaged at present with Lord Caversham, madam.

Turns a cold, glassy eye on HAROLD, *who at once retires.*

MRS. CHEVELEY (*to herself*): How very filial!

PHIPPS: His lordship told me to ask you, madam, to be kind enough to wait in the drawing-room for him. His lordship will come to you there.

MRS. CHEVELEY (*with a look of surprise*): Lord Goring expects me?

PHIPPS: Yes, madam.

MRS. CHEVELEY: Are you quite sure?

PHIPPS: His lordship told me that if a lady called I was to ask her to wait in the drawing-room. (*Goes to the door of the drawing-room and opens it.*) His lordship's directions on the subject were very precise.

MRS. CHEVELEY (*to herself*): How thoughtful of him! To expect the unexpected shows a thoroughly modern intellect. (*Goes towards the drawing-room and looks in.*) Ugh! How dreary a bachelor's drawing-room always looks. I shall have to alter this. (PHIPPS *brings the lamp from the writing-table.*) No, I don't care for that lamp. It is far too glaring. Light some candles.

PHIPPS (*replaces lamp*): Certainly, madam.

MRS. CHEVELEY: I hope the candles have very becoming shades.

PHIPPS: We have had no complaints about them, madam, as yet.

Passes into the drawing-room and begins to light the candles.

MRS. CHEVELEY (*to herself*): I wonder what woman he is waiting for to-night. It will be delightful to catch him. Men always look so silly when they are caught. And they are always being caught. (*Looks about room and approaches the writing-table.*) What a very interesting room! What a very interesting picture! Wonder what his correspondence is like. (*Takes up letters.*) Oh, what a very uninteresting correspondence! Bills and cards, debts and dowagers! Who on earth writes to him on pink paper? How silly to write on pink paper! It looks like the beginning of a middle-class romance. Romance should never begin with sentiment. It should begin with science and end with a settlement. (*Puts letter down, then takes it up again.*) I know that handwriting. That is Gertrude Chiltern's. I remember it perfectly. The ten commandments in every stroke of the pen, and the moral law all over the page. Wonder what Gertrude is writing to him about? Something horrid about me, I suppose. How I detest that woman! (*Reads it.*) 'I trust you. I want you. I am coming to you. Gertrude.' 'I trust you. I want you. I am coming to you.'

A look of triumph comes over her face. She is just about to steal the letter, when PHIPPS *comes in.*

PHIPPS: The candles in the drawing-room are lit, madam, as you directed.

MRS. CHEVELEY: Thank you. (*Rises hastily and slips the letter under a large silver-cased blotting-book that is lying on the table.*)

PHIPPS: I trust the shades will be to your liking, madam. They are the most becoming we have. They are the same as his lordship uses himself when he is dressing for dinner.

MRS. CHEVELEY (*with a smile*): Then I am sure they will be perfectly right.

PHIPPS (*gravely*): Thank you, madam.

MRS. CHEVELEY *goes into the drawing-room.* PHIPPS *closes the door and retires. The door is then slowly opened, and* MRS. CHEVELEY *comes out and creeps stealthily towards the writing-table. Suddenly voices are heard from the smoking-room.* MRS. CHEVELEY *grows pale, and stops. The voices grow louder, and she goes back into the drawing-room, biting her lip.*

Enter LORD GORING *and* LORD CAVERSHAM.

LORD GORING (*expostulating*): My dear father, if I am to get married, surely you will allow me to choose the time, place, and person? Particularly the person.

LORD CAVERSHAM (*testily*): That is a matter for me, sir. You would probably make a very poor choice. It is I who should be consulted, not you. There is property at stake. It is not a matter for affection. Affection comes later on in married life.

LORD GORING: Yes. In married life affection comes when people thoroughly dislike each other, father, doesn't it? (*Puts on* LORD CAVERSHAM'S *cloak for him.*)

LORD CAVERSHAM: Certainly, sir. I mean certainly not, sir. You are talking very foolishly to-night. What I say is that marriage is a matter for common sense.

LORD GORING: But women who have common sense are so curiously plain, father, aren't they? Of course I only speak from hearsay.

LORD CAVERSHAM: No woman, plain or pretty, has any common sense at all, sir. Common sense is the privilege of our sex.

LORD GORING: Quite so. And we men are so self-sacrificing that we never use it, do we, father?

LORD CAVERSHAM: I use it, sir. I use nothing else.

LORD GORING: So my mother tells me.

LORD CAVERSHAM: It is the secret of your mother's happiness. You are very heartless, sir, very heartless.

LORD GORING: I hope not, father.

Goes out for a moment. Then returns, looking rather put out, with SIR ROBERT CHILTERN.

SIR ROBERT CHILTERN: My dear Arthur, what a piece of good luck meeting you on the doorstep! Your servant had just told me you were not at home. How extraordinary!

LORD GORING: The fact is, I am horribly busy to-night, Robert, and I gave orders I was not at home to any one. Even my father had a comparatively cold reception. He complained of a draught the whole time.

SIR ROBERT CHILTERN: Ah! you must be at home to me, Arthur. You are my best friend. Perhaps by to-morrow you will be my only friend. My wife has discovered everything.

LORD GORING: Ah! I guessed as much!

SIR ROBERT CHILTERN (*looking at him*): Really! How!

LORD GORING (*after some hesitation*): Oh, merely by something in the expression of your face as you came in. Who told her?

SIR ROBERT CHILTERN: Mrs. Cheveley herself. And the woman I love knows that I began my career with an act of low dishonesty, that I built up my life upon sands of shame—that I sold, like a common huckster, the secret that had been intrusted to me as a man of honour. I thank heaven poor Lord Radley died without knowing that I betrayed him. I would to God I had died before I had been so horribly tempted, or had fallen so low. (*Burying his face in his hands.*)

LORD GORING (*after a pause*): You have heard nothing from Vienna yet, in answer to your wire?

SIR ROBERT CHILTERN (*looking up*): Yes; I got a telegram from the first secretary at eight o'clock to-night.

LORD GORING: Well?

SIR ROBERT CHILTERN: Nothing is absolutely known against her. On the contrary, she occupies a rather high position in society. It is a sort of open secret that Baron Arnheim left her the greater portion of his immense fortune. Beyond that I can learn nothing.

LORD GORING: She doesn't turn out to be a spy, then?

SIR ROBERT CHILTERN: Oh! spies are of no use nowadays. Their profession is over. The newspapers do their work instead.

LORD GORING: And thunderingly well they do it.

SIR ROBERT CHILTERN: Arthur, I am parched with thirst. May I ring for something? Some hock and seltzer?*

LORD GORING: Certainly. Let me. (*Rings the bell.*)

SIR ROBERT CHILTERN: Thanks! I don't know what to do, Arthur, I don't know what to do, and you are my only friend. But what a friend you are—the one friend I can trust. I can trust you absolutely, can't I?

Enter PHIPPS.

LORD GORING: My dear Robert, of course. (*To* PHIPPS): Bring some hock and seltzer.

PHIPPS: Yes, my lord.

LORD GORING: And Phipps!

PHIPPS: Yes, my lord.

LORD GORING: Will you excuse me for a moment, Robert? I want to give some directions to my servant.

SIR ROBERT CHILTERN: Certainly.

LORD GORING: When that lady calls, tell her that I am not expected home this evening. Tell her that I have been suddenly called out of town. You understand?

PHIPPS: The lady is in that room, my lord. You told me to show her into that room, my lord.

LORD GORING: You did perfectly right. (*Exit* PHIPPS.) What a mess I am in. No; I think I shall get through it. I'll give her a lecture through the door. Awkward thing to manage, though.

SIR ROBERT CHILTERN: Arthur, tell me what I should do. My life seems to have crumbled about me. I am a ship without a rudder in a night without a star.

---

*Rhine wine served with sparkling soda—what is now called a white-wine spritzer.

LORD GORING: Robert, you love your wife, don't you?

SIR ROBERT CHILTERN: I love her more than anything in the world. I used to think ambition the great thing. It is not. Love is the great thing in the world. There is nothing but love, and I love her. But I am defamed in her eyes. I am ignoble in her eyes. There is a wide gulf between us now. She had found me out, Arthur, she has found me out.

LORD GORING: Has she never in her life done some folly—some indiscretion—that she should not forgive your sin?

SIR ROBERT CHILTERN: My wife! Never! She does not know what weakness or temptation is. I am of clay like other men. She stands apart as good women do—pitiless in her perfection—cold and stern and without mercy. But I love her, Arthur. We are childless, and I have no one else to love, no one else to love me. Perhaps if God had sent us children she might have been kinder to me. But God has given us a lonely house. And she has cut my heart in two. Don't let us talk of it. I was brutal to her this evening. But I suppose when sinners talk to saints they are brutal always. I said to her things that were hideously true, on my side, from my standpoint, from the standpoint of men. But don't let us talk of that.

LORD GORING: Your wife will forgive you. Perhaps at this moment she is forgiving you. She loves you, Robert. Why should she not forgive?

SIR ROBERT CHILTERN: God grant it! God grant it! (*Buries his face in his hands.*) But there is something more I have to tell you, Arthur.

Enter PHIPPS *with drinks.*

PHIPPS (*hands hock and seltzer to* SIR ROBERT CHILTERN): Hock and seltzer, sir.

SIR ROBERT CHILTERN: Thank you.

LORD GORING: Is your carriage here, Robert?

SIR ROBERT CHILTERN: No; I walked from the club.

LORD GORING: Sir Robert will take my cab, Phipps.

PHIPPS: Yes, my lord.

Exit.

LORD GORING: Robert, you don't mind my sending you away?

SIR ROBERT CHILTERN: Arthur, you must let me stay for five minutes. I have made up my mind what I am going to do to-night in the House. The debate on the Argentine Canal is to begin at eleven. (*A chair falls in the drawing-room.*) What is that!

LORD GORING: Nothing.

SIR ROBERT CHILTERN: I heard a chair fall in the next room. Some one has been listening.

LORD GORING: No, no; there is no one there.

SIR ROBERT CHILTERN: There is some one. There are lights in the room, and the door is ajar. Some one has been listening to every secret of my life. Arthur, what does this mean?

LORD GORING: Robert, you are excited, unnerved. I tell you there is no one in that room. Sit down, Robert.

SIR ROBERT CHILTERN: Do you give me your word that there is no one there?

LORD GORING: Yes.

SIR ROBERT CHILTERN: Your word of honour? (*Sits down.*)

LORD GORING: Yes.

SIR ROBERT CHILTERN (*rises*): Arthur, let me see for myself.

LORD GORING: No, no.

SIR ROBERT CHILTERN: If there is no one there why should I not look in that room? Arthur, you must let me go into that room and satisfy myself. Let me know that no eavesdropper has heard my life's secret. Arthur, you don't realise what I am going through.

LORD GORING: Robert, this must stop. I have told you that there is no one in that room—that is enough.

SIR ROBERT CHILTERN (*rushes to the door of the room*): It is not enough. I insist on going into this room. You have told me there is no one there, so what reason can you have for refusing me?

LORD GORING: For God's sake, don't! There is some one there. Some one whom you must not see.

SIR ROBERT CHILTERN: Ah, I thought so!

LORD GORING: I forbid you to enter that room.

SIR ROBERT CHILTERN: Stand back. My life is at stake. And I don't care who is there. I will know who it is to whom I have told my secret and my shame. (*Enters room.*)

LORD GORING: Great heavens! his own wife!

SIR ROBERT CHILTERN *comes back, with a look of scorn and anger on his face.*

SIR ROBERT CHILTERN: What explanation have you to give for the presence of that woman here?

LORD GORING: Robert, I swear to you on my honour that that lady is stainless and guiltless of all offence towards you.

SIR ROBERT CHILTERN: She is vile, an infamous thing!

LORD GORING: Don't say that, Robert! It was for your sake she came here. It was to try and save you she came here. She loves you and no one else.

SIR ROBERT CHILTERN: You are mad. What have I to do with her intrigues with you? Let her remain your mistress! You are well suited to each other. She, corrupt and shameful—you, false as a friend, treacherous as an enemy even——

LORD GORING: It is not true, Robert. Before heaven, it is not true. In her presence and in yours I will explain all.

SIR ROBERT CHILTERN: Let me pass, sir. You have lied enough upon your word of honour.

SIR ROBERT CHILTERN *goes out.* LORD GORING *rushes to the door of the drawing-room, when* MRS. CHEVELEY *comes out, looking radiant and much amused.*

MRS. CHEVELEY (*with a mock curtsey*): Good-evening, Lord Goring!

LORD GORING: Mrs. Cheveley! Great heavens . . . May I ask what were you doing in my drawing-room?

MRS. CHEVELEY: Merely listening. I have a perfect passion for listening through keyholes. One always hears such wonderful things through them.

LORD GORING: Doesn't that sound rather like tempting Providence?

MRS. CHEVELEY: Oh! surely Providence can resist temptation by this time. (*Makes a sign to him to take her cloak off, which he does.*)

LORD GORING: I am glad you have called. I am going to give you some good advice.

MRS. CHEVELEY: Oh! pray don't. One should never give a woman anything that she can't wear in the evening.

LORD GORING: I see you are quite as wilful as you used to be.

MRS. CHEVELEY: Far more! I have greatly improved. I have had more experience.

LORD GORING: Too much experience is a dangerous thing. Pray have a cigarette. Half the pretty women in London smoke cigarettes. Personally I prefer the other half.

MRS. CHEVELEY: Thanks. I never smoke. My dressmaker wouldn't like it, and a woman's first duty in life is to her dressmaker, isn't it? What the second duty is, no one has as yet discovered.

LORD GORING: You have come here to sell me Robert Chiltern's letter, haven't you?

MRS. CHEVELEY: To offer it to you on conditions! How did you guess that?

LORD GORING: Because you haven't mentioned the subject. Have you got it with you?

MRS. CHEVELEY (*sitting down*): Oh, no! A well-made dress has no pockets.

LORD GORING: What is your price for it?

MRS. CHEVELEY: How absurdly English you are! The English think that a cheque-book can solve every problem in life. Why, my dear Arthur, I have very much more money than you have, and quite as much as Robert Chiltern has got hold of. Money is not what I want.

LORD GORING: What do you want then, Mrs. Cheveley?

MRS. CHEVELEY: Why don't you call me Laura?

LORD GORING: I don't like the name.

MRS. CHEVELEY: You used to adore it.

LORD GORING: Yes; that's why. (MRS. CHEVELEY *motions to him to sit down beside her. He smiles, and does so.*)

MRS. CHEVELEY: Arthur, you loved me once.

LORD GORING: Yes.

MRS. CHEVELEY: And you asked me to be your wife.

LORD GORING: That was the natural result of my loving you.

MRS. CHEVELEY: And you threw me over because you saw, or

said you saw, poor old Lord Mortlake trying to have a violent flirtation with me in the conservatory at Tenby.

LORD GORING: I am under the impression that my lawyer settled that matter with you on certain terms . . . dictated by yourself.

MRS. CHEVELEY: At that time I was poor; you were rich.

LORD GORING: Quite so. That is why you pretended to love me.

MRS. CHEVELEY (*shrugging her shoulders*): Poor old Lord Mortlake, who had only two topics of conversation, his gout and his wife! I never could quite make out which of the two he was talking about. He used the most horrible language about them both. Well, you were silly, Arthur. Why, Lord Mortlake was never anything more to me than an amusement. One of those utterly tedious amusements one only finds at an English country house on an English country Sunday. I don't think any one at all morally responsible for what he or she does at an English country house.

LORD GORING: Yes. I know lots of people think that.

MRS. CHEVELEY: I loved you, Arthur.

LORD GORING: My dear Mrs. Cheveley, you have always been far too clever to know anything about love.

MRS. CHEVELEY: I did love you. And you loved me. You know you loved me; and love is a very wonderful thing. I suppose that when a man has once loved a woman, he will do anything for her, except continue to love her? (*Puts her hand on his.*)

LORD GORING (*taking his hand away quietly*): Yes; except that.

MRS. CHEVELEY (*after a pause*): I am tired of living abroad. I want to come back to London. I want to have a charming house here. I want to have a salon. If one could only teach the English how to talk, and the Irish how to listen, society here would be quite civilised. Besides, I have arrived at the romantic stage. When I saw you last night at the Chilterns', I knew you were the only person I had ever cared for, if I ever have cared for anybody, Arthur. And so, on the morning of the day you marry me, I will give you Robert Chiltern's letter. That is my offer. I will give it to you now, if you promise to marry me.

LORD GORING: Now?

MRS. CHEVELEY (*smiling*): To-morrow.

LORD GORING: Are you really serious?

MRS. CHEVELEY: Yes, quite serious.

LORD GORING: I should make you a very bad husband.

MRS. CHEVELEY: I don't mind bad husbands. I have had two. They amused me immensely.

LORD GORING: You mean that you amused yourself immensely, don't you?

MRS. CHEVELEY: What do you know about my married life?

LORD GORING: Nothing; but I can read it like a book.

MRS. CHEVELEY: What book?

LORD GORING (*rising*): The Book of Numbers.

MRS. CHEVELEY: Do you think it is quite charming of you to be so rude to a woman in your own house?

LORD GORING: In the case of very fascinating women, sex is a challenge, not a defence.

MRS. CHEVELEY: I suppose that is meant for a compliment. My dear Arthur, women are never disarmed by compliments. Men always are. That is the difference between the two sexes.

LORD GORING: Women are never disarmed by anything, as far as I know them.

MRS. CHEVELEY (*after a pause*): Then you are going to allow your greatest friend, Robert Chiltern, to be ruined, rather than marry some one who really has considerable attractions left. I thought you would have risen to some great height of self-sacrifice, Arthur. I think you should. And the rest of your life you could spend in contemplating your own perfections.

LORD GORING: Oh! I do that as it is. And self-sacrifice is a thing that should be put down by law. It is so demoralising to the people for whom one sacrifices oneself. They always go to the bad.

MRS. CHEVELEY: As if anything could demoralise Robert Chiltern! You seem to forget that I know his real character.

LORD GORING: What you know about him is not his real character. It was an act of folly done in his youth, dishonourable, I admit, shameful, I admit, unworthy of him, I admit, and therefore . . . not his true character.

MRS. CHEVELEY: How you men stand up for each other!

LORD GORING: How you women war against each other!

MRS. CHEVELEY (*bitterly*): I only war against one woman, against Gertrude Chiltern. I hate her. I hate her now more than ever.

LORD GORING: Because you have brought a real tragedy into her life, I suppose.

MRS. CHEVELEY (*with a sneer*): Oh, there is only one real tragedy in a woman's life. The fact that her past is always her lover, and her future invariably her husband.

LORD GORING: Lady Chiltern knows nothing of the kind of life to which you are alluding.

MRS. CHEVELEY: A woman whose size in gloves is seven and three-quarters never knows much about anything. You know Gertrude has always worn seven and three-quarters? That is one of the reasons why there was never any moral sympathy between us. . . . Well, Arthur, I suppose this romantic interview may be regarded as at an end. You admit it was romantic, don't you? For the privilege of being your wife I was ready to surrender a great prize, the climax of my diplomatic career. You decline. Very well. If Sir Robert doesn't uphold my Argentine scheme, I expose him. *Voila tout.**

LORD GORING: You mustn't do that. It would be vile, horrible, infamous.

MRS. CHEVELEY (*shrugging her shoulders*): Oh, don't use big words. They mean so little. It is a commercial transaction. That is all. There is no good mixing up sentimentality in it. I offered to sell Robert Chiltern a certain thing. If he won't pay me my price, he will have to pay the world a greater price. There is no more to be said. I must go. Good-bye. Won't you shake hands?

LORD GORING: With you? No. Your transaction with Robert Chiltern may pass as a loathsome commercial transaction of a loathsome commercial age; but you seem to have forgotten that you came here to-night to talk of love, you whose lips desecrated the word love, you to whom the thing is a book closely sealed, went this afternoon to the house of one of the most noble and gentle women in the world to degrade her husband in her eyes, to try and kill her love for him, to put poison in her heart, and bitterness in her life, to break her idol, and, it may be, spoil her soul. That I cannot forgive you. That was horrible. For that there can be no forgiveness.

---

*That's all.

MRS. CHEVELEY: Arthur, you are unjust to me. Believe me, you are quite unjust to me. I didn't go to taunt Gertrude at all. I had no idea of doing anything of the kind when I entered. I called with Lady Markby simply to ask whether an ornament, a jewel, that I lost somewhere last night, had been found at the Chilterns'. If you don't believe me, you can ask Lady Markby. She will tell you it is true. The scene that occurred happened after Lady Markby had left, and was really forced on me by Gertrude's rudeness and sneers. I called, oh!—a little out of malice if you like—but really to ask if a diamond brooch of mine had been found. That was the origin of the whole thing.

LORD GORING: A diamond snake-brooch with a ruby?

MRS. CHEVELEY: Yes. How do you know?

LORD GORING: Because it is found. In point of fact, I found it myself, and stupidly forgot to tell the butler anything about it as I was leaving. (*Goes over to the writing-table and pulls out the drawers.*) It is in this drawer. No, that one. This is the brooch, isn't it? (*Holds up the brooch.*)

MRS. CHEVELEY: Yes. I am so glad to get it back. It was . . . a present.

LORD GORING: Won't you wear it?

MRS. CHEVELEY: Certainly, if you pin it in. (LORD GORING *suddenly clasps it on her arm.*) Why do you put it on as a bracelet? I never knew it could be worn as a bracelet.

LORD GORING: Really?

MRS. CHEVELEY (*holding out her handsome arm*): No; but it looks very well on me as a bracelet, doesn't it?

LORD GORING: Yes; much better than when I saw it last.

MRS. CHEVELEY: When did you see it last?

LORD GORING (*calmly*): Oh, ten years ago, on Lady Berkshire, from whom you stole it.

MRS. CHEVELEY (*starting*): What do you mean?

LORD GORING: I mean that you stole that ornament from my cousin, Mary Berkshire, to whom I gave it when she was married. Suspicion fell on a wretched servant, who was sent away in disgrace. I recognised it last night. I determined to say nothing about it till I had found the thief. I have found the thief now, and I have heard her own confession.

MRS. CHEVELEY (*tossing her head*): It is not true.

LORD GORING: You know it is true. Why, thief is written across your face at this moment.

MRS. CHEVELEY: I will deny the whole affair from beginning to end. I will say that I have never seen this wretched thing, that it was never in my possession.

MRS. CHEVELEY *tries to get the bracelet off her arm, but fails.* LORD GORING *looks on amused. Her thin fingers tear at the jewel to no purpose. A curse breaks from her.**

LORD GORING: The drawback of stealing a thing, Mrs. Cheveley, is that one never knows how wonderful the thing that one steals is. You can't get that bracelet off, unless you know where the spring is. And I see you don't know where the spring is. It is rather difficult to find.

MRS. CHEVELEY: You brute! You coward! (*She tries again to unclasp the bracelet, but fails.*)

LORD GORING: Oh! don't use big words. They mean so little.

MRS. CHEVELEY (*again tears at the bracelet in a paroxysm of rage, with inarticulate sounds. Then stops, and looks at* LORD GORING): What are you going to do?

LORD GORING: I am going to ring for my servant. He is an admirable servant. Always comes in the moment one rings for him. When he comes I will tell him to fetch the police.

MRS. CHEVELEY (*trembling*): The police? What for?

LORD GORING: To-morrow the Berkshires will prosecute you. That is what the police are for.

MRS. CHEVELEY (*is now in an agony of physical terror. Her face is distorted. Her mouth awry. A mask has fallen from her. She is, for the moment, dreadful to look at*): Don't do that. I will do anything you want. Anything in the world you want.

LORD GORING: Give me Robert Chiltern's letter.

MRS. CHEVELEY: Stop! Stop! Let me have time to think.

LORD GORING: Give me Robert Chiltern's letter.

---

*Probably a curse the audience is unable to hear clearly.

MRS. CHEVELEY: I have not got it with me. I will give it to you to-morrow.

LORD GORING: You know you are lying. Give it to me at once. (MRS. CHEVELEY *pulls the letter out, and hands it to him. She is horribly pale.*) This is it?

MRS. CHEVELEY (*in a hoarse voice*): Yes.

LORD GORING (*takes the letter, examines it, sighs, and burns it over the lamp*): For so well-dressed a woman, Mrs. Cheveley, you have moments of admirable common sense. I congratulate you.

MRS. CHEVELEY (*catches sight of* LADY CHILTERN'S *letter, the cover of which is just showing from under the blotting-book*): Please get me a glass of water.

LORD GORING: Certainly. (*Goes to the corner of the room and pours out a glass of water. While his back is turned* MRS. CHEVELEY *steals* LADY CHILTERN'S *letter. When* LORD GORING *returns with the glass she refuses it with a gesture.*)

MRS. CHEVELEY: Thank you. Will you help me on with my cloak?

LORD GORING: With pleasure. (*Puts her cloak on.*)

MRS. CHEVELEY: Thanks. I am never going to try to harm Robert Chiltern again.

LORD GORING: Fortunately you have not the chance, Mrs. Cheveley.

MRS. CHEVELEY: Well, if even I had the chance, I wouldn't. On the contrary, I am going to render him a great service.

LORD GORING: I am charmed to hear it. It is a reformation.

MRS. CHEVELEY: Yes. I can't bear so upright a gentleman, so honourable an English gentleman, being so shamefully deceived and so——

LORD GORING: Well?

MRS. CHEVELEY: I find that somehow Gertrude Chiltern's dying speech and confession has strayed into my pocket.

LORD GORING: What do you mean?

MRS. CHEVELEY (*with a bitter note of triumph in her voice*): I mean that I am going to send Robert Chiltern the love-letter his wife wrote to you to-night.

LORD GORING: Love-letter?

MRS. CHEVELEY (*laughing*): 'I want you. I trust you. I am coming to you. Gertrude.'

LORD GORING *rushes to the bureau and takes up the envelope, finds it empty, and turns round.*

LORD GORING: You wretched woman, must you always be thieving? Give me back that letter. I'll take it from you by force. You shall not leave my room till I have got it.

He rushes towards her, but MRS. CHEVELEY *at once puts her hand on the electric bell that is on the table. The bell sounds with shrill reverberations, and* PHIPPS *enters.*

MRS. CHEVELEY (*after a pause*): Lord Goring merely rang that you should show me out. Good-night, Lord Goring!

Goes out followed by PHIPPS. *Her face is illumined with evil triumph. There is joy in her eyes. Youth seems to have come back to her. Her last glance is like a swift arrow.* LORD GORING *bites his lip, and lights a cigarette.*

Act Drop

ACT FOUR

SCENE: *Same as Act Two.*

LORD GORING *is standing by the fireplace with his hands in his pockets. He is looking rather bored.*

LORD GORING (*pulls out his watch, inspects it, and rings the bell*): It is a great nuisance. I can't find any one in this house to talk to. And I am full of interesting information. I feel like the latest edition of something or other.

Enter servant.

JAMES: Sir Robert is still at the Foreign Office, my lord.
LORD GORING: Lady Chiltern not down yet?
JAMES: Her ladyship has not yet left her room. Miss Chiltern has just come in from riding.
LORD GORING (*to himself*): Ah! that is something.
JAMES: Lord Caversham has been waiting some time in the library for Sir Robert. I told him your lordship was here.
LORD GORING: Thank you. Would you kindly tell him I've gone?
JAMES (*bowing*): I shall do so, my lord.

Exit servant.

LORD GORING: Really, I don't want to meet my father three days running. It is a great deal too much excitement for any son. I hope to goodness he won't come up. Fathers should be neither seen nor heard. That is the only proper basis for family life. Mothers are different. Mothers are darlings. (*Throws himself down into a chair, picks up a paper and begins to read it.*)

Enter LORD CAVERSHAM.

LORD CAVERSHAM: Well, sir, what are you doing here? Wasting your time as usual, I suppose?

LORD GORING (*throws down paper and rises*): My dear father, when one pays a visit it is for the purpose of wasting other people's time, not one's own.

LORD CAVERSHAM: Have you been thinking over what I spoke to you about last night?

LORD GORING: I have been thinking about nothing else.

LORD CAVERSHAM: Engaged to be married yet?

LORD GORING (*genially*): Not yet; but I hope to be before lunch-time.

LORD CAVERSHAM (*caustically*): You can have till dinner-time if it would be of any convenience to you.

LORD GORING: Thanks awfully, but I think I'd sooner be engaged before lunch.

LORD CAVERSHAM: Humph! Never know when you are serious or not.

LORD GORING: Neither do I, father.

A pause.

LORD CAVERSHAM: I suppose you have read *The Times* this morning?

LORD GORING (*airily*): *The Times?* Certainly not. I only read *The Morning Post*. All that one should know about modern life is where the Duchesses are; anything else is quite demoralising.

LORD CAVERSHAM: Do you mean to say you have not read *The Times* leading article on Robert Chiltern's career?

LORD GORING: Good heavens! No. What does it say?

LORD CAVERSHAM: What should it say, sir? Everything complimentary, of course. Chiltern's speech last night on this Argentine Canal scheme was one of the finest pieces of oratory ever delivered in the House since Canning.*

---

*George Canning (1770–1827), British statesman who served briefly as prime minister in 1827.

LORD GORING: Ah! Never heard of Canning. Never wanted to. And did . . . did Chiltern uphold the scheme?

LORD CAVERSHAM: Uphold it, sir? How little you know him! Why, he denounced it roundly, and the whole system of modern political finance. This speech is the turning-point in his career, as *The Times* points out. You should read this article, sir. (*Opens* The Times.) 'Sir Robert Chiltern . . . most rising of our young statesmen. . . . Brilliant orator. . . . Unblemished career. . . . Well-known integrity of character. . . . Represents what is best in English public life. . . . Noble contrast to the lax morality so common among foreign politicians.' They will never say that of you, sir.

LORD GORING: I sincerely hope not, father. However, I am delighted at what you tell me about Robert, thoroughly delighted. It shows he has got pluck.

LORD CAVERSHAM: He has got more than pluck, sir, he has got genius.

LORD GORING: Ah! I prefer pluck. It is not so common, nowadays, as genius is.

LORD CAVERSHAM: I wish you would go into Parliament.

LORD GORING: My dear father, only people who look dull ever get into the House of Commons, and only people who are dull ever succeed there.

LORD CAVERSHAM: Why don't you try to do something useful in life?

LORD GORING: I am far too young.

LORD CAVERSHAM (*testily*): I hate this affectation of youth, sir. It is a great deal too prevalent nowadays.

LORD GORING: Youth isn't an affectation. Youth is an art.

LORD CAVERSHAM: Why don't you propose to that pretty Miss Chiltern?

LORD GORING: I am of a very nervous disposition, especially in the morning.

LORD CAVERSHAM: I don't suppose there is the smallest chance of her accepting you.

LORD GORING: I don't know how the betting stands to-day.

LORD CAVERSHAM: If she did accept you she would be the prettiest fool in England.

LORD GORING: That is just what I should like to marry. A thoroughly sensible wife would reduce me to a condition of absolute idiocy in less than six months.

LORD CAVERSHAM: You don't deserve her, sir.

LORD GORING: My dear father, if we men married the women we deserved, we should have a very bad time of it.

Enter MABEL CHILTERN.

MABEL CHILTERN: Oh! . . . How do you do, Lord Caversham? I hope Lady Caversham is quite well?

LORD CAVERSHAM: Lady Caversham is as usual, as usual.

LORD GORING: Good-morning, Miss Mabel!

MABEL CHILTERN (*taking no notice at all of* LORD GORING, *and addressing herself exclusively to* LORD CAVERSHAM): And Lady Caversham's bonnets . . . are they at all better?

LORD CAVERSHAM: They have had a serious relapse, I am sorry to say.

LORD GORING: Good-morning, Miss Mabel.

MABEL CHILTERN (*to* LORD CAVERSHAM): I hope an operation will not be necessary.

LORD CAVERSHAM (*smiling at her pertness*): If it is, we shall have to give Lady Caversham a narcotic. Otherwise she would never consent to have a feather touched.

LORD GORING (*with increased emphasis*): Good-morning, Miss Mabel!

MABEL CHILTERN (*turning round with feigned surprise*): Oh, are you here? Of course you understand that after your breaking your appointment I am never going to speak to you again.

LORD GORING: Oh, please don't say such a thing. You are the one person in London I really like to have to listen to me.

MABEL CHILTERN: Lord Goring, I never believe a single word that either you or I say to each other.

LORD CAVERSHAM: You are quite right, my dear, quite right as far as he is concerned, I mean.

MABEL CHILTERN: Do you think you could possibly make your son behave a little better occasionally? Just as a change.

LORD CAVERSHAM: I regret to say, Miss Chiltern, that I have no influence at all over my son. I wish I had. If I had, I know what I would make him do.

MABEL CHILTERN: I am afraid that he has one of those terribly weak natures that are not susceptible to influence.

LORD CAVERSHAM: He is very heartless, very heartless.

LORD GORING: It seems to me that I am a little in the way here.

MABEL CHILTERN: It is very good for you to be in the way, and to know what people say of you behind your back.

LORD GORING: I don't at all like knowing what people say of me behind my back. It makes me far too conceited.

LORD CAVERSHAM: After that, my dear, I really must bid you good-morning.

MABEL CHILTERN: Oh! I hope you are not going to leave me all alone with Lord Goring? Especially at such an early hour in the day.

LORD CAVERSHAM: I am afraid I can't take him with me to Downing Street. It is not the Prime Minister's day for seeing the unemployed.

Shakes hands with MABEL CHILTERN, *takes up his hat and stick, and goes out, with a parting glare of indignation at* LORD GORING.

MABEL CHILTERN (*takes up roses and begins to arrange them in a bowl on the table*): People who don't keep their appointments in the Park are horrid.

LORD GORING: Detestable.

MABEL CHILTERN: I am glad you admit it. But I wish you wouldn't look so pleased about it.

LORD GORING: I can't help it. I always look pleased when I am with you.

MABEL CHILTERN (*sadly*): Then I suppose it is my duty to remain with you?

LORD GORING: Of course it is.

MABEL CHILTERN: Well, my duty is a thing I never do, on principle. It always depresses me. So I am afraid I must leave you.

LORD GORING: Please don't, Miss Mabel. I have something very particular to say to you.

MABEL CHILTERN (*rapturously*): Oh! is it a proposal?

LORD GORING (*somewhat taken aback*): Well, yes, it is—I am bound to say it is.

MABEL CHILTERN (*with a sigh of pleasure*): I am so glad. That makes the second to-day.

LORD GORING (*indignantly*): The second to-day? What conceited ass has been impertinent enough to dare to propose to you before I had proposed to you?

MABEL CHILTERN: Tommy Trafford, of course. It is one of Tommy's days for proposing. He always proposes on Tuesdays and Thursdays, during the Season.

LORD GORING: You didn't accept him, I hope?

MABEL CHILTERN: I make it a rule never to accept Tommy. That is why he goes on proposing. Of course, as you didn't turn up this morning, I very nearly said yes. It would have been an excellent lesson both for him and for you if I had. It would have taught you both better manners.

LORD GORING: Oh! bother Tommy Trafford. Tommy is a silly little ass. I love you.

MABEL CHILTERN: I know. And I think you might have mentioned it before. I am sure I have given you heaps of opportunities.

LORD GORING: Mabel, do be serious. Please be serious.

MABEL CHILTERN: Ah! that is the sort of thing a man always says to a girl before he has been married to her. He never says it afterwards.

LORD GORING (*taking hold of her hand*): Mabel, I have told you that I love you. Can't you love me a little in return?

MABEL CHILTERN: You silly Arthur! If you knew anything about . . . anything, which you don't, you would know that I adore you. Every one in London knows it except you. It is a public scandal the way I adore you. I have been going about for the last six months telling the whole of society that I adore you. I wonder you consent to have anything to say to me. I have no character left at all. At least, I feel so happy that I am quite sure I have no character left at all.

LORD GORING (*catches her in his arms and kisses her. Then there is a pause of bliss*): Dear! Do you know I was awfully afraid of being refused!

MABEL CHILTERN (*looking up at him*): But you never have been refused yet by anybody, have you, Arthur? I can't imagine any one refusing you.

LORD GORING (*after kissing her again*): Of course I'm not nearly good enough for you, Mabel.

MABEL CHILTERN (*nestling close to him*): I am so glad, darling. I was afraid you were.

LORD GORING (*after some hesitation*): And I'm . . . I'm a little over thirty.

MABEL CHILTERN: Dear, you look weeks younger than that.

LORD GORING (*enthusiastically*): How sweet of you to say so! . . . And it is only fair to tell you frankly that I am fearfully extravagant.

MABEL CHILTERN: But so am I, Arthur. So we're sure to agree. And now I must go and see Gertrude.

LORD GORING: Must you really? (*Kisses her.*)

MABEL CHILTERN: Yes.

LORD GORING: Then do tell her I want to talk to her particularly. I have been waiting here all the morning to see either her or Robert.

MABEL CHILTERN: Do you mean to say you didn't come here expressly to propose to me?

LORD GORING (*triumphantly*): No; that was a flash of genius.

MABEL CHILTERN: Your first.

LORD GORING (*with determination*): My last.

MABEL CHILTERN: I am delighted to hear it. Now don't stir. I'll be back in five minutes. And don't fall into any temptations while I am away.

LORD GORING: Dear Mabel, while you are away, there are none. It makes me horribly dependent on you.

Enter LADY CHILTERN.

LADY CHILTERN: Good-morning, dear! How pretty you are looking!

MABEL CHILTERN: How pale you are looking, Gertrude! It is most becoming!

LADY CHILTERN: Good-morning, Lord Goring!

LORD GORING (*bowing*): Good-morning, Lady Chiltern!

MABEL CHILTERN (*aside to* LORD GORING): I shall be in the conservatory, under the second palm tree on the left.

LORD GORING: Second on the left?

MABEL CHILTERN (*with a look of mock surprise*): Yes; the usual palm tree.

Blows a kiss to him, unobserved by LADY CHILTERN, *and goes out.*

LORD GORING: Lady Chiltern, I have a certain amount of very good news to tell you. Mrs. Cheveley gave me up Robert's letter last night, and I burned it. Robert is safe.

LADY CHILTERN (*sinking on the sofa*): Safe! Oh! I am so glad of that. What a good friend you are to him—to us!

LORD GORING: There is only one person now that could be said to be in any danger.

LA.DY CHILTERN: Who is that?

LORD GORING (*sitting down beside her*): Yourself.

LADY CHILTERN: I! In danger? What do you mean?

LORD GORING: Danger is too great a word. It is a word I should not have used. But I admit I have something to tell you that may distress you, that terribly distresses me. Yesterday evening you wrote me a very beautiful, womanly letter, asking me for my help. You wrote to me as one of your oldest friends, one of your husband's oldest friends. Mrs. Cheveley stole that letter from my rooms.

LADY CHILTERN: Well, what use is it to her? Why should she not have it?

LORD GORING (*rising*): Lady Chiltern, I will be quite frank with you. Mrs. Cheveley puts a certain construction on that letter and proposes to send it to your husband.

LADY CHILTERN: But what construction could she put on it? . . . Oh! not that! not that! If I in—in trouble, and wanting your help, trusting you, propose to come to you . . . that you may advise me . . . assist me. . . . Oh! are there women so horrible as that . . . ? And she proposes to send it to my husband? Tell me what happened. Tell me all that happened.

LORD GORING: Mrs. Cheveley was concealed in a room adjoining my library, without my knowledge. I thought that the person who was waiting in that room to see me was yourself. Robert came in unexpectedly. A chair or something fell in the room. He forced his way in, and he discovered her. We had a terrible scene. I still thought it was you. He left me in anger. At the end of everything Mrs. Cheveley got possession of your letter—she stole it, when or how, I don't know.

LADY CHILTERN: At what hour did this happen?

LORD GORING: At half-past ten. And now I propose that we tell Robert the whole thing at once.

LADY CHILTERN (*looking at him with amazement that is almost terror*): You want me to tell Robert that the woman you expected was not Mrs. Cheveley, but myself? That it was I whom you thought was concealed in a room in your house, at half-past ten o'clock at night? You want me to tell him that?

LORD GORING: I think it is better that he should know the exact truth.

LADY CHILTERN (*rising*): Oh, I couldn't, I couldn't!

LORD GORING: May I do it?

LADY CHILTERN: No.

LORD GORING (*gravely*): You are wrong, Lady Chiltern.

LADY CHILTERN: No. The letter must be intercepted. That is all. But how can I do it? Letters arrive for him every moment of the day. His secretaries open them and hand them to him. I dare not ask the servants to bring me his letters. It would be impossible. Oh! why don't you tell me what to do?

LORD GORING: Pray be calm, Lady Chiltern, and answer the questions I am going to put to you. You said his secretaries open his letters.

LADY CHILTERN: Yes.

LORD GORING: Who is with him to-day? Mr. Trafford, isn't it?

LADY CHILTERN: No, Mr. Montford, I think.

LORD GORING: You can trust him?

LADY CHILTERN (*with a gesture of despair*): Oh! how do I know?

LORD GORING: He would do what you asked him, wouldn't he?

LADY CHILTERN: I think so.

LORD GORING: Your letter was on pink paper. He could recognise it without reading it, couldn't he? By the colour?

LADY CHILTERN: I suppose so.

LORD GORING: Is he in the house now?

LADY CHILTERN: Yes.

LORD GORING: Then I will go and see him myself, and tell him that a certain letter, written on pink paper, is to be forwarded to Robert to-day, and that at all costs it must not reach him. (*Goes to the door, and opens it.*) Oh! Robert is coming upstairs with the letter in his hand. It has reached him already.

LADY CHILTERN (*with a cry of pain*): Oh! you have saved his life; what have you done with mine?

Enter SIR ROBERT CHILTERN. *He has the letter in his hand, and is reading it. He comes towards his wife, not noticing* LORD GORING'S *presence.*

SIR ROBERT CHILTERN: 'I want you. I trust you. I am coming to you. Gertrude.' Oh, my love! Is this true? Do you indeed trust me, and want me? If so, it was for me to come to you, not for you to write of coming to me. This letter of yours, Gertrude, makes me feel that nothing that the world may do can hurt me now. You want me, Gertrude.

LORD GORING, *unseen by* SIR ROBERT CHILTERN, *makes an imploring sign to* LADY CHILTERN *to accept the situation and* SIR ROBERT'S *error.*

LADY CHILTERN: Yes.

SIR ROBERT CHILTERN: You trust me, Gertrude?

LADY CHILTERN: Yes.

SIR ROBERT CHILTERN: Ah! why did you not add you loved me?

LADY CHILTERN (*taking his hand*): Because I loved you.

LORD GORING *passes into the conservatory.*

SIR ROBERT CHILTERN (*kisses her*): Gertrude, you don't know what I feel. When Montford passed me your letter across the table—he had opened it by mistake, I suppose, without looking at the hand-writing on the envelope and I read it—oh! I did not care what disgrace or punishment was in store for me, I only thought you loved me still.

LADY CHILTERN: There is no disgrace in store for you, nor any public shame. Mrs. Cheveley has handed over to Lord Goring the document that was in her possession, and he has destroyed it.

SIR ROBERT CHILTERN: Are you sure of this, Gertrude?

LADY CHILTERN: Yes; Lord Goring has just told me.

SIR ROBERT CHILTERN: Then I am safe! Oh! what a wonderful thing to be safe! For two days I have been in terror. I am safe now. How did Arthur destroy my letter? Tell me.

LADY CHILTERN: He burned it.

SIR ROBERT CHILTERN: I wish I had seen that one sin of my youth burning to ashes. How many men there are in modem life who would like to see their past burning to white ashes before them! Is Arthur still here?

LADY CHILTERN: Yes; he is in the conservatory.

SIR ROBERT CHILTERN: I am so glad now I made that speech last night in the House, so glad. I made it thinking that public disgrace might be the result. But it has not been so.

LADY CHILTERN: Public honour has been the result.

SIR ROBERT CHILTERN: I think so. I fear so, almost. For although I am safe from detection, although every proof against me is destroyed, I suppose, Gertrude . . . I suppose I should retire from public life? (*He looks anxiously at his wife.*)

LADY CHILTERN (*eagerly*): Oh yes, Robert, you should do that. It is your duty to do that.

SIR ROBERT CHILTERN: It is much to surrender.

LADY CHILTERN: No; it will be much to gain.

SIR ROBERT CHILTERN *walks up and down the room with a troubled expression. Then comes over to his wife, and puts his hand on her shoulder.*

SIR ROBERT CHILTERN: And you would be happy living somewhere alone with me, abroad perhaps, or in the country away from London, away from public life? You would have no regrets?

LADY CHILTERN: Oh! none, Robert.

SIR ROBERT CHILTERN (*sadly*): And your ambition for me? You used to be ambitious for me.

LADY CHILTERN: Oh, my ambition! I have none now, but that we two may love each other. It was your ambition that led you astray. Let us not talk about ambition.

LORD GORING *returns from the conservatory, looking very pleased with himself, and with an entirely new buttonhole that some one has made for him.*

SIR ROBERT CHILTERN (*going towards him*): Arthur, I have to thank you for what you have done for me. I don't know how I can repay you. (*Shakes hands with him.*)

LORD GORING: My dear fellow, I'll tell you at once. At the present moment, under the usual palm tree . . . I mean in the conservatory . . .

Enter MASON.

MASON: Lord Caversham.

LORD GORING: That admirable father of mine really makes a habit of turning up at the wrong moment. It is very heartless of him, very heartless indeed.

Enter LORD CAVERSHAM. MASON *goes out.*

LORD CAVERSHAM: Good-morning, Lady Chiltern! Warmest congratulations to you, Chiltern, on your brilliant speech last night. I have just left the Prime Minister, and you are to have the vacant seat in the Cabinet.

SIR ROBERT CHILTERN (*with a look of joy and triumph*): A seat in the Cabinet?

LORD CAVERSHAM: Yes; here is the Prime Minister's letter. (*Hands letter.*)

SIR ROBERT CHILTERN (*takes letter and reads it*): A seat in the Cabinet!

LORD CAVERSHAM: Certainly, and you well deserve it too. You have got what we want so much in political life nowadays—high character, high moral tone, high principles. (*To* LORD GORING): Everything that you have not got, sir, and never will have.

LORD GORING: I don't like principles, father. I prefer prejudices.

SIR ROBERT CHILTERN *is on the brink of accepting the Prime Minister's offer, when he sees his wife looking at him with her clear, candid eyes. He then realises that it is impossible.*

SIR ROBERT CHILTERN: I cannot accept this offer, Lord Caversham. I have made up my mind to decline it.

LORD CAVERSHAM: Decline it, sir?

SIR ROBERT CHILTERN: My intention is to retire at once from public life.

LORD CAVERSHAM (*angrily*): Decline a seat in the Cabinet, and retire from public life? Never heard such damned* nonsense in the whole course of my existence. I beg your pardon, Lady Chiltern. Chiltern, I beg your pardon. (*To* LORD GORING): Don't grin like that, sir.

LORD GORING: No, father.

LORD CAVERSHAM: Lady Chiltern, you are a sensible woman, the most sensible woman in London, the most sensible woman I know. Will you kindly prevent your husband from making such a . . . from talking such. . . . Will you kindly do that, Lady Chiltern?

LADY CHILTERN: I think my husband is right in his determination, Lord Caversham. I approve of it.

LORD CAVERSHAM: You approve of it? Good heavens!

LADY CHILTERN (*taking her husband's hand*) I admire him for it. I admire him immensely for it. I have never admired him so much before. He is finer than even I thought him. (*To* SIR ROBERT CHILTERN): You will go and write your letter to the Prime Minister now, won't you? Don't hesitate about it, Robert.

SIR ROBERT CHILTERN (*with a touch of bitterness*): I suppose I had better write it at once. Such offers are not repeated. I will ask you to excuse me for a moment, Lord Caversham.

LADY CHILTERN: I may come with you, Robert, may I not?

SIR ROBERT CHILTERN: Yes, Gertrude.

LADY CHILTERN *goes with him.*

---

*Lord Caversham's expletive is characteristic of the language of the old aristocracy.

LORD CAVERSHAM: What is the matter with this family? Something wrong here, eh? (*Tapping his forehead.*) Idiocy? Hereditary, I suppose. Both of them, too. Wife as well as husband. Very sad. Very sad indeed! And they are not an old family. Can't understand it.

LORD GORING: It is not idiocy, father, I assure you.

LORD CAVERSHAM: What is it then, sir?

LORD GORING (*after some hesitation*): Well, it is what is called nowadays a high moral tone, father. That is all.

LORD CAVERSHAM: Hate these new-fangled names. Same thing as we used to call idiocy fifty years ago. Shan't stay in this house any longer.

LORD GORING (*taking his arm*): Oh! just go in there for a moment, father. Third palm tree to the left, the usual palm tree.

LORD CAVERSHAM: What, sir?

LORD GORING: I beg your pardon, father, I forgot. The conservatory, father, the conservatory—there is some one there I want you to talk to.

LORD CAVERSHAM: What about, sir?

LORD GORING: About me, father.

LORD CAVERSHAM (*grimly*): Not a subject on which much eloquence is possible.

LORD GORING: No, father; but the lady is like me. She doesn't care much for eloquence in others. She thinks it a little loud.

LORD CAVERSHAM *goes into the conservatory.* LADY CHILTERN *enters.*

LORD GORING: Lady Chiltern, why are you playing Mrs. Cheveley's cards?

LADY CHILTERN (*startled*): I don't understand you.

LORD GORING: Mrs. Cheveley made an attempt to ruin your husband. Either to drive him from public life, or to make him adopt a dishonourable position. From the latter tragedy you saved him. The former you are now thrusting on him. Why should you do him the wrong Mrs. Cheveley tried to do and failed?

LADY CHILTERN: Lord Goring?

LORD GORING (*pulling himself together for a great effort, and showing the philosopher that underlies the dandy*): Lady Chiltern, allow me.

You wrote me a letter last night in which you said you trusted me and wanted my help. Now is the moment when you really want my help, now is the time when you have got to trust me, to trust in my counsel and judgment. You love Robert. Do you want to kill his love for you? What sort of existence will he have if you rob him of the fruits of his ambition, if you take him from the splendour of a great political career, if you close the doors of public life against him, if you condemn him to sterile failure, he who was made for triumph and success? Women are not meant to judge us, but to forgive us when we need forgiveness. Pardon, not punishment, is their mission. Why should you scourge him with rods for a sin done in his youth, before he knew you, before he knew himself? A man's life is of more value than a woman's. It has larger issues, wider scope, greater ambitions. A woman's life revolves in curves of emotions. It is upon lines of intellect that a man's life progresses. Don't make any terrible mistake, Lady Chiltern. A woman who can keep a man's love, and love him in return, has done all the world wants of women, or should want of them.*

LADY CHILTERN (*troubled and hesitating*): But it is my husband himself who wishes to retire from public life. He feels it is his duty. It was he who first said so.

LORD GORING: Rather than lose your love, Robert would do anything, wreck his whole career, as he is on the brink of doing now. He is making for you a terrible sacrifice. Take my advice, Lady Chiltern, and do not accept a sacrifice so great. If you do, you will live to repent it bitterly. We men and women are not made to accept such sacrifices from each other. We are not worthy of them. Besides, Robert has been punished enough.

LADY CHILTERN: We have both been punished. I set him up too high.

LORD GORING (*with deep feeling in his voice*): Do not for that reason set him down now too low. If he has fallen from his altar, do not thrust him into the mire. Failure to Robert would be the very mire of shame. Power is his passion. He would lose everything, even his

---

*The "philosopher that underlies the dandy," as Wilde indicates in his stage direction, is curiously conventional.

power to feel love. Your husband's life is at this moment in your hands, your husband's love is in your hands. Don't mar both for him.

Enter SIR ROBERT CHILTERN.

SIR ROBERT CHILTERN: Gertrude, here is the draft of my letter. Shall I read it to you?

LADY CHILTERN: Let me see it.

SIR ROBERT *hands her the letter. She reads it, and then, with a gesture of passion, tears it up.*

SIR ROBERT CHILTERN: What are you doing?

LADY CHILTERN: A man's life is of more value than a woman's. It has larger issues, wider scope, greater ambitions. Our lives revolve in curves of emotions. It is upon lines of intellect that a man's life progresses. I have just learnt this, and much else with it, from Lord Goring. And I will not spoil your life for you, nor see you spoil it as a sacrifice to me, a useless sacrifice!*

SIR ROBERT CHILTERN: Gertrude! Gertrude!

LADY CHILTERN: You can forget. Men easily forget. And I forgive. That is how women help the world. I see that now.

SIR ROBERT CHILTERN (*deeply overcome by emotion, embraces her*): My wife! my wife! (*To* LORD GORING): Arthur, it seems that I am always to be in your debt.

LORD GORING: Oh dear no, Robert. Your debt is to Lady Chiltern, not to me!

SIR ROBERT CHILTERN: I owe you much. And now tell me what you were going to ask me just now as Lord Caversham came in.

LORD GORING: Robert, you are your sister's guardian, and I want your consent to my marriage with her. That is all.

LADY CHILTERN: Oh, I am so glad! I am so glad! (*Shakes hands with* LORD GORING.)

LORD GORING: Thank you, Lady Chiltern.

---

*Here Lady Chiltern telescopes the long speech Lord Goring has recently made in response to her letter requesting his help.

SIR ROBERT CHILTERN (*with a troubled look*): My sister to be your wife?

LORD GORING: Yes.

SIR ROBERT CHILTERN (*speaking with great firmness*): Arthur, I am very sorry, but the thing is quite out of the question. I have to think of Mabel's future happiness. And I don't think her happiness would be safe in your hands. And I cannot have her sacrificed!

LORD GORING: Sacrificed!

SIR ROBERT CHILTERN: Yes, utterly sacrificed. Loveless marriages are horrible. But there is one thing worse than an absolutely loveless marriage. A marriage in which there is love, but on one side only; faith, but on one side only; devotion, but on one side only and in which of the two hearts one is sure to be broken.

LORD GORING: But I love Mabel. No other woman has any place in my life.

LADY CHILTERN: Robert, if they love each other, why should they not be married?

SIR ROBERT CHILTERN: Arthur cannot bring Mabel the love that she deserves.

LORD GORING: What reason have you for saying that?

SIR ROBERT CHILTERN (*after a pause*): Do you really require me to tell you?

LORD GORING: Certainly I do.

SIR ROBERT CHILTERN: As you choose. When I called on you yesterday evening I found Mrs. Cheveley concealed in your rooms. It was between ten and eleven o'clock at night. I do not wish to say anything more. Your relations with Mrs. Cheveley have, as I said to you last night, nothing whatsoever to do with me. I know you were engaged to be married to her once. The fascination she exercised over you then seems to have returned. You spoke to me last night of her as of a woman pure and stainless, a woman whom you respected and honoured. That may be so. But I cannot give my sister's life into your hands. It would be wrong of me. It would be unjust, infamously unjust to her.

LORD GORING: I have nothing more to say.

LADY CHILTERN: Robert, it was not Mrs. Cheveley whom Lord Goring expected last night.

SIR ROBERT CHILTERN: Not Mrs. Cheveley! Who was it then?

LORD GORING: Lady Chiltern.

LADY CHILTERN: It was your own wife. Robert, yesterday afternoon Lord Goring told me that if ever I was in trouble I could come to him for help, as he was our oldest and best friend. Later on, after that terrible scene in this room, I wrote to him telling him that I trusted him, that I had need of him, that I was coming to him for help and advice. (SIR ROBERT CHILTERN *takes the letter out of his pocket.*) Yes, that letter. I didn't go to Lord Goring's, after all. I felt that it is from ourselves alone that help can come. Pride made me think that. Mrs. Cheveley went. She stole my letter and sent it anonymously to you this morning, that you should think. . . . Oh! Robert, I cannot tell you what she wished you to think. . . .

SIR ROBERT CHILTERN: What! Had I fallen so low in your eyes that you thought that even for a moment I could have doubted your goodness? Gertrude, Gertrude, you are to me the white image of all good things, and sin can never touch you. Arthur, you can go to Mabel, and you have my best wishes! Oh! stop a moment. There is no name at the beginning of this letter. The brilliant Mrs. Cheveley does not seem to have noticed that. There should be a name.

LADY CHILTERN: Let me write yours. It is you I trust and need. You and none else.

LORD GORING: Well, really, Lady Chiltern, I think I should have back my own letter.

LADY CHILTERN (*smiling*): No; you shall have Mabel. (*Takes the letter and writes her husband's name on it.*)

LORD GORING: Well, I hope she hasn't changed her mind. It's nearly twenty minutes since I saw her last.

Enter MABEL CHILTERN *and* LORD CAVERSHAM.

MABEL CHILTERN: Lord Goring, I think your father's conversation much more improving than yours. I am only going to talk to Lord Caversham in the future, and always under the usual palm tree.

LORD GORING: Darling! (*Kisses her.*)

LORD CAVERSHAM (*considerably taken aback*): What does this mean, sir? You don't mean to say that this charming, clever young lady has been so foolish as to accept you?

LORD GORING: Certainly, father! And Chiltern's been wise enough to accept the seat in the Cabinet.

LORD CAVERSHAM: I am very glad to hear that, Chiltern . . . I congratulate you, sir. If the country doesn't go to the dogs or the Radicals, we shall have you Prime Minister, some day.

Enter MASON.

MASON: Luncheon is on the table, my Lady! (MASON *goes out.*)

MABEL CHILTERN: You'll stop to luncheon, Lord Caversham, won't you?

LORD CAVERSHAM: With pleasure, and I'll drive you down to Downing Street afterwards, Chiltern. You have a great future before you, a great future. Wish I could say the same for you, sir. (*To* LORD GORING): But your career will have to be entirely domestic.

LORD GORING: Yes, father, I prefer it domestic.

LORD CAVERSHAM: And if you don't make this young lady an ideal husband, I'll cut you off with a shilling.

MABEL CHILTERN: An ideal husband! Oh, I don't think I should like that. It sounds like something in the next world.

LORD CAVERSHAM: What do you want him to be then, dear?

MABEL CHILTERN: He can be what he chooses. All I want is to be . . . to be . . . oh! a real wife to him.

LORD CAVERSHAM: Upon my word, there is a good deal of common sense in that, Lady Chiltern.

They all go out except SIR ROBERT CHILTERN. *He sinks into a chair, wrapt in thought. After a little time* LADY CHILTERN *returns to look for him.*

LADY CHILTERN (*leaning over the back of the chair*): Aren't you coming in, Robert?

SIR ROBERT CHILTERN (*taking her hand*): Gertrude, is it love you feel for me, or is it pity merely?

LADY CHILTERN (*kisses him*): It is love, Robert. Love, and only love. For both of us a new life is beginning.

Curtain

SALOMÉ

A TRAGEDY IN ONE ACT.
TRANSLATED FROM THE
FRENCH OF OSCAR WILDE
BY LORD ALFRED DOUGLAS[1]

THE PERSONS OF THE PLAY*

HEROD ANTIPAS, Tetrarch of Judæa
JOKANAAN, The Prophet
THE YOUNG SYRIAN, Captain of the Guard
TIGELLINUS, A Young Roman
A CAPPADOCIAN
A NUBIAN
FIRST SOLDIER
SECOND SOLDIER
THE PAGE OF HERODIAS
JEWS, NAZARENES, ETC.
A SLAVE
NAAMAN, The Executioner
HERODIAS, Wife of the Tetrarch
SALOMÉ, Daughter of Herodias
THE SLAVES OF SALOMÉ

---

*Among the characters: Herod, a tetrarch, or governor of one-fourth of a province; John the Baptist, whose name Wilde renders in its ancient Hebrew form (Jokanaan); a resident of Nubia, an ancient kingdom in northeastern Africa stretching from southern Egypt into what is now Sudan and Ethiopia, whose people were characteristically depicted as black; a resident of Cappadocia, an ancient kingdom in what is now central Turkey that became part of the Roman Empire in A.D. 17.

SCENE: A great terrace in the Palace of HEROD, *set above the banqueting-hall. Some soldiers are leaning over the balcony. To the right there is a gigantic staircase, to the left, at the back, an old cistern surrounded by a wall of green bronze. Moonlight.*[2]

THE YOUNG SYRIAN: How beautiful is the Princess Salomé to-night!

THE PAGE OF HERODIAS: Look at the moon! How strange the moon seems! She is like a woman rising from a tomb. She is like a dead woman. You would fancy she was looking for dead things.

THE YOUNG SYRIAN: She has a strange look. She is like a little princess who wears a yellow veil, and whose feet are of silver. She is like a princess who has little white doves for feet. You would fancy she was dancing.

THE PAGE OF HERODIAS: She is like a woman who is dead. She moves very slowly.

Noise in the banqueting-hall.

FIRST SOLDIER: What an uproar! Who are those wild beasts howling!

SECOND SOLDIER: The Jews. They are always like that. They are disputing about their religion.

FIRST SOLDIER: Why do they dispute about their religion?

SECOND SOLDIER: I cannot tell. They are always doing it. The Pharisees, for instance, say that there are angels, and the Sadducees* declare that angels do not exist.

---

*Pharisees were members of a Jewish sect that strictly followed religious laws; Sadducees were high priests who rejected anything outside Jewish law (such as the existence of angels or resurrection after death).

FIRST SOLDIER: I think it is ridiculous to dispute about such things.

THE YOUNG SYRIAN: How beautiful is the Princess Salomé to-night!

THE PAGE OF HERODIAS: You are always looking at her. You look at her too much. It is dangerous to look at people in such fashion. Something terrible may happen.

THE YOUNG SYRIAN: She is very beautiful to-night.

FIRST SOLDIER: The Tetrarch has a sombre look.

SECOND SOLDIER: Yes, he has a sombre look.

FIRST SOLDIER: He is looking at something.

SECOND SOLDIER: He is looking at some one.

FIRST SOLDIER: At whom is he looking?

SECOND SOLDIER: I cannot tell.

THE YOUNG SYRIAN: How pale the Princess is! Never have I seen her so pale. She is like the shadow of a white rose in a mirror of silver.

THE PAGE OF HERODIAS: You must not look at her. You look too much at her.

FIRST SOLDIER: Herodias has filled the cup of the Tetrarch.

THE CAPPADOCIAN: Is that the Queen Herodias, she who wears a black mitre sewn with pearls, and whose hair is powdered with blue dust?

FIRST SOLDIER: Yes, that is Herodias, the Tetrarch's wife.

SECOND SOLDIER: The Tetrarch is very fond of wine. He has wine of three sorts. One which is brought from the Island of Samothrace,* and is purple like the cloak of Cæsar.

THE CAPPADOCIAN: I have never seen Cæsar.

SECOND SOLDIER: Another that comes from a town called Cyprus, and is yellow like gold.

THE CAPPADOCIAN: I love gold.

SECOND SOLDIER: And the third is a wine of Sicily. That wine is red like blood.

THE NUBIAN: The gods of my country are very fond of blood.

---

*Greek island in the northeastern Aegean Sea; Wilde's audience would have been familiar with it as the place where the statue Winged Victory (now in the Louvre) was discovered in 1863.

Twice in the year we sacrifice to them young men and maidens; fifty young men and a hundred maidens. But it seems we never give them quite enough, for they are very harsh to us.

THE CAPPADOCIAN: In my country there are no gods left. The Romans have driven them out. There are some who say that they have hidden themselves in the mountains, but I do not believe it. Three nights I have been on the mountains seeking them everywhere. I did not find them. And at last I called them by their names, and they did not come. I think they are dead.

FIRST SOLDIER: The Jews worship a God that you cannot see.

THE CAPPADOCIAN: I cannot understand that.

FIRST SOLDIER: In fact, they only believe in things that you cannot see.

THE CAPPADOCIAN: That seems to me altogether ridiculous.

THE VOICE OF JOKANAAN: After me shall come another mightier than I. I am not worthy so much as to unloose the latchet of his shoes. When he cometh, the solitary places shall be glad. They shall blossom like the lily. The eyes of the blind shall see the day, and the ears of the deaf shall be opened. The new-born child shall put his hand upon the dragon's lair, he shall lead the lions by their manes.*

SECOND SOLDIER: Make him be silent. He is always saying ridiculous things.

FIRST SOLDIER: No, no. He is a holy man. He is very gentle, too. Every day, when I give him to eat he thanks me.

THE CAPPADOCIAN: Who is he?

FIRST SOLDIER: A prophet.

THE CAPPADOCIAN: What is his name?

FIRST SOLDIER: Jokanaan.

THE CAPPADOCIAN: Whence comes he?

FIRST SOLDIER: From the desert, where he fed on locusts and wild honey. He was clothed in camel's hair, and round his loins he had a leathern belt. He was very terrible to look upon. A great multitude used to follow him. He even had disciples.

---

*The prophecy, reminiscent of both the New Testament and Virgil, does not use the uppercase H for "he" or "him" in referring to the Messiah; later, the prophet adopts this capitalization.

THE CAPPADOCIAN: What is he talking of?

FIRST SOLDIER: We can never tell. Sometimes he says terrible things; but it is impossible to understand what he says.

THE CAPPADOCIAN: May one see him?

FIRST SOLDIER: No. The Tetrarch has forbidden it.

THE YOUNG SYRIAN: The Princess has hidden her face behind her fan! Her little white hands are fluttering like doves that fly to their dove-cots. They are like white butterflies. They are just like white butterflies.

THE PAGE OF HERODIAS: What is that to you? Why do you look at her? You must not look at her. . . . Something terrible may happen.

THE CAPPADOCIAN (*pointing to the cistern*): What a strange prison!

SECOND SOLDIER: It is an old cistern.

THE CAPPADOCIAN: An old cistern! It must be very unhealthy.

SECOND SOLDIER: Oh, no! For instance, the Tetrarch's brother, his elder brother, the first husband of Herodias the Queen, was imprisoned there for twelve years. It did not kill him. At the end of the twelve years he had to be strangled.

THE CAPPADOCIAN: Strangled? Who dared to do that?

SECOND SOLDIER (*pointing to the Executioner, a huge Negro**): That man yonder, Naaman.

THE CAPPADOCIAN: He was not afraid?

SECOND SOLDIER: Oh, no! The Tetrarch sent him the ring.

THE CAPPADOCIAN: What ring?

SECOND SOLDIER: The death-ring. So he was not afraid.

THE CAPPADOCIAN: Yet it is a terrible thing to strangle a king.

FIRST SOLDIER: Why? Kings have but one neck, like other folk.

THE CAPPADOCIAN: I think it terrible.

THE YOUNG SYRIAN: The Princess rises! She is leaving the table! She looks very troubled. Ah, she is coming this way. Yes, she is coming towards us. How pale she is! Never have I seen her so pale.

---

*Presumably the Nubian.

THE PAGE OF HERODIAS: Do not look at her. I pray you not to look at her.

THE YOUNG SYRIAN: She is like a dove that has strayed. . . . She is like a narcissus trembling in the wind. . . . She is like a silver flower.

Enter SALOMÉ.

SALOMÉ: I will not stay. I cannot stay. Why does the Tetrarch look at me all the while with his mole's eyes under his shaking eyelids? It is strange that the husband of my mother looks at me like that. I know not what it means. In truth, yes I know it.

THE YOUNG SYRIAN: You have just left the feast, Princess?

SALOMÉ: How sweet the air is here! I can breathe here! Within there are Jews from Jerusalem who are tearing each other in pieces over their foolish ceremonies, and barbarians who drink and drink, and spill their wine on the pavement, and Greeks from Smyrna with painted eyes and painted cheeks, and frizzed hair curled in twisted coils, and silent, subtle Egyptians, with long nails of jade and russett cloaks, and Romans brutal and coarse, with their uncouth jargon. Ah! how I loathe the Romans! They are rough and common, and they give themselves the airs of noble lords.

THE YOUNG SYRIAN: Will you be seated, Princess?

THE PAGE OF HERODIAS: Why do you speak to her? Why do you look at her? Oh! something terrible will happen.

SALOMÉ: How good to see the moon. She is like a little piece of money, you would think she was a little silver flower. The moon is cold and chaste. I am sure she is a virgin, she has a virgin's beauty. Yes, she is a virgin. She has never defiled herself. She has never abandoned herself to men, like the other goddesses.

THE VOICE OF JOKANAAN: The Lord hath come. The son of man hath come. The centaurs have hidden themselves in the rivers, and the sirens* have left the rivers, and are lying beneath the leaves of the forest.

---

*A centaur was a mythical creature with the body of a horse and, from the waist up, the torso, limbs, and head of a man. Sirens were legendary girls who, by singing to lonesome sailors from rocks in the sea, would lure them to destroy their ships.

SALOMÉ: Who was that who cried out?
SECOND SOLDIER: The prophet, Princess.
SALOMÉ: Ah, the prophet! He of whom the Tetrarch is afraid?
SECOND SOLDIER: We know nothing of that, Princess. It was the prophet Jokanaan who cried out.
THE YOUNG SYRIAN: Is it your pleasure that I bid them bring your litter, Princess? The night is fair in the garden.
SALOMÉ: He says terrible things about my mother, does he not!
SECOND SOLDIER: We never understand what he says, Princess.
SALOMÉ: Yes; he says terrible things about her.

Enter a SLAVE.

THE SLAVE: Princess, the Tetrarch prays you to return to the feast.
SALOMÉ: I will not go back.
THE YOUNG SYRIAN: Pardon me, Princess, but if you do not return some misfortune may happen.
SALOMÉ: Is he an old man, this prophet?
THE YOUNG SYRIAN: Princess, it were better to return. Suffer me to lead you in.
SALOMÉ: This prophet . . . is he an old man?
FIRST SOLDIER: No, Princess, he is quite a young man.*
SECOND SOLDIER: You cannot be sure. There are those who say he is Elias.†
SALOMÉ: Who is Elias?
SECOND SOLDIER: A very ancient prophet of this country, Princess.
THE SLAVE: What answer may I give the Tetrarch from the Princess?
THE VOICE OF JOKANAAN: Rejoice not thou, land of Palestine, because the rod of him who smote thee is broken. For from the seed of the serpent shall come forth a basilisk,‡ and that which is born of it shall devour the birds.
SALOMÉ: What a strange voice! I would speak with him.

---

*In this detail, Wilde differs from the usual depiction of John the Baptist.

†The prophet Elijah.

‡Legendary reptile whose breath and gaze could kill humans.

FIRST SOLDIER: I fear it is impossible, Princess. The Tetrarch does not wish any one to speak with him. He has even forbidden the high priest to speak with him.

SALOMÉ: I desire to speak with him.

FIRST SOLDIER: It is impossible, Princess.

SALOMÉ: I will speak with him.

THE YOUNG SYRIAN: Would it not be better to return to the banquet?

SALOMÉ: Bring forth this prophet.

Exit the SLAVE.

FIRST SOLDIER: We dare not, Princess.

SALOMÉ (*approaching the cistern and looking down into it*): How black it is down there! It must be terrible to be in so black a pit! It is like a tomb. . . . (*To the* SOLDIERS): Did you not hear me? Bring out the prophet. I wish to see him.

SECOND SOLDIER: Princess, I beg you do not require this of us.

SALOMÉ: You keep me waiting!

FIRST SOLDIER: Princess, our lives belong to you, but we cannot do what you have asked of us. And indeed, it is not of us that you should ask this thing.

SALOMÉ (*looking at the* YOUNG SYRIAN): Ah!

THE PAGE OF HERODIAS: Oh! what is going to happen? I am sure that some misfortune will happen.

SALOMÉ (*going up to the* YOUNG SYRIAN): You will do this thing for me, will you not, Narraboth? You will do this thing for me. I have always been kind to you. You will do it for me. I would but look at this strange prophet. Men have talked so much of him. Often have I heard the Tetrarch talk of him. I think the Tetrarch is afraid of him. Are you, even you, also afraid of him, Narraboth?

THE YOUNG SYRIAN: I fear him not, Princess; there is no man I fear. But the Tetrarch has formally forbidden that any man should raise the cover of this well.

SALOMÉ: You will do this thing for me, Narraboth, and to-morrow when I pass in my litter beneath the gateway of the idol-sellers I will let fall for you a little flower, a little green flower.

THE YOUNG SYRIAN: Princess, I cannot, I cannot.

SALOMÉ (*smiling*): You will do this thing for me, Narraboth. You know that you will do this thing for me. And to-morrow when I pass in my litter by the bridge of the idol-buyers, I will look at you through the muslin veils, I will look at you, Narraboth, it may be I will smile at you. Look at me, Narraboth, look at me. Ah! you know that you will do what I ask of you. You know it well. . . . I know that you will do this thing.

THE YOUNG SYRIAN (*signing to the third soldier*): Let the prophet come forth. . . . The Princess Salomé desires to see him.

SALOMÉ: Ah!

THE PAGE OF HERODIAS: Oh! How strange the moon looks. You would think it was the hand of a dead woman who is seeking to cover herself with a shroud.*

THE YOUNG SYRIAN: She has a strange look! She is like a little princess, whose eyes are eyes of amber. Through the clouds of muslin she is smiling like a little princess.

The prophet comes out of the cistern. SALOMÉ *looks at him and steps slowly back.*

JOKANAAN: Where is he whose cup of abominations is now full? Where is he, who in a robe of silver shall one day die in the face of all the people? Bid him come forth, that he may hear the voice of him who had cried in the waste places and in the houses of kings.

SALOMÉ: Of whom is he speaking?

THE YOUNG SYRIAN: You never can tell, Princess.

JOKANAAN: Where is she who, having seen the images of men painted on the walls, the images of the Chaldeans limned in colours, gave herself up unto the lust of her eyes, and sent ambassadors into Chaldea?†

SALOMÉ: It is of my mother that he speaks.

THE YOUNG SYRIAN: Oh, no, Princess.

SALOMÉ: Yes, it is of my mother that he speaks.

JOKANAAN: Where is she who gave herself unto the Captains of

---

*The page links the moon, which has already been compared to a pale woman, with death.

†First instance onstage in which the audience hears the prophet decry Herodias.

Assyria, who have baldricks on their loins, and tiaras of divers colours on their heads? Where is she who hath given herself to the young men of Egypt, who are clothed in fine linen and purple, whose shields are of gold, whose helmets are of silver, whose bodies are mighty? Bid her rise up from the bed of her abominations, from the bed of her incestuousness,* that she may hear the words of him who prepareth the way of the Lord, that she may repent her of her iniquities. Though she will never repent, but will stick fast in her abominations; bid her come, for the fan of the Lord is in His hand.

SALOMÉ: But he is terrible, he is terrible!

THE YOUNG SYRIAN: Do not stay here, Princess, I beseech you.

SALOMÉ: It is his eyes above all that are terrible. They are like black holes burned by torches in a Tyrian tapestry. They are like black caverns where dragons dwell. They are like the black caverns of Egypt in which the dragons make their lairs. They are like black lakes troubled by fantastic moons. . . . Do you think he will speak again?

THE YOUNG SYRIAN: Do not stay here, Princess. I pray you do not stay here.

SALOME: How wasted he is! He is like a thin ivory statue. He is like an image of silver. I am sure he is chaste as the moon is.† He is like a moonbeam, like a shaft of silver. His flesh must be cool like ivory. I would look closer at him.

THE YOUNG SYRIAN: No, no, Princess.

SALOMÉ: I must look at him closer.

THE YOUNG SYRIAN: Princess! Princess!

JOKANAAN: Who is this woman who is looking at me? I will not have her look at me. Wherefore doth she look at me with her golden eyes, under her gilded eyelids? I know not who she is. I do not wish to know who she is. Bid her begone. It is not to her that I would speak.

SALOMÉ: I am Salomé, daughter of Herodias, Princess of Judæa.

JOKANAAN: Back! Daughter of Babylon! Come not near the cho-

---

*According to the Old Testament of the Bible, a man who married the widow of his deceased brother was committing incest.

†The moon is now linked to the prophet himself.

sen of the Lord. Thy mother hath filled the earth with the wine of her iniquities, and the cry of her sins hath come up to the ears of God.

SALOMÉ: Speak again, Jokanaan. Thy voice is wine to me.

THE YOUNG SYRIAN: Princess! Princess! Princess!

SALOMÉ: Speak again! Speak again, Jokanaan, and tell me what I must do.

JOKANAAN: Daughter of Sodom,[3] come not near me! But cover thy face with a veil, and scatter ashes upon thine head, and get thee to the desert and seek out the Son of Man.

SALOMÉ: Who is he, the Son of Man? Is he as beautiful as thou art, Jokanaan?

JOKANAAN: Get thee behind me! I hear in the palace the beating of the wings of the angel of death.*

THE YOUNG SYRIAN: Princess, I beseech thee to go within.

JOKANAAN: Angel of the Lord God, what dost thou here with thy sword? Whom seekest thou in this foul palace? The day of him who shall die in a robe of silver has not yet come.

SALOMÉ: Jokanaan!

JOKANAAN: Who speaketh?

SALOMÉ: Jokanaan, I am amorous of thy body! Thy body is white like the lilies of a field that the mower hath never mowed. Thy body is white like the snows that lie on the mountains, like the snows that lie on the mountains of Judæa, and come down into the valleys. The roses in the garden of the Queen of Arabia are not so white as thy body. Neither the roses in the garden of the Queen of Arabia, nor the feet of the dawn when they light on the leaves, nor the breast of the moon when she lies on the breast of the sea. . . . There is nothing in the world so white as thy body. Let me touch thy body.[4]

JOKANAAN: Back! Daughter of Babylon! By woman came evil into the world. Speak not to me. I will not listen to thee. I listen but to the voice of the Lord God.

SALOMÉ: Thy body is hideous. It is like the body of a leper. It is like a plastered wall where vipers have crawled; like a plastered wall

---

*According to three of the Gospels, Jesus utters the same phrase to Peter (regarding the Devil).

where the scorpions have made their nest. It is like a whitened sepulchre full of loathsome things. It is horrible, thy body is horrible. It is of thy hair that I am enamoured, Jokanaan. Thy hair is like clusters of grapes, like the clusters of black grapes that hang from the vine-trees of Edom* in the land of the Edomites. Thy hair is like the cedars of Lebanon, like the great cedars of Lebanon that give their shade to the lions and to the robbers who would hide themselves by day. The long black nights, when the moon hides her face, when the stars are afraid, are not so black. The silence that dwells in the forest is not so black. There is nothing in the world so black as thy hair. . . . Let me touch thy hair.

JOKANAAN: Back, daughter of Sodom! Touch me not. Profane not the temple of the Lord God.

SALOMÉ: Thy hair is horrible. It is covered with mire and dust. It is like a crown of thorns[5] which they have placed on thy forehead. It is like a knot of black serpents writhing round thy neck. I love not thy hair. . . . It is thy mouth that I desire, Jokanaan. Thy mouth is like a band of scarlet on a tower of ivory. It is like a pomegranate cut with a knife of ivory. The pomegranate-flowers that blossom in the garden of Tyre,† and are redder than roses, are not so red. The red blasts of trumpets, that herald the approach of kings, and make afraid the enemy, are not so red. Thy mouth is redder than the feet of those who tread the wine in the wine-press. Thy mouth is redder than the feet of the doves who haunt the temples and are fed by the priests. It is redder than the feet of him who cometh from a forest where he hath slain a lion, and seen gilded tigers. Thy mouth is like a branch of coral that fishers have found in the twilight of the sea, the coral that they keep for the kings . . . ! It is like the vermilion that the Moabites find in the mines of Moab,‡ the vermilion that the kings take from them. It is like the bow of the King of the Persians, that is painted with vermilion, and is tipped with coral. There is nothing in the world so red as thy mouth. . . . Let me kiss thy mouth.

---

*Area between the Dead Sea and the Gulf of Aqaba, in southern Palestine, that originally belonged to Esau, brother of Jacob.

†Ancient Phoenician city in what is now Lebanon.

‡Ancient country to the west of the river Jordan, in what is now the country of Jordan.

JOKANAAN: Never, daughter of Babylon! Daughter of Sodom! Never.

SALOMÉ: I will kiss thy mouth, Jokanaan. I will kiss thy mouth.

THE YOUNG SYRIAN: Princess, Princess, thou who art like a garden of myrrh, thou who art the dove of all doves, look not at this man, look not at him! Do not speak such words to him. I cannot suffer them. . . . Princess, Princess, do not speak these things.

SALOMÉ: I will kiss thy mouth, Jokanaan.

THE YOUNG SYRIAN: Ah!

He kills himself[6] *and falls between* SALOMÉ *and* JOKANAAN.

THE PAGE OF HERODIAS: The young Syrian has slain himself! The young captain has slain himself! He has slain himself who was my friend! I gave him a little box of perfumes and ear-rings wrought in silver, and now he has killed himself! Ah, did he not foretell that some misfortune would happen? I, too, foretold it, and it has happened. Well, I knew that the moon was seeking a dead thing,[7] but I knew not that it was he whom she sought. Ah! why did I not hide him from the moon? If I had hidden him in a cavern she would not have seen him.

FIRST SOLDIER: Princess, the young captain has just killed himself.

SALOMÉ: Let me kiss thy mouth, Jokanaan.

JOKANAAN: Art thou not afraid, daughter of Herodias? Did I not tell thee that I had heard in the palace the beatings of the wings of the angel of death, and hath he not come, the angel of death?

SALOMÉ: Let me kiss thy mouth.

JOKANAAN: Daughter of adultery, there is but one who can save thee, it is He of whom I spake. Go seek Him. He is in a boat on the sea of Galilee, and He talketh with His disciples. Kneel down on the shore of the sea, and call unto Him by His name. When He cometh to thee (and to all who call on Him He cometh) bow thyself at His feet and ask of Him the remission of thy sins.*

SALOMÉ: Let me kiss thy mouth.

---

*Although the audience cannot hear the difference, Wilde now has the prophet capitalize the H in "He," "Him," and "His," reflecting Christ's divinity.

JOKANAAN: Cursed be thou! Daughter of an incestuous mother, be thou accursed!

SALOMÉ: I will kiss thy mouth, Jokanaan.

JOKANAAN: I do not wish to look at thee. I will not look at thee, thou art accursed, Salomé, thou art accursed.

He goes down into the cistern.

SALOMÉ: I will kiss thy mouth, Jokanaan. I will kiss thy mouth.

FIRST SOLDIER: We must bear away the body to another place. The Tetrarch does not care to see dead bodies, save the bodies of those whom he himself has slain.

THE PAGE OF HERODIAS: He was my brother, and nearer to me than a brother.[8] I gave him a little box of perfumes, and a ring of agate that he wore always on his hand. In the evening we used to walk by the river, among the almond trees, and he would tell me of the things of his country. He spake ever very low. The sound of his voice was like the sound of the flute, of a flute player. Also he much loved to gaze at himself in the river. I used to reproach him for that.

SECOND SOLDIER: You are right; we must hide the body. The Tetrarch must not see it.

FIRST SOLDIER: The Tetrarch will not come to this place. He never comes on the terrace. He is too much afraid of the prophet.

Enter HEROD, HERODIAS, *and all the* COURT.

HEROD: Where is Salomé? Where is the Princess? Why did she not return to the banquet as I commanded her? Ah! There she is!

HERODIAS: You must not look at her! You are always looking at her!

HEROD: The moon has a strange look to-night. Has she not a strange look? She is like a mad woman,* a mad woman who is seeking everywhere for lovers. She is naked, too. She is quite naked. The clouds are seeking to clothe her nakedness, but she will not let them. She shows herself naked in the sky. She reels through

---

*The moon suddenly becomes a naked, drunken, mad woman.

the clouds like a drunken woman. . . . I am sure she is looking for lovers. Does she not reel like a drunken woman? She is like a mad woman, is she not?

HERODIAS: No; the moon is like the moon, that is all. Let us go within. . . . You have nothing to do here.

HEROD: I will stay here! Manesseh, lay carpets there. Light torches, bring forth the ivory tables, and the tables of jasper. The air here is delicious. I will drink more wine with my guests. We must show all honours to the ambassadors of Cæsar.

HERODIAS: It is not because of them that you remain.

HEROD: Yes; the air is delicious. Come, Herodias, our guests await us. Ah! I have slipped! I have slipped in blood! It is an ill omen. It is a very evil omen. Wherefore is there blood here . . . ? And this body, what does this body here? Think you that I am like the King of Egypt, who gives no feast to his guests but that he shows them a corpse? Whose is it? I will not look on it.

FIRST SOLDIER: It is our captain, sire. He is the young Syrian whom you made captain only three days ago.

HEROD: I gave no order that he should be slain.

SECOND SOLDIER: He killed himself, sire.

HEROD: For what reason? I had made him captain.

SECOND SOLDIER: We do not know, sire. But he killed himself.

HEROD: That seems strange to me. I thought it was only the Roman philosophers who killed themselves. Is it not true, Tigellinus, that the philosophers at Rome kill themselves?

TIGELLINUS: There are some who kill themselves, sire. They are the Stoics.* The Stoics are coarse people. They are ridiculous people. I myself regard them as being perfectly ridiculous.

HEROD: I also. It is ridiculous to kill oneself.

TIGELLINUS: Everybody at Rome laughs at them. The Emperor has written a satire against them. It is recited everywhere.

HEROD: Ah! he has written a satire against them? Cæsar is wonderful. He can do everything. . . . It is strange that the young Syrian has killed himself. I am sorry he has killed himself. I am very sorry, for he was fair to look upon. He was even very fair. He had

---

*Greek and Roman philosophers who believed in accepting what happened to them without fighting their fates.

very languorous eyes. I remember that I saw that he looked languorously at Salomé. Truly, I thought he looked too much at her.*

HERODIAS: There are others who look at her too much.

HEROD: His father was a king. I drove him from his kingdom. And you made a slave of his mother, who was a queen, Herodias. So he was here as my guest, as it were, and for that reason I made him my captain. I am sorry he is dead. Ho! Why have you left the body here? I will not look at it—away with it. (*They take away the body.*) It is cold here. There is a wind blowing. Is there not a wind blowing?

HERODIAS: No, there is no wind.

HEROD: I tell you there is a wind that blows. . . . And I hear in the air something that is like the beating of wings, like the beating of vast wings.† Do you not hear it?

HERODIAS: I hear nothing.

HEROD: I hear it no longer. But I heard it. It was the blowing of the wind, no doubt. It has passed away. But no, I hear it again. Do you not hear it? It is just like the beating of wings.

HERODIAS: I tell you there is nothing. You are ill. Let us go within.

HEROD: I am not ill. It is your daughter who is sick. She has the mien of a sick person. Never have I seen her so pale.

HERODIAS: I have told you not to look at her.

HEROD: Pour me forth wine. (*Wine is brought.*) Salomé, come drink a little wine with me. I have here a wine that is exquisite. Cæsar himself sent it me. Dip into it thy little red lips, that I may drain the cup.

SALOMÉ: I am not thirsty, Tetrarch.

HEROD: You hear how she answers me, this daughter of yours?

HERODIAS: She does right. Why are you always gazing at her?

HEROD: Bring me ripe fruits. (*Fruits are brought.*) Salomé, come and eat fruit with me. I love to see in a fruit the mark of thy little teeth. Bite but a little of this fruit and then I will eat what is left.

SALOMÉ: I am not hungry, Tetrarch.

---

*Herod echoes Herodias (as she reminds him in her next speech).

†Although a pagan, Herod senses the presence of the angel of death (whom the prophet mentioned earlier).

HEROD (*to* HERODIAS): You see how you have brought up this daughter of yours.

HERODIAS: My daughter and I come of a royal race. As for thee, thy father was a camel driver! He was also a robber!

HEROD: Thou liest!

HERODIAS: Thou knowest well that it is true.

HEROD: Salomé, come and sit next to me. I will give thee the throne of thy mother.

SALOMÉ: I am not tired, Tetrarch.

HERODIAS: You see what she thinks of you.

HEROD: Bring me—what is it that I desire? I forget. Ah! ah! I remember.

THE VOICE OF JOKANAAN: Lo! the time is come! That which I foretold has come to pass, saith the Lord God. Lo! the day of which I spoke.

HERODIAS: Bid him be silent. I will not listen to his voice. This man is for ever vomiting insults against me.

HEROD: He has said nothing against you. Besides, he is a very great prophet.

HERODIAS: I do not believe in prophets. Can a man tell what will come to pass? No man knows it. Moreover, he is for ever insulting me. But I think you are afraid of him. . . . I know well that you are afraid of him.

HEROD: I am not afraid of him. I am afraid of no man.

HERODIAS: I tell you, you are afraid of him. If you are not afraid of him why do you not deliver him to the Jews, who for these six months past have been clamouring for him?

A JEW: Truly, my lord, it were better to deliver him into our hands.

HEROD: Enough on this subject. I have already given you my answer. I will not deliver him into your hands. He is a holy man. He is a man who has seen God.

A JEW: That cannot be.* There is no man who hath seen God since the prophet Elias. He is the last man who saw God. In these days God doth not show Himself. He hideth Himself. Therefore great evils have come upon the land.

---

*The following speeches dramatize the contentiousness of the Jews, who are divided by their differing doctrines.

ANOTHER JEW: Verily, no man knoweth if Elias the prophet did indeed see God. Peradventure it was but the shadow of God that he saw.

A THIRD JEW: God is at no time hidden. He showeth Himself at all times and in everything. God is in what is evil, even as He is in what is good.

A FOURTH JEW: That must not be said. It is a very dangerous doctrine. It is a doctrine that cometh from the schools at Alexandria, where men teach the philosophy of the Greeks. And the Greeks are Gentiles. They are not even circumcised.

A FIFTH JEW: No one can tell how God worketh. His ways are very mysterious. It may be that the things which we call evil are good, and that the things which we call good are evil. There is no knowledge of anything. We must needs submit to everything, for God is very strong. He breaketh in pieces the strong together with the weak, for He regardeth not any man.

FIRST JEW: Thou speaketh truly. God is terrible. He breaketh the strong and the weak as a man brays corn in a mortar. But this man hath never seen God. No man hath seen God since the prophet Elias.

HERODIAS: Make them be silent. They weary me.

HEROD: But I have heard it said that Jokanaan himself is your prophet Elias.

THE JEW: That cannot be. It is more than three hundred years since the days of the prophet Elias.

HEROD: There be some who say that this man is the prophet Elias.

A NAZARENE: I am sure that he is the prophet Elias.

THE JEW: Nay, but he is not the prophet Elias.

THE VOICE OF JOKANAAN: So the day is come, the day of the Lord, and I hear upon the mountains the feet of Him who shall be the Saviour of the world.

HEROD: What does that mean? The Saviour of the world.

TIGELLINUS: It is a title that Cæsar takes.

HEROD: But Cæsar is not coming into Judæa. Only yesterday I received letters from Rome. They contained nothing concerning this matter. And you, Tigellinus, who were at Rome during the winter, you heard nothing concerning this matter, did you?

TIGELLINUS: Sire, I heard nothing concerning the matter. I was explaining the title. It is one of Cæsar's titles.

HEROD: But Cæsar cannot come. He is too gouty. They say that his feet are like the feet of an elephant. Also there are reasons of State. He who leaves Rome loses Rome. He will not come. Howbeit Cæsar is lord, he will come if he wishes. Nevertheless, I do not think he will come.

FIRST NAZARENE: It was not concerning Cæsar that the prophet spake these words, sire.

HEROD: Not of Cæsar?

FIRST NAZARENE: No, sire.

HEROD: Concerning whom, then, did he speak?

FIRST NAZARENE: Concerning Messias* who has come.

A JEW: Messias hath not come.

FIRST NAZARENE: He hath come, and everywhere He worketh miracles.

HERODIAS: Ho! ho! miracles! I do not believe in miracles. I have seen too many. (*To the Page*): My fan!

FIRST NAZARENE: This man worketh true miracles. Thus, at a marriage which took place in a little town of Galilee, a town of some importance, He changed water into wine. Certain persons who were present related it to me. Also He healed two lepers that were seated before the Gate of Capernaum simply by touching them.

SECOND NAZARENE: Nay, it was blind men that he healed at Capernaum.

FIRST NAZARENE: Nay, they were lepers. But He hath healed blind people also, and He was seen on a mountain talking with angels.

A SADDUCEE: Angels do not exist.

A PHARISEE: Angels exist, but I do not believe that this Man has talked with them.

FIRST NAZARENE: He was seen by a great multitude of people talking with angels.

A SADDUCEE: Not with angels.

HERODIAS: How these men weary me! They are ridiculous! (*To*

---

*Messiah.

the Page): Well, my fan! (*The Page gives her the fan.*) You have a dreamer's look; you must not dream. It is only sick people who dream. (*She strikes the Page with her fan.*)

SECOND NAZARENE: There is also the miracle of the daughter of Jairus.

FIRST NAZARENE: Yes, that is sure. No man can gainsay it.

HERODIAS: These men are mad. They have looked too long on the moon. Command them to be silent.

HEROD: What is this miracle of the daughter of Jairus?

FIRST NAZARENE: The daughter of Jairus was dead. He raised her from the dead.

HEROD: He raises the dead?

FIRST NAZARENE: Yea, sire, He raiseth the dead.

HEROD: I do not wish Him to do that. I forbid Him to do that. I allow no man to raise the dead. This Man must be found and told that I forbid Him to raise the dead. Where is this Man at present?

SECOND NAZARENE: He is in every place, my lord, but it is hard to find Him.

FIRST NAZARENE: It is said that He is now in Samaria.*

A JEW: It is easy to see that this is not Messias, if He is in Samaria. It is not to the Samaritans that Messias shall come. The Samaritans are accursed. They bring no offerings to the Temple.

SECOND NAZARENE: He left Samaria a few days since. I think that at the present moment He is in the neighbourhood of Jerusalem.

FIRST NAZARENE: No, he is not there. I have just come from Jerusalem. For two months they have had no tidings of Him.

HEROD: No matter! But let them find Him, and tell Him from me, I will not allow him to raise the dead! To change water into wine, to heal the lepers and the blind. . . . He may do these things if He will. I say nothing against these things. In truth I hold it a good deed to heal a leper. But I allow no man to raise the dead. It would be terrible if the dead came back.[9]

THE VOICE OF JOKANAAN: Ah, the wanton! The harlot! Ah! the daughter of Babylon with her golden eyes and her gilded eye-

---

*Ancient city and former capital of the Northern Kingdom of Israel; Elijah and John the Baptist were said to be buried there.

lids! Thus saith the Lord God, Let there come against her a multitude of men. Let the people take stones and stone her. . . .

HERODIAS: Command him to be silent.

THE VOICE OF JOKANAAN: Let the war captains pierce her with their swords, let them crush her beneath their shields.[10]

HERODIAS: Nay, but it is infamous.

THE VOICE OF JOKANAAN: It is thus that I will wipe out all wickedness from the earth, and that all women shall learn not to imitate her abominations.

HERODIAS: You hear what he says against me? You allow him to revile your wife?[11]

HEROD: He did not speak your name.

HERODIAS: What does that matter? You know well that it is I whom he seeks to revile. And I am your wife, am I not?

HEROD: Of a truth, dear and noble Herodias, you are my wife, and before that you were the wife of my brother.

HERODIAS: It was you who tore me from his arms.

HEROD: Of a truth I was stronger. . . . But let us not talk of that matter. I do not desire to talk of it. It is the cause of the terrible words that the prophet has spoken. Peradventure on account of it a misfortune will come. Let us not speak of this matter. Noble Herodias, we are not mindful of our guests. Fill thou my cup, my well-beloved. Fill with wine the great goblets of silver, and the great goblets of glass. I will drink to Cæsar. There are Romans here; we must drink to Cæsar.

ALL: Cæsar! Cæsar!

HEROD: Do you not see your daughter, how pale she is?

HERODIAS: What is it to you if she be pale or not?

HEROD: Never have I seen her so pale.

HERODIAS: You must not look at her.

THE VOICE OF JOKANAAN: In that day the sun shall become black like the sackcloth* of hair, and the moon shall become like blood, and the stars of the heavens shall fall upon the earth like ripe figs that fall from the fig-tree, and the kings of the earth shall be afraid.

HERODIAS: Ah! Ah! I should like to see that day of which he

---

*Traditionally, Jews in mourning wore garments of sackcloth.

speaks, when the moon shall become like blood, and when the stars shall fall upon the earth like ripe figs. This prophet talks like a drunken man . . . but I cannot suffer the sound of his voice. I hate his voice. Command him to be silent.

HEROD: I will not. I cannot understand what it is that he saith, but it may be an omen.

HERODIAS: I do not believe in omens. He speaks like a drunken man.

HEROD: It may be he is drunk with the wine of God.

HERODIAS: What wine is that, the wine of God? From what vineyards is it gathered? In what winepress may one find it?

HEROD (*from this point he looks all the while at Salomé*): Tigellinus, when you were at Rome of late, did the Emperor speak with you on the subject of . . . ?

TIGELLINUS: On what subject, sire?

HEROD: On what subject? Ah! I asked you a question, did I not? I have forgotten what I would have asked you.

HERODIAS: You are looking again at my daughter. You must not look at her. I have already said so.

HEROD: You say nothing else.

HERODIAS: I say it again.

HEROD: And that restoration of the Temple* about which they have talked so much, will anything be done? They say the veil of the Sanctuary has disappeared, do they not?

HERODIAS: It was thyself didst steal it. Thou speakest at random. I will not stay here. Let us go within.

HEROD: Dance for me, Salomé.

HERODIAS: I will not have her dance.

SALOMÉ: I have no desire to dance, Tetrarch.

HEROD: Salomé, daughter of Herodias, dance for me.

HERODIAS: Let her alone.

HEROD: I command thee to dance, Salomé.

SALOMÉ: I will not dance, Tetrarch.

HERODIAS (*laughing*): You see how she obeys you.

HEROD: What is it to me whether she dance or not? It is naught to

---

*Under Herod, the Second Temple in Jerusalem was rebuilt and expanded.

me. To-night I am happy, I am exceeding happy. Never have I been so happy.

FIRST SOLDIER: The Tetrarch has a sombre look. Has he not a sombre look?

SECOND SOLDIER: Yes, he has a sombre look.

HEROD: Wherefore should I not be happy? Cæsar, who is lord of the world, who is lord of all things, loves me well. He has just sent me most precious gifts. Also he has promised me to summon to Rome the King of Cappadocia, who is my enemy. It may be that at Rome he will crucify him, for he is able to do all things that he wishes. Verily, Cæsar is lord. Thus you see I have a right to be happy. Indeed, I am happy. I have never been so happy. There is nothing in the world that can mar my happiness.

THE VOICE OF JOKANAAN: He shall be seated on this throne. He shall be clothed in scarlet and purple. In his hand he shall bear a golden cup full of his blasphemies. And the angel of the Lord shall smite him. He shall be eaten of worms.

HERODIAS: You hear what he says about you. He says that you will be eaten of worms.

HEROD: It is not of me that he speaks. He speaks never against me. It is of the King of Cappadocia that he speaks; the King of Cappadocia, who is mine enemy. It is he who shall be eaten of worms. It is not I. Never has he spoken word against me, this prophet, save that I sinned in taking to wife the wife of my brother. It may be he is right. For, of a truth, you are sterile.

HERODIAS: I am sterile, I? You say that, you that are ever looking at my daughter, you that would have her dance for your pleasure? It is absurd to say that. I have borne a child. You have gotten no child, no, not even from one of your slaves. It is you who are sterile, not I.

HEROD: Peace, woman! I say that you are sterile. You have borne me no child, and the prophet says that our marriage is not a true marriage. He says that it is an incestuous marriage, a marriage that will bring evils. . . . I fear he is right; I am sure that he is right. But it is not the moment to speak of such things. I would be happy at this moment. Of a truth, I am happy. There is nothing I lack.

HERODIAS: I am glad you are of so fair a humour to-night. It is not your custom. But it is late. Let us go within. Do not forget that we hunt at sunrise. All honours must be shown to Cæsar's ambassadors, must they not?

SECOND SOLDIER: What a sombre look the Tetrarch wears.

FIRST SOLDIER: Yes, he wears a sombre look.

HEROD: Salomé, Salomé, dance for me. I pray thee dance for me. I am sad to-night. Yes, I am passing sad to-night. When I came hither I slipped in blood, which is an evil omen; and I heard, I am sure I heard in the air a beating of wings, a beating of giant wings. I cannot tell what they mean. . . . I am sad to-night. Therefore dance for me. Dance for me, Salomé, I beseech you. If you dance for me you may ask of me what you will, and I will give it you, even unto the half of my kingdom.

SALOMÉ (*rising*): Will you indeed give me whatsoever I shall ask, Tetrarch?

HERODIAS: Do not dance, my daughter.

HEROD: Everything, even the half of my kingdom.

SALOMÉ: You swear it, Tetrarch?

HEROD: I swear it, Salomé.

HERODIAS: Do not dance, my daughter.

SALOMÉ: By what will you swear, Tetrarch?

HEROD: By my life, by my crown, by my gods. Whatsoever you desire I will give it you, even to the half of my kingdom, if you will but dance for me. O, Salomé, Salomé, dance for me!

SALOMÉ: You have sworn, Tetrarch.

HEROD: I have sworn, Salomé.

SALOMÉ: All this I ask, even the half of your kingdom.

HERODIAS: My daughter, do not dance.

HEROD: Even to the half of my kingdom. Thou wilt be passing fair as a queen, Salomé, if it please thee to ask for the half of my kingdom. Will she not be fair as a queen? Ah! it is cold here! There is an icy wind, and I hear . . . wherefore do I hear in the air this beating of wings? Ah! one might fancy a bird, a huge black bird that hovers over the terrace. Why can I not see it, this bird? The beat of its wings is terrible. The breath of the wind of its wings is terrible. It is a chill wind. Nay, but it is not cold, it is hot. I am choking. Pour water on my hands. Give me snow to eat. Loosen my mantle. Quick, quick! Loosen my mantle. Nay, but leave it. It is my garland that hurts me, my garland of roses. The flowers are like fire. They have burned my forehead. (*He tears the wreath from his head and throws it on the table.*) Ah! I can breathe now. How red those petals are! They are like stains of blood on the cloth. That does not matter. You must not find symbols in everything you see. It makes life impossible. It were better to say that stains of blood are as lovely as rose petals. It were better far to say that. . . . But we will not speak of this. Now I am happy, I am passing happy. Have I not the right to be happy? Your daughter is going to dance for me. Will you not dance for me, Salomé? You have promised to dance for me.

HERODIAS: I will not have her dance.

SALOMÉ: I will dance for you, Tetrarch.

HEROD: You hear what your daughter says. She is going to dance for me. You do well to dance for me, Salomé. And when you have danced for me, forget not to ask of me whatsoever you wish. Whatsoever you wish I will give it you, even to the half of my kingdom. I have sworn it, have I not?

SALOMÉ: You have sworn it, Tetrarch.

HEROD: And I have never broken my word. I am not of those who break their oaths. I know not how to lie. I am the slave of my word, and my word is the word of a king. The King of Cappadocia always lies, but he is no true king. He is a coward. Also he owes me money that he will not repay. He has even insulted my ambassadors. He has spoken words that were wounding. But Cæsar will crucify him when he comes to Rome. I am sure that Cæsar will crucify him. And if not, yet will he die, being eaten of worms. The prophet has prophesied it. Well! wherefore dost thou tarry, Salomé?

SALOMÉ: I am waiting until my slaves bring perfumes to me and the seven veils, and take off my sandals. (*Slaves bring perfumes and the seven veils, and take off the sandals of* SALOMÉ.)

HEROD: Ah, you are going to dance with naked feet. 'Tis well! 'Tis well. Your little feet will be like white doves. They will be like little white flowers that dance upon the trees. . . . No, no, she is going to dance on blood. There is blood spilt on the ground. She must not dance on blood. It were an evil omen.

HERODIAS: What is it to you if she dance on blood? Thou hast waded deep enough therein. . . .

HEROD: What is it to me? Ah! Look at the moon! She has become red. She has become red as blood.* Ah! the prophet prophesied truly. He prophesied that the moon would become red as blood. Did he not prophesy it? All of you heard him. And now the moon has become red as blood. Do ye not see it?

HERODIAS: Oh, yes, I see it well, and the stars are falling like ripe figs, are they not? And the sun is becoming black like sackcloth of hair, and the kings of the earth are afraid. That at least one can see. The prophet, for once in his life, was right; the kings of the earth are afraid. . . . Let us go within. You are sick. They will say at Rome that you are mad. Let us go within, I tell you.

THE VOICE OF JOKANAAN: Who is this who cometh from Edom, who is this who cometh from Bozra, whose raiment is dyed with purple, who shineth in the beauty of his garments, who walketh mighty in his greatness? Wherefore is thy raiment stained with scarlet?

HERODIAS: Let us go within. The voice of that man maddens me. I will not have my daughter dance while he is continually crying out. I will not have her dance while you look at her in this fashion. In a word I will not have her dance.

HEROD: Do not rise, my wife, my queen, it will avail thee nothing. I will not go within till she hath danced. Dance, Salomé, dance for me.

HERODIAS: Do not dance, my daughter.

SALOMÉ: I am ready, Tetrarch. (SALOMÉ *dances the dance of the seven veils.*)

HEROD: Ah! Wonderful! Wonderful! You see that she has danced for me, your daughter. Come near, Salomé, come near, that I may give you your reward. Ah! I pay the dancers well. I will pay thee royally. I will give thee whatsoever thy soul desireth. What wouldst thou have? Speak.

SALOMÉ (*kneeling*): I would that they presently bring me in a silver charger . . .

HEROD (*laughing*): In a silver charger? Surely yes, in a silver charger. She is charming, is she not? What is it you would have in

---

*A lighting cue: The stage, which has been flooded with moonlight, now appears red.

a silver charger, O sweet and fair Salomé, you who are fairer than all the daughters of Judæa? What would you have them bring thee in a silver charger? Tell me. Whatsoever it may be, they shall give it to you. My treasures belong to thee. What is it, Salomé?

SALOMÉ (*rising*): The head of Jokanaan.

HERODIAS: Ah! that is well said, my daughter.

HEROD: No, no!

HERODIAS: That is well said, my daughter.

HEROD: No, no, Salomé. You do not ask me that. Do not listen to your mother's voice. She is ever giving you evil counsel. Do not heed her.

SALOMÉ: I do not heed my mother. It is for mine own pleasure that I ask the head of Jokanaan in a silver charger. You have sworn, Herod. Forget not that you have sworn an oath.

HEROD: I know it. I have sworn by my gods. I know it well. But I pray you, Salomé, ask of me something else. Ask of me the half of my kingdom, and I will give it you. But ask not of me what you have asked.

SALOMÉ: I ask of you the head of Jokanaan.

HEROD: No, no, I do not wish it.

SALOMÉ: You have sworn, Herod.

HERODIAS: Yes, you have sworn. Everybody heard you. You swore it before everybody.

HEROD: Be silent! It is not to you I speak.

HERODIAS: My daughter has done well to ask the head of Jokanaan. He has covered me with insults. He has said monstrous things against me. One can see that she loves her mother well. Do not yield, my daughter. He has sworn, he has sworn.

HEROD: Be silent, speak not to me . . . ! Come, Salomé, be reasonable. I have never been hard to you. I have ever loved you. . . . It may be that I have loved you too much. Therefore ask not this thing of me. This is a terrible thing, an awful thing to ask of me. Surely, I think you are jesting. The head of a man that is cut from his body is ill to look upon, is it not? It is not meet that the eyes of a virgin should look upon such a thing. What pleasure could you have in it? None. No, no, it is not what you desire. Hearken to me. I have an emerald, a great round emerald, which Cæsar's minion sent me. If you look through this emerald you can see things which happen at a great distance. Cæsar himself carries such an emerald when he goes to the circus. But my emerald is larger. I know well that it is larger. It is the largest emerald in the whole world. You would like that, would you not? Ask it of me and I will give it you.

SALOMÉ: I demand the head of Jokanaan.

HEROD: You are not listening. You are not listening. Suffer me to speak, Salomé.

SALOMÉ: The head of Jokanaan.

HEROD: No, no, you would not have that. You say that to trouble me, because I have looked at you all this evening. It is true, I have looked at you all evening. Your beauty troubled me. Your beauty has grievously troubled me, and I have looked at you too much. But I will look at you no more. Neither at things, nor at people should one look. Only in mirrors should one look, for mirrors do but show us masks. Oh! oh! bring wine! I thirst. . . . Salomé, Salomé, let us be friends. Come now . . . ! Ah! what would I say? What was't? Ah! I remember . . . ! Salomé—nay, but come nearer to me; I fear you will not hear me—Salomé, you know my white peacocks, my beautiful white peacocks, that walk in the garden between the myrtles and the tall cypress trees. Their beaks are gilded with gold, and the grains that they eat are gilded with gold also, and their feet are stained with purple. When they cry out the rain comes, and the moon shows herself in the heavens when they spread their tails. Two by two they walk between the cypress trees and the black myrtles, and each has a slave to tend it. Sometimes they fly across the trees and anon they crouch in the grass, and round the lake. There are not in all the world birds so wonderful. There is no king in all the world who possesses such wonderful birds. I am sure that Cæsar himself has no birds so fine as my birds. I will give you fifty of my peacocks. They will follow you whithersoever you go, and in the midst of them you will be like the moon in the midst of a great white cloud. . . . I will give them all to you. I have but a hundred, and in the whole world there is no king who has peacocks like unto my peacocks. But I will give them all to you. Only you must loose me from my oath, and must not ask of me that which you have asked of me.

He empties the cup of wine.

SALOME: Give me the head of Jokanaan.

HERODIAS: Well said, my daughter! As for you, you are ridiculous with your peacocks.

HEROD: Be silent! You cry out always; you cry out like a beast of prey. You must not. Your voice wearies me. Be silent, I say. . . . Salomé, think of what you are doing. This man comes perchance from God. He is a holy man. The finger of God has touched him. God has put into his mouth terrible words. In the palace as in the desert God is always with him. . . . At least it is possible. One does not know. It is possible that God is for him and with him. Furthermore, if he died some misfortune might happen to me. In any case, he said that the day he dies a misfortune will happen to some one. That could only be to me. Remember, I slipped in blood when I entered. Also, I heard a beating of wings in the air, a beating of mighty wings. These are very evil omens, and there were others. I am sure there were others, though I did not see them. Well, Salomé, you do not wish a misfortune to happen to me? You do not wish that. Listen to me, then.

SALOMÉ: Give me the head of Jokanaan.

HEROD: Ah! you are not listening to me. Be calm. I—I am calm. I am quite calm. Listen. I have jewels hidden in this place—jewels that your mother even has never seen; jewels that are marvellous. I have a collar of pearls, set in four rows. They are like unto moons chained with rays of silver. They are like fifty moons caught in a golden net. On the ivory of her breast a queen has worn it. Thou shalt be as fair as a queen when thou wearest it. I have amethysts of two kinds, one that is black like wine, and one that is red like wine which has been coloured with water. I have topazes, yellow as are the eyes of tigers, and topazes that are pink as the eyes of a wood-pigeon, and green topazes that are as the eyes of cats. I have opals that burn always with an ice-like flame, opals that make sad men's minds, and are fearful of the shadows. I have onyxes like the eyeballs of a dead woman. I have moonstones that change when the moon changes, and are wan when they see the sun. I have sapphires big like eggs, and as blue as blue flowers. The sea wanders within them and the moon comes never to trouble the blue of their waves. I have chrysolites and beryls and chrysoprases and rubies. I have sardonyx and hyacinth stones, and stones of chalcedony, and I will give them all to you, all, and other things will I add to them. The King of the Indies has but even now sent me four fans fashioned from the feathers of parrots, and the King of Numidia* a garment of ostrich feathers. I have a crystal, into which it is not lawful for a woman to look, nor may young men behold it until they have been beaten with rods. In a coffer of nacre I have three wondrous turquoises. He who wears them on his forehead can imagine things which are not, and he who carries them in his hand can make women sterile. These are great treasures above all price. They are treasures without price. But this is not all. In an ebony coffer I have two cups of amber, that are like apples of gold. If an enemy pour poison into these cups, they become like an apple of silver. In a coffer incrusted with amber I have sandals incrusted with glass. I have mantles that have been brought from the land of the Seres, and bracelets decked about with carbuncles and with jade that come from the city of Euphrates. . . . What desirest thou more than this, Salomé? Tell me the thing that thou desirest, and I will give it thee. All that thou askest I will give thee save one thing. I will give thee all that is mine, save one life. I will give thee the mantle of the high priest. I will give thee the veil of the sanctuary.

THE JEWS: Oh! Oh!

SALOMÉ: Give me the head of Jokanaan.

HEROD (*sinking back in his seat*): Let her be given what she asks! Of a truth she is her mother's child! (*The* FIRST SOLDIER *approaches.* HERODIAS *draws from the hand of the* TETRARCH *the ring of death and gives it to the* SOLDIER, *who straightway bears it to the* EXECUTIONER. *The* EXECUTIONER *looks scared.*) Who has taken my ring? There was a ring on my right hand. Who has drunk my wine? There was wine in my cup. It was full of wine. Some one has drunk it? Oh! surely some evil will befall some one. (*The* EXECUTIONER *goes down into the cistern.*) Ah! Wherefore did I give my oath? Kings ought never to pledge their word. If they keep it not, it is terrible, and if they keep it, it is terrible also.

HERODIAS: My daughter has done well.

HEROD: I am sure that some misfortune will happen.

SALOMÉ (*she leans over the cistern and listens*): There is no sound. I

---

*Ancient North African country located in what is now Algeria.

hear nothing. Why does he not cry out, this man? Ah! if any man sought to kill me, I would cry out, I would struggle, I would not suffer. . . . Strike, strike, Naaman, strike, I tell you. . . . No, I hear nothing. There is a silence, a terrible silence. Ah! something has fallen upon the ground. I heard something fall. It is the sword of the headsman. He is afraid, this slave. He has let his sword fall. He dare not kill him. He is a coward, this slave! Let soldiers be sent. (*She sees the* PAGE OF HERODIAS *and addresses him.*) Come hither, thou wert the friend of him who is dead, is it not so? Well, I tell thee, there are not dead men enough. Go to the soldiers and bid them go down and bring me the thing I ask, the thing the Tetrarch has promised me, the thing that is mine. (*The* PAGE *recoils. She turns to the* SOLDIERS.) Hither, ye soldiers. Get ye down into this cistern and bring me the head of this man. (*The* SOLDIERS *recoil.*) Tetrarch, Tetrarch, command your soldiers that they bring me the head of Jokanaan.

A huge black arm, the arm of the* EXECUTIONER, *comes forth from the cistern, bearing on a silver shield the head of* JOKANAAN. SALOMÉ *seizes it.* HEROD *hides his face with his cloak.* HERODIAS *smiles and fans herself. The* NAZARENES *fall on their knees and begin to pray.*

SALOMÉ: Ah! thou wouldst not suffer me to kiss thy mouth, Jokanaan. Well! I will kiss it now. I will bite it with my teeth as one bites a ripe fruit. Yes, I will kiss thy mouth, Jokanaan. I said it. Did I not say it? I said it. Ah! I will kiss it now. . . . But wherefore dost thou not look at me, Jokanaan? Thine eyes that were so terrible, so full of rage and scorn, are shut now. Wherefore are they shut? Open thine eyes! Lift up thine eyelids, Jokanaan! Wherefore dost thou not look at me? Art thou afraid of me, Jokanaan, that thou wilt not look at me . . . ? And thy tongue, that was like a red snake darting poison, it moves no more, it says nothing now, Jokanaan, that scarlet viper that spat its venom upon me. It is strange, is it not? How is it that the red viper stirs no longer . . . ? Thou wouldst have none of me, Jokanaan. Thou didst reject me. Thou

---

*The executioner's arm emerging from the cistern suggests one of the wings of the angel of death, which have been beating throughout the play.

didst speak evil words against me. Thou didst treat me as a harlot, as a wanton, me, Salomé, daughter of Herodias, Princess of Judæa! Well, Jokanaan, I still live, but thou, thou art dead, and thy head belongs to me. I can do with it what I will. I can throw it to the dogs and to the birds of the air. That which the dogs leave, the birds of the air shall devour. . . . Ah, Jokanaan, Jokanaan, thou wert the only man that I have loved. All other men are hateful to me. But thou, thou wert beautiful! Thy body was a column of ivory set on a silver socket. It was a garden full of doves and of silver lilies. It was a tower of silver decked with shields of ivory. There was nothing in the world so white as thy body. There was nothing in the world so black as thy hair. In the whole world there was nothing so red as thy mouth. Thy voice was a censer that scattered strange perfumes, and when I looked on thee I heard a strange music. Ah! wherefore didst thou not look at me, Jokanaan? Behind thine hands and thy curses thou didst hide thy face. Thou didst put upon thine eyes the covering of him who would see his God. Well, thou hast seen thy God, Jokanaan, but me, me, thou didst never see. If thou hadst seen me thou wouldst have loved me. I, I saw thee, Jokanaan, and I loved thee. Oh, how I loved thee! I loved thee yet, Jokanaan, I love thee only. . . . I am athirst for thy beauty; I am hungry for thy body; and neither wine nor fruits can appease my desire. What shall I do now, Jokanaan? Neither the floods nor the great waters can quench my passion. I was a princess, and thou didst scorn me. I was a virgin, and thou didst take my virginity from me. I was chaste, and thou didst fill my veins with fire. . . . Ah! ah! wherefore didst thou not look at me, Jokanaan? If thou hadst looked at me thou hadst loved me. Well I know that thou wouldst have loved me, and the mystery of love is greater than the mystery of death. Love only should one consider.

HEROD: She is monstrous, thy daughter, she is altogether monstrous. In truth, what she has done is a great crime. I am sure that it was a crime against an unknown God.

HERODIAS: I approve of what my daughter has done. And I will stay here now.

HEROD (*rising*): Ah! There speaks the incestuous wife! Come! I will not stay here. Come, I tell thee. Surely some terrible thing will befall. Manasseth, Issachar, Ozias, put out the torches. I will not look at things, I will not suffer things to look at me. Put out the torches! Hide the moon! Hide the stars! Let us hide ourselves in our palace, Herodias. I begin to be afraid.

*The slaves put out the torches. The stars disappear. The great black cloud crosses the moon and conceals it completely. The stage becomes very dark.** *The* TETRARCH *begins to climb the staircase.*

THE VOICE OF SALOMÉ: Ah! I have kissed thy mouth, Jokanaan. I have kissed thy mouth. There was a bitter taste on thy lips. Was it the taste of blood . . . ? But perchance it is the taste of love. . . . They say that love hath a bitter taste. . . . But what of that? What of that? I have kissed thy mouth, Jokanaan.

A moonbeam falls on SALOMÉ, *covering her with light.*

HEROD (*turning round and seeing* SALOMÉ): Kill that woman!

The soldiers rush forward and crush beneath their shields SALOMÉ, *daughter of* HERODIAS, *Princess of Judæa.*

Curtain

---

*The stage goes from red to black.

ENDNOTES

The Importance of Being Earnest

1. (p. 3) This text of *The Importance of Being Earnest* is the original version of the play. Wilde later combined acts two and three, deleting the roles of Mr. Gribsby and Moulton. The script then comprised three (rather than four) acts. Although the later, "streamlined" version is better known, it omits many lines and exchanges the reader will find wonderful.
2. (p. 51) *"With pleasure"*: This marks the end of the scene; in the revised version, all that follows in this act remains in an expanded act two.
3. (p. 54) *Act Drop:* In the revised version, there is no intermission. The entire action of what follows is played in the garden.
4. (p. 75) *Act Four:* In the revised version, the action included in this segment (which becomes act three) is located in the house.
5. (p. 78) *"victim of a revolutionary outrage?"*: Throughout the late nineteenth century, terrorists used bombs, particularly in Russia, where revolutionaries, including the Nihilists, set off explosions in Saint Petersburg. Wilde had written about these terrorists in his unsuccessful play *Vera*.
6. (p. 82) *"He is an Oxonian"*: Wilde defined himself, at least in part, as an Oxonian; after splitting with his wife, he would spend time with young men at Oxford University. Lady Bracknell's remark is therefore ironic.
7. (p. 88) *"Gower Street omnibus. . . . the explosion of a temperance beverage . . . at Leamington"*: Horse-drawn buses (omnibuses) were common transportation in London. The nonalcoholic soft drink would have been carbonated, hence the explosion. Leamington was a spa that had been made popular by Queen Victoria in the late 1830s.

8. (p. 91) *(Rushes to the bookcase . . .):* The following scene, in which each character looks through a book, is cut from the revised version.

A Woman of No Importance

1. (p. 189) *"an iron Exhibition . . . at that place that has the curious name?":* In 1892 a world's fair (complete with an iron-and-glass exhibition hall) celebrated the 400th anniversary of the discovery of America by Christopher Columbus; the Columbian Exposition was held at the curiously named city of Chicago.

An Ideal Husband

1. (p. 239) *At the top of the staircase . . . loved to paint them:* Wilde's set description, with details of lighting effects, emphasizes the style of the French monarchy before the revolution (l'ancien régime): a tapestry designed by the painter François Boucher (1703–1770), a Louis XVI sofa, the pretty, fragile women whom Antoine Watteau (1684–1721, an artist of the French Regency) would have painted. Indeed, the room depicted, as well as the two ladies, evokes an "affectation of manner" with "a delicate charm."

2. (p. 243) *Sir Robert Chiltern enters. . . . Vandyck would have liked to have painted his head:* Again, Wilde offers a detailed character description; unlike the glamorous women in the room, Chiltern more aptly would be painted by the Flemish portraitist (Sir Anthony Van Dyck, or Vandyck, 1599–1641) who immortalized British aristocrats.

3. (p. 286) *"Blue Book. . . . books . . . in yellow covers":* Mrs. Cheveley jokes that she is unfamiliar with the sorts of political documents the "Blue Books" comprise; her mention of books "in yellow covers" is a reference to the controversial journal *The Yellow Book.* Wilde disliked the magazine but later would be associated with it mistakenly: When he was arrested before his trial, he happened to be carrying a book in a yellow cover, which the newspapers incorrectly reported was *The Yellow Book.*

Salomé

1. (p. 333) *Translated . . . Alfred Douglas:* Although the play's translation is attributed to Wilde's companion, Wilde was unhappy with many aspects of Douglas's English version and made changes to it.

2. (p. 337) *SCENE:. . . Moonlight:* In contrast to the settings in Wilde's more contemporary plays, this scene is described in broad, symbolic terms. Wilde's use of lighting effects, which predates electricity, shows his control throughout the play of the appearance of the overall stage picture.

3. (p. 346) *Sodom:* The reference is to the ancient city destroyed (along with Gomorrah) by God. Sodomites were said to have raped the male angel sent by God; hence, the name of the city and its people had been linked for centuries to homosexuality.

4. (p. 346) *"Let me touch thy body":* Salomé asks first to touch the prophet's body, then to touch his hair, and then to kiss his mouth, a request she goes on to make repeatedly until the end of the play.

5. (p. 347) *"a crown of thorns":* The phrase anticipates the crown Christ would wear on the cross.

6. (p. 348) *He kills himself:* The abrupt suicide should bring the action to a halt, but Salomé's obsession with the prophet is so intense that she is oblivious to the soldier's death.

7. (p. 348) *"I knew that the moon was seeking a dead thing":* The page now associates the moon with death; an implication is that his fascination with the pale, moonlike virgin, Salomé, has killed him.

8. (p. 349) *"He was my brother, and nearer to me than a brother":* The page's longing for his friend suggests that he felt more than collegial love for the soldier.

9. (p. 355) *"It would be terrible if the dead came back":* Herod has ample reason to fear the return of the dead, but at the same time his dismissal of life after death is an outright rejection of one of the central tenets of Christian belief.

10. (p. 356) *"Let the war captains . . . beneath their shields":* In case the audience had any doubt regarding his abilities, the prophet predicts the end of the play, which is now only minutes away.

11. (p. 356) *"You hear . . . him to revile your wife?":* The audience, having heard earlier the prophet's rant against Salomé, realizes that Herodias's interpretation of Jokanaan's scorn is incorrect.

INSPIRED BY OSCAR WILDE AND HIS PLAYS

Film

Oscar Wilde's extraordinary popularity on the stage fittingly has earned him a secure place on the silver screen. The move from stage to screen initially occurred during the silent era, with a British film rendition in 1916 of *Lady Windermere's Fan*, directed by Fred Paul, followed by, in America in 1925, a version directed by cinematic legend Ernst Lubitsch. In Lubitsch's film, Wilde's epigrams appear as they do to readers, as text: intertitles cut among charming scenes in the garden and at the Ascot racetrack. Lubitsch makes use of relatively few of Wilde's dialogue bits, yet he captures Wilde's tone even in the stage directions: "The relations between a man and a woman can be told by the way he presses her doorbell." The rest of the wit is conveyed, to wonderful effect, by innuendo, pregnant glances, and the nuanced movements of the actors. Ronald Colman plays the caddish Lord Darlington; May McAvoy, the coquettish bride of Lord Windermere (Bert Lytell); and Irene Rich, in the performance of her career, Lady Windermere's long-lost mother, Mrs. Erlynne. *Lady Windermere's Fan* was an immediate success and, because it has been carefully preserved, continues to shimmer today. The play was adapted again in 1949—this time with sound, directed by Otto Preminger, and titled *The Fan*; for this production, Wilde's *Windermere* was adapted for the screen in part by Dorothy Parker and was the last film she worked on. Jeanne Crain played Lady Windermere and George Sanders was Lord Darlington.

Director Suri Krishnamma and screenwriter Barry Devlin set their 1994 film *A Man of No Importance* in 1960s Dublin, in an adaptation that stars Albert Finney as Alfie, a Wilde-crazed conductor of a double-decker bus. Every day he delights his passengers—an audience held captive, as it were—by delivering Wilde quotations in hammed-up style. With characteristic Wildean grandeur, Alfie mounts a production of *Salomé*, casting his daily passengers. Among this ragtag bunch are several memorable characters, including the young enchantress Adele (Tara Fitzgerald), whom Alfie wants to play Salomé, and Robbie, the handsome young bus driver on whom Alfie has a crush. Alfie endearingly calls Robbie (played by Rufus Sewell) "Bosie"—Wilde's pet name for his lover Lord Alfred Douglas. The comedy of the situation redoubles as Alfie's sister Lily (Brenda Fricker) is ever on the lookout for a wife for her eccentric middle-aged brother. Exploring the reactions of a conservative Catholic community toward homosexuality and the infamously salacious *Salomé, A Man of No Importance* is a rollick with a conscience, bolstered by Finney's exceptional performance.

An Ideal Husband (1999), adapted and directed by Oliver Parker, is an engaging portrait of a narcissistic, womanizing, yet thoroughly entertaining man about town, that perhaps eclipses even Alexander Korda's 1947 version. Rather than playing up the farce of Wilde's drama, Parker takes a more naturalistic approach that draws parallels between Victorian society and our own. The almost uncannily Wildean Rupert Everett leads an excellent cast as Lord Arthur Goring, "the idlest man in London." Though Goring hopes to talk only about nothing ("It's the only thing I know anything about"), he can't help becoming embroiled in a morass of romance, intrigue, mistaken identities, and a blackmail plot revolving around an Argentine canal. Parker's script enshrines, though it often redistributes, Wilde's dialogue, and creates a universe of unflagging wit, in which Minnie Driver (as Mabel Chiltern), Julianne Moore (Mrs. Laura Cheveley), and Cate Blanchett (Lady Gertrude Chiltern) find themselves very much at home. Parker portrays them dressing, lounging in bed, going to the bathhouses, and riding in carriages, and in the process makes Wilde's hyper-witty characters very convincing.

In 2002 Oliver Parker and Rupert Everett teamed up again to make a droll version of *The Importance of Being Earnest*. Everett plays Algy, and Colin Firth plays his cohort Jack Worthing. Parker's film features a variety of London settings, many of them exterior, and many surfacing in flashback and fantasy sequences (of questionable success). The film's sumptuousness often trumps the power of Wilde's language, painting a world in which characters seem to recite rather than speak. However, the production is elevated by superior acting—Algy's charades include

Judi Dench's imperious Lady Bracknell and Reese Witherspoon's insipid Cecily Cardew.

An earlier, and notable, screen incarnation of *The Importance of Being Earnest* (1952) was adapted and directed by Anthony Asquith (who in 1938 had made *Pygmalion*, based on George Bernard Shaw's play). An interesting note about this film: Asquith, a gay man, was the son of Herbert Asquith, the British home secretary and, later, prime minister who ordered Wilde's arrest, which led to Wilde's conviction of "gross indecency" and subsequent exile. In Asquith's film, Sir Michael Redgrave stars as Jack Worthing and steals the show; Michael Denison breathes sardonic charm into Algernon; the fierce Margaret Rutherford plays Miss Prism with intelligence; and Dame Edith Evans plays Lady Bracknell (Evans had played the icy Bracknell for thirty years onstage prior to the film). Asquith's movie does not depart dramatically from its theater roots; indeed, a Technicolor-red curtain opening and closing on a stage set punctuates the film. Primacy is given to the lines themselves, which are rarely interrupted by fancy camera tricks and distracting interiors.

Opera

Though the stage musical is perhaps the most common translation of Wilde into sonic drama, with half a dozen or so based on *The Importance of Being Earnest* alone, Richard Strauss's operatic adaptation of *Salomé* (1905) has enjoyed the most lasting and significant acclaim. Like Strauss's *Elektra*, the composer's one-act opus *Salomé* delights in the erotic and the violent, and the tension between the two. Writer and composer together distill the quintessential *femme fatale*.

As the curtain opens, lovesick Captain Narraboth sings, "Wie schön ist die Prinzessin Salomé heute Nacht!" (How beautiful is the Princess Salomé tonight!). The triangle of desire emerges as King Herod lusts after his stepdaughter Salomé, while she in turn lusts after John the Baptist. Herod attempts to quell the controversy by having Salomé dance. The result, the "Dance of the Seven Veils," is very sensuous, a sort of Arabian striptease; borrowing from Eastern motifs, it begins gently and builds toward a frenetic cacophony. As a reward for her performance Salomé demands the head of John the Baptist on a silver platter; when the disembodied head appears, she kisses it. Herod, disgusted, orders his soldiers to trample Salomé with their shields, bringing a thunderously violent end to the opera.

Salomé was first performed, in German, by the Dresden Opera in 1905, and it continues to be performed today. With *Salomé* Strauss pioneered a new approach to symphonic music that is akin to realism; he attempted to write musical descriptions in which listeners could tell the difference between a spoon and a fork on the dinner table. Indeed, so precise, vital, and dramatic is Strauss's music that the *Salomé* films made since the debut of the opera pale in comparison, even those that quote liberally from the opera to construct their soundtracks. In a review dated July 17, 1907, the London *Guardian* lauded the production: "The play could thrill no one, but the opera is a succession of 'thrills.' The grinning skeletons start into life, and we get the impression that we are witnessing the play of human passion. It is an amazing transformation."

COMMENTS & QUESTIONS

In this section, we aim to provide the reader with an array of perspectives on the text, as well as questions that challenge those perspectives. The commentary has been culled from sources as diverse as reviews contemporaneous with the work, letters written by the author, literary criticism of later generations, and appreciations written throughout history. Following the commentary, a series of questions seeks to filter Oscar Wilde's The Importance of Being Earnest and Four Other Plays *through a variety of points of view and bring about a richer understanding of these enduring works.*

COMMENTS

George Bernard Shaw

In a certain sense Mr. Wilde is to me our most thorough playwright. He plays with everything: with wit, with philosophy, with drama, with actors and audience, with the whole theater.

—*Saturday Review* (January 12, 1895)

New York Times

"An Ideal Husband," is a very clever play, and admirable in a technical sense. Its most glaring fault is the theatrical use made of Lady Chiltern's pink note in Act III. This is preposterous. But it serves a counter-climax to Goring's bracelet trick for the end of that act, and helps, effectively, to eke out the slender materials of Act IV.

The play would be much better, too, if it were written in simpler language. The illusion of life is missed when people persistently mouth epigrams as surely as when they confine themselves to stale platitudes.

—March 17, 1895

J. T. Grein

In 1895, when "The Importance of Being Earnest" saw the light at the St. James's Theatre, it was voted a perfect farce, and, but for the catastrophe, it would have played for centuries of evenings. I recall this not merely as a chronological fact, but more particularly in order to emphasise the exceeding cleverness of the play since the duality of its fibre escaped most of the critics, and certainly the majority of the public. The practised eye discovered at once that the first and second acts and the third were not of the same mould. They made the impression of wines of different vintages served in the same glasses. Those two acts—perfect, not only as farce, but as comedy, too, for they reflect the manners of the period, and are richly underlaid with humorous current—were written in days when the poet basked in the hot sun of popularity, when his every saying darted like an arrow through the land, when the whole of the English speaking world echoed sallies which, though they were not always Oscar Wilde's, were as *ben trovato* as if they had been his. The third act was—I know it authoritatively—composed under stress of circumstances, when the web was tightening round the man, and menaces of exposure must have rendered his gaiety forced, like that of a being condemned to the stocks. Under pressure a lofty mind often does excellent work, and it is undeniable that in the third act of "The Importance of Being Earnest" there is more cleverness than in one round dozen English comedies *en bloc*. There are epigrams in it for the paternity of which some people would give a few years of their lives, and as a solution to a tangle well-nigh inextricable it is by no means unhappy. Yet it is not of the same quality as those other two acts, in which the real, the probable, and the impossible form a *ménage à trois* of rare felicity. And as we listen to the play, what strikes us most of all is not so much the utterances of a mind which could not fail to be brilliant, but the prospect that this comedy—for I prefer to call it a comedy—will enjoy a kind of perennial youth somewhat akin to Congreve's work or that of Sheridan. It is a bold thing to say, I know, but if there is exaggeration, let it pass, for the sake of the argument that when the artist's working powers were shut off he had not yet thoroughly felt his feet, but was only just beginning to plough his furrow in a new field. "The Importance of Being Earnest" ranks high, not only on account of its gaiety—a gaiety which in many produces the smile of intimate understanding, and in the less *blasé* guffaws straight from a happy mood—but because it satirises vividly, pointedly, yet not unkindly, the mannerisms and foibles of a society which is constantly before the public eye.

—*Dramatic Criticism* (1902)

Arthur Ransome

It is important in considering Wilde's early comedies to remember the character of the audience with which he had to contend. His was a public that asked to feel as well as to smile, a public that had grown accustomed to smile with tears in its eyes, a public that was best pleased to laugh loudly and to sob into handkerchiefs, and judged a play by the loudness of the laughs and the number of the handkerchiefs that made it necessary. He had not a Restoration audience of men and women with sharpened wits and a delight in their exercise, ready to smile and quite unready to take anything seriously except amusement. It is for this reason that he called *Lady Windermere's Fan* "A Play about a Good Woman," instead of making Mrs. Erlynne a Sylvia and punishing Lord Darlington with a marriage. . . .

It is not in the least surprising that *The Importance of Being Earnest*, the most trivial of the social plays, should be the only one of them that gives that peculiar exhilaration of spirit by which we recognize the beautiful. It is precisely because it is consistently trivial that it is not ugly. If only once it marred its triviality with a bruise of passion, its beauty would vanish with the blow. But it never contradicts itself, and it is worth noticing that its unity, its dovetailing of dialogue and plot, so that the one helps the other, is not achieved at the expense of the conversation, but at that of the mechanical contrivances for filling a theatre that Wilde had not at first felt sure of being able to do without. The dialogue has not been weighted to trudge with the plot; the plot has been lightened till it can fly with the wings of the dialogue. The two are become one, and the lambent laughter of this comedy is due to the radio-activity of the thing itself, and not to glow-worms incongruously stuck over its surface.

—*Oscar Wilde: A Critical Study* (1912)

William Saunders

Wilde lived at the time when the Wagnerian influence in music was beginning to make itself universally felt, but this influence was by no means confined to music and musicians alone. The *leit-motif* principle, based as it was upon a foundation of pure artistry, exercised a fascination, not only upon the musicians, but to almost as great an extent upon the writers and poets of the eighties and nineties of the last century. Wilde early evinced a fondness for it. We find it both in *A Woman of No Importance* and in *Lady Windermere's Fan*, the end of Act I, of the former play, for example. . . .

Salomé might as easily have been a tragedy of Euripides as an essay in histrionic creation by the greatest dramatic epigrammatist of the nineteenth century. The tragedy is essentially Greek in character, and after making the necessary allowances for the difference in periods, purely Euripidean in style. From the first word to the last, the inevitability of the tragedy is clearly demonstrable, and the *leit-motifen* merely accentuate the fact. The atmosphere of gloom and tragedy is never absent, but a gleam of light does occasionally fall across the scene,—a spark of wit suddenly flaring up, blazing forth with all the glamour of Wilde's genius for a moment, and then as quickly dying out again; or a flash of passionate love borne along in a chariot of momentary happiness that more than atones for the age of misery it leaves behind,—and there is surely no straining of metaphors in utilizing the moon as the symbol of such resplendent episodes. Like the plot of the Greek tragedy, that of *Salomé* evolves, and develops in a scene of shadow and depression, but if all is darkness, there are yet degrees and differences of its intensity, and there could be no apter exemplification in concrete form of this, than that which the author, with the true and unhesitating confidence of genius, has actually adopted. The point of my argument then centers in this, that the tragedy of *Salomé*, being Greek in conception and character, is dependent to a large extent for its power and terrifying qualities upon figures that are Greek in spirit and pagan in effect. Yet there is a vast difference between pure Hellenic paganism on the one hand, and moral obliquity on the other, and to suggest that the one term connotes the other, or *vice versa*, is indeed merely to attempt the reconciliation of opposites one with another, and the comparison of things that are absolutely unlike. Apart from its alleged moral degeneracy, a fault which, in spite of the *dicta* of some of the so-called greatest men of our time, *Salomé* is one of the greatest tragedies of recent times, and had its author never written another line, there is enough genius embodied in the ninety pages on which it lies,—not embalmed, but a virile and living force for good, and a source of never-ending intellectual joy and satisfaction to all who are capable of appreciating it, to ensure for him an immortality in the world of artistic humanity, and an everlasting niche in the Valhalla of literature, and of pure and unquestioned psychological delineation.

—from his review of *Salomé* in *The Drama* (September 1922)

Questions

1. On the basis of these plays, would you conclude that Oscar Wilde is a moralist, an immoralist, or an amoralist?

2. Try to construct three epigrams in the Wildean manner. Is there a certain frame of mind or attitude toward existence that lies behind his epigrams? What is it?

3. What is it, would you say, that attracted the socialist playwright George Bernard Shaw to Wilde's plays? Was Shaw mistaken in his view of Wilde?

4. The character of the fallen woman continually recurs through late-nineteenth-century literature, from *Madame Bovary* and *Anna Karenina* to *Maggie, a Girl of the Streets.* How is Wilde's take on this common character unusual?

5. Satire is usually thought of as the spoofing of a character or action or institution based on a standard shared by the writer and reader. Does Wilde satirize the English upper class? For what? Based on what standard?

FOR FURTHER READING

By Oscar Wilde

Wilde's drama, fiction, and other writings are available in a variety of editions. Individual works have been brought out by many publishers and can be found in easily affordable paperback form. The collections offered below are recent and critically helpful:

Wilde, Oscar. *The Annotated Oscar Wilde: Poems, Fiction, Plays, Lectures, Essays, and Letters.* Edited by H. Montgomery Hyde. New York: Clarkson N. Potter, 1982.

———. *The Complete Letters of Oscar Wilde.* Edited by Merlin Holland and Rupert Hart-Davis. New York: Henry Holt, 2000.

———. *Complete Shorter Fiction.* Edited by Isobel Murray. Oxford: Oxford University Press, 1979.

———. *"The Picture of Dorian Gray": Authoritative Texts, Backgrounds, Reviews and Reactions, Criticism.* Edited by Donald L. Lawler. New York: W. W. Norton, 1988.

———. *The Works of Oscar Wilde.* Leicester, England: Galley Press, 1987.

Recent Bibliographies of Oscar Wilde's Work and Related Criticism

Fletcher, Ian, and John Stokes. "Oscar Wilde." *Recent Research on Anglo-Irish Writers.* Edited by Richard Finneran. New York: Modern Language Association of America, 1983.

Mikhail, E. H. *Oscar Wilde: An Annotated Bibliography of Criticism.* Totowa, NJ: Rowman and Littlefield, 1978.

Mikolyzk, Thomas A., comp. *Oscar Wilde: An Annotated Bibliography.* Westport, CT: Greenwood Press, 1993.

Recent Books About Oscar Wilde

There is an impressive list of biographies on Wilde. The following have emerged as significant recent additions:

Belford, Barbara. *Oscar Wilde: A Certain Genius.* New York: Random House, 2000.

Ellmann, Richard. *Oscar Wilde.* New York: Alfred A. Knopf, 1987.

Foldy, Michael S. *The Trials of Oscar Wilde: Deviance, Morality, and Late-Victorian Society.* New Haven, CT: Yale University Press, 1997.

Goodman, Jonathan, comp. *The Oscar Wilde File.* London: Allison and Busby, 1988.

Holland, Merlin. *The Wilde Album.* New York: Henry Holt, 1998.

Recent Criticism

There is a wealth of critical studies on Wilde's writings. In addition to book-length studies, articles on Wilde abound. Consult the *MLA International Bibliography* from the Modern Language Association. Here are some recent books that explore his plays and his other works:

Brown, Julia Prewitt. *Cosmopolitan Criticism: Oscar Wilde's Philosophy of Art.* Charlottesville: University Press of Virginia, 1997.

Cohen, William A. *Sex Scandal: The Private Parts of Victorian Fiction.* Durham, NC: Duke University Press, 1996.

Eltis, Sos. *Revising Wilde: Society and Subversion in the Plays of Oscar Wilde.* Oxford: Clarendon Press, 1996.

Freedman, Jonathan, ed. *Oscar Wilde: A Collection of Critical Essays.* Upper Saddle River, NJ: Prentice Hall, 1996.

McCormack, Jerusha, ed. *Wilde the Irishman.* New Haven, CT: Yale University Press, 1998.

Price, Jody. *"A Map with Utopia": Oscar Wilde's Theory for Social Transformation.* New York: Peter Lang, 1996.

Schmidgall, Gary. *The Stranger Wilde: Interpreting Oscar.* New York: E. P. Dutton/William Abrahams Books, 1994.

Title	Author	ISBN	Price
Main Street	Sinclair Lewis	1-59308-036-0	$5.95
Mansfield Park	Jane Austen	1-59308-154-5	$5.95
The Metamorphosis and Other Stories	Franz Kafka	1-59308-029-8	$6.95
Moby-Dick	Herman Melville	1-59308-018-2	$9.95
My Ántonia	Willa Cather	1-59308-202-9	$5.95
Narrative of the Life of Frederick Douglass, an American Slave		1-59308-041-7	$4.95
Notes From Underground, The Double and Other Stories	Fyodor Dostoevsky	1-59308-037-9	$4.95
O Pioneers!	Willa Cather	1-59308-205-3	$5.95
The Odyssey	Homer	1-59308-009-3	$5.95
Oliver Twist	Charles Dickens	1-59308-206-1	$6.95
The Origin of Species	Charles Darwin	1-59308-077-8	$7.95
Paradise Lost	John Milton	1-59308-095-6	$7.95
Persuasion	Jane Austen	1-59308-130-8	$5.95
The Picture of Dorian Gray	Oscar Wilde	1-59308-025-5	$4.95
The Portrait of a Lady	Henry James	1-59308-096-4	$7.95
A Portrait of the Artist as a Young Man and Dubliners	James Joyce	1-59308-031-X	$6.95
Pride and Prejudice	Jane Austen	1-59308-201-0	$5.95
The Prince and Other Writings	Niccolò Machiavelli	1-59308-060-3	$5.95
The Red Badge of Courage and Selected Short Fiction	Stephen Crane	1-59308-119-7	$4.95
Republic	Plato	1-59308-097-2	$6.95
Robinson Crusoe	Daniel Defoe	1-59308-360-2	$5.95
The Scarlet Letter	Nathaniel Hawthorne	1-59308-207-X	$4.95
Sense and Sensibility	Jane Austen	1-59308-125-1	$5.95
Sons and Lovers	D. H. Lawrence	1-59308-013-1	$7.95
The Souls of Black Folk	W. E. B. Du Bois	1-59308-014-X	$5.95
The Strange Case of Dr. Jekyll and Mr. Hyde and Other Stories	Robert Louis Stevenson	1-59308-131-6	$4.95
A Tale of Two Cities	Charles Dickens	1-59308-138-3	$5.95
Tao Te Ching	Lao Tzu	1-59308-256-8	$5.95
The Three Musketeers	Alexandre Dumas	1-59308-148-0	$8.95
The Time Machine and The Invisible Man	H. G. Wells	1-59308-032-8	$4.95
Tom Jones	Henry Fielding	1-59308-070-0	$8.95
Treasure Island	Robert Louis Stevenson	1-59308-247-9	$4.95
The Turn of the Screw, The Aspern Papers and Two Stories	Henry James	1-59308-043-3	$5.95
Twenty Thousand Leagues Under the Sea	Jules Verne	1-59308-302-5	$5.95
Uncle Tom's Cabin	Harriet Beecher Stowe	1-59308-121-9	$7.95
Vanity Fair	William Makepeace Thackeray	1-59308-071-9	$7.95
Villette	Charlotte Brontë	1-59308-316-5	$7.95
The Voyage Out	Virginia Woolf	1-59308-229-0	$6.95
Walden and Civil Disobedience	Henry David Thoreau	1-59308-208-8	$5.95
The War of the Worlds	H. G. Wells	1-59308-085-9	$3.95
Wuthering Heights	Emily Brontë	1-59308-044-1	$4.95

BARNES & NOBLE CLASSICS

If you are an educator and would like to receive an Examination or Desk Copy of a Barnes & Noble Classic edition, please refer to Academic Resources on our website at WWW.BN.COM/CLASSICS or contact us at B&NCLASSICS@BN.COM.

All prices are subject to change.